The Collected Supernatural and Weird Fiction of Edith Nesbit Volume 1

The Collected Supernatural and Weird Fiction of Edith Nesbit Volume 1

One Novel 'Dormant' (a.k.a. 'Rose Royal'), and Eleven Short Tales of the Strange and Unusual including 'The Detective', 'No. 17', 'The Blue Rose' and 'The Haunted House'

Edith Nesbit

LEONAUR

The Collected
Supernatural and Weird
Fiction of
Edith Nesbit
Volume 1
One Novel 'Dormant' (a.k.a. 'Rose Royal'), and Eleven Short Tales of the Strange and
Unusual including 'The Detective', 'No. 17', 'The Blue Rose' and 'The Haunted House'
by Edith Nesbit

FIRST EDITION

Leonaur is an imprint of Oakpast Ltd

Copyright in this form © 2019 Oakpast Ltd

ISBN: 978-1-78282-838-9 (hardcover)
ISBN: 978-1-78282-839-6 (softcover)

http://www.leonaur.com

Publisher's Notes

The views expressed in this book are not necessarily
those of the publisher.

Contents

From the Dead

1

"But true or not true, your brother is a scoundrel. No man—no decent man—tells such things."

"He did not tell me. How dare you suppose it? I found the letter in his desk; and she being my friend and you being her lover, I never thought there could be any harm in my reading her letter to my brother. Give me back the letter. I was a fool to tell you."

Ida Helmont held out her hand for the letter.

"Not yet," I said, and I went to the window. The dull red of a London sunset burned on the paper, as I read in the quaint, dainty handwriting I knew so well and had kissed so often—

Dear, I do—I do love you; but it's impossible. I must marry Arthur. My honour is engaged. If he would only set me free—but he never will. He loves me so foolishly. But as for me, it is you I love—body, soul, and spirit. There is no one in my heart but you. I think of you all day, and dream of you all night. And we must part. And that is the way of the world. Goodbye!—

Yours, yours, yours,

Elvire.

I had seen the handwriting, indeed, often enough. But the passion written there was new to me. That I had not seen.

I turned from the window wearily. My sitting-room looked strange to me. There were my books, my reading-lamp, my untasted dinner still on the table, as I had left it when I rose to dissemble my surprise at Ida Helmont's visit—Ida Helmont, who now sat in my easy-chair looking at me quietly.

"Well—do you give me no thanks?"

"You put a knife in my heart, and then ask for thanks?"

"Pardon me," she said, throwing up her chin. "I have done nothing but show you the truth. For that one should expect no gratitude—may I ask, out of mere curiosity, what you intend to do?"

"Your brother will tell you——"

She rose suddenly, pale to the lips.

"You will not tell my brother?" she began.

"That you have read his private letters? Certainly not!"

She came towards me—her gold hair flaming in the sunset light.

"Why are you so angry with me?" she said. "Be reasonable. What else could I do?"

"I don't know."

"Would it have been right not to tell you?"

"I don't know. I only know that you've put the sun out, and I haven't got used to the dark yet."

"Believe me," she said, coming still nearer to me, and laying her hands in the lightest light touch on my shoulders, "believe me, she never loved you."

There was a softness in her tone that irritated and stimulated me. I moved gently back, and her hands fell by her sides.

"I beg your pardon," I said. "I have behaved very badly. You were quite right to come, and I am not ungrateful. Will you post a letter for me?"

I sat down and wrote—

I give you back your freedom. The only gift of mine that can please you now.

                                                                    Arthur.

I held the sheet out to Miss Helmont, and, when she had glanced at it, I sealed, stamped, and addressed it.

"Goodbye," I said then, and gave her the letter. As the door closed behind her I sank into my chair, and I am not ashamed to say that I cried like a child or a fool over my lost plaything—the little dark-haired woman who loved someone else with "body, soul, and spirit."

I did not hear the door open or any foot on the floor, and therefore I started when a voice behind me said—

"Are you so very unhappy? Oh, Arthur, don't think I am not sorry for you!"

"I don't want anyone to be sorry for me, Miss Helmont," I said.

She was silent a moment. Then, with a quick, sudden, gentle movement she leaned down and kissed my forehead—and I heard the door

8

softly close. Then I knew that the beautiful Miss Helmont loved me.

At first that thought only fleeted by—a light cloud against a grey sky—but the next day reason woke, and said—

"Was Miss Helmont speaking the truth? Was it possible that——?"

I determined to see Elvire, to know from her own lips whether by happy fortune this blow came, not from her, but from a woman in whom love might have killed honesty.

I walked from Hampstead to Gower Street. As I trod its long length, I saw a figure in pink come out of one of the houses. It was Elvire. She walked in front of me to the corner of Store Street. There she met Oscar Helmont. They turned and met me face to face, and I saw all I needed to see. They loved each other. Ida Helmont had spoken the truth. I bowed and passed on. Before six months were gone, they were married, and before a year was over, I had married Ida Helmont.

What did it I don't know. Whether it was remorse for having, even for half a day, dreamed that she could be so base as to forge a lie to gain a lover, or whether it was her beauty, or the sweet flattery of the preference of a woman who had half her acquaintances at her feet, I don't know; anyhow, my thoughts turned to her as to their natural home. My heart, too, took that road, and before very long I loved her as I had never loved Elvire. Let no one doubt that I loved her—as I shall never love again, please God!

There never was anyone like her. She was brave and beautiful, witty and wise, and beyond all measure adorable. She was the only woman in the world. There was a frankness—a largeness of heart—about her that made all other women seem small and contemptible. She loved me and I worshipped her. I married her, I stayed with her for three golden weeks, and then I left her. Why?

Because she told me the truth. It was one night—late—we had sat all the evening in the verandah of our seaside lodging watching the moonlight on the water and listening to the soft sound of the sea on the sand. I have never been so happy; I never shall be happy any more, I hope.

"Heart's heart," she said, leaning her gold head against my shoulder, "how much do you love me?"

"How much?"

"Yes—how much? I want to know what place it is I hold in your heart. Am I more to you than anyone else?"

"My love!"

"More than yourself?"

9

"More than my life!"

"I believe you," she said. Then she drew a long breath, and took my hands in hers. "It can make no difference. Nothing in heaven or earth can come between us now."

"Nothing," I said. "But, sweet, my wife, what is it?"

For she was deathly pale.

"I must tell you," she said; "I cannot hide anything now from you, because I am yours—body, soul, and spirit."

The phrase was an echo that stung me.

The moonlight shone on her gold hair, her warm, soft, gold hair, and on her pale face.

"Arthur," she said, "you remember my coming to you at Hampstead with that letter?"

"Yes, my sweet, and I remember how you——"

"Arthur!"—she spoke fast and low—"Arthur, that letter was a forgery. She never wrote it. I——"

She stopped, for I had risen and flung her hands from me, and stood looking at her. God help me! I thought it was anger at the lie I felt. I know now it was only wounded vanity that smarted in me. That *I* should have been tricked, that *I* should have been deceived, that *I* should have been led on to make a fool of myself! That *I* should have married the woman who had befooled me! At that moment she was no longer the wife I adored—she was only a woman who had forged a letter and tricked me into marrying her.

I spoke; I denounced her; I said I would never speak to her again. I felt it was rather creditable in me to be so angry. I said I would have no more to do with a liar and forger.

I don't know whether I expected her to creep to my knees and implore forgiveness. I think I had some vague idea that I could by-and-by consent with dignity to forgive and forget. I did not mean what I said. No, no; I did not mean a word of it. While I was saying it, I was longing for her to weep and fall at my feet, that I might raise her and hold her in my arms again.

But she did not fall at my feet; she stood quietly looking at me.

"Arthur," she said, as I paused for breath, "let me explain—she—I——"

"There is nothing to explain," I said hotly, still with that foolish sense of there being something rather noble in my indignation, as one feels when one calls one's self a miserable sinner. "You are a liar and forger, and that is enough for me. I will never speak to you again. You have wrecked my life——"

"Do you mean that?" she said, interrupting me, and leaning forward to look at me. Tears lay on her cheeks, but she was not crying now.

I hesitated. I longed to take her in my arms and say—"Lay your head here, my darling, and cry here, and know how I love you."

But instead I kept silence.

"*Do* you mean it?" she persisted.

Then she put her hand on my arm. I longed to clasp it and draw her to me.

Instead, I shook it off, and said—

"Mean it? Yes—of course I mean it. Don't touch me, please! You have ruined my life."

She turned away without a word, went into our room, and shut the door.

I longed to follow her, to tell her that if there was anything to forgive, I forgave it.

Instead, I went out on the beach, and walked away under the cliffs.

The moonlight and the solitude, however, presently brought me to a better mind. Whatever she had done had been done for love of me—I knew that. I would go home and tell her so—tell her that whatever she had done she was my dearest life, my heart's one treasure. True, my ideal of her was shattered, but, even as she was, what was the whole world of women compared to her? I hurried back, but in my resentment and evil temper I had walked far, and the way back was very long. I had been parted from her for three hours by the time I opened the door of the little house where we lodged.

The house was dark and very still. I slipped off my shoes and crept up the narrow stairs, and opened the door of our room quite softly. Perhaps she would have cried herself to sleep, and I would lean over her and waken her with my kisses and beg her to forgive me. Yes, it had come to that now.

I went into the room—I went towards the bed. She was not there. She was not in the room, as one glance showed me. She was not in the house, as I knew in two minutes. When I had wasted a priceless hour in searching the town for her, I found a note on the dressing-table—

"Goodbye! Make the best of what is left of your life. I will spoil it no more."

She was gone, utterly gone. I rushed to town by the earliest morning train, only to find that her people knew nothing of her. Advertisement failed. Only a tramp said he had met a white lady on the cliff, and a fisherman brought me a handkerchief marked with her name that he had found on the beach.

I searched the country far and wide, but I had to go back to London at last, and the months went by. I won't say much about those months, because even the memory of that suffering turns me faint and sick at heart. The police and detectives and the Press failed me utterly. Her friends could not help me, and were, moreover, wildly indignant with me, especially her brother, now living very happily with my first love.

I don't know how I got through those long weeks and months. I tried to write; I tried to read; I tried to live the life of a reasonable human being. But it was impossible. I could not endure the companionship of my kind. Day and night, I almost saw her face—almost heard her voice. I took long walks in the country, and her figure was always just round the next turn of the road—in the next glade of the wood. But I never quite saw her—never quite heard her. I believe I was not altogether sane at that time. At last, one morning as I was setting out for one of those long walks that had no goal but weariness, I met a telegraph boy, and took the red envelope from his hand.

On the pink paper inside was written—

Come to me at once. I am dying. You must come—Ida—Apinshaw Farm, Mellor, Derbyshire.

There was a train at twelve to Marple, the nearest station. I took it. I tell you there are some things that cannot be written about. My life for those long months was one of them, that journey was another. What had her life been for those months? That question troubled me, as one is troubled in every nerve at the sight of a surgical operation or a wound inflicted on a being dear to one. But the overmastering sensation was joy—intense, unspeakable joy. She was alive! I should see her again. I took out the telegram and looked at it: "I am dying."

I simply did not believe it. She could not die till she had seen me. And if she had lived all those months without me, she could live now, when I was with her again, when she knew of the hell, I had endured apart from her, and the heaven of our meeting. She must live. I would not let her die.

There was a long drive over bleak hills. Dark, jolting, infinitely wearisome. At last we stopped before a long, low building, where one or two lights gleamed faintly. I sprang out.

The door opened. A blaze of light made me blink and draw back.

A woman was standing in the doorway.

"Art thee Arthur Marsh?" she said.

"Yes."

"Then, th'art ower late. She's dead."

2

I went into the house, walked to the fire, and held out my hands to it mechanically, for, though the night was May, I was cold to the bone. There were some folks standing round the fire and lights flickering. Then an old woman came forward with the northern instinct of hospitality.

"Thou'rt tired," she said, "and mazed-like. Have a sup o' tea."

I burst out laughing. It was too funny. I had travelled two hundred miles to see *her*; and she was dead, and they offered me tea. They drew back from me as if I had been a wild beast, but I could not stop laughing. Then a hand was laid on my shoulder, and someone led me into a dark room, lighted a lamp, set me in a chair, and sat down opposite me. It was a bare parlour, coldly furnished with rush chairs and much-polished tables and presses. I caught my breath, and grew suddenly grave, and looked at the woman who sat opposite me.

"I was Miss Ida's nurse," said she; "and she told me to send for you. Who are you?"

"Her husband——"

The woman looked at me with hard eyes, where intense surprise struggled with resentment. "Then, may God forgive you!" she said. "What you've done I don't know; but it'll be 'ard work forgivin' you—even for *Him*!"

"Tell me," I said, "my wife——"

"Tell you?" The bitter contempt in the woman's tone did not hurt me; what was it to the self-contempt that had gnawed my heart all these months? "Tell you? Yes, I'll tell you. Your wife was that ashamed of you, she never so much as told me she was married. She let me think anything I pleased sooner than that. She just come 'ere an' she said, 'Nurse, take care of me, for I am in mortal trouble. And don't let them know where I am,' says she. An' me bein' well married to an honest man, and well-to-do here, I was able to do it, by the blessing."

"Why didn't you send for me before?" It was a cry of anguish wrung from me.

"I'd *never* 'a sent for you—it was *her* doin'. Oh, to think as God A'mighty's made men able to measure out such-like pecks o' trouble for us womenfolk! Young man, I dunno what you did to 'er to make 'er leave you; but it muster bin something cruel, for she loved the ground you walked on. She useter sit day after day, a-lookin' at your picture an' talkin' to it an' kissin' of it, when she thought I wasn't takin' no notice, and cryin' till she made me cry too. She useter cry all night 'most. An' one day, when I tells 'er to pray to God to 'elp 'er through 'er trouble, she outs with *your* putty face on a card, she doez, an', says she, with her poor little smile, 'That's my god, Nursey,' she says."

"Don't!" I said feebly, putting out my hands to keep off the torture; "not any more, not now."

"*Don't?*" she repeated. She had risen and was walking up and down the room with clasped hands—"don't, indeed! No, I won't; but I shan't forget you! I tell you I've had you in my prayers time and again, when I thought you'd made a light-o'-love o' my darling. I shan't drop you outer them now I know she was your own wedded wife as you chucked away when you'd tired of her, and left 'er to eat 'er 'art out with longin' for you. Oh! I pray to God above us to pay you scot and lot for all you done to 'er! You killed my pretty. The price will be required of you, young man, even to the uttermost farthing! O God in heaven, make him suffer! Make him feel it!"

She stamped her foot as she passed me. I stood quite still; I bit my lip till I tasted the blood hot and salt on my tongue.

"She was nothing to you!" cried the woman, walking faster up and down between the rush chairs and the table; "any fool can see that with half an eye. You didn't love her, so you don't feel nothin' now; but some day you'll care for someone, and then you shall know what she felt—if there's any justice in heaven!"

I, too, rose, walked across the room, and leaned against the wall. I heard her words without understanding them.

"Can't you feel *nothin'*? Are you mader stone? Come an' look at 'er lyin' there so quiet. She don't fret arter the likes o' you no more now. She won't sit no more a-lookin' outer winder an' sayin' nothin'—only droppin' 'er tears one by one, slow, slow on her lap. Come an' see 'er; come an' see what you done to my pretty—an' then ye can go. Nobody wants you 'ere. *She* don't want you now. But p'r'aps you'd like to see 'er safe underground fust? I'll be bound you'll put a big slab on 'er—to make sure *she* don't rise again."

I turned on her. Her thin face was white with grief and impotent rage. Her claw-like hands were clenched.

"Woman," I said, "have mercy!"

She paused, and looked at me.

"Eh?" she said.

"Have mercy!" I said again.

"Mercy? You should 'a thought o' that before. You 'adn't no mercy on 'er. She loved you—she died lovin' you. An' if I wasn't a Christian woman, I'd kill you for it—like the rat you are! That I would, though I 'ad to swing for it arterwards."

I caught the woman's hands and held them fast, in spite of her resistance.

"Don't you understand?" I said savagely. "We loved each other. She died loving me. I have to live loving her. And it's *her* you pity. I tell you it was all a mistake—a stupid, stupid mistake. Take me to her, and for pity's sake let me be left alone with her."

She hesitated; then said in a voice only a shade less hard—

"Well, come along, then."

We moved towards the door. As she opened it a faint, weak cry fell on my ear. My heart stood still.

"What's that?" I asked, stopping on the threshold.

"Your child," she said shortly.

That, too! Oh, my love! oh, my poor love! All these long months!

"She allus said she'd send for you when she'd got over her trouble," the woman said as we climbed the stairs. "'I'd like him to see his little baby, nurse,' she says; 'our little baby. It'll be all right when the baby's born,' she says. 'I know he'll come to me then. You'll see.' And I never said nothin'—not thinkin' you'd come if she was your leavins, and not dreamin' as you could be 'er husband an' could stay away from 'er a hour—her bein' as she was. Hush!"

She drew a key from her pocket and fitted it to the lock. She opened the door and I followed her in. It was a large, dark room, full of old-fashioned furniture. There were wax candles in brass candle-sticks and a smell of lavender.

The big four-post bed was covered with white.

"My lamb—my poor pretty lamb!" said the woman, beginning to cry for the first time as she drew back the sheet. "Don't she look beautiful?"

I stood by the bedside. I looked down on my wife's face. Just so I had seen it lie on the pillow beside me in the early morning when the wind and the dawn came up from beyond the sea. She did not look like one dead. Her lips were still red, and it seemed to me that a tinge of colour lay on her cheek. It seemed to me, too, that if I kissed her, she would wake, and put her slight hand on my neck, and lay her cheek against mine—and that we should tell each other everything, and weep together, and understand and be comforted.

So, I stooped and laid my lips to hers as the old nurse stole from the room.

But the red lips were like marble, and she did not wake. She will not wake now ever any more.

I tell you again there are some things that cannot be written.

3

I lay that night in a big room filled with heavy, dark furniture, in a great four-poster hung with heavy, dark curtains—a bed the counterpart of that other bed from whose side they had dragged me at last.

They fed me, I believe, and the old nurse was kind to me. I think she saw now that it is not the dead who are to be pitied most.

I lay at last in the big, roomy bed, and heard the household noises grow fewer and die out, the little wail of my child sounding latest. They had brought the child to me, and I had held it in my arms, and bowed my head over its tiny face and frail fingers. I did not love it then. I told myself it had cost me her life. But my heart told me that it was I who had done that. The tall clock at the stair head sounded the hours—eleven, twelve, one, and still I could not sleep. The room was dark and very still.

I had not been able to look at my life quietly. I had been full of the intoxication of grief—a real drunkenness, more merciful than the calm that comes after.

Now I lay still as the dead woman in the next room, and looked at what was left of my life. I lay still, and thought, and thought, and thought. And in those hours, I tasted the bitterness of death. It must have been about two that I first became aware of a slight sound that was not the ticking of the clock. I say I first became aware, and yet I knew perfectly that I had heard that sound more than once before, and had yet determined not to hear it, *because it came from the next room*—the room where the corpse lay.

And I did not wish to hear that sound, because I knew it meant that I was nervous—miserably nervous—a coward and a brute. It meant that I, having killed my wife as surely as though I had put a knife in her breast, had now sunk so low as to be afraid of her dead body—the dead body that lay in the room next to mine. The heads of the beds were placed against the same wall; and from that wall I had fancied

16

I heard slight, slight, almost inaudible sounds. So when I say that I became aware of them I mean that I at last heard a sound so distinct as to leave no room for doubt or question. It brought me to a sitting position in the bed, and the drops of sweat gathered heavily on my forehead and fell on my cold hands as I held my breath and listened.

I don't know how long I sat there—there was no further sound—and at last my tense muscles relaxed, and I fell back on the pillow.

"You fool!" I said to myself; "dead or alive, is she not your darling, your heart's heart? Would you not go near to die of joy if she came to you? Pray God to let her spirit come back and tell you she forgives you!"

"I wish she would come," myself answered in words, while every fibre of my body and mind shrank and quivered in denial.

I struck a match, lighted a candle, and breathed more freely as I looked at the polished furniture—the commonplace details of an ordinary room. Then I thought of her, lying alone, so near me, so quiet under the white sheet. She was dead; she would not wake or move. But suppose she did move? Suppose she turned back the sheet and got up, and walked across the floor and turned the door-handle?

As I thought it, I heard—plainly, unmistakably heard—the door of the chamber of death open slowly—I heard slow steps in the passage, slow, heavy steps—I heard the touch of hands on my door outside, uncertain hands, that felt for the latch.

Sick with terror, I lay clenching the sheet in my hands.

I knew well enough what would come in when that door opened—that door on which my eyes were fixed. I dreaded to look, yet I dared not turn away my eyes. The door opened slowly, slowly, slowly, and the figure of my dead wife came in. It came straight towards the bed, and stood at the bed-foot in its white grave-clothes, with the white bandage under its chin. There was a scent of lavender. Its eyes were wide open and looked at me with love unspeakable.

I could have shrieked aloud.

My wife spoke. It was the same dear voice that I had loved so to hear, but it was very weak and faint now; and now I trembled as I listened.

"You aren't afraid of me, darling, are you, though I am dead? I heard all you said to me when you came, but I couldn't answer. But now I've come back from the dead to tell you. I wasn't really so bad as you thought me. Elvire had told me she loved Oscar. I only wrote the letter to make it easier for you. I was too proud to tell you when you were so angry, but I am not proud any more now. You'll love me again now, won't you, now I'm dead? One always forgives dead people."

The poor ghost's voice was hollow and faint. Abject terror paralyzed me. I could answer nothing.

"Say you forgive me," the thin, monotonous voice went on; "say you love me again."

I had to speak. Coward as I was, I did manage to stammer—

"Yes; I love you. I have always loved you; God help me!"

The sound of my own voice reassured me, and I ended more firmly than I began. The figure by the bed swayed a little unsteadily.

"I suppose," she said wearily, "you would be afraid, now I am dead, if I came round to you and kissed you?"

She made a movement as though she would have come to me.

Then I did shriek aloud, again and again, and covered my face with the sheet, and wound it round my head and body, and held it with all my force.

There was a moment's silence. Then I heard my door close, and then a sound of feet and of voices, and I heard something heavy fall. I disentangled my head from the sheet. My room was empty. Then reason came back to me. I leaped from the bed.

"Ida, my darling, come back! I am not afraid! I love you! Come back! Come back!"

I sprang to my door and flung it open. Someone was bringing a light along the passage. On the floor, outside the door of the death-chamber, was a huddled heap—the corpse, in its grave-clothes. Dead, dead, dead.

★★★★★★

She is buried in Mellor churchyard, and there is no stone over her.

Now, whether it was catalepsy—as the doctors said—or whether my love came back even from the dead to me who loved her, I shall never know; but this I know—that, if I had held out my arms to her as she stood at my bed-foot—if I had said, "Yes, even from the grave, my darling—from hell itself, come back, come back to me!"—if I had had room in my coward's heart for anything but the unreasoning terror that killed love in that hour, I should not now be here alone. I shrank from her—I feared her—I would not take her to my heart. And now she will not come to me anymore.

Why do I go on living?

You see, there is the child. It is four years old now, and it has never spoken and never smiled.

Hurst of Hurstcote

We were at Eton together, and afterwards at Christ Church, and I always got on very well with him; but somehow, he was a man about whom none of the other men cared very much. There was always something strange and secret about him; even at Eton he liked grubbing among books and trying chemical experiments better than cricket or the boats. That sort of thing would make any boy unpopular. At Oxford, it wasn't merely his studious ways and his love of science that went against him; it was a certain habit he had of gazing at us through narrowing lids, as though he were looking at us more from the outside tan any human being has a right to look at any other, and a bored air of belonging to another and a higher race, whenever we talked the ordinary chatter about athletics and the schools.

A wild paper on *Black Magic*, which he read to the Essay Society, filled to overflowing the cup of his college's contempt for him. I suppose no man was ever so much disliked for so little cause.

When we went down, I noticed—for I knew his people at home—that the sentiment of dislike which he excited in most men was curiously in contrast to the emotions which he inspired in women. They all liked him, listened to him with rapt attention, talked of him with undisguised enthusiasm. I watched their strange infatuation with calmness for dislike which he excited in most men was curiously in contrast to the emotions which he inspired in women. They all liked him, listened to him with rapt attention, talked of him with undisguised enthusiasm. I watched their strange infatuation with calmness for several years, but the day came when he met Kate Danvers, and then I was not calm any more. She behaved like all the rest of the women, and to her, quite suddenly, Hurst threw the handkerchief. He was not Hurst of Hurstcote then, but as his family was good, and his means not despicable, so he and she were conditionally engaged.

People said it was a poor match for the beauty of the country; and her people, I know, hoped she would think better of it. As for me—well, this is not the story of my life, but of his. I need only say that I thought him a lucky man.

I went to town to complete the studies that were to make me MD; Hurst went abroad, to Paris or Leipzig or somewhere, to study hypnotism and prepare notes for his book on *Black Magic*. This came out in the autumn, and had a strange and brilliant success. Hurst became famous, famous as men do become nowadays. His writings were asked for by all the big periodicals. His future seemed assured. In the spring they were married; I was not present at the wedding. The practice my father had bought for me in London claimed all my time, I said.

It was more than a year after their marriage that I had a letter from Hurst.

> Congratulate me, old man! Crowds of uncles and cousins have died, and I am Hurst of Hurstcote, which God wot I never thought to be. The place is all to pieces, but we can't live anywhere else. If you can get away about September, come down and see us. We shall be installed. I have everything now that I ever longed for—Hurstcote—cradle of our race—and all that, as the only woman in the world for my wife, and—But that's enough for any man, surely.
>
> John Hurst of Hurstcote

Of course, I knew Hurstcote. Who does not? Hurstcote, which seventy years ago was one of the most perfect, as well as the finest, brick Tudor mansions in England. The Hurst who lived there seventy years ago noticed one day that his chimneys smoked, and called in a Hastings architect.

"Your chimneys," said the local man, "are beyond me, but with the timbers and lead of your castle I can Build you a snug little house in the corner of your park, much more suitable for a residence than this old brick building."

So, they gutted Hurstcote, and built the new house, and faced it with *stucco*. All of the things you will find written in the *Guide to Sussex*. Hurstcote, when I had seen it, had been the merest shell. How would Hurst make it habitable? Even if he had inherited much money with the castle, and intended it restore the building, that would be a work of years, not months. What would he do?

In September I went to see. Hurst met me at Pevensey Station.

"Let's walk up," he said; "there's a cart to bring your traps. Eh, but it's good to see you again, Bernard!"

It was good to see him again. And to see him so changed. And so changed for good, too. He was much stouter, and no longer wore the untidy ill-fitting clothes of the old days. He was rather smartly got up in grey stockings and knee-breeches, and wore a velvet shooting jacket. But the most noteworthy change was in his face; it bore no more the eager, inquiring, half-scornful, half-tolerant look that had won him such ill-will at Oxford. His face now was the face of a man completely at peace with himself and with the world.

"How well you look!" I said, as we walked along the level winding road through the still marshes.

"How much better, you mean!" he laughed. "I know it. Bernard you'll hardly believe it, but I'm on the way to be a popular man."

He had not lost his old knack of reading one's thoughts.

"Don't trouble yourself to find the polite answer to that," he hastened to add. "No-one knows as well as I know how unpopular I was; and no-one knows so well why," he added, in a very low voice. "However," he went on gaily, "unpopularity is a thing of the past. The folk hereabout call on us, and condole with us on our hutch. A thing of the past, as I said—but what a past it was, Eh! You're the only man who ever liked me. You don't know what that's been to me many a dark day and night. When the others were—you know—it was like a hand holding mine, to think of you. I've always thought I was sure of one soul in the world to stand by me."

"Yes," I said, "yes."

He flung his arm over my shoulder with a frank, boyish gesture of affection, quite foreign to his nature as I had known it.

"And I know why you didn't come to our wedding," he went on; "but that's all right now, isn't it?"

"Yes," I said again, for indeed it was. There are brown eyes in the world, after all, as well as blue, and one pair of brown that meant heaven to me as the blue had never done.

"That's well," Hurst answered, and we walked on in satisfied silence, till we passed across the furze-covered ridge, and went down the hill to Hurstcote. It lies in the hollow, ringed round by its moat, its dark red walls showing the sky behind them. There was no welcoming sparkle of early litten candle, only the pale amber of the September evening shining through the gaunt unglazed windows.

Three planks and a rough handrail had replaced the old drawbridge.

We passed across the moat, and Hurst pulled a knotted rope that hung beside the great iron-bound door. A bell clanged loudly inside. In the moment we spent there, waiting, Hurst pushed back a briar that was trailing across the arch, and let it fall outside the handrail.

"Nature is too much with us here," he said, laughing. "The clematis spends its time tripping up, or clawing at one's hair, and we are always expecting the ivy to force itself through the window and make an uninvited third at our dinner-table.

Then the great door of Hurstcote Castle swung back, and there stood Kate, a thousand times sweeter and more beautiful than ever. I looked at her momentary terror and dazzlement. She was indeed much more beautiful than any woman with brown eyes could be. My heart stopped beating

With life or death in the balance. Right!

To be beautiful is not the same thing as to be dear, thank God. I went forward and took her hand with a new heart.

It was a pleasant fortnight I spent with them. They had had one tower completely repaired, and in its queer eight-sided rooms we lived, when we were not out among the marshes, or by the blue sea at Pevensey.

Mrs Hurst had made the rooms quaintly charming by a medley of Liberty stuffs and Wardour Street furniture. The grassy space within the castle walls, with its underground passages, its crumbling heaps of masonry, overgrown with lush creepers, was better than any garden. There we met the fresh morning; there we lounged through lazy noons; there the grey evenings found us.

I have never seen any two married people so utterly, so undisguisedly in love as these were. I, the third, had no embarrassment in so being—for their love had in it a completeness, a childish abandonment, to which the presence of a third—a friend—was no burden. A happiness, reflected from theirs, shone on me. The days went by, dreamlike, and brought the eve of my return to London, and to the commonplaces of life.

We were sitting in the courtyard Hurst had gone to the village to post some letters. A big moon was just showing over the battlements, when Mrs Hurst shivered.

"It's late," she said, "and cold; the summer is gone. Let us go in."

So, we went in to the little warm room, where a wood fire flickered on a brick hearth, and a shaded lamp was already glowing softly. Here we sat on the cushioned seat in the open window, and looked out through the lozenge panes at the gold moon, and ah! the light of her making ghosts in the white mist that rose thick and heavy from the moat.

"I am so sorry you are going," she said presently; "but you will come and skate on the moat with us at Christmas, won't you? We mean to have a medieval Christmas. You don't know what that is? Neither do I; but John does. He is very, very wise."

"Yes," I answered, "he used to know many things that most men don't even dream of as possible to know."

She was silent for a minute, and then shivered again. I picked up a shawl she had thrown down when we came in, and put it round her.

"Thank you! I think—don't you?—that there are some things one is not meant to know, and someone is meant not to know. You see the distinction?"

"I suppose so—yes."

"Did it ever frighten you in the old days," she went on, "to see that John would never—was always—"

"But he has given all that up now?"

"Oh yes, ever since our honeymoon. Do you know, he used to mesmerise me? It was horrible. And that book of his—"

"I didn't know you believed in black magic."

"Oh, I don't—not the least bit. I never was at all superstitious, you know. But those things always frighten me just as much as if I believed in them. And besides—I think they are wicked; but John—Ah, there he is! Let's go and meet him."

His dark figure was outlined against the sky behind the hill. She wrapped the soft shawl more closely around her, and we went out in the moonlight to meet her husband.

The next morning when I entered the room, I found that it lacked its chief ornament. The sparkling white and silver accessories were there, but the deft white hands and kindly welcoming blue eyes of my hostess I looked in vain. At ten minutes past nine Hurst came in looking horribly worried, and more like his old self than I had ever expected to see him.

"I say old man," he said hurriedly, "are you really set on going back to town today—because Kate's awfully queer? I can't think what's wrong. I want you to see her after breakfast."

I reflected a minute. "I can stay if I send a wire," I said.

"I wish you would then," Hurst said, wringing my hand and turning away; "she's been off her head most of the night, talking the most astounding nonsense. You must see her after breakfast. Will you pour out the coffee?"

"I'll see her now, if you like," I said, and he led me up the winding stair to the room at the top of the tower.

I found her quite sensible, but very feverish. I wrote a prescription, and rode Hurst's mare over to Eastbourne to get it made up. When I got back, she was worse. It seemed to be a sort of aggravated marsh fever. I reproached myself with having let her sit by the open window the night before. But I remembered with some satisfaction that I had told Hurst that the place was not quite healthy. I only wished I had insisted on it more strongly.

For the first day or two I thought it was merely a touch of marsh fever, that would pass off with no more worse consequence than a little weakness; but on the third day I perceived that she would die.

Hurst met me as I came from her bedside, stood aside on the narrow landing for me to pass, and followed me down into the little sitting-room, which deprived for three days of her presence, already bore the air of a room long deserted. He came in after me and shut the door.

"You're wrong," he said abruptly, reading my thoughts as usual; "she won't die—she can't die."

"She will," I bluntly answered, for I am no believer in the worst refinement of torture known as 'breaking bad news gently'. "Send for any other man you choose. I'll consult with the whole College of Physicians if you like. But nothing short of a miracle can save her."

"And you don't believe in miracles," he answered quietly. "I do, you see."

"My dear fellow, don't buoy yourself up with false hopes. I know my trade; I wish I could believe I didn't! Go back to her now; you have not very long to be together."

I wrung his hand; he returned the pressure, but said almost cheerfully—"You know your trade, old man, but there are some things you don't know. Mine, for instance—I mean my wife's constitution. Now I know that thoroughly. And you mark my words—she won't die. You might as well say I was not long for this world."

"You," I said with a touch of annoyance; "you're good for another thirty or forty years."

"Exactly so," he rejoined quickly, "and so is she. Her life's as good as mine, you'll see—she won't die."

At dusk on the next day she died. He was with her; he had not left her since he had told me that she would not die. He was sitting by her holding her hand. She had been unconscious for some time, when suddenly she dragged her hand from his, raised herself in the bed, and cried out in a tone of acutest anguish—"John" John! Let me go! For Heaven's sake let me go!"

Then she fell back dead.

He would not understand—would not believe; he still sat by her, holding her hand, and calling on her by every name that love could teach him. I began to fear for his brain. He would not leave her, so by-and-by I brought him a cup of coffee in which I had mixed a strong opiate. In about an hour I went back and found him fast asleep with his face on the pillow close by the face of his dead wife. The gardener and I carried him down to my bedroom, and I sent for a woman from the village.

He slept for twelve hours. When he awoke his first words were—"She is not dead! I must go to her!"

I hoped that the sight of her—pale and beautiful, and still—with the white asters about her, and her cold hands crossed on her breast, would convince him; but no. He looked at her and said—"Bernard you're no fool; you know as well as I do that this is not death. Why treat it so? It is some form of catalepsy. If she should awake and find herself like this the shock might destroy her reason."

And to the horror of the woman from the village, he flung the asters on the floor, covered the body with blankets, and sent for hot-water bottles.

I was now quite convinced that his brain was affected, and I saw plainly enough that he would never consent to take the necessary steps for the funeral.

I began to wonder whether I had not better send for another doctor, for I felt that I did not care to try the opiate again on my own responsibility, and something must be done about the funeral.

I spent the day considering the matter—a day passed by John Hurst beside his wife's body. Then I made up my mind to try all my power to bring him to reason, and to this end I went once more into the chamber of death. I found Hurst talking wildly, in low whispers. He seemed to be talking to someone who was not there. He did not know me, and suffered himself to be led away. He was, in fact, in the first stage of brain fever. I actually blessed his illness, because it opened a way out of the dilemma in which I found myself. I wired for a trained nurse from town, and for the local undertaker. In a week she was buried, and John

Hurst still lay unconscious and unheeding; but I did not look forward to his first renewal of consciousness.

Yet his first conscious words were not the inquiry I dreaded. He only asked whether he had been ill long, and what had been the matter. When I had told him, he just nodded and went off to sleep again.

A few evenings later I found him excited and feverish, but quite himself mentally. I said as much to him in answer to a question which he put to me— "There's no brain disturbance now? I'm not mad or anything?"

"No, no my dear fellow. Everything is as it should be."

"Then," he answered slowly, "I must get up and go to her."

My worst fears were realised.

In moments of intense mental strain, the truth sometimes overpowers all one's better resolves. It sounds brutal, horrible. I don't know what I meant to say; what I said was—"You can't; she's buried."

He sprang up in bed, and I caught him by the shoulders.

"Then it's true!" he cried, "and I'm not mad. Oh, great God in heaven, let me go to her; let me go! It's true! It's true!"

I held him fast, and spoke. "I am strong—you know that. You are weak and ill; you are quite in my power—we're old friends, and there's nothing I wouldn't do to serve you. Tell me what you mean; I will do anything you wish." This I said to soothe him.

"Let me go to her," he said again.

"Tell me all about it," I repeated. "You are too ill to go to her. I will go, if you can collect yourself and tell me why. You could not walk five yards."

He looked at me doubtfully.

"You'll help me? You won't say I'm mad, and have me shut up? You'll help me?"

"Yes, yes—I swear it!" All the time I was wondering what I should do to keep him from his mad purpose.

He lay back on his pillows, white and ghastly; his thin features and sunken eyes showed hawklike above the rough growth of his four weeks' beard. I took his hand. His pulse was rapid, and his lean fingers clenched themselves round mine.

"Look here," he said, "I don't know—There aren't any words to tell you how true it is. I am not mad; I am not wandering. I am as sane as you are. Now listen, and if you've a human heart in you, you'll help me. When I married her, I gave up hypnotism and all the old studies; she hated the whole business. But before I gave it up, I hypnotised her, and when she was completely under my control, I forbade her soul to leave its body till my time came to die."

I breathed more freely. Now I understood why he had said, "She cannot die."

"My dear old man," I said gently, "dismiss these fancies, and face your grief boldly. You can't control the great facts of life and death by hypnotism. She is dead; she is dead, and her body lies in its place. But her soul is with God who gave it."

"No!" he cried, with such strength as the fever had left him. "No! no! Ever since I have been ill, I have seen her, every day, every night, and always wringing her hands and moaning, 'Let me go John—let me go.'"

"Those were her last words, indeed," I said; "it is natural that they should haunt you. See you bade her soul not leave her body. It has left, for she is dead."

His answer came almost in a whisper, borne on the wings of a long breathless pause.

"She is *dead*, but her soul has not *left* her body."

I held his hand more closely, still debating what I should do.

"She comes to me," he went on; "she comes to me continually. She does not reproach, but she implores, 'Let me go, John—let me go!' And I have no more power now; I cannot let her go. I cannot reach her I can do nothing, nothing. Ah!" he cried with a sudden sharp change of voice that thrilled through me to the ends of my fingers and feet: "Ah, Kate, my life, I will come to you! No, no, you shan't be left alone among the dead. I am coming, my sweet."

He reached his arms out towards the door with a look of longing and love, so really, so patently addressed to a sentient presence, that I turned sharply to see if, in truth, perhaps—nothing, of course—nothing.

"She is dead," I repeated stupidly, "I was obliged to bury her."

A shudder ran through him.

"I must go and see for myself," he said.

Then I knew—all in a minute—what to do.

"I will go," I said. "I will open her coffin, and if she is not—is not as other dead folk, I will bring her body back to this house."

"Will you go now?" he asked, with set lips.

It was nigh on midnight. I looked into his eyes.

"Yes, now," I said; "but you must swear to lie still till I return."

"I swear it."

I saw I could trust him, and I went to wake the nurse.

He called weakly after me, "There's a lantern in the tool-shed—and, Bernard—"

"Yes, my poor old chap."

"There's a screwdriver in the sideboard drawer."

I think until he said that I really meant to go. I am not accustomed to lie, even to mad people, and I think I meant it till then.

He leaned on his elbow, and looked at me with wide-open eyes.

"Think," he said, "what she must feel. Out of the body, and yet tied to it, all alone among the dead. Oh, make haste, make haste; for if I am not mad, and I have really fettered her soul, there is but one way."

"And that is?"

"I must die too. Her soul can leave her body when I die."

I called the nurse and left him. I went out, and across the wold to the church, but I did not go in. I carried the screwdriver and the lantern, lest he should send the nurse to see if I had taken them. I leaned on the churchyard wall, and thought of her. I had loved the woman, and I remembered it in that hour.

As soon as I dared, I went back to him—remember I believed him mad—and told the lie that I thought would give him most ease.

"Well?" he said eagerly, as I entered.

I signed the nurse to leave us.

"There is no hope," I said "You will not see your wife again, till you meet her in Heaven."

I laid down the screwdriver and the lantern, and sat down by him.

"You have seen her?"

"Yes."

"And there is no doubt."

"There is no doubt."

"Then I am mad; but you're a good fellow, Bernard, and I'll never forget it in this world or the next."

He seemed calmer, and fell asleep with my hand on his. His last word was a "Thank you", that cut me like a knife.

When I went into his room next morning he was gone. But on his pillow a letter lay, painfully scrawled in pencil, and addressed to me.

"You lied. Perhaps you meant kindly. You didn't understand. She is not dead. She has been with me again. Though her soul may not leave her body, thank God it can still speak to mine. That vault—it is worse than a mere churchyard's grave. Goodbye."

I ran all the way to the church, and entered by the open door. The air was chill and dank after the crisp October sunlight. The stone that closed the vault of the Hursts of Hurstcote had been raised, and was lying beside the dark gaping hole in the chancel floor. The nurse, who had followed me, came in before I could shake off the horror that held me moveless. We both went down into the vault. Weak, exhausted by illness and sorrow, John Hurst had yet found strength to follow his love to the grave. I tell you he had crossed that wold alone, in the grey chill of the dawn; alone he had opened her coffin, and he lay on the floor of the vault with his wife's body in his arms.

He had been dead some hours.

The brown eyes filled with tears when I told my wife this story.

"You were quite right, he was mad," she said. "Poor things! Poor lovers!"

But sometimes when I wake in the grey morning, and between waking and sleeping, think of all those things that I must shut out from my sleeping and my waking thoughts I wonder was I right or was he? Was he mad, or was I idiotically incredulous? For—and it is this thing that haunts me—when I found them dead together in the vault, she had been buried five weeks. But the body that lay in John Hurst's arms, among the mouldering coffins of the Hursts of Hurstcote, was perfect and beautiful as when first he clasped her in his arms, a bride.

In the Dark

It may be that it was a form of madness. Or it may be that he really was what is called haunted. Or it may—though I don't pretend to understand how—have been the development, through intense suffering, of a sixth sense in a very nervous, highly-strung nature. Something certainly led him where They were. And to him they were all one.

He told me the first part of the story, and the last part of it I saw with my own eyes.

1

Haldane and I were friends even in our schooldays. What first brought us together was our common hatred of Visger. He came from our part of the country, and his people knew our people at home, so he was put on to us when he came. He was the most intolerable person, boy and man, that I have ever known. He would not tell a lie. And that is all right, of course. But he didn't stop at that. If he were asked whether any other chap had done anything—been out of bounds, or up to any sort of lark—be would always say: "I don't know, sir, but I believe so." He never did know—we took care of that. But what he believed was always right. I remember Haldane twisting his arm to make him say how he knew about that cherry-tree business, and he only said: "I didn't know—I just felt sure. And I was right, you see." What can you do with a boy like that?

We grew up to be men. At least, Haldane and I did. Visger grew up to be a prig. He was a vegetarian and a teetotaller, and an all-wooler and a Christian Scientist, and all the things that prigs are—but he wasn't a common prig. He knew all sorts of things that he oughtn't to have known, that he *couldn't* have known in any ordinary decent way. It wasn't that he found things out.

He just knew them. Once when I was very unhappy, he came into my rooms—we were all in our last year at Oxford—and talked about things I hardly knew myself. That was really why I went to India that winter. It was bad enough to be unhappy without having that beast knowing all about it.

I was away over a year. Coming back, I thought a lot about how jolly it would be to see old Haldane again. If I thought about Visger at all I wished he was dead. But I didn't think about him much.

I did want to see Haldane. He was always such a jolly chap—gay and kindly and simple, honourable, upright, and full of practical sympathies. I longed to see him, to see the smile in his jolly blue eyes looking out from the net of wrinkles that laughing had made round them, to hear his jolly laugh, and feel the good grip of his big hand. I went straight from the docks to his chambers in Gray's Inn, and I found him cold, pale, anaemic, with dull eyes and a limp hand, and pale lips that smiled without mirth and uttered a welcome without gladness.

He was surrounded by a litter of disordered furniture and personal effects half packed. Some big boxes stood corded, and there were cases of books filled and waiting for the enclosing boards to be nailed on.

"Yes, I'm moving," he said. "I can't stand these rooms. There's something rum about them—something devilish rum. I clear out to-morrow."

The autumn dusk was filling the corners with shadows. "You got the furs," I said, just for something to say, for I saw the big case that had held them lying corded among the others.

"Furs?" he said. "Oh, yes. Thanks, awfully. Yes. I forgot about the furs." He laughed, out of politeness, I suppose, for there was no joke about the furs. They were many and fine—the best I could get for money, and I had seen them packed and sent off when my heart was very sore. He stood looking at me, and saying nothing.

"Come out and have a bit of dinner," I said, as cheerfully as I could.

"Too busy," he answered, after the slightest possible pause and a glance round the room "look here—I'm awfully glad to see you. If you'd just slip over and order in dinner—I'd go myself—only—well, you see how it is."

I went. And when I came back, he had cleared a space near the fire and moved his big gate table into it. We dined there by candlelight I tried to be amusing. He, I am sure, tried to be amused. We did not succeed, either of us. And his haggard eyes watched me all the time, save in those fleeting moments when, without turning his head, he glanced back over his shoulder into the shadows that crowded round the little lighted place where we sat.

When we had dined, and the man had come and taken away the dishes, I looked at him very steadily, so that he stopped in a pointless anecdote and looked interrogation at me.

"Well?" I said.

"You're not listening," he said, petulantly. "What's the matter?"

"That's what you'd better tell me," I said.

He was silent—gave one of those furtive glances at the shadows, and stooped to stir the fire to—I knew it—a blaze that must light every corner of the room.

"You're all to pieces," I said cheerfully. "What have you been up to—whisky, bridge, Stock Exchange? if you won't tell me you'll have to tell your doctor. Why, my dear chap, you're a wreck."

"You're a comfortable friend to have about the place," he said, and smiled a mechanical smile not at all pleasant to see.

"I'm the friend you want, I think," said I. "Do you suppose I'm blind? Something's gone wrong and you've taken to something—morphia, perhaps. And you've brooded over the thing till you've lost all sense of proportion. Out with it, old chap. Bet you half a dollar it's not so bad as you think it."

"If I could tell you—or tell anyone," he said, slowly "it wouldn't be so bad as it is. If I could tell anyone I'd tell you. And even as it is, I've told you more than I've told anyone else."

I could get nothing more out of him. But he pressed me to stay—would have given me his bed and made himself a shake-down, he said. But I had engaged my room at the Victoria, and I was expecting letters. So, I left him, quite late, and he stood on the stairs holding a candle over the banisters to light me down.

When I went back next morning he was gone. Men were moving his furniture into a long van with Somebody's Pantechnicon painted on it in big letters.

He had left no address with the porter, and had driven off in a hansom with two portmanteaux—to Waterloo, the porter thought.

Well, a man has a right to the monopoly of his own troubles if he chooses to have it. And my letters had taught me that I had troubles of my own to keep me busy.

2

It was more than a year later that I saw Haldane again. I had got rooms in the Albany by this time, and he turned up there one morning, very early indeed—before breakfast, in fact. And if he had looked ghastly before, he now looked almost ghostly. His face looked as though it had worn thin, like an oyster-shell that has for years been cast up twice a day by the sea on a shore all pebbly. His hands were thin as a bird's claws, and they trembled like caught butterflies.

I welcomed him with enthusiastic cordiality and pressed breakfast on him. This time, I decided, I would ask no questions. For I saw that none were needed. He would tell me. He intended to tell me. He had come here to tell me, and for nothing else.

I lit the spirit-lamp—I made coffee and small talk for him, and I ate and drank and waited for him to begin. And it was like this that he began.

"I am going," he said, "to kill myself—oh, don't be alarmed"—I suppose I had said or looked something—"I sha'n't do it here, or now. I shall do it when I have to—when I can't bear it any longer. And I want someone to know why. I don't want to feel that I'm the only soul that does know. And I can trust you, can't I?"

I murmured something reassuring.

"I should like you, if you don't mind, to give me your word that you won't tell anyone at all what I'm going to tell you, as long as I'm alive. Afterwards—you can tell whom you please."

I gave him my word.

He sat silent, looking at the fire. Then he shrugged his shoulders.

"It's extraordinary how difficult it is to say it," he said, and smiled. "The fact is—you know that beast George Visger?"

"Yes," I said. "I haven't seen him since I came back. Someone told me he'd gone to some island or other to preach vegetarianism to the cannibals. Anyhow, he's out of the way, bad luck to him."

"Yes," said Haldane, "he's out of the way. But he's not preaching anything. In point of fact, he's dead."

"Dead?" was all I could think of to say.

"Yes," said he; "it's not generally known, but he is."

"What did he die of?" I asked, not that I cared. The bare fact was good enough for me.

"You know what an interfering chap he always was. Always knew everything. Heart-to-heart talks, and have everything open and above-board. Well, he interfered between me and someone else—told her a pack of lies."

"Lies?"

"Well, the *things* were true, but he made lies of them the way he told them—you know." I did. I nodded. "And she threw me over. And she died. And we weren't even friends. I couldn't see her—before—I couldn't even—— Oh, my God! But I went to the funeral. He was there. They'd asked him. And then I came back to my rooms. And I was sitting there, thinking. And he came up."

"He would do. It's just what he would do. The beast. I hope you kicked him out?"

"No. I didn't. I listened to what he'd got to say. He came to say no doubt it was all for the best. And he hadn't known the things he told her. He'd only guessed. He'd guessed right, curse him—like he used to at school—you remember? What right had he to guess right? And he said it was all for the best, because besides that there was madness in my family. He'd found that out too—"

"And is there?"

"If there is, I didn't know it. And that was why it was all for the best. So, then I said, 'There wasn't any madness in my family before; but there is now,' and I got hold of his throat. I am not sure whether I meant to kill him. I ought to have meant to kill him. Anyhow I did kill him. What did you say?"

I had said nothing. It is not easy to think at once of the tactful and suitable thing to say when your old friend tells you that he is a murderer.

"When I could get my hands out of his throat—it was as difficult as it is to drop the handles of a galvanic battery—he was there in a lump on the hearthrug. And I saw what I'd done. How is it that murderers ever get found out?"

"They're careless sometimes, I suppose," I found myself saying, "They lose their nerve."

"I didn't," he said. "I never was calmer. I sat down in the big chair and looked at him and thought it all out. He was just off to that island—I knew that he'd said goodbye to everyone. He'd *told* me that. There was no blood to get rid of—or only just a touch at the corner of his slack mouth. He wasn't going to travel in his own name because of interviewers, Mr, Somebody Something's luggage would he un-claimed and his cabin empty. No one would guess that Mr. Somebody Something was Sir George Visger, Baronet. It was all as plain as plain. There was nothing to get rid of but the man—no weapon, no blood. And I got rid of him all right."

"How?"

He smiled cunningly,

"No, no," he said; "that's where I draw the line. It's not that I doubt your word, but if you talked in your sleep, or had a fever or anything? No, no. As long as you don't know where the body is, don't you see, I'm all right. Even if you could prove that I've said all this, which you can't—it's only the wanderings of my poor unhinged brain. See?"

I saw. And I was very sorry for him. And I did not believe that he had killed Visger, He was not the sort of man who kills people. So, I said:—

"Yes, old chap. I see. Now, look here. Let you and me go away together—travel a bit and see the world, and forget all about that beastly chap."

His eyes lighted up at that.

"Why," he said, "you understand! You don't hate me and shrink from me. I wish I'd told you before—you know'—when you came and I packing up my sticks. But it's too late now."

"Too late? Not a bit of it," I said. "Come, we'll pack right away and be off tonight—out into the unknown, don't you know."

"That's where *I'm* going," he said. "You wait. When you've heard what's been happening to me you won't be so keen to go into the unknown with me."

"But you've told me what's been happening to you," I said. And the more I thought about what he had told me the less I believed it.

"No," he said, slowly, "no; I've told you what happened to *him*. What happened to me is quite different. Did I tell you what his last words were? Just when I was coming at him—before I'd got his throat, you know—he said, 'Look out! You'll never be able to get rid of the body. Besides, anger's sinful.' You know that way he had, like a tract on its hind legs? So afterwards I got thinking of that.

"But I didn't think of it for a year, because I did get rid of his body all right. And then I was sitting in that comfortable chair, and I thought, 'Halloa, it must be about a year now since that——' and I pulled out my pocket-book and went to the window to look at a little almanac I carry about—it was getting dusk—and sure enough it was a year to the day. And then I remembered what he'd said, and I said to myself, 'Not much trouble about getting rid of *your* body, you brute.' And then I looked at the hearthrug, and—— Ah!" he screamed, suddenly and very loud, "I can't tell you—no, I can't!"

My man opened the door—he wore a smooth face over his wriggling curiosity. "Did you call, sir?"

"Yes," I lied. "I want you to take a note to the bank and wait for an answer."

When he was got rid of, Haldane said: "Where was I?"

"You were just telling me what happened after you looked at the almanac. What was it?"

"Nothing much," he said, laughing softly; "oh, nothing much—only that I glanced at the floor; and there *he* was, the man I'd killed a year before. Don't try to explain, or I shall lose my temper. The door was shut. The windows were shut. He hadn't been there a minute before. And he was there then. That's all."

Hallucination was one of the words I stumbled among.

"Exactly what I thought," he said, triumphantly; "but—I touched it. It was quite real. Heavy, you know, and harder than live people are, somehow, to the touch—more like a stone thing covered with kid the hands were, and the arms like a marble statue in a blue serge suit. Don't you hate men who wear blue serge suits?"

"There are hallucinations of touch, too," I found myself saying.

"Exactly what I thought," said Haldane, more triumphant than ever; "but there are limits, you know—limits. So, then I thought someone had got him out—the real him—and stuck him there to frighten me while my back was turned, and I went to the place where I'd hidden him, and he was there—ah—just as I'd left him. Only—it was a year ago. There are two of him there now."

"My dear chap," I said, "this is simply comic."

"Yes," said he, "it is amusing. I find it so myself. Especially in the night when I wake up and think of it, I hope I shan't die in the dark, Winston. That's one of the reasons why I think I shall have to kill myself. I could be sure then of not dying in the dark."

"Is *that* all?" I asked, feeling sure that it must be.

"No," said Haldane at once; "that's not all. He's come back to me again. In a railway carriage it was. I'd been asleep. When I woke up there, he was, lying on the seat opposite me. Looked just the same. Felt just the same. I pitched him out on the line in Red Hill Tunnel. And if I see him again, I'm going out myself. I can't stand it. It's too much. I'd sooner go. Whatever the next world's like there aren't things like that. We leave them here, in graves and boxes, and . . . You think I'm mad, but I'm not. You can't help me—no one can help me. He *knew*, you see. He said I shouldn't be able to get rid of the body. And I can't get rid of it. I can't; I can't. He knew. He always did know things that he *couldn't* know. But I'll cut his game short. After all I've got the ace of trumps, and I play it on his next trick. I give you my word of honour, Winston, that I'm not mad."

"My dear old man," I said, "I don't think you're mad. But I do think your nerves are very much upset. Mine are a bit, too. Do you know why I went to India? It was because of you and her. I couldn't stay and see it, though I wished for your happiness and all that, you know I did. And when I came back, she—and you—Let's see it out together," I said. "You won't keep fancying things if you've got me to talk to. And I always said you weren't half a bad old duffer."

"She liked you," he said.

"Oh, yes," I said, "she liked me."

3

That was how we came to go abroad together. I was full of hope for him. He'd always been such a splendid chap—so sane and strong. I couldn't believe that he was gone mad—gone for ever, I mean, so that he'd never come right again. Perhaps my own trouble made it easy for me to see things not quite straight. Anyhow, I took him away to recover his mind's health, exactly as I should have taken him away to get strong after a fever. And the madness seemed to pass away, and in a month or two we were pretty jolly, and I thought I had cured him. And I was very glad because of that old friendliness of ours, and because she had loved him and liked me.

We never spoke of Visger. I thought he had forgotten all about him. I thought I understood how his mind, overstrained by sorrow and anger, had fixed on the man he hated and woven a nightmare web of horror round that detestable personality. And I had got the whip-hand of my own trouble. And we were as jolly as sandboys—soberish sandboys—together all those months.

And we came to Bruges at last in our travels, and Bruges was very full, because of the exhibition. We could only get one room and one bed, so we tossed for the bed, and the one who lost the toss was to make the best of the night in the armchair. And the bedclothes we were to share equitably.

We spent the evening at a *café chantant* and finished at a beer hall, and it was late and we were sleepy when we got back to the Big Vine. I took our key from its nail in the *concierge's* room and we went up. We talked for a bit, I remember, about the town and the belfry and the Venetian aspect of the canals by moonlight, and then Haldane got into bed and I made a chrysalis of myself with my share of the blankets, and fitted the tight roll into the armchair. I was not at all comfortable, but I was compensatingly tired, and I was nearly asleep when Haldane roused me up to tell me about his will.

"I've left everything to you, old man," he said. "I know I can trust you to see to everything."

"Quite so," said I; "and, if you don't mind, we'll talk about it in the morning."

He tried to go on about it, and about what a friend I'd been, and all that; but I shut him up and told him to go to sleep. But no. He wasn't comfortable, he said; and he'd got a thirst like a lime-kiln. And he'd noticed that there was no water-bottle in the room. "And the water in the jug's like pale soup," he said.

"Oh, all right," said I. "Light your candle and go and get some water, then, in Heaven's name, and let me get to sleep! "

But he said, "No—you light it. I don't want to get out of bed in the dark. I might—I might step on something, mightn't I—or walk into something that wasn't there when I got into bed?"

"Rot," I said; "walk into your grandmother!" But I lit the candle all the same. He sat up in bed, looking at me—very pale—with his hair all tumbled from the pillow and his eyes blinking and shining.

"That's better," he said. And then, "I say—look here. Oh—yes—I see. It's all right. Queer how they mark the sheets here. Blest if I didn't think it was blood, just for the minute."

The sheet was marked, not at the corner, as sheets are marked at home, but right in the middle where it turns down, with big red cross-stitches.

"Yes, I see," I said; "it is a queer place to mark it."

"It's queer letters to have on it," he said. "G.V."

"Grande Vigne," I said. "What letters do you expect them to mark things with? Hurry up."

"You come too," he said. "Yes, it does stand for Grand Vigne, of course. I wish you'd come down too, Winston."

"I'll *go* down," I said, and turned with the candle in my hand.

He was out of bed and close to me in a flash. "No," said he, "I don't want to stay alone in the dark."

He said it just as a frightened child might have done.

"All right, then, come along," I said. And we went. I tried to make some joke, I remember, about the length of his hair and the cut of his pyjamas—but I was sick with disappointment. For it was almost quite plain to me, even then, that all my time and trouble had been thrown away, and that he wasn't cured after all.

We went down as quietly as we could, and got a carafe of water from the long bare dining-table in the *salle à manger*. He got hold of my arm at first, and then he got the candle away from me and went very slowly, shading the light with his hand and looking very carefully all about, as though he expected to see something that he wanted very desperately not to see. And, of course, I knew what that something was. I didn't like the way he was going on. I can't at all express how deeply I didn't like it. And he looked over his shoulder every now and then, just as he did that first evening after I came back from India.

The thing got on my nerves so that I could hardly find the way back to our room. And when we got there, I give you my word I more than half expected to see what *he* expected to see—that, or something like it, on the hearthrug. But, of course, there was nothing.

I blew out the light and tightened my blankets round me—I'd been trailing them after me in our expedition. And I was feeling for my chair when Haldane spoke.

"You've got all the blankets," he said,

"No, I haven't," said I; "only what I've always had."

"I can't find mine, then," he said, and I could hear his teeth chattering. "And I'm cold. I'm—— For God's sake, light the candle! Light it! Light it! Something horrible——"

And I couldn't find the matches.

"Light the candle—light the candle!" he said, and his voice broke, as a boy's does sometimes in chapel. "If you don't hell come to me. It is so easy to come at anyone in the dark. Oh, Winston, light the candle, for the love of God! I can't die in the dark."

"I am lighting it," I said, savagely, and I was feeling for the matches on the marble-topped chest of drawers, on the mantelpiece—everywhere but on the round centre-table where I had put them. "You're not going to die. Don't be a fool," I said. "It's all right. I'll get a light in a second."

He said, "It's cold. It's cold. It's cold," like that; three times. And then he screamed aloud, like a woman, like a child, like a hare when the dogs have got it. I had heard him scream like that once before.

"What is it?" I cried, hardly less aloud. "For God's sake hold your noise! What is it?"

There was an empty silence. Then, very slowly:—

"It's Visger," he said. And he spoke thickly, as through some stifling veil.

"Nonsense. Where?" I asked, and my hand closed on the matches

40

as he spoke.

"Here!" he screamed, sharply, as though he had torn the veil away, "here! Beside me. In the bed."

I got the candle alight. I got across to him.

He was crushed in a heap at the edge of the bed. Stretched on the bed beyond him was a dead man very white and cold.

Haldane had died in the dark.

It was all so simple.

We had come to the wrong room. The man the room belonged to was there, on the bed he had engaged and paid for before he died of heart disease, earlier in the day. A French *commis voyageur* representing soap and perfumery: his name, Felix Leblanc.

Later, in England, I made cautious inquiries. The body of a man had been found in the Red Hill Tunnel—a haberdasher named Simmons, who had drunk spirits of salts, owing to the depression of trade. The bottle was clutched in his dead hand.

For reasons that I had I took care to have a police inspector with me when I opened the boxes that came to me by Haldane's will. One of them was the big box, metal lined, in which I had sent him the skins from India—for a wedding present, God help us all!

It was closely soldered.

Inside were the skins of beasts. No—the bodies of two men. One was identified after some trouble as that of a hawker of pens in City offices—subject to fits. He had died in one, it seemed. The other body was Visger's, right enough. Explain it as you like. I offered you, if you remember, a choice of explanations before I began this story. I have not yet found the explanation that can satisfy me.

John Charrington's Wedding

No one ever thought that May Forster would marry John Charrington; but he thought differently, and things which John Charrington intended had a queer way of coming to pass. He asked her to marry him before he went up to Oxford. She laughed and refused him. He asked her again next time he came home. Again she laughed, tossed her dainty blonde head and again refused. A third time he asked her; she said it was becoming a confirmed bad habit, and laughed at him more than ever.

John was not the only man who wanted to marry her: she was the *belle* of our village *coterie*, and we were all in love with her more or less; it was a sort of fashion, like masher collars or Inverness capes. Therefore we were as much annoyed as surprised when John Charrington walked into our little local Club—we held it in a loft over the saddler's, I remember—and invited us all to his wedding.

'Your wedding?'

'You don't mean it?'

'Who's the happy pair? When's it to be?'

John Charrington filled his pipe and lighted it before he replied. Then he said:

'I'm sorry to deprive you fellows of your only joke—but Miss Forster and I are to be married in September.'

'You don't mean it?'

'He's got the mitten again, and it's turned his head.'

'No,' I said, rising, 'I see it's true. Lend me a pistol, someone—or a first-class fare to the other end of Nowhere. Charrington has bewitched the only pretty girl in our twenty-mile radius. Was it mesmerism, or a love-potion, Jack?'

'Neither, sir, but a gift you'll never have—perseverance—and the best luck a man ever had in this world.'

There was something in his voice that silenced me, and all chaff of the other fellows failed to draw him further.

The queer thing about it was that when we congratulated Miss Forster, she blushed and smiled and dimpled, for all the world as though she were in love with him, and had been in love with him all the time. Upon my word, I think she had. Women are strange creatures.

We were all asked to the wedding. In Brixham everyone who was anybody knew everybody else who was anyone. My sisters were, I truly believe, more interested in the trousseau than the bride herself, and I was to be best man. The coming marriage was much canvassed at afternoon tea-tables, and at our little Club over the saddler's, and the question was always asked, 'Does she care for him?'

I used to ask that question myself in the early days of their engagement, but after a certain evening in August I never asked it again. I was coming home from the Club through the churchyard. Our church is on a thyme-grown hill, and the turf about it is so thick and soft that one's footsteps are noiseless.

I made no sound as I vaulted the low lichened wall, and threaded my way between the tombstones. It was at the same instant that I heard John Charrington's voice, and saw her. May was sitting on a low flat gravestone, her face turned towards the full splendour of the western sun. Its expression ended, at once and for ever, any question of love for him; it was transfigured to a beauty I should not have believed possible, even to that beautiful little face.

John lay at her feet, and it was his voice that broke the stillness of the golden August evening.

'My dear, my dear, I believe I should come back from the dead if you wanted me!'

I coughed at once to indicate my presence, and passed on into the shadow fully enlightened.

The wedding was to be early in September. Two days before I had to run up to town on business. The train was late, of course, for we are on the South-Eastern, and as I stood grumbling with my watch in my hand, whom should I see but John Charrington and May Forster. They were walking up and down the unfrequented end of the platform, arm in arm, looking into each other's eyes, careless of the sympathetic interest of the porters.

Of course I knew better than to hesitate a moment before burying myself in the booking-office, and it was not till the train drew up at the platform, that I obtrusively passed the pair with my Gladstone, and took the corner in a first-class smoking-carriage. I did this with as good an air of not seeing them as I could assume. I pride myself on my discretion, but if John were travelling alone I wanted his company. I had it.

'Hullo, old man,' came his cheery voice as he swung his bag into my carriage; 'here's luck; I was expecting a dull journey!'

'Where are you off to?' I asked, discretion still bidding me turn my eyes away, though I saw, without looking, that hers were red-rimmed.

'To old Branbridge's,' he answered, shutting the door and leaning out for a last word with his sweetheart.

'Oh, I wish you wouldn't go, John,' she was saying in a low, earnest voice. 'I feel certain something will happen.'

'Do you think I should let anything happen to keep me, and the day after tomorrow our wedding day?'

'Don't go,' she answered, with a pleading intensity which would have sent my Gladstone onto the platform and me after it. But she wasn't speaking to me. John Charrington was made differently: he rarely changed his opinions, never his resolutions.

He only stroked the little ungloved hands that lay on the carriage door.

'I must, May. The old boy's been awfully good to me, and now he's dying I must go and see him, but I shall come home in time for ----' the rest of the parting was lost in a whisper and in the rattling lurch of the starting train.

'You're sure to come?' she spoke as the train moved.

'Nothing shall keep me,' he answered; and we steamed out. After he had seen the last of the little figure on the platform he leaned back in his corner and kept silence for a minute.

When he spoke it was to explain to me that his godfather, whose heir he was, lay dying at Peasmarsh Place, some fifty miles away, and had sent for John, and John had felt bound to go.

'I shall be surely back tomorrow,' he said, 'or, if not, the day after, in heaps of time. Thank heaven, one hasn't to get up in the middle of the night to get married nowadays!'

'And suppose Mr Branbridge dies?'

'Alive or dead I mean to be married on Thursday!' John answered, lighting a cigar and unfolding *The Times*.

At Peasmarsh station we said 'goodbye', and he got out, and I saw him ride off; I went on to London, where I stayed the night.

When I got home the next afternoon, a very wet one, by the way, my sister greeted me with:

'Where's Mr Charrington?'

'Goodness knows,' I answered testily. Every man, since Cain, has resented that kind of question.

'I thought you might have heard from him,' she went on, 'as you're to give him away tomorrow.'

'Isn't he back?' I asked, for I had confidently expected to find him at home.

'No, Geoffrey,' my sister Fanny always had a way of jumping to conclusions, especially such conclusions as were least favourable to her fellow-creatures—'he has not returned, and, what is more, you may depend upon it he won't. You mark my words, there'll be no wedding tomorrow.'

My sister Fanny has a power of annoying me which no other human being possesses.

'You mark my words,' I retorted with asperity, 'you had better give up making such a thundering idiot of yourself. There'll be more wedding tomorrow than ever you'll take the first part in.' A prophecy which, by the way, came true.

But though I could snarl confidently to my sister, I did not feel so comfortable when late that night, I, standing on the doorstep of John's house, heard that he had not returned. I went home gloomily through the rain. Next morning brought a brilliant blue sky, gold sun, and all such softness of air and beauty of cloud as go to make up a perfect day. I woke with a vague feeling of having gone to bed anxious, and of being rather averse to facing that anxiety in the light of full wakefulness.

But with my shaving-water came a note from John which relieved my mind and sent me up to the Forsters with a light heart.

May was in the garden. I saw her blue gown through the hollyhocks as the lodge gates swung to behind me. So I did not go up to the house, but turned aside down the turfed path.

'He's written to you too,' she said, without preliminary greeting, when I reached her side.

'Yes, I'm to meet him at the station at three, and come straight on to the church.'

Her face looked pale, but there was a brightness in her eyes, and a tender quiver about the mouth that spoke of renewed happiness.

'Mr Branbridge begged him so to stay another night that he had not the heart to refuse,' she went on. 'He is so kind, but I wish he hadn't stayed.'

I was at the station at half past two. I felt rather annoyed with John. It seemed a sort of slight to the beautiful girl who loved him, that he should come as it were out of breath, and with the dust of travel upon him, to take her hand, which some of us would have given the best years of our lives to take.

But when the three o'clock train glided in, and glided out again having brought no passengers to our little station, I was more than annoyed. There was no other train for thirty-five minutes; I calculated that, with much hurry, we might just get to the church in time for the ceremony; but, oh, what a fool to miss that first train! What other man could have done it?

That thirty-five minutes seemed a year, as I wandered round the station reading the advertisements and the timetables, and the company's bye-laws, and getting more and more angry with John Charrington. This confidence in his own power of getting everything he wanted the minute he wanted it was leading him too far. I hate waiting. Everyone does, but I believe I hate it more than anyone else. The three thirty-five was late, of course.

I ground my pipe between my teeth and stamped with impatience as I watched the signals. *Click.* The signal went down. Five minutes later I flung myself into the carriage that I had brought for John.

'Drive to the church!' I said, as someone shut the door. 'Mr Charrington hasn't come by this train.'

Anxiety now replaced anger. What had become of the man? Could he have been taken suddenly ill? I had never known him have a day's illness in his life. And even so he might have telegraphed. Some awful accident must have happened to him. The thought that he had played her false never—no, not for a moment—entered my head. Yes, some thing terrible had happened to him, and on me lay the task of telling his bride. I almost wished the carriage would upset and break my head so that someone else might tell her, not I, who—but that's nothing to do with this story.

It was five minutes to four as we drew up at the churchyard gate. A double row of eager onlookers lined the path from lychgate to porch. I sprang from the carriage and passed up between them. Our gardener had a good front place near the door. I stopped.

'Are they waiting still, Byles?' I asked, simply to gain time, for of course I knew they were by the waiting crowd's attentive attitude.

'Waiting, sir? No, no, sir; why, it must be over by now.'

'Over! Then Mr Charrington's come?'

To the minute, sir; must have missed you somehow, and I say, sir,' lowering his voice, 'I never see Mr John the least bit so afore, but my opinion is he's been drinking pretty free. His clothes was all dusty and his face like a sheet. I tell you I didn't like the looks of him at all, and the folks inside are saying all sorts of things. You'll see, something's gone very wrong with Mr John, and he's tried liquor. He looked like a ghost, and in he went with his eyes straight before him, with never a look or a word for none of us: him that was always such a gentleman!'

I had never heard Byles make so long a speech. The crowd in the churchyard were talking in whispers and getting ready rice and slippers to throw at the bride and bridegroom. The ringers were ready with their hands on the ropes to ring out the merry peal as the bride and bridegroom should come out.

A murmur from the church announced them; out they came. Byles was right. John Charrington did not look himself. There was dust on his coat, his hair was disarranged. He seemed to have been in some row, for there was a black mark above his eyebrow. He was deathly pale. But his pallor was not greater than that of the bride, who might have been carved in ivory—dress, veil, orange blossoms, face and all.

As they passed out the ringers stooped—there were six of them— and then, on the ears expecting the gay wedding peal, came the slow tolling of the passing bell.

A thrill of horror at so foolish a jest from the ringers passed through us all. But the ringers themselves dropped the ropes and fled like rabbits out into the sunlight. The bride shuddered, and grey shadows came about her mouth, but the bridegroom led her on down the path where the people stood with the handfuls of rice; but the handfuls were never thrown, and the wedding bells never rang. In vain the ringers were urged to remedy their mistake: they protested with many whispered expletives that they would see themselves further first.

In a hush like the hush in the chamber of death the bridal pair passed into their carriage and its door slammed behind them.

Then the tongues were loosed. A babel of anger, wonder, conjecture from the guests and the spectators.

'If I'd seen his condition, sir,' said old Forster to me as we drove off, 'I would have stretched him on the floor of the church, sir, by heaven I would, before I'd have let him marry my daughter!'

Then he put his head out of the window.

'Drive like hell,' he cried to the coachman; 'don't spare the horses.'

He was obeyed. We passed the bride's carriage. I forbore to look at it, and old Forster turned his head away and swore. We reached home before it.

We stood in the doorway, in the blazing afternoon sun, and in about half a minute we heard wheels crunching the gravel. When the carriage stopped in front of the steps old Forster and I ran down.

'Great heaven, the carriage is empty! And yet ----'

I had the door open in a minute, and this is what I saw . . .

No sign of John Charrington; and of May, his wife, only a huddled heap of white satin lying half on the floor of the carriage and half on the seat.

'I drove straight here, sir,' said the coachman, as the bride's father lifted her out; 'and I'll swear no one got out of the carriage.'

We carried her into the house in her bridal dress and drew back her veil. I saw her face. Shall I ever forget it? White, white and drawn with agony and horror, bearing such a look of terror as I have never seen since except in dreams. And her hair, her radiant blonde hair, I tell you it was white like snow.

As we stood, her father and I, half mad with the horror and mystery of it, a boy came up the avenue—a telegraph boy. They brought the orange envelope to me. I tore it open.

Mr Charrington was thrown from the dogcart on his way to the station at half past one. Killed on the spot!

And he was married to May Forster in our parish church at half past three, in presence of half the parish.

'I shall be married, dead, or alive!'

What had passed in that carriage on the homeward drive? No one knows—no one will ever know. Oh, May! oh, my dear!

Before a week was over they laid her beside her husband in our little churchyard on the thyme-covered hill—the churchyard where they had kept their love-trysts.

Thus was accomplished John Charrington's wedding.

Man-Size in Marble

Although every word of this story is as true as despair, I do not expect people to believe it. Nowadays a "rational explanation" is required before belief is possible. Let me then, at once, offer the "rational explanation" which finds most favour among those who have heard the tale of my life's tragedy. It is held that we were "under a delusion," Laura and I, on that 31st of October; and that this supposition places the whole matter on a satisfactory and believable basis. The reader can judge, when he, too, has heard my story, how far this is an "explanation," and in what sense it is "rational." There were three who took part in this: Laura and I and another man. The other man still lives, and can speak to the truth of the least credible part of my story.

I never in my life knew what it was to have as much money as I required to supply the most ordinary needs—good colours, books, and cab-fares—and when we were married we knew quite well that we should only be able to live at all by "strict punctuality and attention to business." I used to paint in those days, and Laura used to write, and we felt sure we could keep the pot at least simmering. Living in town was out of the question, so we went to look for a cottage in the country, which should be at once sanitary and picturesque. So rarely do these two qualities meet in one cottage that our search was for some time quite fruitless. We tried advertisements, but most of the desirable rural residences which we did look at proved to be lacking in both essentials, and when a cottage chanced to have drains it always had stucco as well and was shaped like a tea-caddy. And if we found a vine or rose-covered porch, corruption invariably lurked within.

Our minds got so befogged by the eloquence of house-agents and the rival disadvantages of the fever-traps and outrages to beauty which we had seen and scorned, that I very much doubt whether either of us, on our wedding morning, knew the difference between a house and a haystack. But when we got away from friends and house-agents, on our honeymoon, our wits grew clear again, and we knew a pretty cottage when at last we saw one. It was at Brenzett—a little village set on a hill over against the southern marshes. We had gone there, from the seaside village where we were staying, to see the church, and two fields from the church we found this cottage. It stood quite by itself, about two miles from the village. It was a long, low building, with rooms sticking out in unexpected places. There was a bit of stone-work—ivy-covered and moss-grown, just two old rooms, all that was left of a big house that had once stood there—and round this stone-work the house had grown up. Stripped of its roses and jasmine it would have been hideous.

As it stood it was charming, and after a brief examination we took it. It was absurdly cheap. The rest of our honeymoon we spent in grubbing about in second-hand shops in the county town, picking up bits of old oak and Chippendale chairs for our furnishing. We wound up with a run up to town and a visit to Liberty's, and soon the low oak-beamed lattice-windowed rooms began to be home. There was a jolly old-fashioned garden, with grass paths, and no end of hollyhocks and sunflowers, and big lilies. From the window you could see the marsh-pastures, and beyond them the blue, thin line of the sea. We were as happy as the summer was glorious, and settled down into work sooner than we ourselves expected. I was never tired of sketching the view and the wonderful cloud effects from the open lattice, and Laura would sit at the table and write verses about them, in which I mostly played the part of foreground.

We got a tall old peasant woman to do for us. Her face and figure were good, though her cooking was of the homeliest; but she understood all about gardening, and told us all the old names of the coppices and cornfields, and the stories of the smugglers and highwaymen, and, better still, of the "things that walked," and of the "sights" which met one in lonely glens of a starlight night. She was a great comfort to us, because Laura hated housekeeping as much as I loved folklore, and we soon came to leave all the domestic business to Mrs. Dorman, and to use her legends in little magazine stories which brought in the jingling guinea.

We had three months of married happiness, and did not have a single quarrel. One October evening I had been down to smoke a pipe with the doctor—our only neighbour—a pleasant young Irishman. Laura had stayed at home to finish a comic sketch of a village episode for the Monthly Marplot. I left her laughing over her own jokes, and came in to find her a crumpled heap of pale muslin weeping on the window seat.

"Good heavens, my darling, what's the matter?" I cried, taking her in my arms. She leaned her little dark head against my shoulder and went on crying. I had never seen her cry before—we had always been so happy, you see—and I felt sure some frightful misfortune had happened.

"What is the matter? Do speak."

"It's Mrs. Dorman," she sobbed.

"What has she done?" I inquired, immensely relieved.

"She says she must go before the end of the month, and she says her niece is ill; she's gone down to see her now, but I don't believe that's the reason, because her niece is always ill. I believe someone has been setting her against us. Her manner was so queer—"

"Never mind, Pussy," I said; "whatever you do, don't cry, or I shall have to cry too, to keep you in countenance, and then you'll never respect your man again!"

She dried her eyes obediently on my handkerchief, and even smiled faintly.

"But you see," she went on, "it is really serious, because these village people are so sheepy, and if one won't do a thing you may be quite sure none of the others will. And I shall have to cook the dinners, and wash up the hateful greasy plates; and you'll have to carry cans of water about, and clean the boots and knives—and we shall never have any time for work, or earn any money, or anything. We shall have to work all day, and only be able to rest when we are waiting for the kettle to boil!"

I represented to her that even if we had to perform these duties, the day would still present some margin for other toils and recreations. But she refused to see the matter in any but the greyest light. She was very unreasonable, my Laura, but I could not have loved her any more if she had been as reasonable as Whately.

"I'll speak to Mrs. Dorman when she comes back, and see if I can't come to terms with her," I said. "Perhaps she wants a rise in her screw. It will be all right. Let's walk up to the church."

The church was a large and lonely one, and we loved to go there, especially upon bright nights. The path skirted a wood, cut through it once, and ran along the crest of the hill through two meadows, and round the churchyard wall, over which the old yews loomed in black masses of shadow. This path, which was partly paved, was called "the bier-balk," for it had long been the way by which the corpses had been carried to burial. The churchyard was richly treed, and was shaded by great elms which stood just outside and stretched their majestic arms in benediction over the happy dead. A large, low porch let one into the building by a Norman doorway and a heavy oak door studded with iron. Inside, the arches rose into darkness, and between them the reticulated windows, which stood out white in the moonlight. In the chancel, the windows were of rich glass, which showed in faint light their noble colouring, and made the black oak of the choir pews hardly more solid than the shadows.

But on each side of the altar lay a grey marble figure of a knight in full plate armour lying upon a low slab, with hands held up in everlasting prayer, and these figures, oddly enough, were always to be seen if there was any glimmer of light in the church. Their names were lost, but the peasants told of them that they had been fierce and wicked men, marauders by land and sea, who had been the scourge of their time, and had been guilty of deeds so foul that the house they had lived in—the big house, by the way, that had stood on the site of our cottage—had been stricken by lightning and the vengeance of Heaven. But for all that, the gold of their heirs had bought them a place in the church. Looking at the bad hard faces reproduced in the marble, this story was easily believed.

The church looked at its best and weirdest on that night, for the shadows of the yew trees fell through the windows upon the floor of the nave and touched the pillars with tattered shade. We sat down together without speaking, and watched the solemn beauty of the old church, with some of that awe which inspired its early builders. We walked to the chancel and looked at the sleeping warriors. Then we rested some time on the stone seat in the porch, looking out over the stretch of quiet moonlit meadows, feeling in every fibre of our being the peace of the night and of our happy love; and came away at last with a sense that even scrubbing and blackleading were but small troubles at their worst.

Mrs. Dorman had come back from the village, and I at once invited her to a *tête-à-tête*.

"Now, Mrs. Dorman," I said, when I had got her into my painting room, "what's all this about your not staying with us?"

"I should be glad to get away, sir, before the end of the month," she answered, with her usual placid dignity.

"Have you any fault to find, Mrs. Dorman?"

"None at all, sir; you and your lady have always been most kind, I'm sure—"

"Well, what is it? Are your wages not high enough?"

"No, sir, I gets quite enough."

"Then why not stay?"

"I'd rather not"—with some hesitation—"my niece is ill."

"But your niece has been ill ever since we came."

No answer. There was a long and awkward silence. I broke it.

"Can't you stay for another month?" I asked.

"No, sir. I'm bound to go by Thursday."

And this was Monday!

"Well, I must say, I think you might have let us know before. There's no time now to get anyone else, and your mistress is not fit to do heavy housework. Can't you stay till next week?"

"I might be able to come back next week."

I was now convinced that all she wanted was a brief holiday, which we should have been willing enough to let her have, as soon as we could get a substitute.

"But why must you go this week?" I persisted. "Come, out with it."

Mrs. Dorman drew the little shawl, which she always wore, tightly across her bosom, as though she were cold. Then she said, with a sort of effort—

"They say, sir, as this was a big house in Catholic times, and there was a many deeds done here."

The nature of the "deeds" might be vaguely inferred from the inflection of Mrs. Dorman's voice—which was enough to make one's blood run cold. I was glad that Laura was not in the room. She was always nervous, as highly-strung natures are, and I felt that these tales about our house, told by this old peasant woman, with her impressive manner and contagious credulity, might have made our home less dear to my wife.

"Tell me all about it, Mrs. Dorman," I said; "you needn't mind about telling me. I'm not like the young people who make fun of such things."

Which was partly true.

"Well, sir"—she sank her voice—"you may have seen in the church, beside the altar, two shapes."

"You mean the effigies of the knights in armour," I said cheerfully.

"I mean them two bodies, drawed out man-size in marble," she returned, and I had to admit that her description was a thousand times more graphic than mine, to say nothing of a certain weird force and uncanniness about the phrase "drawed out man-size in marble."

"They do say, as on All Saints' Eve them two bodies sits up on their slabs, and gets off of them, and then walks down the aisle, in their marble"—(another good phrase, Mrs. Dorman)—"and as the church clock strikes eleven they walks out of the church door, and over the graves, and along the bier-balk, and if it's a wet night there's the marks of their feet in the morning."

"And where do they go?" I asked, rather fascinated.

"They comes back here to their home, sir, and if anyone meets them—"

"Well, what then?" I asked.

But no—not another word could I get from her, save that her niece was ill and she must go. After what I had heard I scorned to discuss the niece, and tried to get from Mrs. Dorman more details of the legend. I could get nothing but warnings.

"Whatever you do, sir, lock the door early on All Saints' Eve, and make the cross-sign over the doorstep and on the windows."

"But has anyone ever seen these things?" I persisted.

"That's not for me to say. I know what I know, sir."

"Well, who was here last year?"

"No one, sir; the lady as owned the house only stayed here in summer, and she always went to London a full month afore the night. And I'm sorry to inconvenience you and your lady, but my niece is ill and I must go on Thursday."

I could have shaken her for her absurd reiteration of that obvious fiction, after she had told me her real reasons.

She was determined to go, nor could our united entreaties move her in the least.

I did not tell Laura the legend of the shapes that "walked in their marble," partly because a legend concerning our house might perhaps trouble my wife, and partly, I think, from some more occult reason. This was not quite the same to me as any other story, and I did not want to talk about it till the day was over. I had very soon ceased to think of the legend, however. I was painting a portrait of Laura, against the lattice window, and I could not think of much else. I had got a splendid background of yellow and grey sunset, and was working away with enthusiasm at her lace. On Thursday Mrs. Dorman went. She relented, at parting, so far as to say—

"Don't you put yourself about too much, ma'am, and if there's any little thing I can do next week, I'm sure I shan't mind."

From which I inferred that she wished to come back to us after Hallowe'en. Up to the last she adhered to the fiction of the niece with touching fidelity.

Thursday passed off pretty well. Laura showed marked ability in the matter of steak and potatoes, and I confess that my knives, and the plates, which I insisted upon washing, were better done than I had dared to expect.

Friday came. It is about what happened on that Friday that this is written. I wonder if I should have believed it, if anyone had told it to me. I will write the story of it as quickly and plainly as I can. Everything that happened on that day is burnt into my brain. I shall not forget anything, nor leave anything out.

I got up early, I remember, and lighted the kitchen fire, and had just achieved a smoky success, when my little wife came running down, as sunny and sweet as the clear October morning itself. We prepared breakfast together, and found it very good fun. The housework was soon done, and when brushes and brooms and pails were quiet again, the house was still indeed. It is wonderful what a difference one makes in a house. We really missed Mrs. Dorman, quite apart from considerations concerning pots and pans. We spent the day in dusting our books and putting them straight, and dined gaily on cold steak and coffee. Laura was, if possible, brighter and gayer and sweeter than usual, and I began to think that a little domestic toil was really good for her.

We had never been so merry since we were married, and the walk we had that afternoon was, I think, the happiest time of all my life. When we had watched the deep scarlet clouds slowly pale into leaden grey against a pale-green sky, and saw the white mists curl up along the hedgerows in the distant marsh, we came back to the house, silently, hand in hand.

"You are sad, my darling," I said, half-jestingly, as we sat down together in our little parlour. I expected a disclaimer, for my own silence had been the silence of complete happiness. To my surprise she said—

"Yes. I think I am sad, or rather I am uneasy. I don't think I'm very well. I have shivered three or four times since we came in, and it is not cold, is it?"

"No," I said, and hoped it was not a chill caught from the treacherous mists that roll up from the marshes in the dying light. No—she said, she did not think so. Then, after a silence, she spoke suddenly—

"Do you ever have presentiments of evil?"

"No," I said, smiling, "and I shouldn't believe in them if I had."

"I do," she went on; "the night my father died I knew it, though he was right away in the north of Scotland." I did not answer in words.

She sat looking at the fire for some time in silence, gently stroking my hand. At last she sprang up, came behind me, and, drawing my head back, kissed me.

"There, it's over now," she said. "What a baby I am! Come, light the candles, and we'll have some of these new Rubinstein duets."

And we spent a happy hour or two at the piano.

At about half-past ten I began to long for the goodnight pipe, but Laura looked so white that I felt it would be brutal of me to fill our sitting-room with the fumes of strong cavendish.

"I'll take my pipe outside," I said.

"Let me come, too."

"No, sweetheart, not tonight; you're much too tired. I shan't be long. Get to bed, or I shall have an invalid to nurse tomorrow as well as the boots to clean."

I kissed her and was turning to go, when she flung her arms round my neck, and held me as if she would never let me go again. I stroked her hair.

"Come, Pussy, you're over-tired. The housework has been too much for you."

She loosened her clasp a little and drew a deep breath.

"No. We've been very happy today, Jack, haven't we? Don't stay out too long."

"I won't, my dearie."

I strolled out of the front door, leaving it unlatched. What a night it was! The jagged masses of heavy dark cloud were rolling at intervals from horizon to horizon, and thin white wreaths covered the stars. Through all the rush of the cloud river, the moon swam, breasting the waves and disappearing again in the darkness. When now and again her light reached the woodlands they seemed to be slowly and noiselessly waving in time to the swing of the clouds above them. There was a strange grey light over all the earth; the fields had that shadowy bloom over them which only comes from the marriage of dew and moonshine, or frost and starlight.

I walked up and down, drinking in the beauty of the quiet earth and the changing sky. The night was absolutely silent. Nothing seemed to be abroad. There was no scurrying of rabbits, or twitter of the half-asleep birds. And though the clouds went sailing across the sky, the wind that drove them never came low enough to rustle the dead leaves in the woodland paths. Across the meadows I could see the church tower standing out black and grey against the sky. I walked there thinking over our three months of happiness—and of my wife, her dear eyes, her loving ways. Oh, my little girl! my own little girl; what a vision came then of a long, glad life for you and me together!

I heard a bell-beat from the church. Eleven already! I turned to go in, but the night held me. I could not go back into our little warm rooms yet. I would go up to the church. I felt vaguely that it would be good to carry my love and thankfulness to the sanctuary whither so many loads of sorrow and gladness had been borne by the men and women of the dead years.

I looked in at the low window as I went by. Laura was half lying on her chair in front of the fire. I could not see her face, only her little head showed dark against the pale blue wall. She was quite still. Asleep, no doubt. My heart reached out to her, as I went on. There must be a God, I thought, and a God who was good. How otherwise could anything so sweet and dear as she have ever been imagined?

I walked slowly along the edge of the wood. A sound broke the stillness of the night, it was a rustling in the wood. I stopped and listened. The sound stopped too. I went on, and now distinctly heard another step than mine answer mine like an echo. It was a poacher or a wood-stealer, most likely, for these were not unknown in our Arcadian neighbourhood. But whoever it was, he was a fool not to step more lightly. I turned into the wood, and now the footstep seemed to come from the path I had just left. It must be an echo, I thought. The wood looked perfect in the moonlight. The large dying ferns and the brushwood showed where through thinning foliage the pale light came down.

The tree trunks stood up like Gothic columns all around me. They reminded me of the church, and I turned into the bier-balk, and passed through the corpse-gate between the graves to the low porch. I paused for a moment on the stone seat where Laura and I had watched the fading landscape. Then I noticed that the door of the church was open, and I blamed myself for having left it unlatched the other night. We were the only people who ever cared to come to the church except on Sundays, and I was vexed to think that through our carelessness the damp autumn airs had had a chance of getting in and injuring the old fabric. I went in. It will seem strange, perhaps, that I should have gone half-way up the aisle before I remembered—with a sudden chill, followed by as sudden a rush of self-contempt—that this was the very day and hour when, according to tradition, the "shapes drawed out man-size in marble" began to walk.

Having thus remembered the legend, and remembered it with a shiver, of which I was ashamed, I could not do otherwise than walk up towards the altar, just to look at the figures—as I said to myself; really what I wanted was to assure myself, first, that I did not believe the legend, and, secondly, that it was not true. I was rather glad that I had come. I thought now I could tell Mrs. Dorman how vain her fancies were, and how peacefully the marble figures slept on through the ghastly hour. With my hands in my pockets I passed up the aisle. In the grey dim light, the eastern end of the church looked larger than usual, and the arches above the two tombs looked larger too. The moon came out and showed me the reason. I stopped short, my heart gave a leap that nearly choked me, and then sank sickeningly.

The "bodies drawed out man-size" were gone, and their marble slabs lay wide and bare in the vague moonlight that slanted through the east window.

Were they really gone? or was I mad? Clenching my nerves, I stooped and passed my hand over the smooth slabs, and felt their flat unbroken surface. Had someone taken the things away? Was it some vile practical joke? I would make sure, anyway. In an instant I had made a torch of a newspaper, which happened to be in my pocket, and lighting it held it high above my head. Its yellow glare illumined the dark arches and those slabs. The figures were gone. And I was alone in the church; or was I alone?

And then a horror seized me, a horror indefinable and indescribable—an overwhelming certainty of supreme and accomplished calamity. I flung down the torch and tore along the aisle and out through the porch, biting my lips as I ran to keep myself from shrieking aloud. Oh, was I mad—or what was this that possessed me? I leaped the churchyard wall and took the straight cut across the fields, led by the light from our windows. Just as I got over the first stile, a dark figure seemed to spring out of the ground. Mad still with that certainty of misfortune, I made for the thing that stood in my path, shouting, "Get out of the way, can't you!"

But my push met with a more vigorous resistance than I had expected. My arms were caught just above the elbow and held as in a vice, and the raw-boned Irish doctor actually shook me.

"Would ye?" he cried, in his own unmistakable accents—"would ye, then?"

"Let me go, you fool," I gasped. "The marble figures have gone from the church; I tell you they've gone."

He broke into a ringing laugh. "I'll have to give ye a draught to-morrow, I see. Ye've bin smoking too much and listening to old wives' tales."

"I tell you, I've seen the bare slabs."

"Well, come back with me. I'm going up to old Palmer's—his daughter's ill; we'll look in at the church and let me see the bare slabs."

"You go, if you like," I said, a little less frantic for his laughter; "I'm going home to my wife."

"Rubbish, man," said he; "d'ye think I'll permit of that? Are ye to go saying all yer life that ye've seen solid marble endowed with vitality, and me to go all me life saying ye were a coward? No, sir—ye shan't do ut."

The night air—a human voice—and I think also the physical contact with this six feet of solid common sense, brought me back a little to my ordinary self, and the word "coward" was a mental shower-bath.

"Come on, then," I said sullenly; "perhaps you're right."

He still held my arm tightly. We got over the stile and back to the church. All was still as death. The place smelt very damp and earthy. We walked up the aisle. I am not ashamed to confess that I shut my eyes: I knew the figures would not be there. I heard Kelly strike a match.

"Here they are, ye see, right enough; ye've been dreaming or drinking, asking yer pardon for the imputation."

I opened my eyes. By Kelly's expiring vesta I saw two shapes lying "in their marble" on their slabs. I drew a deep breath, and caught his hand.

"I'm awfully indebted to you," I said. "It must have been some trick of light, or I have been working rather hard, perhaps that's it. Do you know, I was quite convinced they were gone."

"I'm aware of that," he answered rather grimly; "ye'll have to be careful of that brain of yours, my friend, I assure ye."

He was leaning over and looking at the right-hand figure, whose stony face was the most villainous and deadly in expression.

"By Jove," he said, "something has been afoot here—this hand is broken."

And so, it was. I was certain that it had been perfect the last time Laura and I had been there.

"Perhaps someone has tried to remove them," said the young doctor.

"That won't account for my impression," I objected.

"Too much painting and tobacco will account for that, well enough."

"Come along," I said, "or my wife will be getting anxious. You'll come in and have a drop of whisky and drink confusion to ghosts and better sense to me."

"I ought to go up to Palmer's, but it's so late now I'd best leave it till the morning," he replied. "I was kept late at the Union, and I've had to see a lot of people since. All right, I'll come back with ye."

I think he fancied I needed him more than did Palmer's girl, so, discussing how such an illusion could have been possible, and deducing from this experience large generalities concerning ghostly apparitions, we walked up to our cottage. We saw, as we walked up the garden-path, that bright light streamed out of the front door, and presently saw that the parlour door was open too. Had she gone out?

"Come in," I said, and Dr. Kelly followed me into the parlour. It was all ablaze with candles, not only the wax ones, but at least a dozen guttering, glaring tallow dips, stuck in vases and ornaments in unlikely places. Light, I knew, was Laura's remedy for nervousness. Poor child! Why had I left her? Brute that I was.

We glanced round the room, and at first, we did not see her. The window was open, and the draught set all the candles flaring one way. Her chair was empty and her handkerchief and book lay on the floor. I turned to the window. There, in the recess of the window, I saw her. Oh, my child, my love, had she gone to that window to watch for me? And what had come into the room behind her? To what had she turned with that look of frantic fear and horror? Oh, my little one, had she thought that it was I whose step she heard, and turned to meet—what?

She had fallen back across a table in the window, and her body lay half on it and half on the window-seat, and her head hung down over the table, the brown hair loosened and fallen to the carpet. Her lips were drawn back, and her eyes wide, wide open. They saw nothing now. What had they seen last?

The doctor moved towards her, but I pushed him aside and sprang to her; caught her in my arms and cried—-

"It's all right, Laura! I've got you safe, wifie."

She fell into my arms in a heap. I clasped her and kissed her, and called her by all her pet names, but I think I knew all the time that she was dead. Her hands were tightly clenched. In one of them she held something fast. When I was quite sure that she was dead, and that nothing mattered at all any more, I let him open her hand to see what she held.

It was a grey marble finger.

No. 17

I yawned. I could not help it. But the flat, inexorable voice went on.

"Speaking from the journalistic point of view—I may tell you, gentlemen, that I once occupied the position of advertisement editor to the *Bradford Woollen Goods Journal*—and speaking from that point of view, I hold the opinion that all the best ghost stories have been written over and over again; and if I were to leave the road and return to a literary career I should never be led away by ghosts. Realism's what's wanted nowadays, if you want to be up-to-date."

The large commercial paused for breath.

"You never can tell with the public," said the lean, elderly traveller; "it's like in the fancy business. You never know how it's going to be. Whether it's a clockwork ostrich or sometite silk or a particular shape of shaded glass novelty or a tobacco-box got up to look like a raw chop, you never know your luck."

"That depends on who you are," said the dapper man in the corner by the fire. "If you've got the right push about you, you can make a thing go, whether it's a clockwork kitten or imitation meat, and with stories, I take it, it's just the same—realism or ghost stories. But the best ghost story would be the realest one, *I* think."

The large commercial had got his breath.

"I don't believe in ghost stories, myself," he was saying with earnest dullness; "but there was a rather a queer thing happened to a second cousin of an aunt of mine by marriage—a very sensible woman with no nonsense about her. And the soul of truth and honour. I shouldn't have believed it if she had been one of your flighty, fanciful sort."

"Don't tell us the story," said the melancholy man who travelled in hardware; "you'll make us afraid to go to bed."

The well-meant effort failed. The large commercial went on, as I had known he would; his words overflowed his mouth, as his person overflowed his chair. I turned my mind to my own affairs, coming back to the commercial room in time to hear the summing up.

"The doors were all locked, and she was quite certain she saw a tall, white figure glide past her and vanish. I wouldn't have believed it if——" And so on *da capo*, from "if she hadn't been the second cousin" to the "soul of truth and honour."

I yawned again.

"Very good story," said the smart little man by the fire. He was a traveller, as the rest of us were; his presence in the room told us that much. He had been rather silent during dinner, and afterwards, while the red curtains were being drawn and the red and black cloth laid between the glasses and the decanters and the mahogany, he had quietly taken the best chair in the warmest corner. We had got our letters written and the large traveller had been boring for some time before I even noticed that there was a best chair and that this silent, bright-eyed, dapper, fair man had secured it.

"Very good story," he said; "but it's not what I call realism. You don't tell us half enough, sir. You don't say when it happened or where, or the time of year, or what colour your aunt's second cousin's hair was. Nor yet you don't tell us what it was she saw, nor what the room was like where she saw it, nor why she saw it, nor what happened afterwards. And I shouldn't like to breathe a word against anybody's aunt by marriage's cousin, first or second, but I must say I like a story about what a man's seen *himself*."

"So, do I," the large commercial snorted, "when I hear it."

He blew his nose like a trumpet of defiance.

"But," said the rabbit-faced man, "we know nowadays, what with the advance of science and all that sort of thing, we know there aren't any such things as ghosts. They're hallucinations; that's what they are—hallucinations."

"Don't seem to matter what you call them," the dapper one urged. "If you see a thing that looks as real as you do yourself, a thing that makes your blood run cold and turns you sick and silly with fear—well, call it ghost, or call it hallucination, or call it Tommy Dodd; it isn't the *name* that matters."

The elderly commercial coughed and said, "You might call it another name. You might call it——"

"No, you mightn't," said the little man, briskly; "not when the man it happened to had been a teetotal Bond of Joy for five years and is to this day."

"Why don't you tell us the story?" I asked.

"I might be willing," he said, "if the rest of the company were agreeable. Only I warn you it's not that sort-of-a-kind-of-a-somebody-fancied-they-saw-a-sort-of-a-kind-of-a-something-sort-of story. No, sir. Everything I'm going to tell you is plain and straightforward and as clear as a time-table—clearer than some. But I don't much like telling it, especially to people who don't believe in ghosts."

Several of us said we did believe in ghosts. The heavy man snorted and looked at his watch. And the man in the best chair began.

"Turn the gas down a bit, will you? Thanks. Did any of you know Herbert Hatteras? He was on this road a good many years. No? well, never mind. He was a good chap, I believe, with good teeth and a black whisker. But I didn't know him myself. He was before my time. Well, this that I'm going to tell you about happened at a certain commercial hotel. I'm not going to give it a name, because that sort of thing gets about, and in every other respect it's a good house and reasonable, and we all have our living to get. It was just a good ordinary old-fashioned commercial hotel, as it might be this. And I've often used it since, though they've never put me in that room again. Perhaps they shut it up after what happened.

"Well, the beginning of it was, I came across an old schoolfellow; in Boulter's Lock one Sunday it was, I remember. Jones was his name, Ted Jones. We both had canoes. We had tea at Marlow, and we got talking about this and that and old times and old mates; and do you remember Jim, and what's become of Tom, and so on. Oh, you know. And I happened to ask after his brother, Fred by name. And Ted turned pale and almost dropped his cup, and he said, 'You don't mean to say you haven't heard?' 'No,' says I, mopping up the tea he'd slopped over with my handkerchief. 'No, what?' I said.

"'It was horrible,' he said. 'They wired for me, and I saw him afterwards. Whether he'd done it himself or not, nobody knows; but they'd found him lying on the floor with his throat cut.' No cause could be assigned for the rash act, Ted told me. I asked him where it had happened, and he told me the name of this hotel—I'm not going to name it. And when I'd sympathised with him and drawn him out about old times and poor old Fred being such a good old sort and all that, I asked him what the room was like. I always like to know what the places look like where things happen.

"No, there wasn't anything specially rum about the room, only that it had a French bed with red curtains in a sort of alcove; and a large mahogany wardrobe as big as a hearse, with a glass door; and, instead of a swing-glass, a carved, black-framed glass screwed up against the wall between the windows, and a picture of 'Belshazzar's Feast' over the mantelpiece. I beg your pardon?" He stopped, for the heavy commercial had opened his mouth and shut it again.

"I thought you were going to say something," the dapper man went on. "Well, we talked about other things and parted, and I thought no more about it till business brought me to—but I'd better not name the town either—and I found my firm had marked this very hotel—where poor Fred had met his death, you know—for me to put up at. And I had to put up there too, because of their addressing everything to me there. And, anyhow, I expect I should have gone there out of curiosity.

"No. I didn't believe in ghosts in those days. I was like you, sir." He nodded amiably to the large commercial.

"The house was very full, and we were quite a large party in the room—very pleasant company, as it might be tonight; and we got talking of ghosts—just as it might be us. And there was a chap in glasses, sitting just over there, I remember—an old hand on the road, he was; and he said, just as it might be any of you, 'I don't believe in ghosts, but I wouldn't care to sleep in No. 17, for all that'; and, of course, we asked him why. 'Because,' said he, very short, 'that's why.'

"But when we'd persuaded him a bit, he told us.

"'Because that's the room where chaps cut their throats,' he said. "There was a chap called Bert Hatteras began it. They found him weltering in his gore. And since that every man that's slept there's been found with his throat cut.'

"I asked him how many had slept there. 'Well, only two beside the first,' he said; 'they shut it up then.' 'Oh, did they?' said I. 'Well, they've opened it again. No. 17's my room!'

"I tell you those chaps looked at me.

"'But you aren't going to *sleep* in it?' one of them said. And I explained that I didn't pay half a dollar for a bedroom to keep awake in.

"'I suppose it's press of business has made them open it up again,' the chap in spectacles said. 'It's a very mysterious affair. There's some secret horror about that room that we don't understand,' he said, 'and I'll tell you another queer thing. Every one of those poor chaps was a commercial gentleman. That's what I don't like about it. There was Bert Hatteras—he was the first, and a chap called Jones—Frederick

Jones, and then Donald Overshaw—a Scotchman he was, and travelled in children's underclothing.'

"Well, we sat there and talked a bit, and if I hadn't been a Bond of Joy, I don't know that I mightn't have exceeded, gentlemen—yes, positively exceeded; for the more I thought about it the less I liked the thought of No. 17. I hadn't noticed the room particularly, except to see that the furniture had been changed since poor Fred's time. So I just slipped out, by and by, and I went out to the little glass case under the arch where the booking-clerk sits—just like here, that hotel was—and I said:—

"'Look here, miss; haven't you got another room empty except seventeen?'

"'No,' she said; 'I don't think so.'"

"'Then what's that?' I said, and pointed to a key hanging on the board, the only one left.

"'Oh,' she said, 'that's sixteen.'

"'Anyone in sixteen?' I said. 'Is it a comfortable room?'

"'No,' said she. 'Yes; quite comfortable. It's next door to yours—much the same class of room.'

"'Then I'll have sixteen, if you've no objection,' I said, and went back to the others, feeling very clever.

"When I went up to bed, I locked my door, and, though I didn't believe in ghosts, I wished seventeen wasn't next door to me, and I wished there wasn't a door between the two rooms, though the door was locked right enough and the key on my side. I'd only got the one candle besides the two on the dressing-table, which I hadn't lighted; and I got my collar and tie off before I noticed that the furniture in my new room was the furniture out of No. 17; French bed with red curtains, mahogany wardrobe as big as a hearse, and the carved mirror over the dressing-table between the two windows, and 'Belshazzar's Feast' over the mantelpiece. So that, though I'd not got the *room* where the commercial gentlemen had cut their throats, I'd got the *furniture* out of it. And for a moment I thought that was worse than the other. When I thought of what that furniture could tell, if it could speak——

"It was a silly thing to do—but we're all friends here and I don't mind owning up—I looked under the bed and I looked inside the hearse-wardrobe and I looked in a sort of narrow cupboard there was, where a body could have stood upright——"

"A body?" I repeated.

"A man, I mean. You see, it seemed to me that either these poor chaps had been murdered by someone who hid himself in No. 17 to do it, or else there was something there that frightened them into cutting their throats; and upon my soul, I can't tell you which idea I liked least!"

He paused, and filled his pipe very deliberately. "Go, on," someone said. And he went on.

"Now, you'll observe," he said, "that all I've told you up to the time of my going to bed that night's just hearsay. So, I don't ask you to believe it—though the three coroners' inquests would be enough to stagger most chaps, I should say. Still, what I'm going to tell you now's *my* part of the story—what happened to me myself in that room."

He paused again, holding the pipe in his hand, unlighted.

There was a silence, which I broke.

"Well, what *did* happen?" I asked.

"I had a bit of a struggle with myself," he said. "I reminded myself it was not *that* room, but the next one that it had happened in. I smoked a pipe or two and read the morning paper, advertisements and all. And at last I went to bed. I left the candle burning, though, I own that."

"Did you sleep?" I asked.

"Yes. I slept. Sound as a top. I was awakened by a soft tapping on my door. I sat up. I don't think I've ever been so frightened in my life. But I made myself say, 'Who's there?' in a whisper. Heaven knows I never expected anyone to answer. The candle had gone out and it was pitch-dark. There was a quiet murmur and a shuffling sound outside. And no one answered. I tell you I hadn't expected anyone to. But I cleared my throat and cried out, 'Who's there?' in a real out-loud voice. And 'Me, sir,' said a voice. 'Shaving-water, sir; six o'clock, sir.'

"It was the chambermaid."

A movement of relief ran round our circle.

"I don't think much of your story," said the large commercial.

"You haven't heard it yet," said the story-teller, dryly. "It was six o'clock on a winter's morning, and pitch-dark. My train went at seven. I got up and began to dress. My one candle wasn't much use. I lighted the two on the dressing-table to see to shave by. There wasn't any shaving-water outside my door, after all. And the passage was as black as a coal-hole. So, I started to shave with cold water; one has to sometimes, you know. I'd gone over my face and I was just going lightly round under my chin, when I saw something move in the looking-glass. I mean something that moved was reflected in the looking-glass. The big door of the wardrobe had swung open, and by a sort of double reflection I could see the French bed with the red curtains. On the edge of it sat a man in his shirt and trousers—a man with black hair and whiskers, with the most awful look of despair and fear on his face that I've ever seen or dreamt of. I stood paralyzed, watching him in the mirror. I could not have turned round to save my life. Suddenly he laughed. It was a horrid, silent laugh, and showed all his teeth. They were very white and even. And the next moment he had cut his throat from ear to ear, there before my eyes. Did you ever see a man cut his throat? The bed was all white before."

The story-teller had laid down his pipe, and he passed his hand over his face before he went on.

"When I could look around, I did. There was no one in the room. The bed was as white as ever. Well, that's all," he said, abruptly, "except that now, of course, I understood how these poor chaps had come by their deaths. They'd all seen this horror—the ghost of the first poor chap, I suppose—Bert Hatteras, you know; and with the shock their hands must have slipped and their throats got cut before they could stop themselves. Oh! by the way, when I looked at my watch it was two o'clock; there hadn't been any chambermaid at all. I must have dreamed that. But I didn't dream the other. Oh! And one thing more. It was the same room. They hadn't changed the room; they'd only changed the number. *It was the same room!*"

"Look here," said the heavy man; "the room you've been talking about. *My* room's sixteen. And it's got that same furniture in it as what you describe, and the same picture and all."

"Oh, has it?" said the storyteller, a little uncomfortable, it seemed. "I'm sorry. But the cat's out of the bag now, and it can't be helped. Yes, it *was* this house I was speaking of. I suppose they've opened the room again. But you don't believe in ghosts; *you'll* be all right."

"Yes," said the heavy man, and presently got up and left the room.

"He's gone to see if he can get his room changed. You see if he hasn't," said the rabbit-faced man; "and I don't wonder."

The heavy man came back and settled into his chair.

"I could do with a drink," he said, reaching to the bell.

"I'll stand some punch, gentlemen, if you'll allow me," said our dapper story-teller. "I rather pride myself on my punch. I'll step out to the bar and get what I need for it."

"I thought he said he was a teetotaller," said the heavy traveller when he had gone. And then our voices buzzed like a hive of bees. When our storyteller came in again, we turned on him—half-a-dozen of us at once—and spoke.

"One at a time," he said, gently. "I didn't quite catch what you said."

"We want to know," I said, "how it was—if seeing that ghost made all those chaps cut their throats by startling them when they were shaving—how was it *you* didn't cut *your* throat when you saw it?"

"I should have," he answered, gravely, "without the slightest doubt—I should have cut my throat, only," he glanced at our heavy friend, "I always shave with a safety razor. I travel in them," he added, slowly, and bisected a lemon.

"But—but," said the large man, when he could speak through our uproar, "I've gone and given up my room."

"Yes," said the dapper man, squeezing the lemon; "I've just had my things moved into it. It's the best room in the house. I always think it worthwhile to take a little pains to secure it."

The Blue Rose

'Yes, your grandfather he was one o' the old sort—honest as the day, as the sayin' is, an' well brought up, if he wasn't allus easy to live with—an' that set on the truth, an' that pertickler—well, if it 'adn't a bin for 'im bein' that pertickler, you gells would a 'ad a red-'aired woman to your granny instead o' me.'

A smile went round the tea-table; Mrs. Minver's grandchildren nodded, and looked at me—you know the look when there's a story in the air and you're expected to ask for it. But I was too shy. It was my first visit to Myrtle Cottage. Lottie Minver and I were both serving our time with Miss Ellends (*Modes et Robes*), and I was only sixteen then.

'A red-'aired woman,' Mrs. Minver went on, 'an' that would a' been a pity on all accounts, for 'e was a fine man as ever I see, an' me bein' no slip of a chit—'is sons all measured over their six foot—an' all bin measured too—'

She sighed, and looked out through the open door at the narrow strip of back garden where scarlet runners and stocks and reluctant sunflowers had been coaxed to grow. We were having tea in the kitchen. The table was covered with brown oilcloth. The cups were white with mauve spots. We had cresses for tea, and winkles, because it was Sunday.

'A fine man 'e was to be sure,' she went on. 'That's 'is portrait as 'angs to the right o' the parlour chimley piece, just over the crockery lamb yer Aunt Eliza give me the very last fair day afore the Lord took 'er. A fine figure of a man he was, my dears, an' much sought after, but mighty pertickler. An' so 'e married me.'

Mrs. Minver smoothed her black alpaca apron complacently.

'What was it about the red-haired young lady?' I asked.

'Ah! that's a tale, an' it just shows 'ow careful a gell should be when she's courtin'.'

This sounded interesting.

'Do tell us the tale,' I urged.

'Oh! it's nothin' much to tell,' said Mrs. Minver, but she settled herself against the cushions of her Windsor chair and stroked her left mitten with her right hand, in a way that promised.

'Come, granny, tell Lily about the blue roses.'

"'Old yer tongue then, till I can get a word in hedgeways! Blue roses indeed! Spoilin' a story afore it's begun! Well, you must know, young lady, as I was brought up in the country—a reg'lar Kentish apple I was, my man useter say. Our home was in Kent, down among the cherry orchards. We 'ad a nice little orchard oursel's, an' our house it was a wooden 'ouse, all built o' boards-like, not bricks like you see 'em 'ere. An' there was a big pear-tree, as went all up one side of the house—one branch right and one left—even-like, for all the world like a ladder. We useter pick the pears outer our bedroom winder, me and my cousin Hetty did. Jargonels they was, an' a sight sweeter than any as goes to market now-a-days.

'Our garden it wasn't much of a one for size, but for flowers— there! it was a perfect moral—cram full it was—all sorts—pinks an' pansies an' lilies, roses, jassermine, an' sweet willies, an' wallflowers an' daffies and spring flowers, which is my favourites outer all the flowers.'

'What are spring flowers?'

'They're a reg'lar old-fashioned flower—gels used allus to have 'em in their gardens long afore you was thought of, nor me neither, like wallflowers they be, summat, only pink an' yeller, an' only one on a stalk, an' soft like velvet, an' smelling like honey they did. I haven't seen none o' them since I come to live in Bermondsey.

'Well, our little wooden 'ouse it stood on the hill, an' as you come up, whether 'twas by the road, as was white an' windin', or whether 'twas by the shorter way through the medders an' the hop-garden, the first you see of our 'ouse was the white rose-tree. It clomb all over the side of the 'ouse—not the side where the pear-tree was, but the other—there was no windows that side the house—and the rose clomb all along—and blow! it did blow that rose did. Pearl-white the roses was, or what you might call blush-pink, and hundreds of 'em. It was quite a picter. Well, one fine summer every rose as come on that tree wasn't white nor blush-pink any more, but *blue*—a darkish blue at the edges and paler to the middles. Not pretty? Well, p'raps not; but I tell you there never was such a fuss made over any rose as you'd call pretty as there was over that blue rose. Parson, he was always comin' down to see it, an' bringin' his friends, from London sometimes; an' the gentry they drove in their carriages to see our blue rose; an' the tradesmen an' grocers they come in their carts from far an' near, an' they said, "Well, it was a novelty."

'An' they said it would surely take the prize at the flower-show. But it was Hetty's rose-bush. Father'd give it her when first she come to live with us. She come quite little, and she cried at the strange place, an' all she took to was the white roses. So, father he give her the bush—an' next year father 'e died—about cherry time it was.

'So, when they said that about the prize, Hetty said she didn't care about prizes an' flower-shows an' things. It was quite enough to 'ave such a rose-tree for 'er very own.

'The next year the roses come blue again, an' everyone come more 'n ever to look, an' the grocers an' people with carts they come from far an' near, for they said it was a novelty.

'But mother, she was rather quiet-like, an' she didn't say much about the roses; an' one day when she an' me was makin' up the bread—just our two selves, in the back kitchen—she says to me—

'"Addie," she says (my name's Adelaide), "about them blue roses now. If it wasn't that I don't like to think o' a child o' mine bein' up to such tricks, I should say as you or Hetty had been a' borrowed o' my blue-bag."

'"Your blue-bag, mother!" says I. Hard work I had to keep my face, for Hetty she was a makin' faces at me through the winder.

'"Yes, my blue-bag," mother says, lookin' at me very straight.

'"Why, aunt," says Hetty through the window, "if it was the blue-bag, how would all the roses be the same? An' wouldn't it all wash off in the rain? An' you know it's always brighter after a shower," she says. "Besides, would we do such a silly thing if we could, an' keep it up so, an' all? We might do it onst or twice," says she.

'"There's summat in all that," says my mother, going on with the bread. "I misdoubt me it's age turns the roses blue, like it turns folks' hair white. The rose was allus a pearly white or what you might call a blush-pink afore."

'An' the grocers an' people with carts they come from far an' near to see the rose-tree, for it was a novelty, ye see.

'Says I to Hetty that night after I'd said my prayers an' read my chapter—for I was allus properly brought up—"Hetty," I says, "fancy mother saying that about the blue-bag!"

'"Yes, fancy!" says Hetty, laughin'—an' she snuffs out the candle with 'er fingers an' jumps into bed. "I ain't agoin' to 'ave my blue roses run down neither. Why, I'm agoin' to take the prize at the flower-show—I am, with my wonderful blue roses!"

'An' sure enough she told parson the very next day as she would try for the prize at the flower-show.

'It was just about that time she took up with George Winstead. Yes, 'im as come to be your gran'fether instead, an' is lyin' in his grave at Long Mailing this twenty good years. Well, they kep' company together, an' everyone was willin', for he was a godly young man an' taught in Sunday-school, an' had good hopes of his uncle's business, which it was a cornchandler's in Medstone, an' she was a well-lookin' girl enough for all her red hair, which was made fun of then, though I hear it's all the rage now-a-days. I never see a girl so took up with a chap as she was with him. She give up curlin' 'er 'air acause he liked it plain, and she took to readin' the Bible and sayin' her prayers (like I'd allus done, and she'd allus laughed at me afore for it). Why, I've seen her kneel there over 'alf an hour, and then get outer bed again when she thought I was asleep and kneel down on the bare boards by the winder an' cry an' pray an' say, "George, George," an' pray again, not out loud, but so as I could 'ear 'er. Not proper prayers she didn't say like people gets taught, but things outer 'er own 'ead, an' the same things over an' over, till I useter say—

'"Come along ter bed, Hetty, do, for gracious sakes. You'll catch your death o' cold on them boards, an' I'm a-droppin' with sleep."

'Well, as flower-show day come nearer an' nearer, she grew stupider an' stupider, an' more an' more given to prayin', an' used to be all for goin' off by herself and leavin' everything to me—even to makin' our dresses for the flower-show an' lookin' after them roses what was to take the prize. I did it all, a' course—I was allus called a good-natured girl—an' the dresses they looked lovely, an' the roses was bluer than ever, instead o' being a pearly white or a blush-pink, like they should ha' been by rights. An' Hetty she prayed an' cried o' nights till I wonder I ever got a wink o' sleep, an' of a day she'd laugh till she nearly cried again. Well, flower-show day come, an' we 'ad our new sprigged prints—gowns was wore short in the waist then—an' Hetty she looked like a ghost in hers, but they did say mine became me wonderful.

'It was a beautiful day I remember, very sunny an' bright, an' you was glad to walk the shady side o' the way that day, I can tell you. Very hot it was in the big barn where the flower-show was. 'Twas all done up fine with flags an' wreaths an' all sorts, an' it was that hot the flowers was most wilted afore it come time for the prizes. An' everyone was wipin' their faces with their 'andkerchers, an' saying there hadn't been such a day this twenty year.

'When it come time for the prizes, we was all settin' on forms packed close like herr'ns. Mother was there of course, an' George an' his friends, an' Hetty sat nexter me, an' George—that's your gran'father—was settin' the other side of her. An' she kep' edgin' away from him an' getten' close to me, an' crushin' my new print, not to mention 'er own, an' she kep' on 'oldin' my 'and that tight I didn't know 'ow to bear myself, an' I never see a bonnet with pink ribbons look worse on any young woman than it did on her. Mine always suited me. I 'ad it done up with blue the year I was married.

'Presently it come to roses. The barn was full—all the gentry an' the parson an' his friends an' the grocers an' people with carts 'ad come from far an' near.

'Well, the gentleman what was giving out who had got prizes, he takes up the bunch o' blue roses (I'd done 'em up nicely with a white ribbon, for Hetty was in one of her queer fits an' wouldn't touch 'em), an' he says—

'"Hetty Martin—"

'Hetty jumped on her feet. I *felt* what she was a-goin' to do, an' I tried to hold her down, but no. She shook her arm clear o' me, an' she called out in a kind o' sharp shrieky voice as you could a' heard a mile off—

'"Don't you go for to give me no prizes," she says. "It's all a lie—them roses is made up blue. Aunt she just hit it—it was the blue-bag. I never meant to tell, but I can't a-bear it. I made 'em up blue—an' I done it myself, an' I don't care who knows it. There—"

'Yes, my dears—well may you look! She spoke up like that—she did indeed—afore all that barnful! I never see such a gell. Why, I wouldn't never even a' thought o' such a thing, let lone doin' it. Disgraceful, I call it—a gell puttin' 'erself forward afore folks like that!

'You could a' heard a pin drop, as the sayin' is, the place was that quiet, for full 'arf a minute. My 'eart was in my mouth, and for that 'arf minute I didn't know what she'd say next.

'The silly gell! Why, two whole summers we'd blued them roses, an' no one never know'd, an' no one wouldn't never a' known. We useter do it of a mornin' early afore mother come down. Hetty an' me we useter creep down in our stocking feet, so's not to make a clutter, an' afore we raked out the fire or opened the house we'd run round to the rose-tree an' look if there was any more buds out; an' Hetty 'ud say, "Here's another, Addie," an' I'd say, "All right, Hetty, we'll 'ave 'im," an' I'd rub the blue-bag round it once or twice, an' when it rained the blue soaked in more, an' the wet would seem to take it right into the roses' hearts. An' as the rose opened it would be all blue—from us having blued the edges. An' to think we might a' gone on an' on, an' took all the prizes at the flower-shows! I hate a fool.

'Well, that day in the barn it lasted—that kinder quiet like as if we was in church—it lasted for full 'arf a minute, an' it seemed like twenty—an' then there come a buzz, buzz, like a whole bench o' bees when a boy throws an apple at 'em—an' Hetty she says, "*Oh!*" quite soft and frightened-like—as well she might be—an' then, afore any-one could say a word to 'er, she was off, through the big barn door, like a rabbit with the dogs arter it.

'The ole gentleman what give the prizes, he said he'd know'd it all along—but 'e 'adn't, for he'd drove over in his own carriage to see our blue roses, and called them "curious nateral pheno—" suthin' or other.'

'And Hetty didn't tell of *you*, Mrs. Minver? '

'Oh! no, my dear. With all her faults, Hetty was never that sort o' girl.'

'And Mr. George?'

'Oh! he come up that arternoon—I see him from our window by the pear-tree—and Hetty she says—

"'I'm agoin' inter the orchard," she says; "if 'e wants me—but I don't think 'e will want me," says she.

'He did want her though, an' he says to me—

"'You come along, Addie, an' hear what I've got to say."

'We went out inter the cherry-orchard—all the cherries was gath-ered though—an' Hetty was there, walkin' up and down like a ferret as wants to get out of its hutch an' can't. An' George he says—

"' Lookee here, Hetty," he says, "I don't wish no ill-feelin', but you'll see it's best for us to part. I'm sure, if you set any store by me, you wouldn't wish me to keep company with a gell as could act a livin' lie, as parson says. An' I'm sure the Lord wouldn't grant a blessin', an' I wish you well an' goodbye."

'I never see a gell look so plain—for a rather good-looking gell—as Hetty did then, for her eyes was all red an' swelled up with cryin', an' she twisted her nose and mouth up, like as if she was a-goin' to begin again.

'"Goodbye, George," says she. "No, I wouldn't wish it, George," she says, "not if you don't, dear George."

'An' with that she walked away very quiet, an' George, he stood quite still, not looking at anythin' for a minute or two, an' then he give a sorter shrug an' a sorter sigh, an' he went off by the lower gate without as much as a " Good-day to you."

'When tea-time come, mother she says—

'"Enough said about a bit o' gell's nonsense;" an' she ups the stairs to Hetty, and she says at the door—

'"Come down to tea, my gell."

'An' Hetty she says—

'"Don't want no tea, aunt."

'An' mother she goes in, an' there's Hetty lyin' face down on the bed, an' mother she says—

'"Come, child, it's no use a-grislin' over spilt milk; an' arter all—

'*A fault 'ats owned*
Is 'arf atoned.'

'Come along down, an' let's say no more about it."

'But Hetty she says (I was atop o' the stairs an' I heard her)—

'"It ain't no use, aunt," she says, " an' you've been's good's a mother to me, an' I thank you an' I loves you—that I do. But nothin's no good now. You let me be, there's a dear auntie."

'An' mother she left her, just a sayin'—

'"Don't you take on 'bout George, now. He'll come round."

'An' next mornin' when I woke up Hetty was gone, and we never seed her again.'

'Gone? Where to?' I asked.

'To Medstone first, an' then to London; an' mother couldn't never 'ear what come of 'er—but I did 'ear she come to no good.'

'And George? '

'Well, George he took on for a bit, an' didn't take to his victuals as a young man should; but I allus spoke him civil, an' when we was alone I said, "Pore George!" an' "Wasn't it hard when you was fond of a person to have 'em own up a liar quite shameless afore parson an' all!" An' he said, "Yes, 'twas cruel hard." An' next year we was married, George an' me.'

'And I suppose you never told him you had helped to blue the roses?'

'My dear! Now, how could I? an' him that pertickler!'

The Detective
A.k.a. To the Adventurous

1

His mind was made up. There should be no looking back, no weakening, no foolish relentings. Civilisation had no place for him in her scheme of things, and he in his turn would show the jade that he was capable of a scheme in which she had no place, she and her pinchbeck meretricious substitutions of stones for bread, serpents for eggs. What exactly it was that had gone wrong does not matter. There was a girl in it perhaps; a friend most likely. Almost certainly money and pride and the old detestation of arithmetic played their part. His mother was now dead, and his father was dead long since. There was no one nearer than a great uncle to care where he went or what he did; whether he throve or went under, whether he lived or died. Also, it was springtime.

His thoughts turned longingly to the pleasant green country, the lush meadows, the blossoming orchards, nesting birds and flowering thorn, and to roads that should wind slowly, pleasantly between these. The remembrance came to him of another spring day when he had played truant, had found four thrush's nests and a moorhen's, and tried to draw a kingfisher on the back of his Latin prose; had paddled in a mill stream between bright twinkling counterfeits in the glassy water, had been caned at school next day, and his mother had cried when he told her. He remembered how he had said: "I will be good, oh, mother, I will," and then added with one of those odd sudden cautions that lined the fluttering garment of his impulsive soul, "at least, I'll try to be good."

Well, he had tried. For more than a year he had tried, bearing patiently the heavy yoke of ledger and costs book, the weary life of the office the great uncle had found for him. There had been a caged bird at the cobbler's in the village at home, that piped sweetly in its prison and laboured to draw up its own drinking water by slow chained thimblefuls. He sometimes thought that he was like that caged bird, straining and straining forever at the horrible machinery which grudgingly yielded to his efforts the little pittance that kept him alive. And all the while the woods and fields and the long white roads were calling, calling.

And now the chief had been more than usually repulsive, and the young man stood at the top of the stairs, smoothing the silk hat that stood for so much, and remembering in detail the unusual repulsiveness of the chief. An error of two and seven-pence in one column, surely a trivial error, and of two hundred pounds in another, quite an obvious error that, and easily rectified, had been the inspiration of the words that sang discordantly to his revolted soul. He suddenly tossed his hat in the air, kicked it as it fell, black and shining, and sent it spinning down the stars. The office boy clattered; thin-necked, red-eared, slack mouth well open.

"My hat!" was his unintentionally appropriate idiom.

"Pardon me, *my* hat," said the young man suavely. But the junior was genuinely shocked.

"I say, Mr Sellinge," he said solemnly, "it'll never be the same again, that tile won't. Ironing it won't do it, no, nor yet blocking."

"Bates," the young man retorted with at least equal solemnity, "I shall never wear that hat again. Remove your subservient carcase. I'm going back to tell the chief."

"About your hat?" the junior asked, breathless, incredulous.

"About my hat," Sellinge repeated.

The chief looked up a little blankly. Clerks who had had what he knew well that they called the rough side of his tongue rarely returned to risk a second heling. And now this hopeless young incompetent, this irreverent trifler with the columns of the temple of the gods *L. s.* and *d.*, was standing before him, and plainly, standing there to speak, not merely to be spoken to.

"Well, Sellinge," he said, frowning a little, but not too much, lest he should scare away an apology more ample than that with which Sellinge had met the rough side. "Well, what is it?"

Sellinge, briefly, respectfully, but quite plainly told him what it was. And the chief listened, hardly able to believe his respectable ears.

"And so," the tale ended. "I should like to leave at once, please, sir."

"Do you realise, young man," the head of the firm asked heavily, "that you are throwing away your career?"

Sellinge explained what he did realise.

"Your *soul*, did you say?" The portly senior looked at him through gold-rimmed glasses. "I never heard of such a thing in my life."

Sellinge waited respectfully, and the head of the house looked suddenly older. The unusual is the disconcerting. The chief was not used to hearing souls mentioned except on Sundays. Yet the boy was the grand-nephew of an old friend, a valued and useful business friend, a man whom it would be awkward for him to offend or annoy. This is the real meaning of friendship in the world of business. So, he said, "Come, come, now, Sellinge; think it over. I've had occasion to complain, but I've not complained unjustly, not unjustly, I think. Your opportunities in this office—what did you say?"

The young man had begun to say, quite politely, what he thought of the office.

"But God bless my soul," said the older man, quite flustered by this impossible rebellion. "What is it you want? Come now," he said, remembering the usefulness of that eminent great-uncle, and unbending as he remembered, "if this isn't good enough for you a respectable solicitor's office and every chance of rising, every chance," he repeated pensively, oblivious now of all that the rough side had said; "if this isn't good enough for you what is? What *would* you like?" he asked, with a pathetic mixture of hopelessness, raillery, and the certitude that his question was unanswerable.

"I should like," said Sellinge slowly, "to be a tramp, or a burglar—" ("Great Heavens!" said the chief.)

"—or a detective. I want to go about and do things. I want—"

"A detective?" said the chief. "Have you ever—"

"No," said Sellinge, "but I could."

"A new Sherlock Holmes, eh?" said the chief, actually smiling.

"Never," said the clerk firmly, and he frowned. "May I go now, sir? I've no opening in the burgling or detective line, so I shall be a tramp for this summer at least. Perhaps I'll go to Canada. I'm sorry I haven't been a success here. Bates is worth twice my money. He never wavers in his faith. Seven nines are always sixty-three with Bates."

Again, the chief thought of his useful city friend.

"Never mind Bates," he said. "Is the door closed? Right. Sit down, if you please, Mr Sellinge. I have something to say to you."

Sellinge hesitated, looked round at the dusty leather-covered furniture, the worn Turkey carpet, the black, shiny deed-boxes, and the shelves of dull blue and yellow papers. The brown oblong of window framed a strip of blue sky and a strip of the opposite office's dirty brickwork. A small strayed cloud, very white and shining, began to cross the strip of sky.

"It's very kind of you, sir," said Sellinge, his mind more made up than ever, "but I wouldn't reconsider my decision for ten times what I've been getting.

"Sit down," said the chief again. "I assure you I do not propose to raise your salary, nor to urge you to reconsider your decision. I merely wish to suggest an alternative, one of your own alternatives," he added persuasively.

"Oh!" said Sellinge, sitting down abruptly, "which?"

2

And now behold the dream realised. A young man with bare sun-bleached hair that looks as though it had never known the shiny black symbol of civilisation, boots large and dusty, and on his back the full equipment of an artist in oils; a little too new the outfit, but satisfactory and complete. He goes slowly along through the clean white dust of the roads, and his glance to right and left embraces green field and woodland with the persuasive ardour of a happy lover. The only blot on the fair field of life outspread before him the parting words of the chief:

"It's a very simple job for a would-be detective. Just find out whether the old chap's mad or not. You get on with the lower orders, you tell me. Well, get them to talk to you. And if you find that out, well, there may be a career for you. I've long been dissatisfied with the ordinary enquiry agent. Yes, two pounds a week and expenses. But in reason. Not first-class, you know."

This much aloud. To himself he had said:

"A simpleton's useful sometimes, if he's honest. And if he doesn't find out anything, we shall be no worse off than we were before, and I shall be able to explain to his uncle that I really gave him exceptional opportunities—exceptional."

Sellinge also, walking along between the dusty powdered white-flowered hedges, felt that the opportunity was exceptional. All his life people had told him things, and the half-confidences of two people often make up a complete sphere of knowledge, if only the confidant possess the power of joining the broken halves. This power Sellinge had. He knew many things; the little scandals, the parochial intrigues and intricacies of the village where he was born were clearer to him than the principal performers. He looked forward pleasantly to the lodging in the village ale-house, and to the slow gossip on the benches by the door.

The village (he was nearing it now) was steep and straggling, displaying its oddly assorted roofs amid a flutter of orchard trees, a carpet of green spaces. The Five Bells stood to the left, its tea-gardens beside it, cool and alluring.

Sellinge entered the dark sandy passage where the faint smell of last night's tobacco and this morning's beer contended with the fresh vigour of a bunch of wallflowers in a blue jug on the ring-marked bar.

Within ten minutes he had engaged his room, a little hot white attic under the roof, and had learned it was Squire who lived in the big house, and that there was a lot of tales, so there was, but it didn't do to believe all you heard, nor yet more'n half you see, and least said soonest mended, and the house was worth looking at, or so people said as took notice of them old ancient tumble-down places. No, it wasn't likely you could get in. Used to be open of a Thursday, the 'ouse and grounds, but been closed to visitors this many year. Also, that, for all it looked so near, the house was a good four and a half miles by the road.

"And Squire's mighty good to the people in the village," the pleasant-faced old landlady behind the bar went on: "pays good wages, 'e does, and if anyone's in trouble he's always got his hand in 'is pocket. I don't believe he spends half on himself to what he gives away. It'll be a poor day for Jevington when anything happens to him, sir, you take that from me. No harm in your trying to see the house, sir, but as for seeing him, he never sees no one. Why listen,"—there was the sound of hoofs and wheels in the road—"look out, sir, quick."

Sellinge looked out to see an old-fashioned carriage and pair sweep past, in the carriage a white-haired old man with a white thin face and pale clouded eyes.

"That's him," said the landlady beside him, ducking as the carriage passed. "Yes, four and a half miles by the road, sir."

Harnessed n his trappings of colour-box and easel, the young detective set out. There was about him none of the furtivity of your stage detective. His disguise was perfect, mainly because it was not a disguise. Such disguise as there was hung over his soul, which was pretending to itself that the errand was one of danger and difficulty. The attraction of the detective's career was to him not so much the idea of hunting down criminals as the dramatic attitude of one who goes about the world with a false beard and a make-up box in one hand and his life in the other. To find out the truth about an old gentleman's eccentricities was quite another pair of sleeves, but of these, as yet, our hero perceived neither the cut nor the colour. He had wanted to be a tramp or a detective and here he was, both. One has to earn one's bread, and what better way than this?

A smooth worn stile prefaced a path almost hidden in grass up for hay, a blaze of red sorrel, buttercups, ox-eyed daisies in the feathery foam of flowered grasses. The wood of the stile was warm to his hands, and the grasses that met over the path powdered his boots with their little seeds.

Then there was a copse, and a rabbit warren, and a short crisp grass dry on the chalk it thinly covered. The sun shone hardly in a sky of brass. The wayfarer panted for shade. It showed far ahead like a mirage in a desert, a group of pines, a flat whiteness of pond-water, a little house. One might ask the way at that house, and get—talk.

He fixed his eyes on it and walked on, the leather straps hot on his shoulders, his oak stick-handle hoe in his hand. Then suddenly he saw on the hill, pale beyond the pines, someone coming down the path. He knew the magnet that a planted easel is to rustic minds. This might perhaps be, after all, the better way. Never did artist prepare so rapidly the scene that should attract the eye of the rustic gazer, the lingering but inevitable approach of the rustic foot.

In three minutes, he was seated on his camp-stool, a canvas before him, his palette half-set. Four minutes saw a good deal of blue on the canvas. Purple, too, at the fifth minute, because the sky and turned that colour in the west, purple and, moreover, a strange threatening tint that called for burnt sienna and mid chrome and a dash of madder. The white advancing figure had disappeared among the pines. He madly squeezed green paint on to the foreground; one must at least have a picture begun. And the sun searched intolerably every bit of him as he sat in the shadeless warren awaiting the passing of the other.

And then, more sudden than an earthquake or the birth of love, a mighty rushing wind fell on him, caught up canvas and easel, even colour-box and oak staff, and whirled them away like leaves in an autumn equinox. His hat went too, not that that mattered, and the virgin sketch book whirled white before a wind that, the papers said next day, travelled at the rate of five-and-fifty miles an hour. The wonderful purple and copper of the west rushed up across the sky, a fierce spatter of rain stung face and hands. He pursued the colour-box, which had lodged in the front entry of a rabbit's house, caught at the canvas, whose face lay closely pressed to a sloe-bush, and ran for the nearest shelter, the house among the pines. In a rain like that one had to run head down or be blinded, and so he did not see till he drew breath in the mouldering rotten porch of it that his shelter was not of those from which hospitality can be asked.

A little lodge it was, long since deserted; walls and ceilings bulging and discoloured with damp, its latticed windows curtained only by the tapestry of the spider, its floors carpeted with old dust and drift of dry pine needles, and on its hearth the nests of long-fledged birds had fallen on the ashes of a fire gone out a very long time ago. A blazing lightning-flash dazzled him as he tried the handle of the door, and the door, hanging by one rusty hinge, yielded to his push as the first shattering peal of thunder clattered and cracked overhead. But a shelter it was, though the wind drove the rain almost horizontally through the broken window and across the room.

He reached through the casement, and at the cost of a soaked coat sleeve pulled to a faded green shutter and made this fast. Then he explored the upper rooms. Holes in the thatch had let through the weather, and the drop, drop of the water that wears away stone had worn away the boards of the floor, so that they bent dangerously to his tread. The halfway landing of the little crooked staircase seemed the driest place. He sat down there with his back against the wall and listened to the cracking and blundering of the thunder, watched through the skylight the lightning shoot out of the clouds, rapid and menacing as the tongue from the mouth of a snake.

No man who is not a dreamer chooses as a symbolic rite the kicking of a tall black hat down the stairs of the office he has elected to desert. Sellinge, audience at first to the glorious orchestra, fell from hearing to a waking dream, and the waking dream merged in a dreamless sleep.

When he awoke, he knew at once that he was not alone in the little forgotten house. A tramp perhaps, a trespasser almost certainly. He had not had time to move under this thought before the other overpowered it. It was *he* who was the tramp, the trespasser. The other might be the local police. Have you ever tried to explain anything to the police in a rural district? It would be better to lie quietly, holding one's breath, and so, perhaps, escape an interview that could not be to his advantage, and might, in view of the end he pursued, be absolutely the deuce-and-all.

So he lay quietly, listening. To almost nothing. The other person, whoever it was, moved hardly at all; or perhaps the movements were drowned in the mutter of the thunder and the lashing of the rain, for Sellinge had not slept out the storm. But its violence had lessened while he slept, and presently the great thunders died away in slow sulky mutterings, and the fierce rain settled to a steady patter on the thatch and a slow drip, drip from the holes in the roof to the rotting boards below. And the dusk was falling; shadows were setting up their tents in the corners of the stairs and of the attic whose floor was on a level with his eyes. And below, through the patter of the rain, he could hear soft movements. How soft, his strained ears hardly knew till the abrupt contrast of a step on the earth without reminded him of the values of the ordinary noises that human beings make when they move.

The step on the earth outside was heavy and plashy in the wet mould; the touch on the broken door was harsh, and harshly the creaking one hinge responded. The footsteps on the boarded floor of the lower room were loud and echoing. Those other sounds had been as the half-heard murmur of summer woods in the ears of one half asleep. This was definite, undeniable as the sound of London traffic.

Suddenly all sounds ceased for a moment, and in that moment Sellinge found time to wish that he had never found this shelter. The wildest, wettest, stormiest weather out under the sky seemed better than this little darkening house which he shared with these two others. For there were two. He knew it even before the man began to speak. But he had not known till then that the other, the softly moving first-comer, was a woman, and when he knew it, he felt, in a thrill of impotent resentment, the shame of his situation and the impossibility of escaping from it. He was an eavesdropper.

He had not, somehow, thought of eavesdropping as incidental to the detective career. And there was nothing he could do to make things better which would not, inevitably, make them worse. To declare himself now would be to multiply a thousandfold everything which he desired to minimise. Because the first words that came to him from the two below were love-words, low, passionate, and tender, in the voice of a man. He could not hear the answer of the woman, but there are ways of answering which cannot be heard.

"Stay just as you are," he heard the man's voice again, "and let me stay here at your feet and worship you."

And again, "Oh, my love, my love, even to see you like this. It's all so different from what we used to think it would be; but it's heaven compared with everything else in the world."

Sellinge supposed that the woman answered, though he caught no words, for the man went on: "Yes, I know it's hard for you to come, and you come so seldom. And even when you're not here, I know you understand. But life's very long and cold, dear. They talk about death being cold. It's life that's the cold thing, Anna."

Then the voice sank to a murmur, cherishing, caressing, hardly articulate, and the shadows deepened, deepened inside the house. But outside it grew lighter because the moon had risen and the clouds and rain had swept away, and sunset and moonrise were mingling in the clear sky.

"Not yet; you'll not send me away yet," he heard. "Oh, my love, such a little time, and all the rest of life without you. Ah! Let me stay beside you a little while."

The passion and the longing of the voice thrilled the listener to an answering passion of pity. He himself had read of love, thought of it, dreamed of it; but he had never heard it speak; he had not known that its voice could be like this.

A faint whispering sound came to him; the woman's answer, he thought, but so low was it that it was lost even as it reached him in the whisper of a wet ivy branch at the window. He raised himself gently and crept on hands and knees to the window of the upper room. His movements made no sound that could have been heard below. He felt happier there, looking out on the clear, cold, wedded lights, and also, he was as far as he could be, in the limits of that house, from those two lovers.

Yet he still heard the last words of the man, vibrant with the agony of a death-parting.

"Yes, yes, I will go." Then, "Oh, my dear, dear love; goodbye, good-bye."

The sound of footsteps on the floor below, the broken hinged door was opened and closed again from without, he heard its iron latch click into place. He looked from the window. The last indiscretion of sight was nothing to the indiscretions of hearing that had gone before, and he wanted to see this man to whom all his soul had gone out in sympathy and pity. He had not supposed that he could ever be sorry for anyone.

He looked to see a young man bowed under a weight of sorrow, and he saw an old man bowed with the weight of years. Silver-white was the hair in the moonlight, thin and stooping the shoulders, feeble the footsteps, and tremulous the hand that closed the gate of the little enclosure that had been a garden. The figure of a sad old man went away alone through the shadows of the pine trees.

And it was the figure of the old man who had driven by The Five Bells in the old-fashioned carriage, the figure of the man he had come down to watch, to spy upon. Well, he had spied, and he had found out—what?

He did not wait for anyone else to unlatch that closed door and come out into the moonlight below the window. He thinks now that he knew even then that no one else would come out. He went down the stairs in the darkness, careless of the sound of his feet on the creaking boards. He lighted a match and held it up and looked round the little bare room with its shuttered window and its one door, close latched. And there was no one there, no one at all. The room was as empty and cold as any last year's nest.

He got out very quickly and got away, not stopping to shut the door or gate nor to pick up the colour-box and canvas from the foot of the stairs where he had left them. He went very quickly back to The Five Bells, and he was very glad of the lights and the talk and the smell and sight and sound of living men and women.

It was next day that he asked his questions; this time of the round-faced daughter of the house.

"No," she told him, "Squire wasn't married," and "Yes, there was a sort of story."

He pressed for the story, and presently got it.

"It ain't nothing much. Only they say when Squire was a young man there was some carrying on with the gamekeeper's daughter up at the lodge. Happen you noticed it, sir, an old tumble-down place in the pine woods."

Yes, he did happen to notice.

"Nobody knows the rights of it now," the girl told him; "all them as was in it's under the daisies this long-time, except Squire. But he went away and there was some mishap; he got thrown from his horse and didn't come home when expected, and the girl she was found drownded in the pond nigh where she used to live. And Squire he waren't never the same man. They say he hangs about round the old lodge to this day when it's full moon. And they do say— But there, I dunno, it's all silly talk, and I hope you won't take no notice of anything I've said. One gets talking."

Caution, late born, was now strong in her, and he could not get any more.

"Do you remember the girl's name?" he asked at last, finding all assaults vain against the young woman's discretion.

"Why, I wasn't born nor yet thought of," she told him, and laughed and called along the fresh sanded passage:

"Mother, war was that girl's name, you know, the one up at the lodge that—"

"Ssh!" came back the mother's voice, "you keep a still tongue, Lily; it's all silly talk."

"All right, mother, but what *was* her name?"

"Anna," came the voice along the fresh sanded passage.

Sellinge's report, written the next day. Ran:

"Dear Sir, I have made enquiries and find no ground for supposing the gentleman in question to be otherwise than of sound mind. He is much respected in the village and very kind to the poor. I remain here awaiting instructions."

While he remained there awaiting the instructions, he explored the neighbourhood, but he found nothing of much interest except the grave on the north side of the churchyard, a grave marked by no stone, but covered anew every day with fresh flowers. It had been so covered every day, the sexton told him, for fifty years.

"A long time, fifty years," said the man, "a long time, sir. A lawyer in London, he pays for the flowers, but they do say—"

"Yes," said Sellinge quickly, "but then people say all sorts of things, don't they?"

"Some on 'em's true though," said the sexton.

The Ebony Frame

To be rich is a luxurious sensation—the more so when you have plumbed the depths of hard-up-ness as a Fleet Street hack, a picker-up of unconsidered pars, a reporter, an unappreciated journalist—all callings utterly inconsistent with one's family feeling and one's direct descent from the Dukes of Picardy.

When my Aunt Dorcas died and left me seven hundred a year and a furnished house in Chelsea, I felt that life had nothing left to offer except immediate possession of the legacy. Even Mildred Mayhew, whom I had hitherto regarded as my life's light, became less luminous. I was not engaged to Mildred, but I lodged with her mother, and I sang duets with Mildred, and gave her gloves when it would run to it, which was seldom. She was a dear good girl, and I meant to marry her someday. It is very nice to feel that a good little woman is thinking of you—it helps you in your work—and it is pleasant to know she will say "Yes" when you say "Will you?"

But, as I say, my legacy almost put Mildred out of my head, especially as she was staying with friends in the country just then.

Before the first gloss was off my new mourning I was seated in my aunt's own armchair in front of the fire in the dining-room of my own house. My own house! It was grand, but rather lonely. I *did* think of Mildred just then.

The room was comfortably furnished with oak and leather. On the walls hung a few fairly good oil-paintings, but the space above the mantelpiece was disfigured by an exceedingly bad print, "The Trial of Lord William Russell," framed in a dark frame. I got up to look at it. I had visited my aunt with dutiful regularity, but I never remembered seeing this frame before. It was not intended for a print, but for an oil-painting. It was of fine ebony, beautifully and curiously carved.

I looked at it with growing interest, and when my aunt's housemaid—I had retained her modest staff of servants—came in with the lamp, I asked her how long the print had been there.

"Mistress only bought it two days afore she was took ill," she said; "but the frame—she didn't want to buy a new one—so she got this out of the attic. There's lots of curious old things there, sir."

"Had my aunt had this frame long?"

"Oh yes, sir. It come long afore I did, and I've been here seven years come Christmas. There was a picture in it—that's upstairs too—but it's that black and ugly it might as well be a chimley-back."

I felt a desire to see this picture. What if it were some priceless old master in which my aunt's eyes had only seen rubbish?

Directly after breakfast next morning I paid a visit to the lumber-room.

It was crammed with old furniture enough to stock a curiosity shop. All the house was furnished solidly in the early Victorian style, and in this room everything not in keeping with the "drawing-room suite" ideal was stowed away. Tables of *papier-mâché* and mother-of-pearl, straight-backed chairs with twisted feet and faded needlework cushions, fire screens of old-world design, oak bureaux with brass handles, a little work-table with its faded moth-eaten silk flutings hanging in disconsolate shreds: on these and the dust that covered them blazed the full daylight as I drew up the blinds. I promised myself a good time in re-enshrining these household gods in my parlour, and promoting the Victorian suite to the attic. But at present my business was to find the picture as "black as the chimley-back;" and presently, behind a heap of hideous still-life studies, I found it.

Jane the housemaid identified it at once. I took it downstairs carefully and examined it. No subject, no colour were distinguishable. There was a splodge of a darker tint in the middle, but whether it was figure or tree or house no man could have told. It seemed to be painted on a very thick panel bound with leather. I decided to send it to one of those persons who pour on rotting family portraits the water of eternal youth—mere soap and water Mr. Besant tells us it is; but even as I did so the thought occurred to me to try my own restorative hand at a corner of it.

My bath-sponge, soap, and nailbrush vigorously applied for a few seconds showed me that there was no picture to clean! Bare oak presented itself to my persevering brush. I tried the other side, Jane watching me with indulgent interest. The same result. Then the truth dawned on me. Why was the panel so thick? I tore off the leather binding, and the panel divided and fell to the ground in a cloud of dust. There were two pictures—they had been nailed face to face. I leaned them against the wall, and the next moment I was leaning against it myself.

For one of the pictures was myself—a perfect portrait—no shade of expression or turn of feature wanting. Myself—in a cavalier dress, "love-locks and all!" When had this been done? And how, without my knowledge? Was this some whim of my aunt's?

"Lor', sir!" the shrill surprise of Jane at my elbow; "what a lovely photo it is! Was it a fancy ball, sir?"

"Yes," I stammered. "I—I don't think I want anything more now. You can go."

She went; and I turned, still with my heart beating violently, to the other picture. This was a woman of the type of beauty beloved of Burne Jones and Rossetti—straight nose, low brows, full lips, thin hands, large deep luminous eyes. She wore a black velvet gown. It was a full-length portrait. Her arms rested on a table beside her, and her head on her hands; but her face was turned full forward, and her eyes met those of the spectator bewilderingly. On the table by her were compasses and instruments whose uses I did not know, books, a goblet, and a miscellaneous heap of papers and pens. I saw all this afterwards. I believe it was a quarter of an hour before I could turn my eyes away from hers. I have never seen any other eyes like hers. They appealed, as a child's or a dog's do; they commanded, as might those of an empress.

"Shall I sweep up the dust, sir?" Curiosity had brought Jane back. I acceded. I turned from her my portrait. I kept between her and the woman in the black velvet. When I was alone again, I tore down "The Trial of Lord William Russell," and I put the picture of the woman in its strong ebony frame.

Then I wrote to a frame-maker for a frame for my portrait. It had so long, lived face to face with this beautiful witch, that I had not the heart to banish it from her presence; from which, it will be perceived that I am by nature a somewhat sentimental person.

The new frame came home, and I hung it opposite the fireplace. An exhaustive search among my aunt's papers showed no explanation of the portrait of myself, no history of the portrait of the woman with the wonderful eyes. I only learned that all the old furniture together had come to my aunt at the death of my great-uncle, the head of the family; and I should have concluded that the resemblance was only a family one, if everyone who came in had not exclaimed at the "speaking likeness." I adopted Jane's "fancy ball" explanation.

And there, one might suppose, the matter of the portraits ended. One might suppose it, that is, if there were not evidently a good deal more written here about it. However, to me, then, the matter seemed ended.

I went to see Mildred; I invited her and her mother to come and stay with me. I rather avoided glancing at the picture in the ebony frame. I could not forget, nor remember without singular emotion, the look in the eyes of that woman when mine first met them. I shrank from meeting that look again.

I reorganised the house somewhat, preparing for Mildred's visit. I turned the dining-room into a drawing-room. I brought down much of the old-fashioned furniture, and, after a long day of arranging and re-arranging, I sat down before the fire, and, lying back in a pleasant languor, I idly raised my eyes to the picture. I met her dark, deep hazel eyes, and once more my gaze was held fixed as by a strong magic—the kind of fascination that keeps one sometimes staring for whole minutes into one's own eyes in the glass. I gazed into her eyes, and felt my own dilate, pricked with a smart like the smart of tears.

"I wish," I said, "oh, how I wish you were a woman, and not a picture! Come down! Ah, come down!"

I laughed at myself as I spoke; but even as I laughed, I held out my arms.

I was not sleepy; I was not drunk. I was as wide awake and as sober as ever was a man in this world. And yet, as I held out my arms, I saw the eyes of the picture dilate, her lips tremble—if I were to be hanged for saying it, it is true. Her hands moved slightly, and a sort of flicker of a smile passed over her face.

I sprang to my feet. "This won't do," I said, still aloud. "Firelight does play strange tricks. I'll have the lamp."

I pulled myself together and made for the bell. My hand was on it, when I heard a sound behind me, and turned—the bell still unrung. The fire had burned low, and the corners of the room were deeply shadowed; but, surely, there—behind the tall worked chair—was something darker than a shadow.

"I must face this out," I said, "or I shall never be able to face myself again." I left the bell, I seized the poker, and battered the dull coals to a blaze. Then I stepped back resolutely, and looked up at the picture. The ebony frame was empty! From the shadow of the worked chair came a silken rustle, and out of the shadow the woman of the picture

96

was coming—coming towards me.

I hope I shall never again know a moment of terror so blank and absolute. I could not have moved or spoken to save my life. Either all the known laws of nature were nothing, or I was mad. I stood trembling, but I am thankful to remember, I stood still, while the black velvet gown swept across the hearthrug towards me.

Next moment a hand touched me—a hand soft, warm, and human—and a low voice said, "You called me. I am here."

At that touch and that voice the world seemed to give a sort of bewildering half-turn. I hardly know how to express it, but at once it seemed not awful—not even unusual—for portraits to become flesh—only most natural, most right, most unspeakably fortunate.

I laid my hand on hers. I looked from her to my portrait. I could not see it in the firelight.

"We are not strangers," I said.

"Oh no, not strangers." Those luminous eyes were looking up into mine—those red lips were near me. With a passionate cry—a sense of having suddenly recovered life's one great good, that had seemed wholly lost—I clasped her in my arms. She was no ghost—she was a woman—the only woman in the world.

"How long," I said, "O love—how long since I lost you?"

She leaned back, hanging her full weight on the hands that were clasped behind my head.

"How can I tell how long? There is no time in hell," she answered.

It was not a dream. Ah, no—there are no such dreams. I wish to God there could be. When in dreams, do I see her eyes, hear her voice, feel her lips against my cheek, hold her hands to my lips, as I did that night—the supreme night of my life? At first, we hardly spoke. It seemed enough—

After long grief and pain,
To feel the arms of my true
Love round me once again.

★★★★★★

It is very difficult to tell this story. There are no words to express the sense of glad reunion, the complete realisation of every hope and dream of a life, that came upon me as I sat with my hand in hers and looked into her eyes.

How could it have been a dream, when I left her sitting in the straight-backed chair, and went down to the kitchen to tell the maids

I should want nothing more—that I was busy, and did not wish to be disturbed; when I fetched wood for the fire with my own hands, and, bringing it in, found her still sitting there—saw the little brown head turn as I entered, saw the love in her dear eyes; when I threw myself at her feet and blessed the day I was born, since life had given me this?

Not a thought of Mildred: all the other things in my life were a dream—this, its one splendid reality.

"I am wondering," she said after a while, when we had made such cheer each of the other as true lovers may after long parting—"am wondering how much you remember of our past."

"I remember nothing," I said. "Oh, my dear lady, my dear sweetheart—I remember nothing but that I love you—that I have loved you all my life."

"You remember nothing—really nothing?"

"Only that I am yours; that we have both suffered; that——Tell me, my mistress dear, all that you remember. Explain it all to me. Make me understand. And yet——No, I don't want to understand. It is enough that we are together."

If it was a dream, why have I never dreamed it again?

She leaned down towards me, her arm lay on my neck, and drew my head till it rested on her shoulder. "I am a ghost, I suppose," she said, laughing softly; and her laughter stirred memories which I just grasped at, and just missed. "But you and I know better, don't we? I will tell you everything you have forgotten. We loved each other—ah! no, you have not forgotten that—and when you came back from the war we were to be married. Our pictures were painted before you went away. You know I was more learned than women of that day. Dear one, when you were gone, they said I was a witch. They tried me. They said I should be burned. Just because I had looked at the stars and had gained more knowledge than they, they must needs bind me to a stake and let me be eaten by the fire. And you far away!"

Her whole body trembled and shrank. O love, what dream would have told me that my kisses would soothe even that memory?

"The night before," she went on, "the devil did come to me. I was innocent before—you know it, don't you? And even then, my sin was for you—for you—because of the exceeding love I bore you. The devil came, and I sold my soul to eternal flame. But I got a good price. I got the right to come back, through my picture (if anyone looking at it wished for me), as long as my picture stayed in its ebony frame. That frame was not carved by man's hand. I got the right to come back to you. Oh, my heart's heart, and another thing I won, which you shall hear *anon.* They burned me for a witch, they made me suffer hell on earth. Those faces, all crowding round, the crackling wood and the smell of the smoke———"

"O love! no more—no more."

"When my mother sat that night before my picture she wept, and cried, 'Come back, my poor lost child!' And I went to her, with glad leaps of heart. Dear, she shrank from me, she fled, she shrieked and moaned of ghosts. She had our pictures covered from sight and put again in the ebony frame. She had promised me my picture should stay always there. Ah, through all these years your face was against mine."

She paused.

"But the man you loved?"

"You came home. My picture was gone. They lied to you, and you married another woman; but someday I knew you would walk the world again and that I should find you."

"The other gain?" I asked.

"The other gain," she said slowly, "I gave my soul for. It is this. If you also will give up your hopes of heaven, I can remain a woman, I can move in your world—I can be your wife. Oh, my dear, after all these years, at last—at last."

"If I sacrifice my soul," I said slowly, with no thought of the imbecility of such talk in our "so-called nineteenth century"—"if I sacrifice my soul, I win you? Why, love, it's a contradiction in terms. You *are* my soul."

Her eyes looked straight into mine. Whatever might happen, whatever did happen, whatever may happen, our two souls in that moment met, and became one.

"Then you choose—you deliberately choose—to give up your hopes of heaven for me, as I gave up mine for you?"

"I decline," I said, "to give up my hope of heaven on any terms. Tell me what I must do, that you and I may make our heaven here—as now, my dear love."

"I will tell you tomorrow," she said. "Be alone here tomorrow night—twelve is ghost's time, isn't it?—and then I will come out of the picture and never go back to it. I shall live with you, and die, and be buried, and there will be an end of me. But we shall live first, my heart's heart."

I laid my head on her knee. A strange drowsiness overcame me. Holding her hand against my cheek, I lost consciousness. When I awoke the grey November dawn was glimmering, ghost-like, through the uncurtained window. My head was pillowed on my arm, which rested—I raised my head quickly—ah! not on my lady's knee, but on the needle-worked cushion of the straight-backed chair. I sprang to my feet. I was stiff with cold, and dazed with dreams, but I turned my eyes on the picture. There she sat, my lady, my dear love. I held out my arms, but the passionate cry I would have uttered died on my lips. She had said twelve o'clock. Her lightest word was my law. So, I only stood in front of the picture and gazed into those grey-green eyes till tears of passionate happiness filled my own.

"Oh, my dear, my dear, how shall I pass the hours till I hold you again?"

No thought, then, of my whole life's completion and consummation being a dream.

I staggered up to my room, fell across my bed, and slept heavily and dreamlessly. When I awoke it was high noon. Mildred and her mother were coming to lunch.

I remembered, at one shock, Mildred's coming and her existence.

Now, indeed, the dream began.

With a penetrating sense of the futility of any action apart from *her*, I gave the necessary orders for the reception of my guests. When Mildred and her mother came, I received them with cordiality; but my genial phrases all seemed to be someone else's. My voice sounded like an echo; my heart was other where.

Still, the situation was not intolerable until the hour when afternoon tea was served in the drawing-room. Mildred and her mother kept the conversational pot boiling with a profusion of genteel commonplaces, and I bore it, as one can bear mild purgatories when one is in sight of heaven. I looked up at my sweetheart in the ebony frame, and I felt that anything that might happen, any irresponsible imbecility, any bathos of boredom, was nothing, if, after it all, *she* came to me again.

And yet, when Mildred, too, looked at the portrait, and said, "What a fine lady! One of your flames, Mr. Devigne?" I had a sickening sense of impotent irritation, which became absolute torture when Mildred—how could I ever have admired that chocolate-box barmaid style of prettiness?—threw herself into the high-backed chair, covering the needlework with her ridiculous flounces, and added, "Silence gives consent! Who is it, Mr. Devigne? Tell us all about her: I am sure she has a story."

Poor little Mildred, sitting there smiling, serene in her confidence that her every word charmed me—sitting there with her rather pinched waist, her rather tight boots, her rather vulgar voice—sitting in the chair where my dear lady had sat when she told me her story! I could not bear it.

"Don't sit there," I said; "it's not comfortable!"

But the girl would not be warned. With a laugh that set every nerve in my body vibrating with annoyance, she said, "Oh, dear! mustn't I even sit in the same chair as your black-velvet woman?"

I looked at the chair in the picture. It *was* the same; and in her chair Mildred was sitting. Then a horrible sense of the reality of Mildred came upon me. Was all this a reality after all? But for fortunate chance might Mildred have occupied, not only her chair, but her place in my life? I rose.

"I hope you won't think me very rude," I said; "but I am obliged to go out."

I forget what appointment I alleged. The lie came readily enough.

I faced Mildred's pouts with the hope that she and her mother would not wait dinner for me. I fled. In another minute I was safe, alone, under the chill, cloudy autumn sky—free to think, think, think of my dear lady.

I walked for hours along streets and squares; I lived over again and again every look, word, and hand-touch—every kiss; I was completely, unspeakably happy.

Mildred was utterly forgotten: my lady of the ebony frame filled my heart and soul and spirit.

As I heard eleven boom through the fog, I turned, and went home.

When I got to my street, I found a crowd surging through it, a strong red light filling the air.

A house was on fire. Mine.

I elbowed my way through the crowd.

The picture of my lady—that, at least, I could save!

As I sprang up the steps, I saw, as in a dream—yes, all this was *really* dream-like—I saw Mildred leaning out of the first-floor window, wringing her hands.

"Come back, sir," cried a fireman; "we'll get the young lady out right enough."

But *my* lady? I went on up the stairs, cracking, smoking, and as hot as hell, to the room where her picture was. Strange to say, I only felt that the picture was a thing we should like to look on through the

long glad wedded life that was to be ours. I never thought of it as being one with her.

As I reached the first floor, I felt arms round my neck. The smoke
was too thick for me to distinguish features.

"Save me!" a voice whispered. I clasped a figure in my arms, and,
with a strange disease, bore it down the shaking stairs and out into
safety. It was Mildred. I knew *that* directly I clasped her.

"Stand back," cried the crowd.

"Everyone's safe," cried a fireman.

The flames leaped from every window. The sky grew redder and
redder. I sprang from the hands that would have held me. I leaped up
the steps. I crawled up the stairs. Suddenly the whole horror of the
situation came on me. "*As long as my picture remains in the ebony frame.*"
What if picture and frame perished together?

I fought with the fire, and with my own choking inability to fight
with it. I pushed on. I must save my picture. I reached the drawing-
room.

As I sprang in, I saw my lady—I swear it—through the smoke and
the flames, hold out her arms to me—to me—who came too late to
save her, and to save my own life's joy. I never saw her again.

Before I could reach her, or cry out to her, I felt the floor yield
beneath my feet, and I fell into the fiery hell below.

★★★★★★

How did they save me? What does that matter? They saved me
somehow—curse them. Every stick of my aunt's furniture was destroyed. My friends pointed out that, as the furniture was heavily in-
sured, the carelessness of a nightly-studious housemaid had done me
no harm.

No harm!

That was how I won and lost my only love.

I deny, with all my soul in the denial, that it was a dream. There are
no such dreams. Dreams of longing and pain there are in plenty, but
dreams of complete, of unspeakable happiness—ah, no—it is the rest
of life that is the dream.

But if I think that, why have I married Mildred, and grown stout
and dull and prosperous?

I tell you it is all *this* that is the dream; my dear lady only is the
reality. And what does it matter what one does in a dream?

The Five Senses

Professor Boyd Thompson's services to the cause of science are usually spoken of as inestimable, and so indeed they probably are, since in science, as in the rest of life, one thing leads to another, and you never know where anything is going to stop. At any rate, inestimable or not, they are world-renowned, and he with them. The discoveries which he gave to his time are a matter of common knowledge among biological experts, and the sudden ending of his experimental activities caused a few days' wonder in even lay circles. Quite unintelligent people told each other that it seemed a pity, and persons on omnibuses exchanged commonplaces starred with his name.

But the real meaning and cause of that ending have been studiously hidden, as well as the events which immediately preceded it. A veil has been drawn over all the things that people would have liked to know, and it is only now that circumstances so arrange themselves as to make it possible to tell the whole story. I propose to avail myself of this possibility.

It will serve no purpose for me to explain how the necessary knowledge came into my possession; but I will say that the story was only in part pieced together by me. Another hand is responsible for much of the detail and for a certain occasional emotionalism which is, I believe, wholly foreign to my own style. In my original statement of the following facts I dealt fully, as I am, I may say without immodesty, qualified to do, with all the scientific points of the narrative. But these details were judged, unwisely as I think, to be needless to the expert, and unintelligible to the ordinary reader, and have therefore been struck out; the merest hints have been left as necessary links in the story. This appears to me to destroy most of its interest, but I admit that the elisions are perhaps justified. I have no desire to assist or encourage callow students in such experiments as those by which Professor Boyd

Thompson brought his scientific career to an end.

Incredible as it may appear, Professor Boyd Thompson was once a little boy who wore white embroidered frocks and blue sashes; in that state he caught flies and pulled off their wings to find out how they flew. He did not find out, and Lucilla, his little girl-cousin, also in white frocks, cried over the dead, dismembered flies, and buried them in little paper coffins. Later, he wore a holland blouse with a belt of leather, and watched the development of tadpoles in a tin bath in the stable yard. A microscope was, on his eighth birthday, presented to him by an affluent uncle. The uncle showed him how to surprise the secrets of a drop of pond water, which, limpid to the eye, confessed under the microscope to a whole cosmogony of strenuous and undesirable careers.

At the age of ten, Arthur Boyd Thompson was sent to a private school, its Headmaster an acolyte of Science, who esteemed himself to be a high priest of Huxley and Tyndal, a devotee of Darwin. Thence to the choice of medicine as a profession was, when the choice was insisted on by the elder Boyd Thompson, a short, plain step. Inorganic chemistry failed to charm, and under the cloak of Medicine and Surgery the growing fever of scientific curiosity could be sated on bodies other than the cloak-wearer's. He became a medical student and an enthusiast for vivisection.

The bow of Apollo was not always bent. In a rest-interval, the summer vacation, to be exact, he met again the cousin—second, once removed—Lucilla, and loved her. They were betrothed. It was a long, bright summer full of sunshine, garden-parties, picnics, archery—a decaying amusement—and croquet, then coming to its own. He exulted in the distinction already crescent in his career, but some half-formed wholly unconscious desire to shine with increased lustre in the eyes of the beloved caused him to invite, for the holiday's ultimate week, a fellow student, one who knew and could testify to the quality of the laurels already encircling the head of the young scientist. The friend came, testified, and in a vibrating interview under the lime-trees of Lucilla's people's garden, Mr. Boyd Thompson learned that Lucilla never could, never would, love or marry a vivisectionist.

The moon hung low and yellow in the spacious calm of the sky; the hour was propitious, the lovers fond. Mr. Boyd Thompson vowed that his scientific research should henceforth deal wholly with departments into which the emotions of the non-scientific cannot enter. He went back to London, and within the week bought four dozen frogs, twelve guinea-pigs, five cats, and a spaniel. His scientific aspirations met his love-longings, and did not fight them. You cannot fight beings of another world. He took part in a debate on 'Blood Pressure', which created some little stir in medical circles, spoke eloquently, and distinction surrounded him with a halo.

He wrote to Lucilla three times a week, took his degree, and published that celebrated paper of his which set the whole scientific world by the ears; *The Action of Choline on the Nervous System* I think its name was.

Lucilla surreptitiously subscribed to a press-cutting agency for all snippets of print relating to her lover. Three weeks after the publication of that paper, which really was the beginning of Professor Boyd Thompson's fame, she wrote to him from her home in Kent.

Arthur,
You have been doing it again. You know how I love you, and I believe you love me; but you must choose between loving me and torturing dumb animals. If you don't choose right, then it's goodbye, and God forgive you.
Your poor Lucilla,
who loved you very dearly.

He read the letter, and the human heart in him winced and whined. Yet not so deeply now, nor so loudly, but that he bethought himself to seek out a friend and pupil, who would watch certain experiments, attend to the cutting of certain sections, before he started for Tenterden, where she lived. There was no station at Tenterden in those days, but a twelve-mile walk did not dismay him.

Lucilla's home was one of those houses of brave proportions and an inalienable *bourgeois* stateliness, which stand back a little from the noble High Street of that most beautiful of Kentish towns. He came there, pleasantly exercised, his boots dusty, and his throat dry, and stood on the snowy doorstep, beneath the Jacobean lintel. He looked down the wide, beautiful street, raised eyebrows, and shrugged uneasy shoulders within his professional frock-coat.

'It's all so difficult,' he said to himself.

Lucilla received him in a drawing-room scented with last year's rose leaves, and fresh with chintz that had been washed a dozen times. She stood, very pale and frail; her blonde hair was not teased into fluffiness, and rounded over the chignon of the period but banded Madonna-wise, crowning her with heavy burnished plaits. Her gown was of white muslin, and round her neck black velvet passed, supporting a gold locket. He knew whose picture it held. The loose bell sleeves fell away from the slender arms with little black velvet bracelets, and she leaned one hand on a chiffonier of carved rosewood, on whose marble top stood, under a glass case, a Chinese *pagoda*, carved in ivory, and two Bohemian glass vases with medallions representing young women holding pigeons. There were white curtains of darned net, in the fireplace white ravelled muslin spread a cascade brightened with threads of tinsel. A canary sang in a green cage, wainscoted with yellow tarlatan, and two red rosebuds stood in lank specimen glasses on the mantelpiece.

Every article of furniture in the room spoke eloquently of the sheltered life, the iron obstinacy of the well-brought-up.

It was a scene that invaded his mental vision many a time, in the laboratory, in the lecture-room. It symbolised many things, all dear, and all impossible.

They talked awkwardly, miserably. And always it came round to this same thing.

'But you don't mean it,' he said, and at last came close to her.

'I do mean it,' she said, very white, very trembling, very determined.

'But it's my life,' he pleaded; 'it's the life of thousands. You don't understand.'

'I understand that dogs are tortured. I can't bear it.'

He caught at her hand.

'Don't,' she said. 'When I think what that hand does!'

'Dearest,' he said very earnestly, 'which is the more important, a dog or a human being?'

'They're all God's creatures,' she flashed, unorthodoxly unorthodox. 'They're all God's creatures.' With much more that he heard and pitied and smiled at miserably in his heart.

'You don't understand,' he kept saying, stemming the flood of her rhetorical pleadings. 'Spencer Wells alone has found out wonderful things, just with experiments on rabbits.'

'Don't tell me,' she said. 'I don't want to hear.'

The conventions of their day forbade that he should tell her anything plainly. He took refuge in generalities. 'Spencer Wells, that operation he perfected, it's restored thousands of women to their husbands—saved thousands of women for their children.'

'I don't care what he's done—it's wrong if it's done in that way.'

It was on that day that they parted, after more than an hour of mutual misunderstood reiteration. He, she said, was brutal. And, besides, it was plain that he did not love her. To him she seemed unreasonable, narrow, prejudiced, blind to the high ideals of the new science.

'Then it's goodbye,' he said at last. 'If I gave way, you'd only despise me, because I should despise myself. It's no good. Goodbye, dear.'

'Goodbye,' she said. 'I know I'm right. You'll know I am, someday.'

'Never,' he answered, more moved and in a more diffused sense than he had ever believed he could be. 'I can't set my pleasure in you against the good of the whole world.'

'If that's all you think of me,' she said, and her silk and her muslin whirled from the room.

He walked back to Staplehurst, thrilled with the conflict. The thrill died down, went out, and left as ashes a cold resolve.

That was the end of Mr. Boyd Thompson's engagement.

It was quite by accident that he made his greatest discovery. There are those who hold that all great discoveries are accident—or Providence. The terms are, in this connection, interchangeable. He plunged into work to wash away the traces of his soul's wounds, as a man plunges into water to wash off red blood. And he swam there, perhaps, a little blindly. The injection with which he treated that white rabbit was not compounded of the drugs he had intended to use. He could not lay his hand on the thing he wanted, and in that sort of frenzy of experiment, to which no scientific investigator is wholly a stranger, he cast about for a new idea. The thing that came to his hand was a drug that he had never in his normal mind intended to use—an unaccredited, wild, magic medicine obtained by a missionary from some savage South Sea tribe and brought home as an example of the ignorance of the heathen.

And it worked a miracle.

He had been fighting his way through the unbending opposition of known facts, he had been struggling in the shadows, and this discovery was like the blinding light that meets a man's eyes when his pick-axe knocks a hole in a dark cave and he finds himself face to face with the sun. The effect was undoubted. Now it behoved him to make sure of the cause, to eliminate all those other factors to which that effect might have been due. He experimented cautiously, slowly. These things take years, and the years he did not grudge. He was never tired, never impatient; the slightest variations, the least indications, were eagerly observed, faithfully recorded.

His whole soul was in his work. Lucilla was the one beautiful memory of his life. But she was a memory. The reality was this discovery, the accident, the Providence.

Day followed day, all alike, and yet each taking almost unperceived, one little step forward; or stumbling into sudden sloughs, those losses and lapses that take days and weeks to retrieve. He was Professor, and his hair was grey at the temples before his achievement rose before him, beautiful, inevitable, austere in its completed splendour, as before the triumphant artist rises the finished work of his art.

He had found out one of the secrets with which Nature has crammed her dark hiding-places. He had discovered the hidden possibilities of sensation. In plain English, his researches had led him thus far; he had found—by accident or Providence—the way to intensify sensation. Vaguely, incredulously, he had perceived his discovery; the rabbits and guinea-pigs had demonstrated it plainly enough. Then there was a night when he became aware that those results must be checked by something else. He must work out in marble the form he had worked out in clay. He knew that by this drug, which had, so to speak, thrust itself upon him, he could intensify the five senses of any of the inferior animals.

Could he intensify those senses in man? If so, worlds beyond the grasp of his tired mind opened themselves before him. If so, he would have achieved a discovery, made a contribution to the science he had loved so well and followed at such a cost, a discovery equal to any that any man had ever made.

Ferrier, and Leo, and Horsley; those he would outshine. Galileo, Newton, Harvey; he would rank with these.

Could he find a human rabbit to submit to the test?

The soul of the man Lucilla had loved, turned and revolted. No: he had experimented on guinea-pigs and rabbits, but when it came to experimenting on men, there was only one man on whom he chose to use his new-found powers. Himself.

At least she would not have it to say that he was a coward, or unfair, when it came to the point of what a man could do and dare, could suffer and endure.

His big laboratory was silent and deserted. His assistants were gone, his private pupils dispersed. He was alone with the tools of his trade. Shelf on shelf of smooth stoppered bottles, drugs and stains, the long bench gleaming with beakers, test tubes, and the glass mansions of costly apparatus. In the shadows at the far end of the room, where the last going assistant had turned off the electric lights, strange shapes lurked: wicker-covered carboys, kinographs, galvanometers, the faintly threatening aspect of delicate complex machines all wires and coils and springs, the gaunt form of the pendulum myographs, and certain well-worn tables and copper troughs, which for the moment had no use.

He knew that this drug with others, diversely compounded and applied, produced in animals an abnormal intensification of the senses; that it increased—nay, as it were, magnified a thousandfold, the hearing, the sight, the touch—and, he was almost sure, the senses of taste and smell. But of the extent of the increase he could form no exact estimate.

Should he tonight put himself in the position of one able to speak on these points with authority? Or should he go to the Royal Society's meeting and hear that ass Netherby maunder yet once again about the secretion of lymph?

He pulled out his notebook and laid it open on the bench. He went to the locked cupboard, unfastened it with the bright key that hung instead of seal or charm at his watch-chain. He unfolded a paper and laid it on the bench where no one coming in could fail to see it. Then he took out little bottles, three, four, five, polished a graduated glass and dropped into it slow, heavy drops. A larger bottle yielded a medium in which all mingled. He hardly hesitated at all before turning up his sleeve and slipping the tiny needle into his arm. He pressed the end of the syringe. The injection was made.

Its effect, though not immediate, was sudden. He had to close his eyes, staggered indeed and was glad of the stool near him, for the drug coursed through him as a hunt in full cry might sweep over untrodden plains. Then suddenly everything seemed to settle; he was no longer helpless but was once again Professor Boyd Thompson, who had injected a mixture of certain drugs and was experiencing their effect.

His fingers, still holding the glass syringe, sent swift messages to his brain. When he looked down at his fingers, he saw that what they grasped was the smooth, slender tube of clear glass. What he felt that they held was a tremendous cylinder, rough to the touch. He wondered, even at the moment, why, if his sense of touch were indeed magnified to this degree, everything did not appear enormous—his ring, his collar. He examined the new phenomenon with cold care. It seemed that only that was enlarged on which his attention, his mind, was fixed. He kept his hand on the glass syringe, and thought of his ring, got his mind away from the tube, back again in time to feel it small between his fingers, grow, increase, and become big once more.

'So *that's* a success,' he said, and saw himself lay the thing down. It lay just in front of the rack of test tubes, to the eye, just that little glass cylinder. To the touch it was like a water-pipe on a house side, and the test tubes, when he touched them, like the pipes of a great organ.

'Success,' he said again, and mixed the antidote. For he had found the antidote in one of those flashes of intuition, imagination, genius, that light the ways of science as stars light the way of a ship in dark waters. The action of the antidote was enough for one night. He locked the cupboard, and, after all, was glad to listen to the maunderings of Netherby. It had been lonely there, in the atmosphere of complete success.

One by one, day by day, he tested the action of his drugs on his other senses. Without being technical, I had perhaps better explain that the compelling drug was, in each case, one and the same. Its action was directed to this set of nerves or that by means of the other drugs mixed with it. I trust this is clear?

The sense of smell was tested, and its laboratory, with its mingled odours, became abominable to him. Hardly could he stay himself from rushing forth into the outer air to wash his nostrils in the clear coolness of Hampstead Heath. The sense of taste gave him, magnified a thousand times, the flavour of his after-dinner coffee, and other tastes, distasteful almost beyond the bearing point.

But 'Success,' he said, rinsing his mouth at the laboratory sink after the drinking of the antidote, 'all along the line, success.'

Then he tested the action of his discovery on the sense of hearing. And the sound of London came like the roar of a giant, yet when he fixed his attention on the movements of a fly all other sounds ceased, and he heard the sound of the fly's feet on the shelf when it walked. Thus, in turn, he heard the creak of boards expanding in the heat, the movement of the glass stoppers that kept imprisoned in the proper bottles the giants of acid and alkali.

'Success!' he cried aloud, and his voice sounded in his ears like the shout of a monster overcoming primeval forces. 'Success! Success!'

There remained only the eyes, and here, strangely enough, the Professor hesitated, faint with a sudden heart-sickness. Following a intensification there must be reaction. What if the reaction exceeded that from which it reacted, what if the wave of tremendous sight stemmed by the antidote ebbing, left him blind? But the spirit of the explorer in science is the spirit that explores African rivers, and sail amid white bergs to seek the undiscovered Pole.

He held the syringe with a firm hand, made the required puncture, and braced himself for the result. His eyes seemed to swell to great globes, to dwindle to microscopic globules, to swim in a flood of fire, to shrivel high and dry on a beach of hot sand. Then he *saw*, and the glass fell from his hand. For the whole of the stable earth seemed to be suddenly set in movement, even the air grew thick with vast overlapping shapeless shapes. He opined later that these were the microbes and *bacilli* that cover and fill all things in this world that looks so clean and bright.

Concentrating his vision, he saw in the one day's little dust on the bottles, myriads of creatures, crawling and writhing, alive. The proportions of the laboratory seemed but little altered. Its large lines and forms remained practically unchanged. It was the little things that were no longer little, the invisible things that were now invisible no longer. And he felt grateful for the first time in his life for the limits set by Nature to the powers of the human body. He had increased those powers. If he let his eye stray idly about, as one does in the waltz, for example, all was much as it used to be. But the moment he looked steadily at any one thing it became enormous.

He closed his eyes. Success here had gone beyond his wildest dreams. Indeed, he could not but feel that success, taking the bit between its teeth, had perhaps gone just the least little bit too far.

And on the next day he decided to examine the drug in all its aspects, to court the intensification of all his senses, which should set him in the position of supreme power over men and things, transform him from a professor into a demi-god.

The great question was, of course, how the five preparations of his drug would act on or against each other. Would it be intensification, or would they neutralise each other? Like all imaginative scientists, he was working with stuff perilously like the spells of magic, and certain things were not possible to be foretold. Besides, this drug came from a land of mystery and the knowledge of secrets which we call magic. He did not anticipate any increase in the danger of the experiment. Nevertheless, he spent some hours in arranging and destroying papers, among others certain pages of the yellow notebook. After dinner he detained his man as, laden with the last tray, he was leaving the room.

'I may as well tell you, Parker,' the professor said, moved by some impulse he had not expected, 'that you will benefit to some extent by my will. On conditions. If any accident should cut short my life, you will at once communicate with my solicitor, whose name you will now write down.'

The model man, trained by fifteen years of close personal service, drew forth a notebook neat as the professor's own, wrote in it neatly the address the professor gave.

'Anything more, sir?' he asked, looking up, pencil in hand.

'No,' said the professor, 'nothing more. Goodnight, Parker.'

'Goodnight, sir,' said the model man.

******

The next words the model man opened his lips to speak were breathed into the night tube of the nearest doctor.

'My master, Professor Boyd Thompson; could you come round at once, sir. I'm afraid it's very serious.'

It was half past six when the nearest doctor—Jones was his unimportant name—stooped over the lifeless body of the professor.

He shook his head as he stood up and looked round the private laboratory on whose floor the body lay.

'His researches are over,' he said. 'Yes, he's dead. Been dead some hours. When did you find him?'

'I went to call my master as usual,' said Parker; 'he rises at six, summer and winter, sir. He was not in his room, and the bed had not been slept in. So, I came in here, sir. It is not unusual for my master to work all night when he has been very interested in his experiments, and then he likes his coffee at six.'

'I see,' said Doctor Jones. 'Well, you'd better rouse the house and fetch his own doctor. It's heart failure, of course, but I daresay he'd like to sign the certificate himself.'

'Can nothing be done?' said Parker, much affected.

'Nothing,' said Doctor Jones. 'It's the common lot. You'll have to look out for another situation.'

'Yes, sir,' said Parker; 'he told me only last night what I was to do in case of anything happening to him. I wonder if he had any idea?'

'Some premonition, perhaps,' the doctor corrected.

The funeral was a very quiet one. So, the late Professor Boyd Thompson had decreed in his will. He had arranged all details. The body was to be clothed in flannel, placed in an open coffin covered only with a linen sheet, and laid in the family mausoleum, a moss-grown building in the midst of a little park which surrounded Boyd Grange, the birthplace of the Boyd Thompsons. A little property in

Sussex it was. The Professor sometimes went there for weekends. He had left this property to Lucilla, with a last love-letter, in which he begged her to give his body the hospitality of the death-house, now hers with the rest of the estate. To Parker he left an annuity of two hundred pounds, on the condition that he should visit and enter the mausoleum once in every twenty-four hours for fourteen days after the funeral.

To this end the late professor's solicitor decided that Parker had better reside at Boyd Grange for the said fortnight, and Parker, whose nerves seemed to be shaken, petitioned for company. This made easy the arrangement which the solicitor desired to make—of a witness to the carrying out by Parker of the provisions of the dead man's will. The solicitor's clerk was quite good company, and arm in arm with him Parker paid his first visit to the mausoleum. The little building stands in a glade of evergreen oaks. The trees are old and thick, and the narrow door is deep in shadow even on the sunniest day. Parker went to the mausoleum, peered through its square grating, but he did not go in. Instead, he listened, and his ears were full of silence.

'He's dead, right enough,' he said, with a doubtful glance at his companion.

'You ought to go in, oughtn't you?' said the solicitor's clerk;

'Go in yourself if you like, Mr. Pollack,' said Parker, suddenly angry; 'anyone who likes can go in, but it won't be me. If he was alive, it 'ud be different. I'd have done anything for him. But I ain't going in among all them dead and mouldering Thompsons. See? If we both say I did, it'll be just the same as me doing it.'

'So, it will,' said the solicitor's clerk; 'but where do I come in?'

Parker explained to him where he came in, to their mutual consent.

'Right you are,' said the clerk; 'on those terms I'm fly. And if we both say you did it, we needn't come to the beastly place again,' he added, shivering and glancing over his shoulder at the door with the grating.

'No more we need,' said Parker.

Behind the bars of the narrow door lay deeper shadows than those of the ilexes outside. And in the blackest of the shadow lay a man whose every sense was intensified as though by a magic potion. For when the professor swallowed the five variants of his great discovery, each acted as he had expected it to act. But the union of the five vehicles conveying the drug to the nerves, which served his five senses, had paralysed every muscle. His hearing, taste, touch, scent, and sight were intensified a thousandfold—as they had been in the individual experiments—but the man who felt all this exaggerated increase of sensation was powerless as a cat under curare. He could not raise a finger, stir an eyelash. More, he could not breathe, nor did his body advise him of any need of breathing.

And he had lain thus immobile and felt his body slowly grow cold, had heard in thunder the voices of Parker and the doctor, had felt the enormous hands of those who made his death-toilet, had smelt intolerably the camphor and lavender that they laid round him in the narrow, black bed; had tasted the mingled flavours of the drug and its five mediums; and, in an ecstasy of magnified sensation, had made the lonely train journey which coffins make, and known himself carried into the mausoleum and left there alone. And every sense was intensified, even his sense of time, so that it seemed to him that he had lain there for many years. And the effect of the drugs showed no sign of any diminution or reaction.

Why had he not left directions for the injection of the antidote? It was one of those slips which wreck campaigns, cause the discovery of hidden crimes. It was a slip, and he had made it. He had thought of death, but in all the results he had anticipated death's semblance had found no place. Well, he had made his bed, and he must lie on it. This narrow bed, whose scent of clean oak and French polish was distinct among the musty, intolerable odours of the charnel house.

It was perhaps twenty hours that he had lain there, powerless, immobile, listening to the sounds of unexplained movements about him, when he felt with joy, almost like delirium, a faint quivering in the eyelids.

They had closed his eyes, and till now, they had remained closed. Now, with an effort as of one who lifts a grave-stone, he raised his eyelids. They closed again quickly, for the roof of the vault, at which he gazed earnestly, was alive with monsters; spiders, earwigs, crawling beetles, and flies, far too small to have been perceived by normal eyes, spread giant forms over him. He closed his eyes and shuddered. It felt like a shudder, but no one who had stood beside him could have noted any movement.

It was then that Parker came—and went.

Professor Boyd Thompson heard Parker's words, and lay listening to the thunder of Parker's retreating feet. He tried to move—to call out. But he could not. He lay there helpless, and somehow, he thought of the dark end of the laboratory, where the assistant before leaving had turned out the electric lights.

He had nothing but his thoughts. He thought how he would lie there, and die there. The place was sequestered; no one passed that way. Parker had failed him, and the end was not hard to picture. He might recover all his faculties, might be able to get up, able to scream, to shout, to tear at the bars. The bars were strong, and Parker would not come again. Well, he would try to face with a decent bravery whatever had to be faced.

Time, measureless, spread round. It seemed as though someone had stopped all the clocks in the world, as though he were not in time but in eternity. Only by the waxing and waning light he knew of the night and the day.

His brain was weary with the effort to move, to speak, to cry out. He lay, informed with something like despair—or fortitude. And then Parker came again. And this time a key grated in the lock. The professor noted with rapture that it sounded no louder than a key should sound, turned in a lock that was rusty. Nor was the voice other than he had been used to hear it, when he was man alive and Parker's master. And——

'You can go in, of course, if you wish it, miss,' said Parker disapprovingly; 'but it's not what I should advise myself. For me it's different,' he added, on a sudden instinct of self-preservation; 'I've got to go in. Every day for a fortnight,' he added, pitying himself.

'I will go in, thank you,' said a voice. 'Yes, give me the candle, please. And you need not wait. I will lock the door when I come out.' Thus, the voice spoke. And the voice was Lucilla's.

In all his life the professor had never feared death or its trappings. Neither its physical repulsiveness, nor the supernatural terrors which cling about it, had he either understood or tolerated. But now, in one little instant, he did understand.

He heard Lucilla come in. A light held near him shone warm and red through his closed eyelids. And he knew that he had only to unclose those eyelids to see her face bending over him. And he could unclose them. Yet he would not. He lay there, still and straight in his coffin, and life swept through him in waves of returning power. Yet he lay like death. For he said, or something in him said:

'She believes me dead. If I open my eyes it will be like a dead man looking at her. If I move it will be a dead man moving under her eyes. People have gone mad for less. Lie still, lie still,' he told himself; 'take any risks yourself. There must be none for her.'

She had taken the candle away, set it down somewhere at a distance, and now she was kneeling beside him and her hand was under his head. He knew he could raise his arm and clasp her—and Parker would come back perhaps, when she did not return to the house, come back to find a man in grave-clothes, clasping a mad woman. He lay still. Then her kisses and tears fell on his face, and she murmured broken words of love and longing. But he lay still. At any cost he must lie still. Even at the cost of his own sanity, his own life. And the warmth of her hand under his head, her face against his, her kisses, her tears, set his blood flowing evenly and strongly. Her other arm lay on his breast, softly pressing over his heart. He would not move. He would be strong. If he were to be saved, it must be by some other way, not this.

Suddenly tears and kisses ceased; her every breath seemed to have stopped with these. She had drawn away from him. She spoke. Her voice came from above him. She was standing up.

'Arthur!' she said. 'Arthur!' Then he opened his eyes, the narrowest chink. But he could not see her. Only he knew she was moving towards the door. There had been a new quality in her tone, a thrill of fear, or hope was it? or at least of uncertainty? Should he move; should he speak? He dared not. He knew too well the fear that the normal human being has of death and the grave, the fear transcending love, transcending reason. Her voice was further away now. She was by the door. She was leaving him. If he let her go, it was an end of hope for him. If he did not let her go, an end, perhaps, of reason, for her. No.

'Arthur,' she said, 'I don't believe . . . I believe you can hear me. I'm going to get a doctor. If you *can* speak, speak to me.'

Her speaking ended, cut off short as a cord is cut by a knife. He did not speak. He lay in conscious, forced rigidity.

'Speak if you can,' she implored, 'just one word!'

Then he said, very faintly, very distinctly, in a voice that seemed to come from a great way off, 'Lucilla!'

And at the word she screamed aloud pitifully, and leaped for the entrance; and he heard the rustle of her crape in the narrow door. Then he opened his eyes wide, and raised himself on his elbow. Very weak he was, and trembling exceedingly. To his ears her scream held the note of madness. Vainly he had refrained. Selfishly he had yielded. The cold band of a mortal faintness clutched at his heart.

'I don't want to live now,' he told himself, and fell back in the straight bed.

Her arms were round him.

'I'm going to get help,' she said, her lips to his ear; 'brandy and things. Only I came back. I didn't want you to think I was frightened. Oh, my dear! Thank God, thank God!' He felt her kisses even through the swooning mist that swirled about him. Had she really fled in terror? He never knew. He knew that she had come back to him.

★★★★★★

That is the real, true, and authentic narrative of the events which caused Professor Boyd Thompson to abandon a brilliant career, to promise anything that Lucilla might demand, and to devote himself entirely to a gentlemanly and unprofitable farming, and to his wife. From the point of view of the scientific world it is a sad ending to much promise, but at any rate there are two happy people hand in hand at the story's ending.

There is no doubt that for several years Professor Boyd Thompson had had enough of science, and, by a natural revulsion, flung himself into the full tide of commonplace sentiment. But genius, like youth, cannot be denied. And I, for one, am doubtful whether the professor's renunciation of research will be a lasting one. Already I have heard whispers of a laboratory which is being built on the house, beyond the billiard-room.

But I am inclined to believe the rumours which assert that, for the future, his research will take the form of extending paths already well-trodden; that he will refrain from experiments with unknown drugs, and those dreadful researches which tend to merge the chemist and biologist in the alchemist and the magician. And he certainly does not intend to experiment further on the nerves of any living thing, even his own. The professor had already done enough work to make the reputation of half-a-dozen ordinary scientists. He may be pardoned if he rests on his laurels, entwining them, to some extent, with roses.

The bottle containing the drug from the South Seas was knocked down on the day of his death and swept up in bits by the laboratory boy. It is a curious fact that the professor has wholly forgotten the formulae of his experiment, which so nearly was his last. This is a great satisfaction to his wife, and possibly to the Professor. But of this I cannot be sure; the scientific spirit survives much.

To the unscientific reader, the strangest part of this story will perhaps be the fact that Parker is still with his old master, a wonderful example of the perfect butler. Professor Boyd Thompson was able to forgive Parker because he understood him. And he learned to under-stand Parker in those moments of agony, when his keen intellect and his awakened heart taught him, through his love for Lucilla, the depth of that gulf of fear which lies between the quick and the dead.

The Haunted House

It was by the merest accident that Desmond ever went to the Haunted House. He had been away from England for six years, and the nine months' leave taught him how easily one drops out of one's place.

He had taken rooms at the Greyhound before he found that there was no reason why he should stay in Elmstead rather than in any other of London's dismal outposts. He wrote to all the friends whose addresses he could remember., and settled himself to await their answers.

He wanted someone to talk to, and there was no one. Meantime he lounged on the horsehair sofa with the advertisements, and his pleasant grey eyes followed line after line with intolerable boredom. Then, suddenly, "Halloa!" he said, and sat up. This is what he read:—

A Haunted House—Advertiser is anxious to have phenomena investigated. Any properly-accredited investigator will be given full facilities. Address, by letter only, Wildon Prior, 237, Museum Street, London.

"That's rum!" he said. Wildon Prior had been the best wicket-keeper in his club. It wasn't a common name. Anyway, it was worth trying, so he sent off a telegram.

Wildon Prior, 237, Museum Street, London, May I come to you for a day or two and see the ghost?—William Desmond.

On returning next day from a stroll there was an orange envelope on the wide Pembroke table in his parlour.

Delighted—expect you today. Book to Crittenden from Charing Cross. Wire train—Wildon Prior, Ormehurst Rectory, Kent.

"So that's all right," said Desmond, and went off to pack his bag and ask in the bar for a timetable, "Good old Wildon; it will be ripping, seeing him again."

A curious little omnibus, rather like a bathing-machine, was waiting outside Crittenden Station, and its driver, a swarthy, blunt-faced little man, with liquid eyes, said, "You a friend of Mr, Prior, sir?" shut him up in the bathing-machine, and banged the door on him. It was a very long drive, and less pleasant than it would have been in an open carriage.

The last part of the journey was through a wood; then came a churchyard and a church, and the bathing-machine turned in at a gate under heavy trees and drew up in front of a white house with bare, gaunt windows.

"Cheerful place, upon my soul!" Desmond told himself, as he tumbled out of the back of the bathing-machine.

The driver set his bag on the discoloured doorstep and drove off. Desmond pulled a rusty chain, and a big-throated bell jangled above his head.

Nobody came to the door, and he rang again. Still nobody came, but he heard a window thrown open above the porch. He stepped back on to the gravel and looked up.

A young man with rough hair and pale eyes was looking out. Not Wildon, nothing like Wildon. He did not speak, but he seemed to be making signs; and the signs seemed to mean, "Go away!"

"I came to see Mr. Prior," said Desmond. Instantly and softly the window closed.

"Is it a lunatic asylum I've come to by chance?" Desmond asked himself, and pulled again at the rusty chain.

Steps sounded inside the house, the sound of boots on stone. Bolts were shot back, the door opened, and Desmond, rather hot and a little annoyed, found himself looking into a pair of very dark, friendly eyes, and a very pleasant voice said

"Mr. Desmond, I presume? Do come in and let me apologise."

The speaker shook him warmly by the hand, and he found himself following down a flagged passage a man of more than mature age, well-dressed, handsome, with an air of competence and alertness which we associate with what is called "a man of the world." He opened a door and led the way into a shabby, bookish, leathery room.

"Do sit down, Mr. Desmond."

"This must be the uncle, I suppose," Desmond thought, as he fitted himself into the shabby, perfect curves of the armchair.

"How's Wildon?" he asked, aloud. "All right, I hope?"

The other looked at him. "I beg your pardon," he said, doubtfully.

"I was asking how Wildon is?"

"I am quite well, I thank you," said the other man, with some formality.

"I beg your pardon"—it was now Desmond's turn to say it—"I did not realise that your name might be Wildon, too, I meant Wildon Prior."

"I am Wildon Prior," said the other, and you, I presume, are the expert from the Psychical Society?"

"Good Lord, no!" said Desmond. "I'm Wildon Prior's friend, and, of course, there must be two Wildon Priors."

"You sent the telegram? You are Mr, Desmond? The Psychical Society were to send an expert, and I thought—"

"I see," said Desmond; "and I thought you were Wildon Prior, an old friend of mine—a young man," he said, and half rose.

"Now, don't," said Wildon Prior. "No doubt it is my nephew who is your friend. Did he know you were coming? But of course, he didn't. I am wandering. But I'm exceedingly glad to see you. You will stay, will you not? If you can endure to be the guest of an old man. And I will write to Will tonight and ask him to join us."

"That's most awfully good of you," Desmond assured him, "I shall be glad to stay. I was awfully pleased when I saw Wildon's name in the paper, because—"

And out came the tale of Elmstead, its loneliness and disappointment.

Mr. Prior listened with the kindest interest. "And you have not found your friends? How sad! But they will write to you. Of course, you left your address?"

"I didn't, by Jove!" said Desmond. "But I can write. Can I catch the post?"

"Easily," the elder man assured him. "Write your letters now. My man shall take them to the post, and then we will have dinner, and I will tell you about the ghost."

Desmond wrote his letters quickly, Mr. Prior just then reappearing.

"Now I'll take you to your room," he said, gathering the letters in long, white hands. "You'll like a rest. Dinner at eight."

The bedchamber, like the parlour, had a pleasant air of worn luxury and accustomed comfort.

"I hope you will be comfortable," the host said, with courteous solicitude. And Desmond was quite sure that he would.

Three covers were laid, the swarthy man who had driven Desmond from the station stood behind the host's chair, and a figure came towards Desmond and his host from the shadows beyond the yellow circles of the silver-sticked candles.

"My assistant, Mr. Verney," said the host, and Desmond surrendered his hand to the limp, damp touch of the man who had seemed to say to him, from the window above the porch, "Go away!" Was Mr. Prior perhaps a doctor who received "paying guests," persons who were, in Desmond's phrase, "a bit balmy"? But he had said "assistant."

"I thought," said Desmond, hastily, "you would be a clergyman. The Rectory, you know—I thought Wildon, my friend Wildon, was staying with an uncle who was a clergyman."

"Oh, no," said Mr. Prior. "I rent the Rectory. The rector thinks it is damp. The church is disused, too. It is not considered safe, and they can't afford to restore it. Claret to Mr. Desmond, Lopez." And the swarthy, blunt-faced man filled his glass.

"I find this place very convenient for my experiments. I dabble a little in chemistry, Mr. Desmond, and Verney here assists me."

Verney murmured something that sounded like "only too proud," and subsided.

"We all have our hobbies, and chemistry is mine," Mr. Prior went on. "Fortunately, I have a little income which enables me to indulge it. Wildon, my nephew, you know, laughs at me, and calls it the science of smells. But it's absorbing, very absorbing."

After dinner Verney faded away, and Desmond and his host stretched their feet to what Mr. Prior called a "handful of fire," for the evening had grown chill.

"And now," Desmond said, "won't you tell me the ghost story?"

The other glanced round the room.

"There isn't really a ghost story at all. It's only that—well, it's never happened to me personally, but it happened to Verney, poor lad, and he's never been quite his own self since."

Desmond flattered himself on his insight.

"Is mine the haunted room?" he asked.

"It doesn't come to any particular room," said the other, slowly, "nor to any particular person."

"Anyone may happen to see it?"

"No one sees it. It isn't the kind of ghost that's seen or heard."

122

"I'm afraid I'm rather stupid, but I don't understand," said Desmond, roundly. "How can it be a ghost, if you neither hear it nor see it?"

"I did not say it was a ghost," Mr. Prior corrected. "I only say that there is something about this house which is not ordinary. Several of my assistants have had to leave; the thing got on their nerves."

"What became of the assistants?" asked Desmond.

"Oh, they left, you know; they left," Prior answered, vaguely. "One couldn't expect them to sacrifice their health. I sometimes think—village gossip is a deadly thing, Mr. Desmond—that perhaps they were prepared to be frightened; that they fancy things. I hope the Psychical Society's expert won't be a neurotic. But even without being a neurotic one might—but you don't believe in ghosts, Mr. Desmond. Your Anglo-Saxon common sense forbids it."

"I'm afraid I'm not exactly Anglo-Saxon," said Desmond. "On my father's side I'm pure Celt; though I know I don't do credit to the race."

"And on your mother's side?" Mr. Prior asked, with extraordinary eagerness; an eagerness so sudden and disproportioned to the question that Desmond stared. A faint touch of resentment as suddenly stirred in him, the first spark of antagonism to his host.

"Oh," he said, lightly, "I think I must have Chinese blood, I get on so well with the natives in Shanghai, and they tell me I owe my nose to a Red Indian great grandmother."

"No negro blood, I supposed" the host asked, with almost discourteous insistence.

"Oh, I wouldn't say that," Desmond answered. He meant to say it laughing, but he didn't. "My hair, you know—it's a very stiff curl it's got, and my mother's people were in the West Indies a few generations ago. You're interested in distinctions of race, I take it?"

"Not at all, not at all," Mr. Prior surprisingly assured him; "but, of course, any details of your family are necessarily interesting to me. I feel," he added, with another of his winning smiles, "that you and I are already friends."

Desmond could not have reasoningly defended the faint quality of dislike that had begun to tinge his first pleasant sense of being welcomed and wished for as a guest.

"You're very kind," he said; "it's jolly of you to take in a stranger like this."

Mr. Prior smiled, handed the cigar-box, mixed whisky and soda,

123

and began to talk about the history of the house.

"The foundations are almost certainly thirteenth century. It was a priory, you know. There's a curious tale, by the way, about the man Henry gave it to when he smashed up the monasteries. There was a curse; there seems always to have been a curse—"

The gentle, pleasant, high-bred voice went on. Desmond thought he was listening, but presently he roused himself and dragged his attention back to the words that were being spoken.

"—that made the fifth death. . . .There is one every hundred years, and always in the same mysterious way."

Then he found himself on his feet, incredibly sleepy, and heard himself say:—

"These old stories are tremendously interesting. Thank you very much. I hope you won't think me very uncivil, but I think I'd rather like to turn in; I feel a bit tired, somehow."

"But of course, my dear chap."

Mr. Prior saw Desmond to his room.

"Got everything you want? Right. Lock the door if you should feel nervous. Of course, a lock can't keep ghosts out, but I always feel as if it could," and with another of those pleasant, friendly laughs he was gone.

William Desmond went to bed a strong young man, sleepy indeed beyond his experience of sleepiness, but well and comfortable. He awoke faint and trembling, lying deep in the billows of the feather bed; and lukewarm waves of exhaustion swept through him. Where was he? What had happened? His brain, dizzy and weak at first, refused him any answer. When he remembered, the abrupt spasm of repulsion which he had felt so suddenly and unreasonably the night before came back to him in a hot, breathless flush. He had been drugged, he had been poisoned!

"I must get out of this," he told himself, and blundered out of bed towards the silken bell-pull that he had noticed the night before hanging near the door.

As he pulled it, the bed and the wardrobe and the room rose up round him and fell on him, and he fainted.

When he next knew anything, someone was putting brandy to his lips. He saw Prior, the kindest concern in his face. The assistant, pale and watery-eyed. The swarthy manservant, stolid, silent, and expressionless. He heard Verney say to Prior:—

"You see it was too much—I told you—"

"Hush," said Prior, "he's coming to."

★★★★★★

Four days later Desmond, lying on a wicker chair on the lawn, was a little disinclined for exertion, but no longer ill. Nourishing foods and drinks, beef-tea, stimulants, and constant care—these had brought him back to something like his normal state. He wondered at the vague suspicions, vaguely remembered, of that first night; they had all been proved absurd by the unwavering care and kindness of everyone in the Haunted House.

"But what caused it?" he asked his host, for the fiftieth time. "What made me make such a fool of myself?" And this time Mr. Prior did not put him off, as he had always done before by begging him to wait till he was stronger.

"I am afraid, you know," he said, "that the ghost really did come to you. I am inclined to revise my opinion of the ghost."

"But why didn't it come again?"

"I have been with you every night, you know," his host reminded him. And, indeed, the sufferer had never been left alone since the ringing of his bell on that terrible first morning.

"And now," Mr. Prior went on, "if you will not think me inhospitable, I think you will be better away from here. You ought to go to the seaside."

"There haven't been any letters for me, I suppose?" Desmond said, a little wistfully.

"Not one. I suppose you gave the right address? Ormehurst Rectory, Crittenden, Kent?"

"I don't think I put Crittenden," said Desmond. "I copied the address from your telegram." He pulled the pink paper from his pocket.

"Ah, that would account," said the other.

"You've been most awfully kind all through," said Desmond, abruptly.

"Nonsense, my boy," said the elder man, benevolently. "I only wish Willie had been able to come. He's never written, the rascal! Nothing but the telegram to say he could not come and was writing."

"I suppose he's having a jolly time somewhere," said Desmond, enviously; "but look here—do tell me about the ghost, if there's anything to tell. I'm almost quite well now, and I *should* like to know what it was that made a fool of me like that."

"Well"—Mr, Prior looked round him at the gold and red of dahlias and sunflowers, gay in the September sunshine—"here, and now, I don't know that it could do any harm. You remember that story of the man who got this place from Henry VIII. and the curse? That man's wife is buried in a vault under the church. Well, there were legends, and I confess I was curious to see her tomb. There are iron gates to the vault. Locked, they were. I opened them with an old key—and I couldn't get them to shut again."

"Yes?" Desmond said,

"You think I might have sent for a locksmith; but the fact is, there is a small crypt to the church, and I have used that crypt as a supplementary laboratory. If I had called anyone in to see to the lock they would have gossiped. I should have been turned out of my laboratory—perhaps out of my house,"

"I see."

"Now, the curious thing is," Mr. Prior went on, lowering his voice, "that it is only since that grating was opened that this house has been what they call 'haunted.' It is since then that all the things have happened."

"What things?"

"People staying here, suddenly ill—just as you were. And the attacks always seem to indicate loss of blood. And—" He hesitated a moment, "That wound in your throat, I told you you had hurt yourself falling when you rang the bell. But that was not true. What *is* true is that you had on your throat just the same little white wound that all the others have had. I wish"—he frowned—"that I could get that vault gate shut again. The key won't turn."

"I wonder if I could do anything?" Desmond asked, secretly convinced that he *had* hurt his throat in falling, and that his host's story was, as he put it, "all moonshine." Still, to put a lock right was but a slight return for all the care and kindness. "I'm an engineer, you know;" he added, awkwardly, and rose. "Probably a little oil. Let's have a look at this same lock."

He followed Mr. Prior through the house to the church. A bright, smooth old key turned readily, and they passed into the building, musty and damp, where ivy crawled through the broken windows, and the blue sky seemed to be laid close against the holes in the roof. Another key clicked in the lock of a low door beside what had once been the Lady Chapel, a thick oak door grated back, and Mr. Prior stopped a moment to light a candle that waited in its rough iron candlestick on a ledge of the stonework. Then down narrow stairs, chipped a little at the edges and soft with dust. The crypt was Norman, very simply beautiful. At the end of it was a recess, masked with a grating of rusty ironwork.

"They used to think," said Mr. Prior, "that iron kept off witchcraft. This is the lock," he went on, holding the candle against the gate, which was ajar.

They went through the gate, because the lock was on the other side. Desmond worked a minute or two with the oil and feather that he had brought. Then with a little wrench the key turned and returned.

"I think that's all right," he said, looking up, kneeling on one knee, with the key still in the lock and his hand on it.

"May I try it?"

Mr. Prior took Desmond's place, turned the key, pulled it out, and stood up. Then the key and the candlestick fell rattling on the stone floor, and the old man sprang upon Desmond.

"Now I've got you," he growled, in the darkness, and Desmond says that his spring and his clutch and his voice were like the spring and the clutch and the growl of a strong savage beast.

Desmond's little strength snapped like a twig at his first bracing of it to resistance. The old man held him as a vice holds. He had got a rope from somewhere. He was tying Desmond's arms.

Desmond hates to know that there in the dark he screamed like a caught hare. Then he remembered that he was a man, and shouted "Help! Here! Help!"

But a hand was on his mouth, and now a handkerchief was being knotted at the back of his head. He was on the floor, leaning against something. Prior's hands had left him.

"Now," said Prior's voice, a little breathless, and the match he struck showed Desmond the stone shelves with long things on them—coffins he supposed. "Now, I'm sorry I had to do it, but science before friendship, my dear Desmond," he went on, quite courteous and friendly. "I will explain to you, and you will see that a man of honour could not act otherwise. Of course, you having no friends who know where you are is most convenient. I saw that from the first. Now I'll explain. I didn't expect you to understand by instinct. But no matter. I am, I say it without vanity, the greatest discoverer since Newton. I know how to modify men's natures.

"I can make men what I choose. It's all done by transfusion of blood. Lopez—you know, my man Lopez—I've pumped the blood of dogs into his veins, and he's my slave—like a dog. Verney, he's my slave, too—part dog's blood and partly the blood of people who've come from time to time to investigate the ghost, and partly my own, because I wanted him to be clever enough to help me. And there's a bigger thing behind all this. You'll understand me when I say"—here he became very technical indeed, and used many words that meant nothing to Desmond, whose thoughts dwelt more and more on his small chance of escape.

To die like a rat in a hole, a rat in a hole! If he could only loosen the handkerchief and shout again!

"Attend, can't you?" said Prior, savagely, and kicked him. "I beg your pardon, my dear chap," he went on, suavely, "but this is important. So, you see the elixir of life is really the blood. The blood is the life, you know, and my great discovery is that to make a man immortal, and restore his youth, one only needs blood from the veins of a man who unites in himself blood of the four great races—the four colours, black, white, red, and yellow. Your blood unites these four. I took as much as I dared from you that night. I was the vampire, you know." He laughed pleasantly. "But your blood didn't act. The drug I had to give you to induce sleep probably destroyed the vital germs. And, besides, there wasn't enough of it. Now there is going to be enough!"

Desmond had been working his head against the thing behind him, easing the knot of the handkerchief down till it slipped from head to neck. Now he got his mouth free, and said, quickly:—

"That was not true what I said about the Chinamen and that. I was joking. My mother's people were all Devon."

"I don't blame you in the least," said Prior, quietly. "I should lie myself in your place."

And he put back handkerchief. The candle was now burning clearly from the place where it stood—on a stone coffin. Desmond could see that the long things on the shelves were coffins, not all of stone. He wondered what this madman would do with his body when everything was over. The little wound in his throat had broken out again. He could feel the slow trickle of warmth on his neck. He wondered whether he would faint. It felt like it.

"I wish I'd brought you here the first day—it was Verney's doing, my tinkering about with pints and half-pints. Sheer waste—sheer wanton waste!"

Prior stopped and stood looking at him.

Desmond, despairingly conscious of growing physical weakness, caught himself in a real wonder as to whether this might not be a dream—a horrible, insane dream—and he could not wholly dismiss the wonder, because incredible things seemed to be adding themselves to the real horrors of the situation, just as they do in dreams. There seemed to be something stirring in the place—something that wasn't Prior. No—nor Prior's shadow, either. That was black and sprawled big across the arched roof. This was white, and very small and thin. But it stirred, it grew—now it was no longer just a line of white, but a long, narrow, white wedge—and it showed between the coffin on the shelf opposite him and that coffin's lid.

And still Prior stood very still looking down on his prey. All emotion but a dull wonder was now dead in Desmond's weakened senses. In dreams—if one called out, one awoke—but he could not call out. Perhaps if one moved—— But before he could bring his enfeebled will to the decision of movement—something else moved. The black lid of the coffin opposite rose slowly—and then suddenly fell, clattering and echoing, and from the coffin rose a form, horribly white and shrouded, and fell on Prior and rolled with him on the floor of the vault in a silent, whirling struggle. The last thing Desmond heard before he fainted in good earnest was the scream Prior uttered as he turned at the crash and saw the white-shrouded body leaping towards him.

"It's all right," he heard next. And Verney was bending over him with brandy. "You're quite safe. He's tied up and locked in the laboratory. No. That's all right, too." For Desmond's eyes had turned towards the lidless coffin. "That was only me. It was the only way I could think of, to save you. Can you walk now? Let me help you, so. I've opened the grating. Come."

Desmond blinked in the sunlight he had never thought to see again. Here he was, back in his wicker chair. He looked at the sundial on the house. The whole thing had taken less than fifty minutes.

"Tell me," said he. And Verney told him in short sentences with pauses between.

"I tried to warn you," he said, "you remember, in the window. I really believed in his experiments at first—and—he'd found out something about me—and not told. It was when I was very young. God knows I've paid for it. And when you came, I'd only just found out what really had happened to the other chaps. That beast Lopez let it out when he was drunk. Inhuman brute! And I had a row with Prior that first night, and he promised me he wouldn't touch you. And then he did."

"You might have told me."

"You were in a nice state to be told anything, weren't you? He promised me he'd send you off as soon as you were well enough. And he had been good to me. But when I heard him begin about the grating and the key I knew—so I just got a sheet and—"

"But why didn't you come out before?"

"I didn't dare. He could have tackled me easily if he had known what he was tackling. He kept moving about. It had to be done suddenly. I counted on just that moment of weakness when he really thought a dead body had come to life to defend you. Now I'm going to harness the horse and drive you to the police-station at Crittenden. And they'll send and lock him up. Everyone knew he was as mad as a hatter, but somebody had to be nearly killed before anyone would lock him up. The law's like that, you know."

"But you—the police—won't they—"

"It's quite safe," said Verney, dully. "Nobody knows but the old man, and now nobody will believe anything he says. No, he never posted your letters, of course, and he never wrote to your friend, and he put off the Psychical man. No, I can't find Lopez; he must know that something's up. He's bolted."

But he had not. They found him, stubbornly dumb, but moaning a little, crouched against the locked grating of the vault when they came, a prudent half-dozen of them, to take the old man away from the Haunted House. The master was dumb as the man. He would not speak. He has never spoken since.

Dormant
(A.k.a. Rose Royal)

Contents

CHAPTER 1

Malacca Wharf

Malacca Wharf lies on a little creek of the great muddy river, a creek into which the ooze has silted till it is, at low water, merely a stretch of smooth glistening mud, and even when the tide is high the water that looks so profound has not the depth that shall float an un-laden barge. The wharf has dropped out of its place in the great come and go, the round game of trade with the round world, where fate and tide and the winds deal the cards, and, sooner or later, every player loses. It had been worth no one's while to spend a fortune on clearing the creek. So, the wharf and its warehouses stood deserted, decaying.

At night, lit by the dipping lanterns on the ships at anchor in the stream, and by the gas lamp in the rough road outside the great shut gates, the place was still imposing enough. Seen thus, it might have been a wharf where ships bound for the Fortunate Islands took on their lovely varied freights, where scented cargoes from tropic lands were unloaded from strange ships of unfamiliar rig, manned by out-land men with musical speech and daggers in their boots. The dark buildings might have held bloomy tea, rich silk from the Flowery Land, carpets from Persian looms, broideries worked in *purdah* by hid-den Indian beauties, and sent out across two continents to lie among strange wonders in that tall house of treasure from over-seas.

But dawn tore down the kind shadows, and the mystery of the darkness turned, in the daylight, to ancient disorder and a decay al-most complete enough to be called ruin. Grass grew between the cobble-stones of the yard; the timbers at the water's edge were rotting apart. On the heap of old barrels, cracked and distorted, black moss grew. The warehouses and sheds showed grey light through many chinks and rifts, and in their roofs were squares of grey light, the places whence slates had slipped in old storms; in the dulled windows cobwebs replaced the shattered panes. All the wooden buildings were broken, crooked, settling into dissolution. Only the large brick-built warehouse and the little house by the yard gate were still whole, and, whether their windows were broken or not, they kept their secrets behind close-nailed boards and heavy shutters.

On the other side of a desolate, sordid, waste space, where weeds and sickly grass strove with old tins and broken crockery, lay the mean nearest street. The more adventurous of the children, whose home this street was, had been used to leave the waste space, their playground, to seek the keener joys of play in the deserted wharf. The smaller sheds could be explored; a loose plank or a hole in the masonry let in the little, curious, prying, human animals. But the big warehouse and the little square house resisted firmly, It was fun to creep through the little door in the great gate—there was a hole that you could put your hand through and so draw the bolts—and to hide when you heard the far-away, unmistakable boots of the rare policeman. To the unwashed, ill-smelling, ragged, bright-eyed boys the old wharf was the greatest wonder of their world—a quiet, secret place where you could do what you liked, and nobody scolded or swore at you except your friends and equals, on whom you could joyously and confidently re-taliate. Malacca Wharf had always been there, it always would be there.

There was a board up that said, "To Let," but no one ever answered what it said. And year after year the woodwork and the stonework and the bricks and the slates and the tiles, under sun and frost, moved a little—a very little—nearer the time when they should all be dust to-gether. And the boys played there. It was with a shock of surprise that they found one day the big gates closed, and when the daring leader climbed to the top of the wall and looked down, he almost fell from that eminence, and the word "Jimminy!" sprang unbidden to his lips.

"What's up, Aelf?" asked his followers from below.

"It's a chap. In a napron. Puttin' in the windows!"

"They've got thome fool to take it," suggested a business-like child with a straight nose and beautiful dark eyes. "Won't 'e be gay when 'e findth out about the thallow water?"

"There's another chap with a paint pot," said the leader, in low, awe-struck tones. "Green paint. 'E's doing the door-posts."

"Letth 'ave a thquint," said the business-like child, pulling at the leg of the leader, who fell off the wall. And before he had picked himself out of the mud, the dark-eyed one was in his place, the only place where the broken bottles were broken enough to be disregarded.

"Let's come when these chaps is gone an' bust all the winders," suggested an undistinguished boy.

"No profith in that," said he on the wall; "thome of uth might get

136

took on 'ere before they knowth about the water. 'Twouldn't latht, but there'd be thomething thticking to it. I thay, mithter," he added over the wall, addressing the "chap in a napron," "want anyone to lend a hand?"

The glazier, used to the boys of the neighbourhood, answered by a brief description of the inquirer's character, delivered without malice; and the business child retorted, also without malice, but with a superior vocabulary.

The glazier replied, the boy rejoined, while the deposed leader and the others listened admiringly. The glazier was the first to weary of the complimentary exchange.

"Here, you run along home, you young unmentionable," he said amiably.

"Tell uth who'th took the old pig-thtye," said the boy persuasively.

"If I tell you, will you cut along and not come back? Not today anyhow."

"If you tellth me enough, I will," said the child, pleased with any bargain in which he might gain more than he gave.

"Well, then—no one's took it."

"That ain't enough, not for me to cut along on."

"Well, then; the owner's a-coming to live 'ere."

"That's a lie," said half-a-dozen voices from beyond the wall.

"It's gospel truth," said the glazier; "now, hook it!"

With much talk, and very slowly, they did hook it, and the glazier went on with his work. The painter went on with his too, and so did the plasterer and the bricklayer; and when the boys came next day firm set cement and a *chevaux-de-frise* of bottles said "No!" very sharply to their curiosity. Also, the loose bricks had been replaced in the wall, and there was no foothold. And after a day or two it did not seem to be worthwhile to take half-an-hour out of your free time just to cut across to Malacca and shout abuse outside a very high brick wall.

And inside the wall the workmen went on working, and late one night, when there were no boys about, a little van-load of furniture came along the old broken road that skirted the desolate waste space, and "The Owner" set up housekeeping in the little house by the gate, and there were muslin curtains and window-boxes, and a wire netting over the windows that did not look on the yard. So that it was no use to throw stones. Carter Paterson was always leaving boxes and things there. But no one could say what trade the owner proposed to ply.

The boys watched in vain for the first barge to come sailing up the creek, for no barge came. And then they watched for the owner, and weeks went on, and presently it was no secret that the owner was a woman, and lived there alone.

This news decided the gang. The very next Sunday they repaired to the wharf to enjoy themselves. They had not quite decided what form the enjoyment should take—vaguely it was phrased as "letting her have it." To this end they collected a good many stones. And one of the boys, whose father was often out at night and exercised a profession involving unusual implements, brought a cold chisel to knock out the newly inserted bricks. Another brought a piece of old carpet for the negotiating of the bottles on the top of the wall.

The campaign was opened by yells, a few snatches of unsavoury comic songs, and a shower of stones at the great gates. Then Benny, the business-like child, began to use the chisel, and the rest collected more stones. They had just collected a nice heap, and a brick was getting quite loose, when there was a sound from within—bolts were being withdrawn. The besieging army drew back, a little uncertain. One or two of the more stalwart stooped for stones. One stone was thrown. It was a very fair shot. It hit the little door in the big gate just under the keyhole, and the marksman stooped for another stone. But before he could grasp it the little door was opened, and a young woman in a blue dress stood there looking at them.

They looked at her, doubtful, astonished, grave, hostile. She smiled brilliantly at them. It is a very difficult thing to smile in the face of serious hostility, but she did it. She did more. She threw back the door, and said amazingly—

"Won't you come in?"

No one moved.

"Do come in," she said. "Come and look at my funny garden. It's so pretty. I've been wanting to show it to someone. You'll come, won't you?" She turned the appeal of voice and eye and smile directly on the beautiful Benjamin, standing chisel in hand.

"I don't mind," he said, "tho long ath ith understood you arthkt uth. It ain't trethpath, you know, Mith, tho if you've got the copperth up your thleeve we ain't done nothing. Thee?"

"Of course, you haven't done anything," she said; "but there's something I wish you *would* do. I want to move one of my trees, and it's too heavy for me. Would you mind helping me?" "What'll you give uth?" asked the child.

"I was asking you as a friend," she said reproachfully. And for a moment it was touch and go. A rowdy guffaw answered her; a snigger answered the guffaw, and a voice cried—

"Ho, yus; let's be friends, lidy;" and a voice uplifted in song urged—

Let us be true,
Me and you,
Ever the best of friends.

But her fearless eyes conquered. After all, they were only a lot of children.

"Come on," she said. "Don't let's waste time in talking. You come in," she said to Benny, "and I'll leave the door open, and the rest of you can come in just when you like. See!"

She held out her hand to the business-like child, and he took it, and stepped across the wooden threshold.

"This is the tree," she said, putting her hand on the smooth stem of a little bay tree in a green tub. "And I want to move it as far as this." She indicated the spot with the tip of a real Sunday shoe. "Lend me a hand, won't you?"

Benny, with a vision of red and blue and yellow and great cleanness dazzling his dark eyes, lent a hand.

When the tub had been moved, the lady looked round, and the little yard was dark with crowding boys.

"Are we all in?" she asked, and half-a dozen voices answered, "Yus, lidy." Half-a-dozen others said, "Yus, teacher."

"Good," she said; "then shut the door, one of you."

The door was shut, and the Lady of the Malacca turned to her guests.

"Now," she said, "isn't it pretty?"

It was. On the flagged pavement of her little yard stood four bay trees in tubs. All round was a narrow border of black mould, trimmed with red and white geraniums and lobelias and calceolarias. The windows of the house had white curtains, and each window had its window-box, ardent with primary colours. A wall with a door in it divided the little sunny yard from the big cobbled yard of the wharf. It, with all the woodwork in sight, was painted a soft, bright, pleasant green. And in the middle stood the lady in blue, smiling.

"I can't ask you all to tea," she said, "because I haven't enough milk."

Somebody said, "Never mind about milk."

"Or enough tea, or sugar, or teacups, or anything. But there's one thing I have got enough of. That's biscuits. Hands up for biscuits."

Hands were up.

"Then I'll go and get them." She went into her house, leaving them awestruck. When she came back, a scuffle was just reaching its climax in the banging and locking of the little door.

"All right, lidy," several breathless voices assured her. "'E pinched one of yer flowers, and we chucked 'im aat!"

"Thank you," she said; "it's kind of you to take care of my garden. But shall we let him come back? I don't think he'll pick any more."

Reluctantly they opened the gate.

"She says you can come in again if you'll keep your hands to yourself."

"I don't want to come in," he said. "Silly billy!" he added bitterly, and trailed away across the waste.

But he came again the next Sunday when the rest of the boys, by special invitation, went to Malacca Wharf for what the lady called another biscuit party.

Thus, did the lady, partly by luck and partly by that incalculable thing we call personality, defend herself against the child-hooligans of the waste.

It was after the second party that she told the tale to a friend of hers.

"I really was rather frightened," she said, "but I took the bull in both hands and tried loving my enemies—or, at any rate, acting as if I loved them. And then afterwards I found I really did. And they're quite dears, some of them; and I'm going to have biscuit parties once a week. I can't afford real tea-parties. And you and some of the others might come down sometimes, and help me play with them. Why have I gone to live there? I thought you knew. Oh! I forgot; you've been in Cornwall all the while, haven't you? Well, I've been coming of age, and then they told me what my little bit of money comes from. It's rents in the East End. And Malacca is part of my property, only it won't let. So, I thought I'd live there and save rent. I've been waiting for you to come back, to have my house-warming."

"It isn't safe," said the friend, crumbling his bread. They were dining at a little restaurant in Soho. "You oughtn't to live there alone."

"I'm not alone," she said. "I've got a lovely charwoman. She has the loveliest voice. She used to sing in the streets. She happened to be out that day, but she's a tower of strength, really."

"She can't defend you from big hooligans," he said. "You don't

140

know what those East End roughs are."

"Well, never mind," she said comfortably, "come to my house-warming and see my little hooligans. Thank you, Alphonse, one *mille-feuille* and one *petit suisse*."

She smiled on the waiter as she had smiled on the boys.

"Everyone's moving," said her friend. "Sullivan's going to America, and Anthony's got the kick-out from his place. Can't stand the smells. I warned him they wouldn't. Why do chemists always insist on using the drugs that are stenches? They must know before they begin what the things in the bottles smell like."

"Where's he going?" she asked, ignoring the more abstruse question.

"I don't know. Can't find anyone who'll have him. His candid nature compels him. He can't exaggerate the smells, but I believe he would if he could—in the service of truth."

"Will he ever find out anything?" she asked.

"Yes, lots of things. Whether they'll be what he wants . . ."

"What sort of place does he want?"

"Oh! big, and no questions asked—and cheap. That sort of place doesn't go begging. Have some coffee?"

"Please—white coffee. No, that sort of place doesn't," she said thoughtfully.

"If you're going straight home," he said, after the coffee, "I'll see you there. May I? And walk back. I want a walk."

When coffee was over, he paid his reckoning, she hers. For this was not an assignation dinner, but a mere chance rencounter at a little French eating-house where, that night, no other of the friends of either happened to be. The reckoning paid, he saw her home, to the house on the creek in the far east, by the ugliest of the many ugly lines that worm their dirty way out of London. Both were thoughtful. He walked home.

On the next Sunday the little hooligans were dazzled by two more lidies and four gents, who taught them new and wonderful games, and played with them.

When the party had culminated in biscuits and the ragged guests gone, the Lady in blue took her friends to see her little house and her big studio—the top floor of the warehouse on the far side of the inner court. It was reached by an outside stairway of stone that ran up the side of the building.

And all her friends admired everything very much. Especially Anthony Drelincourt.

"I wish I could find a place like this," he told her, as he and she came down the stairs after the others.

"There are two floors below and a basement," she said. "You could have either or both or all three."

"Do you mean it?" he said eagerly. "It's the ideal place. But I should be in your way. And the rent. Couldn't afford it."

"If I don't let it to a friend, I shan't let it to anyone," she said shortly; "and you wouldn't be in my way. There's an inner staircase to the other two floors. We needn't see each other even, if we don't want to."

"Are you sure?" he asked.

And she laughed. "Of course, I'm sure," she said.

"What is the rent?" he asked.

"Fifteen pounds a year," she said, since that was what he paid for the attic he was leaving. "Fifteen pounds and nothing found."

"I could get the gas laid on?"

"Of course. There is water laid on."

"I will, then. It's jolly decent of you, Rose. Sure, I won't be a nuisance."

"When you've set the Thames on fire with your great discovery, and they are all writing your biography, they'll say, 'His landlady was called Rose Royal.'"

"And when you've set the Thames on fire with your pictures, they'll write, 'She had a tenant called Anthony Drelincourt.'"

When Rose announced the tenancy to William Bats, he said, "Oh!" and then, after a quite perceptible pause, "so now you'll have someone to see you home occasionally. That's all right. And a man within call. Get him to fix a telephone between your place and his."

"Nonsense!" said Rose. But before he had been in the place a week the telephone was fixed.

And now all that was nearly a year ago. For a year these two earnestly unconventional young people had been neighbours in that far eastern country. He had not been in her way. But she had found it necessary to exert her will to keep out of his. She bought an old, round-nosed punt for thirty-five shillings, because she knew it would amuse him to paddle about in it, and tried not to be in sight whenever he stooped to loosen it from its moorings. She lent him her charwoman, and would have lent or given him almost anything else.

But he never asked for anything else. And now the cold, yellow, foggy light of a March dawn shines upon Miss Royal going across the large courtyard with something in each hand—something which she carries carefully. She sets the things down at the door of the warehouse, takes out a little key and opens the door, goes in, and shuts it. A few minutes later she comes out, and goes quietly and quickly back to her little square house with the muslin-and-geranium windows.

Anthony Drelincourt had made himself a nest of such materials as his kind uses for nest-building. The ground floor he kept locked always. No one but himself ever went in, and no one knew for certain what he did there. Most of the big first floor of the warehouse, with its row of grey, uncurtained, unshuttered windows, was sheer laboratory, with the usual medley of bright porcelain and glass. Two large distilling flasks, holding bright-coloured liquids, formed, with their condensers and receiving flasks, an imposing group; and, together with a large filter full of dubious-looking mess, plainly said "organic chemist" to any well-informed observer. To Rose they simply said, "Anthony as usual." A small, dirty, copper oven stood as a sort of connecting link to the oddly domestic-looking saucepans and cake-tins which make such good water-baths. Shelves of labelled bottles, clean test tubes and dirty test tubes, a few stray dry cells and accumulators, a few odd tools scattered about, bits of insulated wire, cork-borers and corks, made a harmonious background.

A large square table, covered with papers, was under one window. Under another the microscope had a little table to its brassy self. On a third a bright balance glittered attractively. In one corner a little room stood out; it had been a counting-house in the days when Malacca Wharf *was* a wharf, not a derelict. This room, with the space near it, surrounding the fireplace, and in, but not of, the laboratory proper, was a sort of shabby oasis furnished with odd jetsam from the domestic life of an age not his—a lady's silk welled work-table, a *prie-Dieu* chair with lilies worked on it in beads, a tall, crimson banner-screen, two gilded Empire chairs, a round table of *papier-maché*, lacquered with golden birds, that stood upright like a great black and yellow sunflower, a shelf of crockery, another of pots and pans, a worn Aubusson carpet, once of delicate beauty, and, against the wall, shelves and shelves of books.

The light grew. But it was still twilight in the quiet laboratory when Anthony came in from his bedroom in his dressing-gown to light the fire, so that the kettle should be boiling by the time he had dressed and shaved. He reached for the matches, which should have been on the little work-table. He did not find them. Instead, his hand struck against something cold and unfamiliar which fell over with a crash, and something cold and wet flooded his hand and the table. He said something, and fetched the matches from his bedroom. His lamp, lighted quickly, showed him that he had upset a tall, straight, green vase in which two red roses had been standing. They lay on the floor now among a shining shatter of glass, and table and carpet were drenched with the water from the vase. A squat pot full of violets had escaped, and stood solidly. A drowned white thing caught his eye. It was a paper on which he read the words—

Happy birthday. R. R.

"Oh, bother the girl!" said Anthony, as he mopped up the water. It was not till after breakfast that he began to feel how kind it was of her. He wrote a little note.

A thousand thanks! How do you manage always to think of such pretty things and such pretty ways of doing them? I thought the fairies had been here. But it was only you.

Fortunately, he read this over, and changed the ending to—

I thought a good fairy had been here. And I was right.

Which was much better.

You do not know what any of these people looked like. You shall quite soon, now. Myself, I never want to know what people look like until I know where they live, and what they do and say and think, and whether they are rich or poor. Nobody has done or said or thought much so far, but, at any rate, we know where Rose Royal lives, and that she has a wharf and an income. And we know where Anthony Drelincourt lives; but even he himself never could estimate his income, which, with his expenditure, varied too much to be estimable. Anyhow he was very poor. And Rose Royal was much too poor to be buying red roses at a shilling apiece and round-nosed punts at thirty-five shillings. She had not, however, spent the last of her month's money on the violets and the red roses. She proposed to spend some of the rest on things to eat for a party she was going to that night. And some she meant to spend on a real birthday present for her tenant. The roses and violets, in her opinion, were not real presents.

"I wish," she said, throwing down her palette after a hopeless morning, "that I had a thousand pounds. Then I could buy something worth giving to a person. Roses and rubbish! It's hateful to be poor.

When I give a present, I should like it to be a present that there isn't another of in the world. And there are thousands and millions of any of the sort of things that I can afford to buy for any one. And I wish," she added, still more fervently, "that it didn't always rain whenever I want it not to. I think it's going to stop," she said, flattening her nose against the grey square of window, "only I know it isn't."

It wasn't.

CHAPTER 2

A Book Like Another

You know Charlotte Street, Fitzroy Square. It is not a pretty street, and on a wet day it is of course uglier than ever. The rain came straight down and steady, without pause, for it had its work to do—and without haste, for there was plenty of time to do it in. Most of the foot passengers appeared merely as trousers or skirts surmounted by umbrellas.

Inside the entries of those Swiss boarding-houses where young waiters wait, desiring situations and sinking day by day more deeply into the *patron's* debt, groups of anaemic, unshaved youths watched with dull eyes the stream of sordid traffic, and talked in strange tongues of unemployment and the English climate. From out these doorways rank cigarette smoke eddied into the rain, and with it came intermittent weary criticism of the passers-by. These English—they were sad, they were stupid, they were unintelligent, everything which the Swiss exile from Swiss scenery esteemed himself as not being.

"And the women," said a lank man, with oily hair and a long yellow face. "Women? Camels!"

"Their eyes—like blue porcelain."

"Their hands—like hams for largeness."

"Their feet—like the foot of elephant."

"Their teeth—as is one who has swallowed a pianoforte not completely."

So arose the chorus of detraction, justified, perhaps, by the thin stream of worn-out working women that trickled along Charlotte Street towards those strange courts which hide in the square bounded by Goodge Street, Howland Street, and the Tottenham Court Road.

"Since I am here—ten interminable days," a pink-faced, square-faced boy went on, shrugging round, broad shoulders, "I see not one woman that one may call a woman, that is not French or Swiss or German. Thou hast reason. The Englishwomen are camels, and the reason . . ."

"But hold," the yellow-faced lounger interrupted, resettling his hat at an alluring angle—"*en voici une*, for example."

A thrill of self-consciousness electrified the languid group. It was like seeing dogs prick up their ears. And all eyes turned to where, between black mud and grey sky, came a young woman, who trod the pavement with the freedom of a boy and the assurance of a maiden goddess. Her skirts were short and straight—none of that flow and draggle and dip that Goodge Street knows so well—and skirt as well as coat was of brown corduroy. A three-cornered hat of brown felt was set firmly on coils of black hair, and the rain had lit to radiance that skin of white and rose which belongs to Irish eyes. The girl looked about her as she went, with no roving weakness, but with a keen interest and observation. Her hands were bare, slender, and pink in the rain, and they held many parcels.

The pink-faced youth spat reflectively.

"The first," he said, "the first I see who is worthy a thought from a son of Helvetia."

"Almost I follow her," said the yellow-faced man, "yet no. It is not worth the trouble. Nothing is worth the trouble in this land abominable. Yet she has charm—I tell it you—I, Achille."

"You have not the courage to say her good-day," said an under-sized, dark boy, frowning. "Why vaunt yourself? You are a waiter. And she is a queen."

"Thou sayest?" The yellow-faced Achille plumed himself like a bantam cock. "Thou shalt see. If she repasses by here, I address her the speech. Do I not? For *vingt centimes*."

"I bet you *cinquante* you dare not," said the boy, who was an ugly boy with large ears, "and if you win the *cinquant centimes*, I pay. Also, I fight."

A roar of laughter went up, laughter without beauty, without mirth, the ugly laughter of ugly souls who laugh at the real things of life.

"The little Sebastien! Behold him at last *épris*! See she has entered Vandenhauten's. She goes to buy the *patisserie* for the *noces* with the *gentil petit* Sebastien."

Sebastien drew into his jacket and seemed to grow smaller. He hoped she would not come back that way. He hoped he should not have to fight Achille. He hoped he should win Achille's fifty *centimes*. He hoped many things.

The girl in the brown dress and the Napoleon hat came out of Vandenhauten's, and the parcels she carried were more than ever. She stood a moment undecided, and in that moment, Sebastien found time to put up a prayer to his patron saint. He was young, and was not long from home; to him his patron saint was still a force that ill-doers had to reckon with. Also, he confusedly implored the consideration of Saint Agnes and Saint Ursula, so evidently the lady's patrons, to turn the lady's steps in any direction other than that of the Hôtel Simplon.

The saints seldom answer a prayer as one answers a request for bread and butter. There is always a little subtlety about the saints. The boy got what he wished—and not what he asked for.

She turned and came back along the pavement. The yellow Achille pulled up his collar and ran fat yellow fingers through the oily black curls above his ears. Sebastien trembled, and wondered how it felt to carry a knife in one's waist-belt, over the right hip, as some men did.

And the girl came on, unconscious, nearer, nearer. Now she was almost opposite the door, and Achille made a half step forward. Sebastien caught at his arm.

But the saints had not been idle; their unseen fingers no doubt had been busy with the strings of all these parcels, and that was why, at this very moment of all moments, something gave way among the parcels and half of them fell and clattered and slid on the slimy pavement of Charlotte Street.

Sebastien was first. He had picked up the square Vandenhauten box, and the packet that felt like *charcuterie*, before the others were there, quite wordless, but enthusiastically helpful, picking up the brown paper packets, wiping the mud from them, and restoring them, with every manifestation of respectful regret, to their owner. Sebastien picked up the last parcel as well as the first, and as he gave it to her his fingers touched hers. It was an accident. Or did the saints throw it in as a make-weight?

Then suddenly the girl looked from one to another of the group and smiled. She looked at the mud on the handkerchiefs they held, and smiled a little more. Then she said—

"I thank you infinitely, *Messieurs*. Good morning!" and was gone. And then they all were on the pavement saying, "*Il n'y a pas de quoi, Mademoiselle*," and "*De rien, Mademoiselle*," with their hats in their hands, and their cigarettes nowhere.

Achille had won his bet. He had spoken to her. He had said, "*Pas de quoi, Mademoiselle*," with the others. But Sebastien promised his patron a little candle for next Sunday, all the same. He paid his *centimes* like a man, and Achille took them.

147

"All the same, it is to thee the psychologic victory," he said handsomely. "Thou hadst reason. She is a queen. I add my fifty, and we have all a bock, and drink to the *Reine Inconnue*."

This toast they drank, by the sticky marble tables of Cellini near to hand, with intense seriousness and their hands on their hearts. They were only boys after all, even the large yellow Achille, and one does not see a goddess every day.

So, the smile that conquered the little East End hooligans served as a protecting halo in Fitzroy Street, and illustrates the sort of effect Rose Royal had on people, and tells you more about her than you would learn by a complete catalogue of her more habitual conquests.

Rose had been the reigning beauty of the Slade, but then quite ugly girls have been that. She was the leader in her set, but then charm is not always of the essence of a leader. She had received from two to five offers of marriage every year since she was seventeen, and at least twice as many offers of platonic friendship; declarations of impermanent adoration at various temperatures were to her common incidents of life, to be laughed at or to despise, according to the circumstances of the declaration and the nature of the declarer. She had girl friends by dozens, who worshipped and obeyed, and she had not more than half-a-dozen enemies, and all of these were women, and none of them whole-hearted foes. She was poor, proud, and energetic; had versatility and initiative, a good temper and perfect health. It was always she who said, "Let's!" and her friends who said, "Yes, do let's." As for her faults, I fear they stick out of this catalogue of her endowments.

She walked on. Her arms were now uncomfortably full of parcels, and one more purchase remained to be made, the gift for her tenant. The parcels she already had, had cost her all the money left of her month's income, save and except the four shillings which were the price of a birthday present not yet bought. The paper of the parcels was getting wet; corners of their insides protruded through the softened wrappings. One saw the gleam of a sardine tin, the spring tint of a lettuce.

"Oh, bother!" she said, and let the parcels fall from her arms on the mat of an open doorway. Then she made an apron of her dress, lifting it with one hand and dropping the parcels in it, and so carried the load along Goodge Street, brave in crimson petticoat and lifted skirt.

In Tottenham Court Road she saw a taximeter cab. The driver caught her eye and raised his hand. Quite without meaning to nod, she nodded, and the taxi slid to the edge of the pavement and stopped in front of her.

"Oh, bother!" she said, tumbling the parcels on to the floor of the cab. "Two thousand St. Martin's Lane."

She leaned back against the air cushions enjoying the luxury of such soft rest, for she was tired, and the parcels had been many and awkward, and while her body luxuriated, her mind scowled.

"Just like you," it said, "to tire yourself out grubbing round, so as to save eighteenpence; and just when the whole beastly business is nearly over, you weaken, hail a taxi, and throw everything away. You might as well have taken one to begin with, and saved yourself all this fag. For you can't buy the book now." This theme, with the interminable variations on it so familiar to all of us who are not millionaires or consistent economists, occupied her till the cab set her down before the second-hand-bookshop in face of whose window she always spent, in passing, a few covetous moments.

"It's no good," she said, "but one might as well try it on."

And she went in. The stout, black-bearded, black-skullcapped man turned keen eyes on her behind his large spectacles.

"Oh, Mr. Abrahamson, good morning!" she said. "May I look at that book again? You know, the one about precious stones and things, with the pages written in at the end? I want to buy it to give to a friend for a birthday present."

He stretched a hand to a dusty shelf.

"I do like the smell of your shop," she said, reaching out her hand for the book he now held; "it's not only the old leather, it's something that's like a dream of a dream."

"It is perhaps the fragrance of the past, Miss Royal," said he.

"Of course, it is," she said, and flashed her smile at him. "I wish I could interest you in the fragrance of the future."

She always interested him, as she interested most men. He would not have said so. What he said was, "Proceed, Lady Sybilla."

"Yes, I know I'm mysterious," she said, "but the fact behind the mystery is that I want this book most awfully—and it's four shillings."

"And what is four shillings," Mr. Abrahamson asked, "to one with the princess's chariot awaiting her? He glanced through the light-lines between the brown prints wafered against the window, at the waiting taxi-cab.

"That's just it," said the girl, yielding to an inspiration of truth-telling: "I had got just four shillings left, and I had such a heap of parcels, and the insides were worming out of them because of their getting wet. Perhaps you haven't noticed how it's raining, Mr. Abrahamson?"

"It is the inclement weather," he said, "which is usual in this land of melancholy liberty. And so . . ."

"And then the taxi hailed me, and before I knew where I was, I said, 'Yes.' And that means, will you take two shillings for the book, because really and truly that's all I've got."

The old man raised his eyebrows slowly.

"So," he said, and paused on the word.

"What do you say?" said Rose, consciously and unconsciously using all her power, all her charm, on this old dry-as-dust.

"I say not 'No,'" said Mr. Abrahamson.

"Ah!" said Rose, and he raised a hand. "Also, I say not 'Yes.' I have other books, very good books, at the two shilling price. The friend will be very pleased with the book at two shillings that I shall sell you."

"It's that book I want," the girl told him.

"But why *that* book? Is it by chance very rare and valuable, and I do not know it? And Miss Royal knows it, and seeks to make her profit of old Abrahamson."

"Of course, it isn't!" she impetuously answered; "and there's the taxi eating its head off at two pence a second, or whatever it is. It's only that it's got my friend's name in it—the friend I want to give it to for a *birthday* present—and the bookplate and all. Perhaps it belonged to an ancestor or something. Will you take two shillings?"

He took, for the moment, not two shillings, but the book from her hand, and, looking down obliquely through his spectacles, read aloud, "*Ex Libris Antonii Drelincourt.*"

Then he looked at her.

The same lack of self-control that had driven her into her taxi drove her now on the mercy of the second-hand-bookseller. A flash of crimson illumined the face whose eyes brightened and drooped suddenly.

"So!" said Mr. Abrahamson, and Miss Royal understood that her secret was not any longer her secret.

"You fool, you born-blind idiot," she silently called herself.

"My dear young lady," said the bookseller, dandling the brown *octavo* in his hand, as a grandmother dandles her first grandchild; "I love all books, and this I very much love, because I do not understand it. It was my son, Gideon, who price it four shillings. For me forty, I should have said, or perhaps forty pounds. Who knows? There are in this book secrets, old secrets, precious to men a long time dead."

He whirred the leaves with accustomed thumb, and ended with an open gesture which displayed pages of twisted characters in faded brown ink. "It is the *manuscriptum*," he said, "and the finest works they are, the ones that never were printed."

"But if I've only got two shillings left," said Miss Royal, her eyes on the book.

"You come another time. I keep it for you," said Mr. Abrahamson, his eyes on hers.

"But it's his birthday today," she said.

"The same name and arms?" he said.

"Yes; of course, that's just it," she said.

"I see," said he. And there was a pause. Outside, the blurred sound of London traffic swept by.

"Well?" said Miss Royal.

"Well," said Nathan Abrahamson.

And again, London's voices spoke.

"His name—it is just the same, Antonio?"

"Antony, yes."

"He is an artist like Miss Royal?"

"He's a chemist. An experimental chemist. And physics and physiology, all those sort of scientific things. He's always trying to find out secrets, secrets of Nature, you know."

"This book also, it deals with the experimental chemistry and secret ways. If once it belonged to one of your friend's family, that shows the taste for the experimental and the secret is inherited."

"Yes," she said. His tone when he said, "Your friend," brushed softly and kindly on the quivering surface of her revealed secret. She looked at him with eyes whose deep appeal was no longer conscious.

"*Et in arcadio ego*," he murmured.

"What did you say?" said she.

"I said that I could not abate the price," Mr. Abrahamson answered; "but I know Miss Royal. Take it, and pay me when you can."

"I've got two shillings," she said, showing them.

"Those you keep," said the bookseller; "who knows, you may need another taxi!"

"It's awfully good of you," said the girl. "Of course, you know . . . you know I shall pay you all right."

"I know," he said; "at the same time I think the little accommodation I give you deserves a bonus. If this book is of service to your friend Antonio, if by it the secret he searches for reveal itself and he grows rich, you give me one hundred pounds. He give me one hundred pounds. Is it so?"

"A hundred pounds!" Rose Royal said, leaning her elbows on the counter, rubbed smooth by so many elbows of persons who desired—or despaired of various items of Mr. Abrahamson's stock.

"If he get two thousand, I get one hundred. Only a little five *per cent.*, is it not?"

She saw that he smiled, and she also smiled.

"A hundred pounds," she said, "if he gets two thousand out of the book? Rather!"

"The notes," said the bookseller, fluttering the leaves, "the marginal notes and the *manuscriptum*! It is these that your friend should study."

The intonation of "your friend" brought the blood to her face again.

"Thank you," she said, "I'll bring the money early in April—the four shillings, I mean."

"I know you will," he said, "and for the friend . . . hide everything. I am an old man, and I know. I also in Arcadia have been. Reveal nothing. Let nothing be shown. Keep your secret, my young Lady Royal. Can he read this?"

"I don't know," she said; "can anybody?"

"If I were a beautiful young lady who gave a present," said he, "I would learn first to read what I gave. There are those who teach such things."

"But I've got to give the present today," she said; "it's his birthday. There isn't time to learn anything. Oh! what are we talking about? It's just a book like any other book! It's a birthday present for him."

"Yes," said Mr. Abrahamson, "just a book like any other book; just a birthday present to a friend."

"Thank you so very much," she said conventionally, all the unconventionality of the interview suddenly coming home to her.

"Not at all, Miss Royal," he said, matching her mood. She went back to the taxi-cab with its burden of little parcels, bearing with her the old brown leather-covered book, and the knowledge that her heart's most intimate secret was given away to an old second-hand-bookseller in St. Martin's Lane.

The old man followed her across the pavement to her cab door.

"Courage!" he said; "with courage, all is well. Someday I read the beautiful Miss Royal's fortune? I lay out the cards for her? No? Some day when it is not the friend's birthday, and your heart is free for new things. Abrahamson knows the cards. I could make much money in Bond Street telling the fortunes of the ladies with dyed hair who are no longer young and desire the heritage of youth. But I only lay out the cards for hope and beauty and youth and the strength of youth. You come again for that?"

"Thank you," she said. "Oh, thank you very much! But I think people make their own fortunes, don't they?"

"So, say always the beloved of the gods," the old man answered, "but the Fates decree otherwise."

Some impulse, for ever unexplained, brought Rose Royal's hand out to the seller of second-hand books.

"Thank you," she said, not knowing why, "thank you."

"Ah!" said Mr. Abrahamson, taking it carefully. "You have one gift, the greatest; you know your friends."

CHAPTER 3

The Septet

If you mount the steps of the Falstaffe Theatre under the glass roof where the pink geraniums and white daisies make a light that you can see from the end of the street, you will find between the box office and the pit entrance a door, and beside it the legend "Falstaffe Chambers." When the theatre is closed, as it quite often is, the ragged children of Soho play about the entrance, and on the lower steps of that staircase elderly little girls sit nursing heavy babies and scolding their little brothers, and the door of Falstaffe Chambers serves them as shelter, ambush, and hiding-place.

It is an untidy doorway, through whose door, mostly open, the wind blows dust and straws and scraps of paper. If, picking your way through the clusters of infants, you go up a flight of stone steps, you pass, on your right, the fine rooms where the Management does its business, when it has any. Still ascending, you pass another plate on the door of Mr. Ben Burt, where to his name are added the significant words "Correspondence only." On the floor above you find a brown door on which is whitely painted the word *Monolith*, and below it "William Bats, Editor."

If you knock at the door and ask for a copy of the *Monolith*, Mr. Bats, if he be at home, will tell you that the paper has ceased to appear. If you are annoyed at this, you ask him why he has not taken the name off the door, and he will smile and say he is sorry you should have been disappointed. But he will not tell you the truth, which is that he is too lazy to send a postcard to Mr. Musto of Great Ormond Street, asking him to come and paint out the name of that unfortunate journal. Nor will he tell you—as indeed why should he?—that even Mr. Musto's moderate charges are charges which are beyond his means.

As your boots echo down the uncarpeted stair, Mr. William Bats will close the door and return to his books.

And Mr. Bats' books are worth going back to. They line that large, low, upper room from floor to ceiling, and their bindings are old and brown and smell of the past. He is known to every second-hand-bookseller in London, and to many provincial ones beside. His morning post brings him those pleasant catalogues which spin out breakfast to somewhere too near lunch, as one turns their pages and wishes one were rich enough to buy this *Elzevir* or that first edition of *Montaigne*. Mr. Bats is a friend of Mr. Abrahamson's in St. Martin's Lane. He is also the friend of Rose Royal.

The room is the last room you would expect to find in that house. It is, as I said, brown with books, and but for those it might be a room in a farmhouse. For all its furniture is old and solid and heavy, from the settle that stands out from the wall at right angles to the fireplace, the gate-legged table, the oak church-table on which Mr. Bats keeps his pens and inks and papers. A tall clock ticks near the door. It has a silver face, and a painted moon and sun mark the hours of day and night. There is a round mirror over the mantelpiece, and there are some comfortable round-bodied Windsor chairs, shaped cunningly to support the back. The divan with the leopard skin looks like a happy accident. The windows are curtained with cotton fabric of a pleasant green colour, and on one window-ledge a blue-lustre mug stands, and in it, all the year round, a few cheap flowers. On the floor is a Persian carpet.

A door opens from this room into a dining-room, white walled and furnished with beautiful simplicity. A dark dresser holds pleasant red and blue crockery and Nuremberg glass; the chairs are of apple-wood, rush-seated and ladder-backed; the floor is covered with a pale India matting. On the mantelshelf are brass candlesticks and crockery greyhounds with crockery hares in their mouths. This room, with the small bedroom and the smaller kitchen, makes up the home of Mr. William Bats. It is the neatest home in the world. Everything has its place, and is in it, from the stick of sealing-wax and the ball of string displayed in the silver snuffer-tray on the writing-table, to the ties and shirts concealed in the tall-boys beyond the closed bedroom door.

The only things that are out of place are the books with which Mr.

Bats is always surrounded.

"Another half-hour," said Mr. William Bats, glancing at the silver-faced clock—"another half-hour before I need even begin to think of putting them away."

And even as he thought it, a step came up the stair, past the gorgeous rooms of the Management, past the mysterious rooms where business was done by correspondence only, up the last flight of stairs.

The little brass lion-headed knocker sounded on his outer door, and he got up. You would have said that something very pleasant had happened, pleasant and unforeseen. Yet when he opened the door all he said was—

"You? You're nearly an hour too early!"

And Rose Royal stood before him with her skirt full of parcels. "I know I'm early. Don't be cross. How jolly your wallflowers smell. And the tobacco and the old books! They ought to sell it in bottles. I'm so tired, and I've spent all my money, and it's raining like mad and—"

She came into the room, and advanced towards the gate table.

"Don't put them down there," he said, and opened the door into the dining-room.

"Don't be cross," she said again. "I'll go away if you insist. But you'd better get back to your work, and let me set the table."

She was drawing the pins out of her hat with the air of being very much at home.

"I'm all to pieces, I know," she said. "Such a day!" She felt in her pocket and brought out a little mirror.

"Pause!" said Mr. Bats. "You little know your blessings. I got this expressly for you."

He showed an oval looking-glass with a frame of carved wood, that hung behind the door.

"How beautiful!" said Rose, looking in and not at the glass. "I knew I was all to pieces." Her hands were busy with her hair, and his with the parcels on the table. "How did you think of such a simple and charming idea? It's nothing less than genius. And what a beautiful frame!" she added, giving it the briefest glance.

"I've been convinced for the last six months that you wouldn't be happy till you got it. My mind moves slowly, as you know. Only today the conviction crystallised in action. Say you're pleased."

"You're an angel," she told him, her eyes still on the glass. "Haven't I brought nice things to eat?"

"You always do," he said; "much too nice," and folded the discarded papers neatly, and rolled the string into little self-contained circlets. "What's the book?"

"Oh, that's for Tony! That's really why I came early. If it hadn't been for that, I could have walked round and round Soho Square, getting wetter and wetter, till it was real right time to arrive. I wanted to show it to you, to see if it's any good. It looks as if it might be the real original key to the real original Bacon-Shakespeare cypher."

"You excite me almost beyond endurance," he said placidly, putting the string and paper into the proper drawer for such things. "I'll put your hat in my room, shall I?"

"No, I'll hang it on the hat-stand in the hall," she said. "It'll be handier if I have to rush out for anything. And may I wash the lettuce while you look at the book?"

"Don't let the tap splash," he said; "if you hold the basin under it for a moment, it won't."

The hat-stand in the hall was a nail driven into the back of the door of the tiny kitchen.

"Don't watch me," she said, dabbling among the wet lettuces. "You always make me feel so large, and clumsy and awkward."

"Yes, I'm a delicate little thing, aren't I?" he said, leaning a lazy six feet against the kitchen door.

"If I didn't like you so much, I should hate you," she said. "When you're not there, I am neat, orderly, competent, adequate, worthy. When I'm with you, I'm a worm—an untidy, expansive worm. You ought to curb your moral nature, and not make people so uncomfortable. I say, *do* look at that book instead of talking to me. It's got 'Antonii Drelincourt' on the book-plate, and the same coat-of-arms that's on Tony's snuff-box that was his grandfather's."

"A romance! Cheers from the bystanders," remarked Mr. Bats. "Long lost heir mercifully restored. Triumphant arches, garlands. Downtrodden tenantry. Sycophantic cheers. Don't I see the *Daily Mail*, foaming at the headlines."

"Just as you like," said Rose, putting the lettuce on the dresser. "Only the others will be here directly. And I can lay a table when your eye isn't on me. And I know where everything is." She opened the smooth-sliding drawer of the Welsh dresser, and took out a folded tablecloth. "If you watch me, I'll drop the glasses. You might be fifty brothers rolled into one, instead of a perfect stranger, if one judged by your attitude of criticism."

"You remember," he said, turning the pages of the book, "that the

Septet was formed on the distinct basis of our all being as disagreeable as we liked to each other, and I'm the only one who has ever tried to live up to the old ideal. All the others merely grovel before you, wormlike. How you can stand it, I can't think!"

"I don't. I mean, they don't. Don't be silly."

"Who don't? Lena does, frankly. Esther and Milton also, after their kind. Tony, of course, does too, or he wouldn't be human."

He so obviously refrained from looking at her when he said this, that he might as well have stared her out of countenance with his deep-set alert eyes.

She thought of Mr. Abrahamson. Did her silly secret then, she asked herself, stick out of her, as Mr. Henry James puts it?

"Of course, he adores me," she answered hardily, and she might just as well have denied it for any screen she got. "And so," she added, helplessly trying for words that should not let silence close round her last ones, "and so do you. Only you don't know it yet. But you will someday. And I adore you all, of course!" She got away from the subject on that, and breathed a little quickly.

"You are very discerning," said Mr. Bats. "I did not know that you knew of my adoration. Concealment being at an end, let me remark that you have not put the tablecloth on straight."

"Trust me not at all, or all in all." She pushed him gently to the door. "Do go and look at the book, there's an angel, and hide it if—if anyone comes in."

"Don't drop the salt-cellars as you did the other day," he said, as the door closed upon him.

"You look at the book," she called after him. "Don't go into a dream about something else."

Whatever dream he may have gone into, it was at least brief, for when she went into the room, he was deep in the book; so deep that he did not raise his head when she came in—did not even hear her when she asked reproachfully where he kept the mustard now.

In Gower Street, Bloomsbury, stands, as you may or may not know, University College; and there, swarm students of all degrees; students of Art and Literature, and Law and Language, Medicine and Chemistry, and Engineering and Semitic Epigraphy, Physics and Mathematics; young men and women of all types and tastes. Some of them desire to learn and some desire to appear to have learnt, but all, or almost all, desire, deeply and with the whole heart, to enjoy themselves. This they do, each in 'his own way. You have heard of the strawberry teas;

perhaps you have passed along Gower Street, gazed curiously through the iron railings, and beheld young women in bright muslins adorning the steps and the green sward in front of the Art School, and dispensing tea and chatter to lounging youths.

You cannot be ignorant of the brilliance and charm of Slade dances; and the story of the Brown Dog statue is next door to history. But there are other ways in which the students of University College seek to wring the full perfume from life. There used to be clubs: one, I remember, met in two horrid little rooms over a railway collecting-office near Euston, and gave musical teas. There were never enough cups, and the things to eat were like Lockhart's things, but I believe the members thought they were living their own lives—always an invigorating conviction. And there was another club where they had bent-wood chairs and smoking was forbidden. But that was very select, and I never went to it. Besides the clubs, there are Societies, Debating Societies and Critical Societies, the Chemical and Physical Society, the Christian Association, the Literary Society, where people go for tea and gas, the Natural Science, which is very young and takes itself seriously, and the Mathematical Society, which is serious.

The members of the Septet, for which Rose Royal was laying the table, had all "lived their own lives "in most of the respectable ways dictated by the student convention. They had had, and given, strawberry teas, they had got up dances, they had opened debates on Capital Punishment and the Right of Women to the Suffrage. One had even read a paper on "Bacon: our Shakespeare" to an exasperated Literary Society. In living, even your own life, you do, as the proverb says, learn. These young people had learned several things, the most important being that clubs and societies are things which bores infest. Further, that they none of them bored each other. Acting on these two discoveries, they formed a society of their own, whose membership should be strictly limited to eight, and those eight the founders.

Now that Sullivan had gone to America, there were only seven, and these met every Tuesday in term time at the rooms of one or other of them, ate together, drank together, and took it in turns to suggest the evening's amusement. And it was a point of honour with the Septet to carry out the suggestion made by the Ruler of the Evening. They had done most of the amusing silly things you can think of, from making toffee over Rose Royal's studio fire, to going from Hammersmith to Gravesend on a stone-barge. And in the intervals of doing the silly amusing things, they talked and talked and talked, which always sounds dull, but sometimes isn't. And they all got to know each other very well indeed.

"Where do you keep the mustard *now?*" repeated Rose, and William, with the book in his hand, got up and found the mustard, in its right place of course, and went back to his reading-chair without a word.

And then there came other steps on the stairs, and Rose snatched the book from Mr. Bats.

"Is it any good?" she asked; "it looks like a lunatic's diary in cypher."

"It's all right," said Mr. Bats; "but it's not much use to Tony. He can't read it."

"Can you?" she asked.

"More or less, given time," he told her. "But present it. The name and the coat-of-arms will be enough to endear it."

Then Anthony Drelincourt came in, and the rest of the members followed him so quickly that there was no time to present the book before they all arrived, all talking, and all talking at once.

And now you see them seated at the long narrow table, Bats at one end and Drelincourt at the other. Rose at Anthony's right hand, and on his left Linda Smith, small, delicate, pale, with fair hair, and an embroidery of soft blues and purples round the shoulders of her gown of soft green. It is Linda's trade to make embroidered dresses.

"Oh yes, I went to the Slade, and I meant to be an artist," she will tell you (if she likes you well enough to tell you anything), "but I soon found there was no money in it," she will add with the jolly laugh that is such an odd surprise from that thin-lipped, severely cut mouth," and I'm not doing so badly."

Just now she is pleased with her dress. Also, she is pleased that she is sitting next to Anthony and opposite Rose.

On her other side is Wilfred Wilton; he is just going up for his final, and the others find it amusing to call him Doctor.

Esther Raven sits by William Bats. She has her trade, like the rest, and her trade is journalism. She is a regular contributor to *Home Drivel* and *Woman in Chains*. In secret she writes verses, and is very sorry that she was not born beautiful. She wears tweed coats and skirts, and knows that they do not suit her.

There is one other man. They call him the Outsider and the Copy Cat, and he laughs and does not mind. He never thinks of anything for himself, but he is quite good at carrying out other people's ideas. He is very kind and admiring and soothing. William Bats once got him out of a scrape, and it was like saving a dog—a very nice, thoroughbred dog—from drowning. He has no trade, and has more money than any of the others. That is why he is always shabbier than they are. He tries to live up to them and their poverty, and is very grateful to them for receiving him on terms of equality in spite of his money. His name is Mullinger, and his father was Mullinger's Matchless Vermin Killer, Swift and Sure. You know the poster?—rats, mice, bats, and smaller things that creep and jump, and fly and bite, all done very large and plain on a pale blue background, with the motto, "*Death to Pests: harmless to children and domestic animals.*"

These were the seven young people who ate and drank, and talked and laughed in the back-room of Mr. William Bats on that March evening. You will have noticed, perhaps with a pained surprise, that I have omitted to name or describe the chaperon. Well—there wasn't one. Among young people who work, or are training to work, for their living, the idea has somehow ceased to obtain that when seven young people spend an evening together, the fires of youth blaze up so fiercely that only a wet blanket can avert the regrettable.

When the meal was over, they washed up in the little kitchen, and William Bats saw to it that each crock and cup, and spoon and glass returned to its appointed place.

And then they grouped themselves about the sitting-room, Rose and Linda lounging on the divan, Esther very upright on a high-backed chair, smoking cigarettes and wishing she had been born picturesque.

In the middle of the half circle round the fire sat Drelincourt, who is, I suppose, the hero of this romance. At any rate it was to him that most of the happenings came. Women said he was interesting. This meant that he was pale and thin and dark, and had grey eyes that did not always see what they seemed to be looking at. His hands were long and thin, and his face was clean-shaven, and a little hollow in the cheek.

He rapped on the arm of his Windsor chair.

"The business of the evening will now begin," he said; "Miss Raven has kindly consented to address the meeting."

"Don't be silly," said Miss Raven. "I know it is my turn to say what we shall do tonight. But the fire's so ripping. My landlady's callous—no fires after March. She has the chimneys swept on the first. Couldn't we just sit here and jaw?"

160

"Forbidden by the rules," said more than one voice.

"Sloth and luxury," said William Bats regretfully, "are shocking vices."

"Well, then," said Miss Raven, "suppose we pretend we're in a Dickens Christmas Number, and each tell the sad sweet story of our lives."

"We shouldn't have time to make them up," said Rose.

"No, we shouldn't—should we?" said the Outsider thoughtfully.

"Well, then, let's each tell a story that's *not* the sad sweet, and write them afterwards, and print them and divide the money."

"The *Monolith* has cured most of us of that illusion. But I suppose the fact that you get paid for your stuff blinds you to the fact that other people don't."

"I could tell you a dissecting-room story," said the doctor, "but—"

"No, you don't," said Anthony firmly. "Miss Raven will now come to the point of her remarks. So far, I find myself in entire agreement with the lecturer. If we could do *anything* that would end in our dividing any money, I for one should ask no better of Fate. I may remind the meeting that the chairman's watch and chain have been in seclusion since last April."

"Beastly bad form to brag about your jewellery," said Wilton.

"There's a certain affluence attached to a state in which one no longer needs one's medical library," said the chairman. "Proceed, Miss Raven."

"Well, look here," said Miss Raven, "I'll tell you what—" and stopped short.

"No hurry," said the chairman, settling his back against the Windsor chair.

"All right! I'll think of something in a minute. Look here! Let's all answer advertisements. 'Home work. How to make fifty pounds a week in your spare time without hindrance to present employment.'"

"I've done that," said Linda. "It turned out to be sewing jet beads on to net to dress fat Jewesses in. You might earn five shillings a week if you really stuck at it."

"Chair!" said Drelincourt. "Is this really your decision, Miss Raven? Is this the way in which you decree that seven sane persons shall spend an evening which, once wasted, can never be recalled?"

"I can't think of anything else," she said. "Do stop rotting, Tony. If you can think of anything else, say so. If not—"

"As chairman of the evening," said he, "I am expressly debarred from thinking. Rather will I call upon Mr. William Bats to produce seven pens, seven inks, and seven sheets of notepaper, seven envelopes, and seven copies of the Daily Whatsitsname."

"You'll have to send out for those," said Mr. Bats.

"I'll go," said Mullinger, getting up at once.

"It's all right," Miss Raven assured him. "I bought seven evening papers, all different."

"And suppose we'd agreed to sit and jaw as you suggested?" Linda asked.

"That would have been cheap at threepence halfpenny, don't you think?"

And now with rustlings and white wavings the company vanished behind newspapers.

"Of course," said Miss Raven warningly, "we aren't to tell each other what advertisement we answer."

"And suppose we all answer the same one?"

"The more the merrier."

"This," said Rose over the top of her paper, "is the dullest game I ever played."

"Oh no!" Linda protested: "dull? How can you?"

"By the way," Mr. Bats asked carelessly, "may we answer any advertisement, or only the ones about spare time?"

"Oh, any," answered Miss Raven, absorbed in her paper.

"Right O!" said Mr. Bats, "I shall answer an agony one."

But no one paid any attention. And presently pens scratched, and wandering eyes, vaguely seeking the right word, met and fixed other eyes in that blank mutual glare which attains perfection only across a writing-table.

And when all the letters were written, Miss Raven collected all the newspapers and put them away neatly.

"Girl after my own heart!" said Mr. William Bats.

"I only do it to avoid fuss," said Miss Raven, "not because I'm really tidy."

"It shall go no further," said Bats.

"Now all the letters are done, we can jaw," said Linda luxuriously. "Anthony shall play to us."

She reached down the old viol-di-gamba which hung on the wall, as it had once hung on the wall of a great lady's ante-room in the days when James the First was king, for the entertainment of guests waiting for an audience.

"Why, where is he?"

"He wrote his letter and stamped it, and took it and went ten minutes ago," said Mr. Bats, "only you were all so busy you never noticed him."

Miss Royal opened her lips, and shut them again without speaking, and Mr. Bats said, also without speaking,

"Yes, I know you saw him go."

"He whispered a parting word in my ear," Mr. Bats went on; "two in fact. 'Blazing headache' was what he said."

"I'm afraid the advertisement game bored him," said Miss Raven, "but I really couldn't think of anything else."

"He's been looking ill for a long time," said Linda Smith; "he ought to see a doctor."

"He's seen me," said Wilton, "and I've seen him. What he wants is what we all want."

"What's that?"

"A settled income," said the doctor.

"Yes, isn't it a shame?" Miss Raven said; "here's a man, really a genius in his own line, they say, hung up every half minute for want of money—money for chemicals and instruments and things. It's enough to give any one a headache."

"He can work at the College Lab., you know," Wilton reminded her.

"Not his sort of work," said the Outsider. "The things he's got at Malacca must have cost pounds and pounds."

"I only wish someone would leave one of us a fortune; we'd make it all right for him then," said Linda.

"You know very well he wouldn't let you," said Rose.

"No, indeed," said Mullinger. in a heartfelt tone, so that everyone looked kindly at him.

"One never knows whether he means what he says," said Linda thoughtfully. "He told me the other day that, if he couldn't soon pull off some experiment, or other—you know, the one he's always just going to pull off, and then he doesn't—if he couldn't pull that off, he should join an Arctic expedition and become a naturalised Eskimo."

"Of course, he didn't mean it," said Miss Royal a little sharply.

"You never know," said Linda perseveringly.

"Well, don't let his absence cast a blight," said Bats. "Esther, have some more cigarettes. Take a lot, take two; and let's enjoy ourselves. Wilton, just buttle a little, will you? There's some claret left on the dresser. And I'll get out the cherry brandy. Let us drink Mr. Anthony Drelincourt's health again. Begone, dull care!"

"Yes, let's," said everyone. But all the same everyone had left before eleven, and in rather low spirits.

"Some evenings are like that, you know. All flat, somehow," said Linda at the corner of the Tottenham Court Road where you wait for omnibuses.

"Oh! do you think so?" Rose roused herself to say gaily. "Why, I've enjoyed myself most awfully. Goodnight, dear."

Still smiling, she sprang to the step of her moving omnibus, and found a seat. A grizzled South Sea missionary opposite her thought he had never seen so gay and beautiful a face. He turned his eyes away because one must not stare—at white people anyhow. The next time he ventured to look at her he knew, with a sudden shock, that he had never seen a face so beautiful and so sad.

Mr. William Bats, left alone, was re-reading the inscription on a slip of paper which Anthony Drelincourt had silently laid before him at the moment of whispering in his ear that lie about the headache. It said:

Come straight on to me as soon as the others go. Something very odd has happened. I want to tell you. Don't let anything stop your coming—A. D.

CHAPTER 4

The Advertisement

"Come along in, do," said Anthony, holding the door open at the top of the stairs; "I thought you were never coming. Did you lock the gate and the front door?"

"Yes," said William Bats, "I did. And I'm tired and cross, and it's late, and this is a hell of a place to get to, Tony. It's not many chaps—"

"No, I know. The fire's burning up. Make yourself comfortable." He set the bottle and glasses on the work-table. "Because I propose to tell you things, and it may take some time."

Bats was sniffing at a couple of limp red roses that lay beside a contented-looking pot of violets on the table.

"Yes," said Drelincourt, "and that's another thing. She put them there—my wretched birthday, you know—I wrote my name in some idiotic little book—jolly kind of her, and all that. She's always doing nice things. And I wish she wouldn't."

"Makes you feel small, eh? Considering how little you do for other people."

"Makes me feel helpless and resentful," Drelincourt answered; "mother's-little-boy feeling, don't you know? You feel she'll know it if you get your feet wet."

"You don't know it when you're well off," said the other. "You don't deserve—"

"Well, I said it was jolly kind of her, didn't I? And if there was anything, I could do for her, I would. But there isn't. And that's what makes it so hateful."

"If," said William Bats, beginning to light his pipe, "you brought me to this beastly hole to tell me that Rose Royal was jolly kind, and you were jolly ungrateful, you needn't have troubled. I could have been trusted to find out a little thing like that for myself."

"But she is," said Drelincourt with a sort of wilful stupidity. "It's not only me. She's looking after all the brutes who are in those houses she owns, as well as the biscuit boys. She's lowered their rents, and given each house a fireguard because of the kids, and a brass paraffin lamp because glass receivers are dangerous. She's started a sewing class and a competitive baby exam on Saturdays. She's jolly kind."

"Now, I wonder," Mr. Bats asked himself, "whether this is because she really does fill his mind so that he must talk about her, or whether he's just doing it because he must talk about anything rather than the thing his mind is full of?" Aloud he said—

"Carried unanimously. And then—"

"Look here," said Drelincourt, laying down the pipe he had been pretending to light; "we've always got on pretty well together."

"Ever since we was boys," said the other. "I have nine pounds seventeen in the bank, if that's any good."

"It isn't, thanks," said Drelincourt. "Look here," he said again, and took up the pipe. "I must talk about it to someone, and I can't think of anyone but you."

"Flattered, and all that," said Bats.

And again, everything hung fire. It is like that sometimes, you know. One wants to talk, the other wants to listen, and yet it's impossible. The atmosphere is wrong, somehow. Vague remembrances came to Bats of things he had heard about the methods of priests at the confessions of shy penitents.

"Look here," he said; "it's not money, you say?"

"Not more than it always is. My mother left me a little money, you

165

know. I've been spending the capital, and there's precious little left, but it's not that. No."

"It's not Rose?"

"Not more than usual."

"Some other girl. Some woman?"

"No," said Drelincourt. "Good Lord, no!"

The Father Confessor would probably have been able to think of other things that it might be, but William Bats could not; he had not been trained to the profession of confessor.

"Oh, spit it out," he said wearily. "I never guessed a riddle in my life."

"You see," said Drelincourt, "there's rather a lot in it. I don't know where to begin."

"Begin in the middle," said his friend.

"All right, I will. You know that silly answering advertisements? Well, I was looking for one to answer, and I found one, by Jove!"

He took the folded paper from the pocket of his great-coat, peered at it a moment, and handed it to Bats, who read—

"If Anthony Drelincourt, son of Bartholomew Drelincourt, will communicate with Messrs. Wigram and Bucks, Solicitors, Lewes, he will hear of something to his advantage."

"Well?" he said, "it looks like the long-lost heir possibility cropping up again. You'll apply in person tomorrow, of course."

"Shall I?" said Drelincourt slowly, "shall I? That's just it."

"Why not?"

"Well, I don't know whether they mean me. And if they do mean me, I don't know what they want me for."

"For your advantage, of course. And you are the son of Bartholomew Drelincourt, aren't you?"

"Suppose I am; suppose it was to my advantage; suppose it was money—lots of it; that would be all right. But suppose it meant perhaps just a little money, and being bothered with relations I've never seen. It would play the deuce with my work. And you know, Bill, I'm on the edge of something big this time. Yes—I know I've said that before, but this time there's something different. I wouldn't have that interfered with, for all the advantages that all the solicitors in England could offer."

"You're sure this time?"

"Hang it, man!"—Drelincourt stretched his feet to the fire which had grown red and comforting—"don't throw my failures in my face.

I know you think it's rubbish, but those old alchemists weren't such fools as you think."

"True," said Bats; "how do we know there isn't an elixir of life and a philosopher's stone into the bargain?"

"Laugh if you like, if it amuses you, but I couldn't have my work interfered with. On the other hand, perhaps I'm not the man that the advantages are for. I've never told anyone what I'm going to tell you, but I want to tell you."

"Fire ahead."

"I've never had any relations but my mother. We lived very quietly at Lewisham, you know. Her father left her a little—the interest was just enough to keep us. He was killed out hunting when I was quite a baby. He was a farmer. My own father was killed in the Zulu war in 1885, so I don't remember him. My mother used to talk about him to me when I was quite a kiddie, but after I began to go to school, she would not talk about him anymore. But once she told me that she hated all his relations. There was no portrait of him about the house. But after my mother died—I was fifteen then—I found a portrait of him in her desk, and a snuff-box that I remembered I had seen when I was a little chap, and she'd told me it was my grandfather's. It had a coat-of-arms on it, and I found out that it was the coat of the Drelincourts, and I looked them up in Burke, and there was a Bartholomew Drelincourt, younger son of the Baronet, who died in 1885."

"Well, that's all right."

"Is it? You see, Burke says he died unmarried."

There was a silence. Then—

"I see," said Bats.

"You see," Drelincourt repeated, his eyes on the fire, "if it wasn't all right about my mother, I'd rather not know it. Because if she'd wanted me to know it, she'd have told me. I don't want to find out things she didn't want me to know. For myself, of course, nothing could make any difference. I *knew* her. She was the best—" he stopped. "All the same, it would be pleasant to be quite sure that one's father wasn't a scoundrel."

"I see," said Bats again.

"I've been thinking it over for the last two or three hours," said Drelincourt. "And I see that I can't *write*. Don't you think I could sort of go disguised, you know—no, I don't mean a false beard and glasses; I mean just not giving my real name till I saw what was up. I thought if you'd give me one of your cards—would you mind? Then I'd go down to Lewes and see."

"I see."

"But there's another difficulty. I feel in my bones that if I went away for more than a day—and if I once get caught in the machinery—law business and so on, I might not be able to get back at once. If I went away for more than a day, that girl would tidy up this place and have it cleaned out."

"Well?"

"Well, I shouldn't mind so much about this floor. But the ground floor. You know one has to make experiments if one is ever to find out anything. And if she got into the downstairs rooms and found a dead guinea-pig or a dissecting-knife—well, you know what girls are."

"Lock it up," suggested Bats.

"I lock this up. But she got in with those roses. I suppose she has duplicate keys or something. No, the only thing is, could you come and stay here while I'm away. I *might* only be away a few hours. But would you come?"

"Of course," said Bats, and a soft warmth that was not that of the coal-fire crept to neck and cheek, "certainly I would."

"You know I've got all sorts of things going on. There are one or two things I should have to ask you to do for me, and things to attend to. There's a monkey that has to be fed. Oh no"—in answer to a little shrug of the other's shoulders—"he's all right—jolly as a sandboy. You aren't going to begin believing those Brown Dog stories at this time of day, Bill?"

"All right," said Bats, "just show me what to do. I'll be here by ten tomorrow if that's all right."

"You don't think I'm a fool not to just write a letter and jump at the 'advantage' whatever it is?" Drelincourt asked a little wistfully.

"On the contrary," said Bats, rousing himself from his thoughts, "I'm lost in admiration of a caution and foresight hitherto quite foreign to your character. Yes, thanks. Two fingers, and half the soda—oh—well, water, then."

"And you won't let anyone in while I'm away. Not even Rose?"

"Not even Rose," said William Bats, picking up his great-coat.

Drelincourt turned to feel in the pocket of his.

"By the way," he said, "before you go; I found this in my pocket, coming home. It's from Rose, a birthday present. It looks interesting, only I can't make anything out of it. And it's got the Drelincourt arms in."

Bats took the book.

"Yes, she showed it to me. About the properties of precious stones. And the manuscript pages at the end? They're in cypher, of course."

"Well, I'll leave it for you to look at. Perhaps some of your Bacon-Shakespeare cypher will fit it."

"It's probably about your sort of subject," said Bats. "All right, I'll see if I can make anything out of it. And I say, old chap," he added, pausing by the door; "of course, if it is a piece of luck—well, I'm jolly glad and all that, don't you know?"

And on that he went. When he got home the fire was nearly out. But he roused it cunningly, and when its heart was red again, he burned in it two soft fading red roses.

CHAPTER 5

Family Secrets

Toyshops look innocent enough. But you never know. It was from a toyshop that came the guiding inspiration of Anthony Drelincourt's life. Bookshops are dangerous, of course; they are full of ideas, and ideas are explosive. And the bookshops came in later, and did their part. But the very beginning of all was the toyshop.

Looking back into the past, as one looks at things through the wrong end of a telescope, Anthony could see himself a little boy in a little bed in a little room in a little house in Lewisham. The little boy was cool and comfortable now, but there had been days and nights when everything had been otherwise. In a word, he had had the measles. And now he was what his mother called "nicely better," and tomorrow was his birthday, and Mother had been to London on purpose to buy him a present; and there it was, large and rectilinear on the chest of drawers, between the medicine bottle and the embossed green plate with grapes on it.

"I won't see it till tomorrow, shall I, Mother?" he asked.

"No, dearest," said his mother; "tomorrow's your birthday, you know."

"Yes," said little Tony, deliberate and thoughtful.

"I do hope you'll like it," said she wistfully.

It is dreadful when you save up to buy a present for your little boy, go without a few things that you want rather badly, so as to have enough money to buy it; spend an hour of agonised indecision among the bewildering temptations of Hamley's; and then, after all, your little boy rewards you with a lifeless "Thank you," and you perceive that he is disappointed, and would much rather have tin soldiers for his birthday present.

"Mother," said Anthony, "I've thought of a new game. You think of something, and I'll try to guess what it is. Like 'Twenty Questions,' you know."

"Very well; I've thought of something."

"Is it my present?"

"No." "Oh, but it must be! I don't want to play unless it's my present you're thinking of. Now you are, aren't you?"

And she was, of course.

"Is it wood?"

"Partly."

"But you ought to say just only Yes or No."

"I can't when it isn't."

"Well, then, is it blocks?"

"No; you've got lots of blocks, Tony."

"Bricks?"

"They're all wood, and you've got lots of them too."

"No, they aren't. There's little bits of glass in the windows."

"Well, it isn't bricks, dear."

"Is it puzzle maps?"

"No; you've got all the nice ones."

And indeed, he had; for this denying oneself to get presents for the child was no new game to the child's mother.

"Is it metal?"

"Partly."

"Not tops?"

"No."

"Railways?"

"No."

"A paint-box? No, it's too big. There *couldn't* be a paint-box so beautiful big as all that, could there, Mother?"

"I don't know," she laughed; "there might be. Only there isn't this time. You'll never guess. I will make you comfy now, and then you'll go to sleep, and it'll be morning before you know where you are."

"Will it?" he asked doubtfully. "Sometimes I know where I am *long* before it's morning, and I keep knowing it for ages and ages."

"Well, I'm going to wash you and make you all comfy for the night. We can go on playing just the same. It's all sorts of different things," she said, bringing the basin and the warm water with the seven drops of sweet scent in it. "Shut your eyes, or the soap will get into them."

"Is it soldiers?" he asked with his eyes shut.

"No, dear."

"Not marbles?"

"Of course not."

"Then I don't see what it can be. I've thought of *everything*," he said, through the towel.

"Not quite."

"It isn't books?"

"No. Now your handies."

"Not a model farm?"

"You've got that."

"Do tell me. No, don't tell me. I will guess."

But the evening toilet was completed, and the gas was lowered to a blue bead, and Mother was gone down to her supper. And still he had not guessed.

And now he lay alone in the darkened room wondering, and the wonder made his head ache and his hands hot, and bed was not the comfortable place it had been.

"I'm sure it's making me feverish," he told himself. "Mother wouldn't like me to be feverish. And I mustn't be selfish and disturb her at her meals. Gwendolen said so."

He sat up in the bed and listened. There was no sound in the house except the faint swish of Gwendolen's scrubbing brush on the kitchen floor. She was late with her work that night, because she had sat with him while Mother was out.

"I'll just take one little feel," he said, and got out of bed. His legs felt soft and tingly, and it was difficult to stand up straight, but he held on to the bedpost, and got to the chest of drawers. He felt the parcel. There was a box in it. Beyond doubt a box. He tore the paper at the corner. A wooden shiny box. Parlour croquet, perhaps?

He pulled the box towards him, and the medicine bottle fell over softly on a pile of clean handkerchiefs. He pulled the box to the edge, and it fell heavily into his arms. He only just saved it from falling noisily on to the floor, and stood swaying and hugging it to him.

"I believe it's carving tools," said he, and reeled back with it to the bed. He had to lie there quietly for a few minutes, the sharp angles of the box running into side and arm, before he had strength to sit up and tear off the paper.

"I'll tell Mother when she comes up," he said. "She won't mind if I tell her I couldn't bear the suspense."

The paper, scrabbled off by hot eager fingers, disclosed a polished wooden case. It had doors in the front that opened like the ones of stationery cabinets. Inside was much stuffing, tiny shavings, tow and tissue paper wrappings. Inside one of the doors a card, nailed at the corners. It said:

The Young Chemist's Practical Cabinet, Contains Sixty Different Chemicals, with full instructions for use. With pestle and mortar.

He read no more, but began pulling the packets out. There were little bottles and pill-boxes, and round wooden boxes, all neatly labelled. "Sulphate of Copper," they said, and "Chromate of Potash," and "Alum," and interesting words like that. And there were little bottles which said the same sort of things in the same sort of language—a new and beautiful language, but to Tony, as yet, a foreign one. There was a pestle and mortar, and a graduated glass, and a little pair of wire tweezers, and a little pair of scales with tiny weights in tissue paper inside a pill-box, and there was one test-tube.

The things lay over the bed all mixed up with the tow, and Tony took up the blue-covered book of "full instructions." Most of the instructions seemed difficult. But there was one:

If a piece of camphor be placed in a basin of pure water, and then ignited, it will dart about as though alive. If a drop of oil be placed in the water, the motion of the camphor will immediately cease.

"I could try that," said Tony. "I saw camphor just now." He found the camphor in its pink and white pill-box, and there were matches. . . .

He drew himself from the bed as a dagger is drawn from the sheath, so as not to disturb the lovely freight of his counterpane, and stood on the mat beside. He reached the matches from the mantelpiece near his bedhead.

"I will light the camphor first," he said, "and then take it to the basin."

So, he lighted the camphor, and it flared up with instant magnificence and burnt his fingers, so that he screamed and threw it from him. It fell among the tow and shavings on the bed, and instantly it was a bed of flames, that leaped up and hotly licked his face, and neck,

172

and hands

His mother was there before the echo of his scream had died away, and she and Gwendolen put the fire out. And Anthony's burns were not very bad ones. But his mother would not buy him another Chemical Cabinet. Only when he first saw the laboratory at St. Edward's he felt curiously at home. He had seen these sort of things before. And the mischief was done. That box had implanted in him the seed of an imperishable desire to mess about with chemicals.

And the book that his schoolmistress sent for his birthday held another seed, from which grew another life-purpose, intertwining for ever with the first, sometimes overgrown by the strong tendrils and heavy leaves of scientific attainments, but every now and then unfolding in the midst of all the things that everybody saw, sudden starry flowers that no one else could see. If that second life-purpose could ever have been imagined by the masters and professors who assisted in the development of the first, I don't know what would have happened. Probably some well-meaning person would have tried to persuade his mother to place him in a home for the mentally afflicted.

But he kept his secret, even from his mother, even, later, from Bats. He knew from the first, quite inexplicably and quite surely, that no one else would believe in it. He believed in it. Children have so many strange new things to believe, things that grown-ups tell them, about China and Peru, botany and geology, and the births of religions and the deaths of kings, that to believe a few things more, comes, as it were, in the day's work. And as he grew older and perceived that things are not necessarily true because they are in printed books, it seemed to him that that secret belief of his was no more dreamlike and wonderful than the things they taught him about radium and electrons, and polarised light, and all the things that to the unscientific sound so like incredible fairy tales.

The book the schoolmistress had sent was a book called something-or-other Magic—not for years did Anthony recall its real name—and it ought to have been a book called *Natural Magic*—a nice little childish book about birds' eggs and spiders' webs, and the respectable conduct of the ant. Only it wasn't. By some error of the bookseller it was this other book. And before the error was discovered and rectified by the authorities, there had been born in the little Anthony a deep unassuageable desire, an almost ignorance that there was no ignoring, a longing beyond all mundane longings, for . . . what that book talked about. Beautiful things that you didn't understand at all, but that made you think of other things. It was a wonderful book that made even sums interesting. Can one put the fascination more strongly? A book that made one long for it to be Revelations and not anything else for the second lesson in Church; that set one to reading one's Bible in a way that made one's mother weep tears of joy, pious and amazed; that lit the stars anew, and put new names to the dullest words, new crowns to the simplest numbers.

He had done wonders on the scientific side at St. Edward's School, and when he left with a scholarship for University College, old Mug, the headmaster, made him a little pleasant speech about Fame and Newton, and Faraday and original work and natural aptitude, a speech so flattering that he could never have repeated it to anyone except his mother. But his mother was dead.

He thought of that year after his mother's death, and before his scholarship at University College. There had been another scholarship, a travelling one. And he had travelled, straight to a place that later, in the rush and tumble of his student life, he had not dared to think of—had only felt as one feels a hand in the dark. A quite ordinary place, a whitewashed villa in a little French town near the forest of Fontainebleau, with a walled garden above whose gate wisteria drooped, faintly purple like grapes in a dream, much sunlight, green shutters, the splendour and mystery of the forest, world-old rocks and world-old secrets, the disciple who inquired, the Master who knew.

Then came University College and hard facts, physics, mathematics, chemistry, life transfigured. And the call of the blood, recognized consciously and consciously not responded to. And the outside veneer of a life that was like acting a charade. And the steady purpose maturing, the growth of the idea, the development of the invention, the unfolding, leaf by leaf, of the wonder-flower of the world. Anthony felt that he was not one, but two; the physicist-chemist-mathematician, and that other thing that refused to be tied down and bound by a name. Also, he was another thing—not a *duad*, but a *triad*. There was in him, deep and desperate, the desire to be as other men, to rejoice in their joys, grieve as they grieved. He summoned up the third Anthony when he said once to Bats—

"If I could only see what you fellows see in these actresses and people, I shouldn't mind. But I can't."

"Neither can I," said Bats. "At least I can. But I don't want to see any more."

"That's just it," said Anthony. "I don't see. And I wish I could."

174

He remembered all this now, as he sat staring out of the window of his third-class carriage at the woods and fields, pale in the March sunshine. He had the carriage to himself, and he remembered many things in that noisy quiet. He remembered his mother—little, thin, energetic, with bright eyes and smooth, hard, gentle, busy, little hands; and he understood just a little of the love that had wrapped the child round (as precious things are folded in cotton wool) to keep away all hard things that might hurt.

"I wish you were here," he said aloud. "I hope you won't mind what I'm doing. I hope that if you do mind, something will happen to prevent my finding out anything that you don't want me to know."

He often spoke to her. It seemed to him impossible that the love that had made so soft a nest should now have either ceased to be, or should be where it could no longer reach him.

"I don't believe in death, you see," he said once to Bats. "Things change, but they don't cease to be. And some things don't change: it's the surroundings that change. You don't persuade me that if you get near enough to people to love them, and go on loving them till you die, that then your love's turned off like a tap. I'm not at all sure that dead people don't stay near the people they love. You can't prove that they don't."

"I can't prove that you're a morbid ass," Bats answered, "and I don't need to. I should have thought that your scientific rot would have knocked all that rot out of your head."

"And this from one who can believe as many as six impossible things about Bacon and Shakespeare before breakfast! But why expect anything from a Baconian but a grunt?"

"And now you're coarse, and not even original. That's the kind of joke that all the Shakespearians like and the kind of argument they use."

"But what I said about dead people was true, and you can't prove it isn't. You modern people think you know everything about life and death. Your old Francis wouldn't have been so cocksure."

"I'm an awkward idiot," said Bats, answering something that was not the other's speech. But all that had happened years ago.

Anthony had found out many things since then, things old and new; and now he was alone in the train, going perhaps to find out something very new indeed. He looked out across the grey green fields, where little old farm buildings lay humped up under leafless trees. The quiet and peace of the country reached out to him, and he wondered half wistfully how it would have been with him if his grandfather, the Sussex farmer, had not died in the hunting field. Would he have been brought up on the farm, to order the sowing and the reaping, and think only of the condition of beasts and the rotation of crops. He would have ridden to hounds like his grandfather, and come home tired and splashed to take off his muddy boots in the firelit farm-kitchen. Would he have ever wanted anything, not better but different? Would he have longed so to "find out" if it had not been for the box of mystery from the toyshop?

"I think I should," he said. "I think it's like a fire in my blood. Something would have lighted the fire and set it blazing. Ah!"

A thrill ran through him; the train had swung round a curve, and a great shoulder of Down rose vast and quiet before his eyes. He looked, and loved it.

"And that's in my blood, too," he said, remembering that somewhere on those South Downs was the farm where his mother was born, and where, but for the stumble of a horse at a hedge, he might have lived his own life. He did not know where that farm was. She had never told him.

If he had been a farmer he would have married. He thought of the firelit farm-kitchen again, a woman coming in to put her arms round his neck, and ask if they had had a good run—a woman gentle, dark-eyed, fragile, enchanting, as no woman was that he had ever met.

No, a farmer's wife would have had to be energetic, vital, managing and organising, a woman like Rose Royal. Then he thought of her for a little while. "Well, anyway I couldn't afford to marry any one now," he told himself, "even if—" and stopped the thought there.

And then it was Lewes, and he was out of the train and beholding the full revelation of great curves and chalk cuttings, the massive splendour of the Down country.

He asked a porter the way to the office of Messrs. Wigram & Bucks, and went out into the streets. A girl fleeting by on a bicycle slowed down a little to look at him, and thought that he looked very sad, and that if a really nice girl were to be fond of him, she could make a great difference in his life. This was exactly what every girl thought who ever came near enough to him to see his eyes. But the girl on the bicycle did not know this. She went by slowly, and even looked back at him, which is "not done," and her bicycle swerved and ran over a stone, and she nearly fell off. So, she said, "Serve me right," and went on quickly, feeling hot and uncomfortable.

"What a fool he'll think me," she told herself. But he had not even seen her.

One lawyer's office is very like another—the same smell of dusty leather, the same posters which, at the first glance, look like play-bills, but which really deal, not with the details of the drama, but with the sale of acres and stock and estates and messuages.

There is the same very young clerk, casual to exasperation, the same delay, the same certainty that the man you have come to see will have gone out to lunch.

Anthony had to wait, and through a partly-opened door he got a glimpse of Turkey carpet, roll-topped desk, and black tin boxes that had Drelincourt Estate on them in white letters.

"So, it is my father's people," he told himself, and hated the thought of what he might have to hear. He imagined a repentant father providing on his death-bed for the son of the woman his youth had wronged. Anthony ground his teeth, and the clerk offered him the *Lewes Gazette.* Perhaps—his eyes occupied with its advertisement columns-his thoughts were still free, but he called them back and chained them to the leading article. He had finished this as well as the reports of a Conservative meeting, a bazaar, and the fire in the High Street, before the door swung open, and portly, frock-coated, high-batted, a presence appeared in the doorway, passed Anthony with unseeing eyes, and disappeared into the inner room. The small clerk, alacritously obsequious, followed. There was a subdued murmur, the door was flung back, and Anthony, requested to step this way, stepped.

"Mr. Drelincourt, sir," said the small clerk, and went out, shutting the door, almost.

"Take a seat, Mr. Drelincourt," said the august frock-coated one, got up from the chair, and closed the door quite.

Anthony took the client's chair facing the light by the roll-topped desk, and looked across its angle at the large calm face of the solicitor who was rearranging papers on his desk. There was a silence. Anthony did not like his reception. He felt as might one who has been invited to dinner, and whose hostess should meet him with a tacit inquiry as to what had procured her this unexpected pleasure. So, he broke the silence, and broke it curtly.

"I am here in response to your advertisement," he said.

"Quite so, quite so," said the solicitor, still arranging his papers.

There was another silence. Anthony rose.

"You seem to be busy," he said; "please don't trouble to explain why you advertised. Good morning."

Mr. Wigram looked at him over his spectacles, and said—

"All in good time, Mr. Drelincourt. Pray resume your seat. I have here a paper of notes which concerns the matter in hand. Ah! here it is."

Anthony sat down again, abashed by portly superiority.

"Ah, yes. Quite so. I advertised for Anthony Drelincourt. That is your name?"

"Yes," said Anthony.

"The name of your mother?"

"Why do you want to know that?"

The solicitor raised fine eyebrows.

"The name of your father, then?"

"Before I tell you anything, I must know why you want to know."

"And before I tell you anything," said Mr. Wigram, laying down the papers with an air of finality, "you must give me some guarantee that you are the person whom you represent yourself to be. Have you your birth certificate? The certificate of the marriage of your parents? Any letters or mementoes of your parents to prove your identity?"

"I have no intention," said Drelincourt deliberately, "of telling you anything until you have told me your reason for advertising."

"It is," said the lawyer, "something to your advantage, if you are the person for whom we advertised."

"Our ideas of advantage may not be identical," said Anthony.

"It is a question of property," said Mr. Wigram.

"Quite so," said Anthony, "and if you feel that you are doing your duty by advertising for me, and then refusing me any information when I call upon you, well—you and your conscience must settle it between you."

"Come, come, Mr. Drelincourt," the lawyer spoke with some warmth, "you cannot expect me to confide family secrets to you until you have shown me that you are a member of the family."

"Oh! there's a family secret, is there," said Anthony; "well, I don't think I want to hear it."

Mr. Wigram supposed the young man to be mad; and at the same moment ceased to suppose him to be an impostor.

"There is family property awaiting Mr. Anthony Drelincourt," he said.

Anthony looked at him.

"You mean there's money left to me?"

"Mr. Anthony Drelincourt inherits money—yes."

"Well, if I can't have it without hearing something I'd rather not hear, I'd rather not have it."

"You can't expect me to know what you'd rather not hear, don't you know?" said the lawyer, dropping, in his mystification, into the colloquial. Anthony wondered whether he was being more than usually silly. Surely if there were anything—he looked at the other man, and saw no embarrassment behind that calm mask, no intolerable knowingness, no insolent pity.

"He looks just ordinary," Anthony told himself. But he was not skilled in the penetration of the masks of solicitors. What the other man was thinking was—

"Mad as a hatter. Well, that's evidence, as far as it goes. They all have bees of one kind or other in their bonnets."

"What I mean," said Anthony, twisting his hands between his knees, "is that I don't want to hear anything about dead people that they'd rather I didn't hear. If this money was left by someone who did wrong, and then was sorry—look here, I won't have the money at all. I'm sorry I came. I'll go. Let the rightful heirs have it."

He got up so quickly that Mr. Wigram had to get up too, and catch him by the arm to keep him from going. And on Mr. Wigram's face was the decorous smile of sudden and complete enlightenment.

"My dear sir," he said, "we seem to have been at cross-purposes. There is nothing, absolutely nothing, to cause you a moment's uneasiness. If you can establish your identity—as I feel sure you can," he added comfortably, "you inherit by succession a title and a considerable property. You are a very fortunate young gentleman. Now be reasonable, my dear sir. Sit down, and tell me all about yourself. Where you were born, for instance?"

"Somewhere near here, I believe," Anthony answered.

"Good," the other nodded. "Your mother's name was—?"

"Frewen. Her father was a farmer somewhere near here."

"Quite so. And your father?"

"He died in the Zulu war in 1881."

"Exactly. Then it is only a matter of a few certificates—easily obtainable."

"I haven't my mother's marriage certificate," said Anthony, not having meant to say anything of the kind.

"But I have," said Mr. Wigram. "There is no reasonable doubt, my dear sir, that you are the heir to the Drelincourt title and estates."

Anthony suddenly produced a silver snuff-box.

"These are my father's arms, I believe," he said.

"Quite so, quite so," said the solicitor. "And now," he said, "do you wish to hear the family secrets? Your mother's marriage certificate is in that black box," he added, hastily forestalling some possible imminent Quixotry.

"If you please," said Anthony.

"Your father," said the solicitor, "was the youngest son of Sir Hamnet Drelincourt. He married in defiance of his father's wishes, and Sir Hamnet Drelincourt refused to recognize your father's wife, or to make the young couple any allowance. When your father, Mr. Bartholomew Drelincourt, was killed in the Zulu war, your paternal grandfather wrote to your mother offering her an allowance on condition that she took another name, and never claimed for you any relationship with your father's family."

"Brute!" said the grandson.

"*De mortuis*—" said the solicitor.

"Your mother indignantly refused. And before time had had—in short—time to soften these regrettable animosities, your maternal grandfather—by the way, do you know how he met his death?"

"In the hunting field," said Anthony. "Go on."

"Quite so," said Mr. Wigram, "and on his decease your mother disappeared and could not be traced."

"I don't suppose they tried much," said Anthony,

"Perhaps their efforts were not very whole-hearted," Mr. Wigram admitted. "At any rate, she, with her baby, disappeared. On the death of Sir Hamnet Drelincourt, his eldest son succeeded; the second and third sons have succumbed to the lot of all men."

"You mean they died?"

"Quite so. Without issue. And now, on the decease of Sir Jocelyn, your paternal uncle, the title and the property devolve upon the eldest son of the late Bartholomew Drelincourt. I feel convinced that a few simple formalities will establish your claim, which, indeed, there is none to dispute. Sir Anthony Drelincourt, allow me to congratulate you."

"Is there much money?" Anthony asked across the sudden handshake.

"The estates bring in something between six and seven thousand a year, and the late Sir Jocelyn Drelincourt having lived well within his income, there is a considerable amount invested in sound securities."

"You mean," said Anthony abruptly, "that I am rich, and I am Sir Anthony Drelincourt."

"I believe that to be the case. A very few days will suffice to make everything quite certain."

Anthony smiled for the first time during the interview.

"I'm glad," he said. "I'm afraid I behaved rather foolishly just now, but—but—"

"Not another word," said the solicitor. "My dear Sir Anthony, I understand perfectly."

"Not you," said Anthony to himself.

But of course, Mr. Wigram did understand thoroughly. Anthony, on the other hand, did not even begin to understand what it was which he so suddenly and astonishingly inherited.

CHAPTER 6

All Nonsense

"Here's some coffee!"

"Hold on a minute."

Rose Royal stood at the top of the rickety wooden stairs holding a tray. William Bats responded from the other side of the locked laboratory door, which presently he opened a very little.

"Aren't you going to let me in?" she asked, standing radiant and distracting with the tray in her hands.

"No," said William Bats, reaching for the tray; "but if you'll let me carry this back to your house and invite me to share it—"

"You're sillier than I should have believed possible, even for a Baconian," said Rose Royal ; "and why mayn't I come in, please? Tony always lets me."

"Tony's not here, and his last conscious words ere leaving this scene expressly forbade it."

"Nonsense! Why?"

"He is experimenting on the brains of mummies, and he knows you would turn their heads; and just now it is most important that they should preserve their agelong immobility."

"And you know *that's* nonsense."

"Granted, lidy ! But it has a lining of sense—a *doublure*, as the French have it. He really has some experiments going. And you know he's morbidly sensitive about his experiments." "How silly! Of course, I shouldn't touch any of his wretched experiments."

"You'd put things down on things; you always do."

"No, but really—oh, take the tray if you like. There isn't really anything, is there? Guinea-pigs without brains, or anything horrible like that?"

"Agreeable Rose, please don't. You know our Anthony's tender sympathetic nature. Give me the tray."

"The coffee's getting cold," she said; "let me come in and talk."

Bats closed the door, and its Yale lock clicked softly. Then he sat down abruptly against it. "Sit on the stairs," he said. "If you won't invite me to your house, we'll have a picnic."

"Yes; but—" she said, letting him take the tray and sinking among green draperies on the top step. "I don't want guinea-pigs to be cut up."

"You're not alone in the kindly thought. But pour out the coffee. We're not here to discuss guinea-pigs. Though if it hadn't been for them, Linda would probably have gone out that time she had diphtheria."

"The question is, whether it wouldn't have been better for—yes, even for Linda to die than to have those poor little beasts, thousands of them, tortured——"

"They aren't tortured. Don't be silly. No, don't fetch a cup; I prefer to drink out of the saucer. And think of the things you accept without turning a hair. Have you ever been made at all uncomfortable by Harvey's theory of the Circulation of the Blood?"

"Of course not," said Rose, pouring coffee. "Why?"

"Oh, nothing. Only he left some notes of his methods. Most explicit. They daren't publish them. There were no anaesthetics in those days, Rose."

She shuddered.

"I don't believe it," she said.

"Shall I describe the pavilion at the end of the garden where he kept his subjects—till he was ready for them? The good time he gave them until he was ready. The sudden summons. The—"

"I do hate you," she said. Tony-——"

"On the contrary. That's just what I'm trying to make you see. All the great big cruel experiments are over; and you never knew. And now whatever's done doesn't hurt. And anyhow, Anthony doesn't keep guinea pigs, and why row? And it's very draughty, too. Won't you ask me to come to your house, kind lidy?"

"No," she said firmly. "Either let me in, or we'll sit here and drink our coffee and catch our deaths of—"

"*Mademoiselle en est l'arbitre,*" he said. And she told him she had not known that he knew his Villette.

And they drank their coffee and were gay. And then the biscuit boys came, and he entertained them. And Rose sent off a telegram by one of the biscuit boys. And presently a telegram came to her:

Please send drawings at once. *Glorious Weekly.*

And when she asked William Bats what on earth she was to do since she had no one to send with the drawings, he made the obvious suggestion and locked up the laboratory; and she gave him a brown paper parcel and saw him off at the gate.

The moment he was out of sight she got rid of the biscuit boys, and, key in hand, flew to the door of Anthony's laboratory. She opened it, and went in. There were some violets, withered and ill-smelling, in a squat bowl. Nothing else which, with the best will in the world, she could connect with anything vital and real.

"What on earth did he make such a fuss for, then?" she asked. The place looked just as it always looked, only tidier in the oasis where the table and chairs were, "You don't mean that because William Bats was living in it and not Drelincourt. She sat down in the armchair and pleated the faded silk of the work-table in her fingers, and wondered whether it had belonged to Anthony's mother. And then she thought of Anthony, if that can be called thinking which is no ordered se- quence of ideas but only confused hopes, dreams, and longings strung at random on the string of memory.

He had been gone now three days. He had sent a long telegram to William Bats saying, "All right," and asking for a portmanteau and clothes to be sent by passenger train to Lewes. Rose had wondered why he had gone to Lewes, and William Bats had let her wonder. Whatever it was, he ought to be home soon. When he came she would ask him to dinner—a very nice dinner—and get the whole story out of him: why he had gone away, and where he had been, and who he had been with? Relations possibly. But she had never heard that he had any relations. Cousins, perhaps; girl cousins.

"Nonsense," she told herself. "You can't expect him to live in a glass case and never even see other girls. Don't be an idiot."

But you know the sort of things that girls think. And time went on.

The sound of boots on the flagstones outside made her start guiltily.

"William! He's come back for something." And at once she felt that distressing hollow sensation which is the portion of the thoroughly found out. Anthony had not wanted her to come in, and she had come. It was a mean thing to do, and now William Bats would know. And she had not found anything out either. So that she was not only mean but silly. And now the boots were on the stairs.

She sprang up. She must go. Better meet him on the stairs than here. It was on the landing that she met—not Mr. Bats, but another.

"Oh, how do you do?" she said.

"I seek Mr. Bats," said the other. "He gave me this address, and I have business in this part, so I come to show him a book of beauty— the *De Augmentis*, 1623 edition, with marginal notes by the hand of the great Bacon himself written."

"He's not in," said Rose; "will you leave the book in case he wants to buy it?"

"No, no," the other laughed. "He will not buy it. It is for the very rich or the public library. I only come to show it. He love to see the beauty book, even if he cannot buy. And since I am here, Miss Royal, shall I tell that fortune of the which we speak?"

"Oh, Mr. Abrahamson!" said Rose; "thank you, but—yes—I should love it, only—yes, come over to my house. I live in the little house by the gate."

"It is here," said the bookseller, waving his hand towards the laboratory door; "it is here, that is the atmosphere congenial to the fortune-telling. Not in little houses by gates. We go in. Yes?"

"But I don't think there are any cards here."

"It is not with cards I tell today," he said, and led the way into the quiet large room adorned with the gleaming machinery of science. After all, she could not explain that Anthony did not want her in his rooms could not at any rate explain it to this old man already too well-informed in matters that she would have desired to keep secret even from herself.

He closed the door.

"What a place of wonder!" he said. "So must the rooms of old alchemists have been. Is it not? What miracles are the dreams of men!"

"I don't believe in miracles," she said.

"And yet you see them every day. Yes, and you work them," he told her. "Your boy savages that you have trained. Oh! you do well not to believe in miracles."

"They're dear boys," she said.

"They are what you are making them. We all shape each other's destiny. And then the stupid—wise ones talk of praise and blame, and crime and virtue, and reward and punishment. And another thing I tell before I tell your fortune, there exists a young man who adores you."

"That ought to be part of the fortune."

"I think, indeed, it might be. But it is not the love-adoring. It is as you Christians adore your saints. He is not of your class."

"I don't know anyone," she was beginning, but he interrupted.

"That makes nothing," he said. "If some day you need a slave, a watch-dog. If your friend no longer lives here, and you need a—how do you say?—Takecarer for this building, then you tell me, and I tell you where to find a good watchdog devoted to your service. And now sit you down here, Miss Royal, you who do not believe in miracles, and we shall try to show you one—a little pretty miracle for you alone."

He pushed forward the chair in which she had been sitting.

"So! And now," he said, "I make the little confession. I come not only to bring the book to Mr. Bats —that was the excuse; the reason—"

"What was the reason?" she asked, defensively struggling to feel commonplace, and not to think about miracles.

"The reason was the unreasoning impulse, the strongest reason in the world. I come, because I knew I find you. And this day and this hour are those propitious to the fortune-reading for you. The stars are for you this day. This is a great day in your life, and today the powers lift a little the veil, and I am permitted to behold."

"Really and truly," said Rose, "I don't believe in these things."

"What things?"

"Fortune-telling and fate and miracles and stars, you know," she told him, her heart fluttering a little.

"But you do believe," he said calmly, and felt in his pocket; "and yet, more, you shall believe. Give me your hand." He set something cold and round in it. "Hold the crystal, and I will light the lamp."

It was a little brass lamp, that he took from the black bag he carried. From that also he took the black velvet cloth which he spread on the table, and the long-handled incense tray like a toy brass frying-pan with a foot.

"Think of what you wish for most," he said, shaking from a folded paper some grey rough powder into the brass tray thing; "and hold the crystal tightly with both hands."

He pulled down the wide dark blue blinds till the place was all dark. Then he unscrewed the top of the spirit lamp, and lighted it.

And little answering sparks of reflected light sprang up among the crowded mystery of bench and shelves, from strange shapes of glass and metal. He lighted the incense, and its sweet thick smoke swirled about among the sparks of reflected light.

"Now," he said, "lay the crystal on the table, and gaze into it with all your heart. Think of nothing else. See nothing else."

"I don't see anything," she said at once.

"You have not yet looked. Patience! Continue to look," he said, "and when the vision appears tell me what you see."

"There isn't any vision," she said, "only clouds and lights."

"That comes first," he said. "Now you shall speak no more till I speak."

There was a silence in the laboratory—a long silence. Then, "Now speak," said he. "What is the vision you behold?"

"A white road; no, it's only the incense smoke; yes it is, a white road winding and great hills. Now it looks like a face. It is—I don't want to see any more." She pushed the crystal away.

The bookseller caught her hand and held it strongly.

"Be still," he said, in a tone of authority. "I will look for you."

Again, there was silence. Rose's heart felt as though it were beating in her throat. For the face she had seen, plain, distinct as a miniature, lighted as by clear pale sunlight, alive as her own face, was the face of Anthony. And his eyes had looked at her as his eyes had never yet looked.

The bookseller was speaking.

"I see a face also, pale, with dark eyes. The face of a man you think you love. Today he will tell you he loves you. There is wealth coming to him, but with it a strange sorrow. There is something here which I do not understand. A beautiful woman dead. No, it is not *your* face. I see—" He stopped abruptly, and bent silently over the crystal; then rose, and drew up the blinds. The pale dusky light crept in. The incense was burnt out, and he replaced the brass vessel and the crystal in his bag, and began to fold up the velvet cloth.

"Well," she said, "did you see anymore?"

"I tell you no more," he said, and there was a new agitation in his voice; "but I confess you this. I did not think I should see so much. Always I believed in the crystal when I have seen in it hints and half-hints, wandering shapes like dreams just distinguished. But this time I see it all so plain as how I see you, and I now believe no more. It is impossible. Illusion."

"Do tell me what you saw," she said, hiding an agitation not less than his own.

"No, it is not good. If someday a terrible trouble comes, ask me, and perhaps I may tell. But not now. I do not believe. But if I did believe—"

"Well, if you did?" she persisted, still consciously calm.

"If I did believe, I should entreat you to love only a poor man, and if wealth should come to your lover, wealth that he has not earned, bid him refuse it, reject it; have nothing to do with the accursed thing."

He spoke strongly, vehemently.

"Oh!" said Rose, with a laboured lightness, "of course that's just your Socialism coming out."

"It is not Socialism, nor any politics-affair. I tell you it is life and death; or would be, if I believed it."

"But what is it?" she persisted.

"Life and death. I can no more than that tell you. It is death, and life, and joy, and horror, and sorrow for you, and worse than sorrow for him."

"*What* is? You must tell me. You mean if I marry him." Rose was being shaken out of her reticences. "Will that bring sorrow?"

"There is no sorrow in your marriage," he said. "It is the wealth. For him wealth is the beginning of tragedy. But why say all this?—I do not believe it; it is only a game we play in sport. There are no such miracles. It is as you say. I act no more on impulse, Miss Royal. This place has the atmosphere too congenial to the magic. I regret I came to it."

"Oh, don't say that," said Rose, trying to speak and feel as she usually spoke and felt. It had for her the effect of repeating a lesson learnt by heart. "It was very kind of you; very kind indeed. Won't you come to the little house by the gate? It is quite a good house for having tea in; even if it's no good for fortune-telling. Let me give you some tea"?

"But Mr. Abrahamson picked up his bag and his parcel, and said "Goodbye!"

"It's all dreams, and not to be believed," he said; "think no more of it, Miss Royal."

And of course, she thought of nothing else. She put all in order to leave the laboratory as she had found it, passed out, locked the door, and went to her own neat, matted-floored, airy room, thinking all the time.

"It has been a day," she said, lighting the two candles on the man-

187

telpiece that cast such pleasant reflections in her sparse polished furniture. But the reflections reminded her. She lighted the green-shaded lamp. She drew the curtains, coaxed the neglected fire to little blue and red activities, and set out the simple supper she would eat later—bread, milk, and Tasmanian apples. And still she thought—if, as I said, you can call it thinking.

Then she pulled out the table, and sat down to work at some pen-and-ink drawings to illustrate a story of Esther Raven's. For Rose was a worker, and the fact that in the daytime she painted ambitious amateurish pictures which nobody bought, and dreamed of fame, did not at all prevent her working in the evening at the clever little illustrations which people *did* buy. She had the confessed desire to make money; and the secret dream of making enough to be useful to Anthony transfigured and vitalized the sordid details of business. For she knew that he needed money—would always need it—for the scientific work that was his life. Since he had lived at Malacca Wharf, he had fallen into the habit of coming for odd half-hours to sit in that little parlour of hers, whose unnatural neatness was her own protest and revolt against her own innate untidiness.

"I'll have one room tidy anyhow," she told herself. And she had. You can easily keep one room tidy by the simple process of carrying everything out of it every morning except the furniture, and just dumping down what you have carried out in the other rooms. Only, of course, the other rooms suffer. You know the things one cannot somehow get rid of? Piles of newspapers and pamphlets, brown paper, cardboard boxes, pictures that you don't want to hang, odds and ends left over from dressmaking, music that wants mending, books that want binding, lace that wants ironing, letters that you mean to answer sometime, photographs of people you only care a little about, bits of ribbon, ends of sealing-wax. Rose always seemed to have more of these things than other people. It is an effect untidy people give.

But her parlour was tidy, and she sat in it working quickly and neatly. All the neatness of her seemed to be spent on her dress and her work, and, by an effort of will, on that parlour.

Presently she heard the yard gate click.

"William," she told herself.

Footsteps came to her door, and when she opened it she found herself for the second time that day confronting someone who was not William. But this time it was Anthony.

"Oh, you!" she said, with an indescribable intonation. "Oh, come in."

It was that intonation that decided him. For he had come to her after hours of indecision. He came in, shut the door, and followed her into the room.

"Now sit down," she said comfortably, "and tell me all about it. What was it, and was it to your advantage?"

He looked round the pleasant familiar room; he looked at the beautiful familiar face. It was like coming home. These four days in Lewes had been very long, lonely ones.

"I will tell you," he said; "but there is something else I want to tell you first. I've been thinking all the way up." He stood by the mantelpiece, fingering the brass candlesticks. "I should like always to come home to you. Life's a lonely thing."

"You've got your experiments to come home to," said Rose clumsily, with the sudden sense of things happening.

"Don't you care about me, then?" he asked, like a child, wounded, incredulous.

"Of course, I care," she said; "we've always been such friends."

"Oh, don't be silly," he said. "You know I'm trying to ask you to marry me."

"No—I mean, you don't really mean it," she said, still clumsy with what was half hurt and half happiness; "no one could possibly believe that you—What are you asking me for?"

"Because I want you," he said, still fumbling with the candlesticks. "Rose, I feel so lost—as if I were going to Australia by myself in a convict ship. It was so lonely down there."

"It's just a mood. You don't mean it. You'll wish you hadn't tomorrow. I mean you would, if I said Yes. You're asking me for some other reason. Someone's been saying something about our living down at Malacca Wharf, or something. No. It's not good enough, Tony. I don't care two pence what people say, and you don't either. You don't love me, and I'm not going to pretend to believe you do. I'll get some supper, and then you'll feel better."

"Bother supper," he said.

"Oh, don't be silly," she said. "How can I?—when you don't really want me to. You don't really love me a little bit."

"Love's such a great thing," he said. "It's dangerous to use the great names."

"There," she said. "You see. You don't care—or you couldn't talk like that."

She knew now what it was to have the wine of life offered in a cup to which she could not bring herself to put her lips.

"No, thank you," she said bitterly.

Then for the first time he looked at her.

"My beautiful Rose," he said. "I do love you. But I don't want to love you too much. I want to keep my head for my work. Oh yes, I love you, and you must know it; just as I know you love me. Promise that you'll marry me, and nothing shall come between us."

And still she would not take the cup.

"If you really mean it," she said, "you can ask me again in—oh, in June, and I'll tell you then."

"No," said he, "that's not a game I can play, Rose; and it's a game you couldn't play either. Oh, I'm so tired. Be good to me. I know I've told you in a silly sort of way. But I want you more than anything."

Suddenly he was kneeling beside her, and her arms went round his neck.

"This is worth everything," he said, "to come home to this."

"And," he said presently, "there's no more worry about money—I'm rich, rich, rich! No more work that we don't want to do. Only the real things of life, the work we want to do. What's the matter?" For she had moved uneasily.

"Nothing," she said, and stroked his hair gently; "only everything's so different from what you'd think it would be."

But in her heart, she was remembering the crystal and the prophecy that had already come true. And she remembered the warning and his face as she had seen it in the crystal.

"Let me look at you," she said, and he raised his face. But it did not look as the face had looked which had, from the crystal, gazed answering love into her eyes.

CHAPTER 7

The Day After

"It's a beastly shame," Bats was saying: "you don't care two pence about her. You told me you didn't."

"I never did. I do care very much," said Drelincourt shortly.

"Not you. You were wishing you could do something for her. When you got your miserable money you thought—'Hullo! I can make her Lady Drelincourt and give her diamonds.'"

"Shut up," said Anthony.

"Oh, don't I see it," said Bats, his back to the laboratory fire. "You went away feeling gloomy—you grew gloomier. The gloomy fit culminated in an access of sentiment, and you're going to tie that glorious girl to a dead fish. You're no better."

Drelincourt laughed.

"No good, my dear chap. I have the prize. You may have the grumble. It's only fair. I have love, money, and the opportunity of work. What more can anyone want? But if you're interested in psychology—allow me to adopt the classic manner. I am, as you say, formed by nature to attract young ladies. My path of life is, as you justly remark, strewn with the victims of my fatal beauty. Haughty, unresponsive, I pass on my way heedless of the broken hearts which encumber it. It's quite difficult, as you say, to avoid treading on some of them. But their sufferings are nothing to me. I see, far above me, a star, and worship it. One day when I am feeling rather lost and pathetic, I have a sudden access of mad courage and faith. I call to the star, and it slides down the ladder of its own rays and permits me to call it mine. There you have the whole thing."

"Rot!" said Bats, very much disturbed. It was the morning after Anthony's return, and the "two men were at the end of a late breakfast. "You told me the night before you went away—"

"Surely a man may mask his most sacred emotions even from you?"

"You don't kid me," said Bats. "And it's not fair to the girl."

"She thinks it is."

"She won't think so long."

"Does it occur to your super-sensitive mind," Anthony asked, "that if anything's not fair to her it's our talking her over like this?"

"I'm not talking her over. I'm talking you over. Don't you see—I want her to be happy? And she won't be, with you."

"She thinks she will."

"She won't think so long," said Bats again. "When are you going to be married?"

"Quite soon. There's nothing to wait for."

The fire-flame flickered, and tobacco smoke circled quietly above the dialogue. Bats was silent a moment.

"Look here," he spoke with a hesitation unusual to him, and new in this talk. "Look here. I don't want to shove my oar in. But will you wait—only wait? Don't spoil her life just because you happen to have felt that you could help her *not* to spoil it."

"If you're asking me to give her up," said Drelincourt.

"Don't be an ass. Of course, I don't want you to give her up. Just wait. Don't announce the engagement. She won't be keen on announcing it."

"Won't she?"

"No—she'll be only too glad to keep the beautiful secret a secret; at least I should think that's how a girl would feel about it."

"Well?"

"Well—that's all. If you'd only not announce the engagement. And don't get married for six months. In six months, you'll both know where you are. If she still thinks she wants you, then—well, anyway you'll both know your own minds for certain. You see—you may protest till you're black in the face, but I know you don't love her."

"And I know I do," said Drelincourt quietly. "Look here. Did it ever strike you as odd that I'm twenty-five, and I've never had a love-affair-not the ghost of one?"

"It has been the talk of the schools."

"No—rotting apart. I'm not the sort of man that catches fire as the rest of you seem to do. I simply don't understand it. I'm not sure that it isn't just the literary influence with you others. The Romeo and Juliet business, you know. I'm simply not there. It's in another world to the one I live in. If there really is that sort of love, and the poets haven't just invented it—well, the capacity for it was left out of me—that's all. And Rose isn't silly in that sort of way either. She's always had heaps of men at her feet, and kept them there. And I believe she and I are the normal people, and the desperate flaming wild passionate business is all moonshine out of the poets. I never cared two pence for anyone but Rose. She never cared two pence for anyone but me."

"That's true enough."

"And we're perfectly contented and perfectly happy."

"Humph!" said William Bats. "But all the same I do see there's something in what you say. You know mine's a trade that teaches patience. One can never hurry. One must always be quite sure. But, then, I can't suggest waiting—to her. But if she *should* suggest it, I'll agree. I can't say more. And the same about announcing the engagement. But I don't think she *will* suggest it; I think you're wrong about that."

"Perhaps I am," Bats admitted. "Anyhow, it's well there's no more to be said. You know I wish you happiness, and all that sort of thing."

"Yes," said Drelincourt. "Yes—and I say, it's all right your saying what you did. I don't mind; I know it's just out of decent feeling and all that. But— We'll not talk about her again, do you mind? It doesn't seem straight somehow."

"I don't want to talk about her. I've said all I've got to say. And too much, I expect. Well, I must get back to work. And you'll be going to see her, of course."

"Ought I to? So soon?"

Bats laughed aloud.

"Go over and say good morning, you old owl," he said. "And take her some flowers or something."

"Flowers don't grow here, you know; at least, not profusely," Anthony reminded him.

"Well, take her a culture or an ion or an electron or a guinea-pig's ear, or whatever your sort finds as a gift for his fair. And if you can't find anything else, take her your invaluable self, and say you've not been able to sleep for thinking how happy you are."

"She wouldn't believe me," said Drelincourt.

"No," said his friend. "I shouldn't be surprised if she didn't. I'm off. Goodbye."

Drelincourt went across to Rose's little house. He kissed her with respectful tenderness, and asked her if she had slept well. It was the first commonplace that occurred to him.

"Not very," she admitted. "I was thinking about you."

"That was very dear of you."

She smiled.

"Now look here, Tony," she said. "We're engaged to be married, it's true; but you're under no contract to make those sort of speeches to me. Let's go out in the boat, and I'll tell you my ideas about being engaged and married, and all that."

They went out, and between blue March sky and black Thames water they threaded the boat's way among moored ships and slow stately barges, and the little busy dangerous tugs that were everywhere.

"Now," he said, shifting his oars in a quiet place between two empty barges high and sheltering to the water between.

"Well, then. I want it to go on just exactly as we have been doing. I want to keep it all to ourselves just for a little."

"You do?" he said, astounded by this proof of the insight of Bats.

"Yes—we won't tell anyone——"

"I've told Bill."

"Oh, Bill doesn't count. Tell him not to tell the others. They'll have quite enough to amuse them with your pretty money and your pretty estates without this."

"It's just as *you* like, of course," he told her. "And when shall we be married? It was June we said last night, wasn't it?"

"Was it? But I've been thinking. Wouldn't it be jollier just to go on as we are till you've finished the great experiment—it is nearly done, isn't it? and then we could go off to Rome, or Venice, or China, or Peru, or somewhere, and see the big round world."

"Would you really like that best?" he asked.

"Yes, much. But, Tony, I see a sort of strained stupidness growing on you. You feel that you've got to behave as though you were engaged, and you don't know how exactly. And if you keep that up, you'll be unbearable. You see, we've been chums for ages. I don't want to lose all that just because we've decided to get married someday. I want to go on being chums, and for you only to remember we're engaged when you—when you want very much to remember it. See."

"You've arranged it all very neatly. You have a talent for arranging things."

"And you haven't. That's why we ought to get on. We always have got on, haven't we?"

If her tone was wistful, there was no one to hear it except Anthony, and he did not. He said—

"Get on is hardly the term. You've been the light of my life from the beginning."

"That's better," she said. And they both laughed. "I like you to say things like that, that sound nice and that we both know the other one knows is nonsense."

"Is that grammar?" he asked.

"Good enough for my humble needs. What's the good of grammar so long as people understand what you say? And let's just go on with our work just as usual. And you mustn't come to see me in the mornings, and—oh, Tony! do you really care about me at all?"

"You know I do," he answered, and laid his hand in hers. The most impassioned lover could have done little more in such a moment.

"If you found you'd found out that you didn't, you'd tell me, wouldn't you?" she asked, and this time he heard the wistful note.

"I should hasten to you at once with the glad news," he assured her; "even calling in the morning for the purpose. Rose of the world, your fur is trailing in the water."

"Then it's all settled."

"Yes; all settled. Beautifully settled. Only it won't really be like that. Going on as we did before, I mean; because I've got to go down and take possession of my Ancestral Halls. And then there'll be a week or two of the settled part. And then my experience will be complete. And then you'll come and stay at the A.H. Shall we ask the Septet?"

"That would be ripping," she asserted rather than admitted. "But you'll be having County Families there, won't you? Aren't chaperons *de rigueur* in those exalted circles which my Lord is going to move in?"

"There *is* a chaperon," he said; "at least there's a Lady Blair, a second cousin once removed of mine, who kept house for my uncle—she's still there."

"What *is* a second cousin once removed?"

"Lady Blair is. I could show you exactly with pencil and paper, or with bits of bread if we were at dinner, but not in the Muddy Duck."

"I hope she'll not be very harsh. Titles are so alarming. I suppose they're really almost human, like monkeys, these lords and ladies. But I always feel that you and I and all the rest of the human people are somewhere halfway between the English Aristocracy and the apes—don't you think? I expect they look on villa-dwellers as we do on Zoo-dwellers, and now you're going to be one of them."

"You wander in your speech," he said. "I am neither lord nor monkey-a mere laboratory dweller. Wigram & Bucks think Lady Blair eccentric, if that's any comfort to you. Anyhow, if you don't like her, we'll send her off, and import a tame chaperon from the British Museum Reading Room." "What a lot of jolly things one could do with money," she mused. "Just think of one of those poor old dears who live in one room and go to the Museum in the winter, to save fires. You know they spend half the time in the ladies' cloak-room gossiping together. Just think of one of them if a glorious Apollo of a chemist came suddenly up to them, when they were crumbling buns in bags in the Assyrian Gallery, and said: 'Madam, pardon the intrusion. I am Sir Anthony Drelincourt, and I venture to ask whether you would be disposed to undertake the duties of housekeeper at Drelincourt at a salary of one hundred pounds a year, beer and washing found.' It would be almost enough to make one endure having her there afterwards—just the sight of her face when you said it."

"I think I hope it mayn't come to that. Lady Blair's face when I introduced her supplanter might be less alluring."

"But she'll have to go some time, I suppose?"

"When we're married," he said. "Yes, of course. I forgot that."

The pause was imperceptible to him that divided his words from her next ones, which were—

"How glorious it is out here. Look at the water—it looks like an enchanted river of silver—and everything is so clearly drawn—I should like to stay here all day."

"Why not?" said he.

"Because there's work to do," she answered gaily, "paid work, Tony. Oh, I forgot that doesn't appeal to you now. I've got some illustrations to finish, and back we go, alas!"

He put out the sculls. "I've got a lot of things on too," he said, "but we'll have tea together, shall we? May I come?"

"Of course," she said. And they rowed back along the silver river to Malacca Wharf.

Chapter 8
Mystery

The law business took longer than anyone expected. And it was not till May that Anthony Drelincourt went down to the house where his father had been born. But thanks to Messrs. Wigram & Bucks, who not only consented to advance cash for present expenses but positively pressed loans upon him, Anthony passed the month of April very pleasantly. He worked hard, but the play time that lay between the work times was a very different play time to any he had ever had. He was able to take cabs now, taxi-cabs which Rose adored. The modern drama was now accessible from the stalls instead of from the gallery. One could dine, take Rose to dine, which was much more important, instead of merely eating. Also, one could buy clothes, and one did.

"You know," Rose said quite early in the engagement, "you ought to get some new clothes *now*. Then you won't be bran-new when you go down."

"Some of them will, if I get many; though, of course, I might wear three suits at a time, to try and shab them a little before I display them to the lynx eyes of Lady Blair."

"Oh," she said, "I expect even the aristocracy have new clothes *sometimes*. They must, if you come to think of it; or, perhaps, their valet or valets wear them first to take the newness off. By the way, Tony, you ought to have a valet."

"The question is," he put it to her, "is one bound to do just as all other baronets do? Or can one still live one's own life when one has ceased to be Mr. and become Sir Anthony? I only ask for information."

"If it was me," she told him, "I should try doing as they do—just to show them you know how."

"But I don't," he interrupted.

"And, then, if you don't like it, you can always start living your own life at any moment.You must get some clothes, Anthony; let's go and buy some *now*."

"Even at my worst I have not bought reach-me-downs," he said. "Men's clothes are not 'bought,' my child.They are ordered. From the most expensive tailors, I presume," he added dreamily. "And hats are built."

"I didn't mean dull coats and hats," she said, "but the nice things. Ties and socks and dressing-cases, and Gladstone bags and interesting shirts, with violet and green stripes, and the ties and socks match, you know, like Americans."

"Do Americans match?"

"Yes—come along.You know the shop—in Shaftesbury Avenue." They were in Regent Street.

"If I allow you to come and see me buy my socks and ties, you must let me buy you something first. A quiet little tiara now, just to wear of a morning?"

"The very thing!" she said, and they stood gazing in at the window where the diamonds lie and look more beautiful on their cream-coloured velvet beds than ever they will on the mottled necks of the aged rich for whom they are so largely designed.

"There's one thing I would like," she said. "I'll have it instead of the tiara, if you don't mind."

"What is it? Come to think of it, I've never bought you anything, except things to eat."

"And rides in cabs. I want a ring!"

"An engagement ring! Idiot! Of course, I ought to have come with that in my pocket that night. Come along in," he said eagerly.

He would have bought her half-a-dozen of the bright circlets displayed. But she drew back.

"There's one at a shop in Vigo Street," she said; "an old one—I'd rather have that. And it's got *A.D.* inside it, and 1866. And *A.D.* stands for you."

"As well as for the year of our Lord. Come on.What stone is it?"

"It's greeny, with diamonds round. It's rather expensive," she told him.

It was a beryl, set as she had said. And he bought it without asking the price, which was less than he expected.

"Thank you very, very," she said, walking down the street beside him pulling on her glove.

"It was idiotic of me not to get you a ring off my own bat," he said; "but, you see, I've never been engaged before. And it was much jollier to get you something you really liked than to come along like a roaring Jew, oozing diamonds from every pore. All the same—"

Then they went and bought ties and socks, and trunks and portmanteaus, and suit-cases and dressing-cases, and things like that.

"Let's get second-hand bags and boxes," she said. "You simply *mustn't* look new all over."

A fortnight later he brought her a necklace that he had had made for her.

"I got the idea of it out of that book you gave me. Bats read it to me. All the stones mean something. And the lot of them bring luck—so they say; you'll live and die loving and beloved. Only you mustn't ever take it off. I ought to have it welded on, oughtn't I?"

"And about that 'valet or valets," she said, the day before he left for Drelincourt. "How does one get a valet?"

"You really insist?"

"I do."

This time they were in Soho.

"There are registry offices in Charlotte Street. Oh!"

"Yes?"

"Mr. Abrahamson said there was a young man who was devoted to me. It would be nice if your valet or valets were devoted to me, wouldn't it?"

"I really don't think I want one."

"Nonsense," she insisted, "you simply must. We'll go to old Abrahamson, and ask who it is."

The old bookseller looked at them Over his spectacles with wise eyes.

"So?" he said.

"Yes," said Rose. "I must tell *you*, but we aren't telling anyone else yet. Mr. Abrahamson told my fortune, Tony, and he foretold—you!"

"I wish you every happiness," said the Jew very quietly.

"Thank you," they said. And told why they had come.

The valet was that same young Sebastien who had risked and lost his fifty *centimes*, and had called on the saints for the sake of Rose Royal. And he was still in the hands of the patron of the Hôtel Simplon—very deeply in, for he owed him a month's pension.

He flushed a deep pink when he entered the large oilcloth carpeted room with the bent-wood chairs, where clients and servants meet and engage, or do not engage.

"I remember you," said Rose. "You picked up some parcels for me one day in the mud."

"*Au service*," said Sebastien, red to the ears.

"*Ce Monsieur*," said Rose, "wants a valet."

"*Au service*," said Sebastien, and ten minutes later Sebastien, alone, in his mean little bedroom, agonised with relief, gratitude, and romantic joy, was informing Saints Ursula, Agnes, and Sebastien that, thanks entirely to their good offices, he was now free of the Hotel Simplon, and was, moreover, devoted to the service of *Monsieur*, who was himself devoted to the service of *Mademoiselle*.

And so, it was Sebastien who travelled with Anthony when first he went to Drelincourt.

He wrote to Rose:

It was rummer than rum, going down first-class, and all the station people behaving like worms. I'm not sure I like it. There was a glorious creature in top-boots touching a hat I should be proud to be seen with—and a 'bang-up horse in a slap-up dog-cart,' and village people ducking and touching foreheads. And the lodge-gates—more ducking from an old woman—a green park, trees just coming out. You'd love it. One of those parks like billiard tables, with trees like cauliflowers. And then the house—a dream, a long terrace with urns, rather like the picture of Sir Leicester's place in Lincolnshire.

A being at the door to welcome me. (I wish I could overcome my nervous terror of butlers. I don't even know the thing's name yet.) Rows of servants to welcome me. At the end of the row a little lady like a Dresden shepherdess grown old, gracefully holding out two perfect little hands to welcome me.

'Lady Blair,' I said—not another word. 'Second cousin once removed,' I added. 'Thank Heaven, you're not the hag I have sometimes feared you might be,' or other words to that effect.

'*You're* not such a bounder as I was afraid you might be,' she answered (or words to that effect).

Then (when she had dissipated the cloud of footmen and things) we had tea. She is quite an old dear. You'll like her. And no old museum rat will ever get the surprise we planned for her. I am writing this at a Buhl table in a library sixty feet long. The inkstand is silver, and this pen the worst I have ever used. Sebastien has disappeared. I suppose he's all right. He knows a valet's place well enough. I only wish I knew a baronet's. But Lady Blair will see me through. I wish you were here. I want to talk to you. It's rather fine, you know, this coming back to the Ancestral Hall. I shall have a lab. fitted up here, and finish the experiment. It only went wrong last time through my having to go and answer that advertisement. But this time I really shall pull it off. My beautiful Rose, I never wanted you as much as I do at this moment.

More tomorrow. A howling dervish of a gong has just said, 'Get dressed, you scientific outsider, and dine with the really select.'

Goodbye—   Your Tony.

P.S.—My beautiful Rose, I do hope I'm not getting too fond of you.

"Not you," said Rose, as she refolded the letter. "'He seems extraordinarily gay," she told herself. "I think he's only really fond of me when he's very happy or very miserable. The rest of the time it's all habit." She thought a minute, twisting the letter in her fingers, "Anyhow," she said, "I'm the only one. If he doesn't care for me, he doesn't care for anyone. It's the second best. But if there is no best. . . . Don't be an idiot."

She fingered the necklace softly for a moment and then sat down to write to her lover.

He wrote again the next day:—

It's all very like a dream. Lady Blair does not appear till the middle of the day I spent my morning with my agent—me with an agent!—a Balliol man of agreeable exterior and perfect manners. He hardly showed at all that I corresponded in no particular with his idea of a baronet.

We drove round the estate. If my grandfather had not broken his neck hunting, I should have been able to ride a horse like any other fool. However, that can be mended. But it will be years before I know my own farms and fields.

It was jolly to get your note this morning.

Lady Blair appeared at luncheon—fresh and smiling as the dawn. Afterwards we walked on the terrace in the sunshine, and she told me family stories. We seem to have been the rummest lot! One of the ancestors, it seems, was a friend of Bill's friend, Bacon. There's a picture of him in a ruff in the picture gallery. Did I tell you there was a P.G.? But I can't tell you the half of it. I can't begin to tell you—you must come and see. Lady Blair has the most beautiful manners in the world, except perhaps the butler's. I have found out his name, and I feel weighted with so great a knowledge. His name is Wilkes.

There is a secret staircase, only it's no secret, though I thought it was when I found it. It ended in Wilkes' room, and he was reading the *Daily Mail* in his shirt sleeves. I felt as though I had caught a bishop without his gaiters. He was smoking a cigar when I tumbled in on him. He forgave me at once. What noble natures these butlers have! I could never have forgiven anyone who had found me without my halo.

The agent is coming to dinner tonight. You should see the drawing-room; it's as big as a barn, with cabinets, and sofas, and tables, and Chinese vases as big as you are, and Chinese cabinets as big as pianos. And the windows go up to the ceiling, and the curtains are brocade-the sort of stuff most people make dresses of.

I haven't told Lady Blair about you yet. But I shall tomorrow, and arrange about your coming home. I still feel as though it were her house, not mine. She is most awfully decent to me, and I like her. She talks awfully well. Chooses her words like that American girl. I expect it comes of being seventy-two, as she tells me she is. She looks any age you please down to thirty. I had no idea old ladies could be so nice to talk to. Tea.—More later.

Later.—I am not suspicious, as you know; but I have just told her about you, because she was telling me more than I could endure how charming some Emmeline or other is, and I find the Emmeline is her niece. She said I must marry well. Then she talked about hunting, and then she talked about archery and the days of her youth, and the Empress Eugénie; and then she got back to Emmeline. But I wasn't going to have any more Emmeline. So, I just told her. She was quite nice, but—*surprised.* I can't think why. Ought I to have told her right away?

My beautiful Rose, I shall write to you every day. I never wanted you so much.

Everything I have ever done and been seems long ago and far away—even my work. No, that doesn't express it. It's really more as though I were taking part in a charade. I feel like somebody else.

And that doesn't express it either.

I'm horribly glad all this is mine-and yours; and yet I feel that I have perhaps sold my soul. We've always been so down on rich people. And now I'm rich myself. I don't know what I mean or what I feel, except that I feel rather as a kettle must the first time it boils. Things will settle down presently, and I shall be able to think again and to work. Just now I only know that I wish everyone had all this. Only of course they can't have. It's very difficult. Will you and the others come down next week?

Another letter fits in here:—

Dear Rose of the World,—Here's a go ! It's only ten o'clock, but I must write to you. What do you think? Mysteries of Udolpho! Drelincourt, the Home of Mystery! But I'll tell you from the beginning.

Your letter came this morning. The excellent Sebastien—you were quite right, I should never have got on without him-brought it up when he called me.

I read it before I dressed, and I took it to the window because the room is very large and dark and the bed miles from the window. It's a big bed, like a four-post hearse. And the sun was jolly, and the park like a fire-new toy out of a box for a giant baby; and I read your letter and put it on the window ledge, and went to my bath. There's a bathroom opening out of my bedroom; Sebastien turns on the water and hovers with warm towels. But everything is simply the Lap Of.

When I came back from the bath your letter was nowhere to be seen. (That's the dramatic, mysterious touch; eh, what?)

So, of course, I looked for it all about the room. Nowhere! Then the awful truth flashed across me—it must have flown out of the window. There was a pretty strong wind blowing, and no doubt when the bathroom door was opened . . . you see? Your letter, blowing about the terrace for the under-gardener to read! (Bear up. It wasn't really, but I thought it was.)

I dressed like the wind (does it?) and flew down. Your letter was not on the terrace nor among the flowerbeds. I looked and looked. I was just going in to enlist Sebastien in a search party when I saw something white sticking in the ivy under my window.

What could it be? My style is getting too dramatic—I mean, of course, it was your letter. So, I went through the shrubs and tried to reach up to it. No go!

So, then I started to climb up the ivy. It was very strong and old, and quite easy going. And I got your letter all right.

And then I noticed—now I'm coming to it—a ridge of stone, and the ivy not quite so thick. A bit of it came away in my hand, but I was holding on by the other hand all right.

And then I saw—what do you think?

But I cannot wait for you to guess. It was a window ledge, the stone ridge, and above it a window boarded up.

Then when I'd got down, I looked up at that place where the ivy grew so thickly. In fact, in the symmetry of that side of the Ancestral Hall a window is missing. Of course, I went in at once to see which it was.

But Wilkes caught me in the hall, and I was ashamed not to have breakfast. I felt he knew all about my letter. I had asked a gardener if he had seen it.

But after breakfast!—Oh, I asked Wilkes what window it was that had been boarded up. And he said, 'None in my time, Sir Anthony.'

And he's been here twenty-two years!

And I can't ask Lady Blair till she comes down, can I? It's a glorious mystery. I did wish you were here.

Because I explored the house, and there does really seem to be a lump *missing* between the library and the outside. Only the house is such an odd shape—it's been built on to at odd times, you know. It was an abbey once, and every Drelincourt since Henry VIII.'s time seems to have added his little bit. I'll finish this when I've seen Lady Blair, and found out if there really is anything.

Later.

It's a much more glorious mystery than I thought. I've explored a bit more, and I'm practically certain there *is* a bit missing, just where that window is, outside. And I've asked Lady Blair. And here I insist on being dramatic.

ME. 'What is that window that was blocked up?'

HER. 'What window?'

ME. 'Just below my room.'

HER. 'Surely you are mistaken. There are no windows there.' (And she has known the house ever since she was a kiddie.)
ME. 'But surely——'
HER. 'There's nothing but ivy and the wall. The house, you know, is very irregularly built.'
ME. 'Yes. I see. Thank you.'
End of dramatic bit.

But I don't really see at all, of course: I don't see why she doesn't know about the window. And if she does know, I don't know why she doesn't want me to know. As Mr. Edgar Jepson would say, 'It partakes of the nature of the distinctly rum.' I don't know, as I say. But I'm going to know. Oh, Rose, it only wanted this. I had everything else—and now, in my own house, I've got life's crowning joy—a mystery!—Yours exultantly,

A. D.

P.S.—I've just read this over. I seem to have felt jolly when I wrote it. But I've been fumbling round all the afternoon, and now I somehow feel as though I'd just as soon the house knew its own mind, and reconciled its inside with its outside. '*You* don't know your own mind,' I hear you say. True. I don't.

CHAPTER 9

The Great Discovery

"It's no use," Linda Smith told Esther Raven; "it can't be the same again ever. I wish it hadn't happened."

The two were the first arrivals at Rose's house with the window-boxes. They had found a paper on the door, and the paper said—

To the Septet.
Gone to buy things.
La clef dans le
usual endroit.

And they had found the key wedged between window-box and brick and let themselves in, and taken their hats off and re-arranged their hair.

"*I* wish it hadn't happened," said Esther, "and a couple of spiteful cats we are to wish it. And of course, things'll never be the same. Why should they? The Septet was too nearly the Real Right thing to last. I knew something would happen, but I didn't think it would be this."

"What did you think it would be?"

"An engagement of course. It always is an engagement that breaks up Societies."

"But who? Rose and Anthony?"

"Not much," said Esther scornfully; "he doesn't care for anything but his chemical rubbish."

"Who then?" Linda asked.

"Oh, Rose and the Outsider—or you and Bats. Or me and the whole lot of them—how should I know?"

"I should have thought Rose and Anthony—" Linda persisted.

"Then you'd have thought wrong," said Miss Raven shortly. "One has to notice things if one writes—and I tell you if I had a thousand a year to be paid so long as Rose and Anthony weren't engaged, I should feel that I'd got it for life."

"I wonder!" Linda was busy with a strip of red and green embroidery. She always filled up odd waiting moments with embroidery, and carried a thimble in her pocket, as our grandmothers used to do. "I hope it never does happen. I hope they never *will* get engaged."

"Why?" Esther asked sharply.

"Because they wouldn't be happy. At least I don't think so."

"They'd be as happy as most people, I suppose," said Esther.

"I sometimes think," Linda went on, very intent on her work, "that Anthony's different from other people."

"Of course, he is: we all are."

"No—but really different from all of us. Like a changeling, you know. Perhaps he is a changeling."

"Perhaps you're a goose," said Esther. "I'm sorry he won't be here. He's come more regularly lately."

"Yes," said Linda.

"But of course," Esther added, "we can't expect him to be keen on a two-penny-halfpenny Septet when he's got an income, and estates, and a title, and all that."

"Anyone would think you grudged it—only, of course I know you don't."

"How do you know I don't?" Esther flamed out; "because I do. I want it much more than he does. So, do you. Why should he have everything? He was all right. He was doing the work he wanted to do-he loves his work. Now I hate mine, and you hate yours. We ought to have had it."

"Or Rose, or William, or the doctor?"

"No, they've all got what they like to do. It's you and I that are out in the cold. As for Rose, she's a beauty and she has a settled income, and she does the work she likes doing, and she doesn't know how bad her work is. What more does she want? I call that being in Heaven. I hate my work—and I know how bad it is. And when she falls in love, she'll get the man she wants by just holding up her little finger. Now you and I——"

"Thank you," said Linda with decision, "speak for yourself. I don't want to hear about what won't happen when I hold up my little finger, because I never shall. As for Rose—she's a darling, and I hope she'll get the man she wants, if she ever does want one!"

"Loyal and deserving Linda! Of course, she's a darling. But all the same, if I didn't love her so much, I should hate her."

From which it will be seen that the secret of the betrothal of the occupants of Malacca Wharf had been well kept.

"I don't know what you mean," said Linda, deeply loyal.

"No—but Rose will. Here she comes. Rose!" she called, as the door opened, "I was just saying that if I didn't love you so much, I should hate you."

"It sounds very subtle. How are you?" said Rose, coming in with many parcels. "Yes, awfully subtle and clever. So clever, that I'm sure it's been used half a dozen times already. So, don't put it in one of your stories as a novelty. The answer to the subtlety is, 'Of course, dear, you would—that's the only real basis for friendship,' and the subtler in the book is always frightfully impressed."

"I am," Esther owned, "and here comes William looking like a Scilly gardener with daffodils in both hands."

"Coals to—" Esther said; "look at her flower beds."

The narrow borders had put on the pink and yellow and white and blue pattern that bulbs are meant to make.

"I don't often make floral offerings," Bats said, "and when I saw your flower beds I felt—well, there!"

"You can't have too much of a good thing," said Rose, "and that's another clever thing that's been used before, so you can't have it for your book, Esther. You get the table ready while I put the flowers in water."

The Septet was met to tell of the outcome of its advertisement, but the only advertisement that has anything to do with the story was the one answered by Anthony Drelincourt. But the recountal of the others' answerings made the evening a merry one.

Rose, as Ruler of the Feast, decided that the Tales of the Adventures of the Advertisement Answerers was enough event for one evening, and when she had served coffee, they all went across the yard and down to the wharf, and packed themselves into the long round-nosed punt.

"Is there room?" Mullinger asked, "because really I don't a bit mind if I sit here and smoke. I can read, too. 'A book of verses underneath the bough—'"

"I'm sure you *can* read. But you needn't. There's room for eight or nine of you if you only sit still. The Muddy Duck's as fine a craft as there is on the river," said the doctor, who had a boat about twenty-five feet long which he called a yacht, and had sailed to Flanders in—his proudest achievement.

"What an evening!" said Mullinger. "Anthony ought to be here."

"Anthony," said Esther Raven, "is in the lap of luxury, and lost to us forever. And I think there ought to be a new rule. Nobody ought ever to say they wish someone else was here. It's a reflection on present company."

"It wouldn't be a bad rule for *all* parties of pleasure—not just the Septet," said Rose. "Let's go up the river and look at the sky."

"Then the doctor and Mullinger can't see it if they're rowing," said Bats perversely.

"Oh, but the sky is just as beautiful the other way, you know," Mullinger hastened to protest; "look at the rosy flush in the north—not by eastern windows, only, you know."

So, they went upstream singing harmoniously, which is unusual in those waters, charming the ears of all such masters of small craft as were not, at that hour, too drunk for appreciation. And a man has to be very drunk indeed not to appreciate good singing-in fact, up to a certain point, the drunker the more appreciative. When it grew dusk, they rigged a spare scull as a mast, and hung a big red and gold and blue Chinese lantern upon it, and so back along the gleaming, darkling, dirty, beautiful river, singing the last song. You know it, of course. It is the first effort of every young glee club. But even that cannot spoil its beauty. Let us have it from the beginning as six of the Septet had it that April night:—

> O who will o'er the Downs so free,
> O who will with me ride,
> O who will up and follow me
> To win a blooming bride?

Her father he has locked the door,
Her mother keeps the key,
But neither bolts nor bars shall keep
My own true love from me.

I saw her bower at break of day,
'Twas guarded safe and sure;
I saw her bower at twilight hour,
'Twas guarded then no more.
The varlets they were all asleep,
And there was none to see
The greeting fair that passed there
Between my love and me.

I promised her to come again
With comrades brave and true,
A gallant band with sword in hand
To break her prison through.
I promised her to come at night—
She's waiting now for me;
And ere the dawn of morning light
I'll set my true love free.

And ere the dawn of morning light
I'll set my true love free,

The voices repeated in the darkness, and with the last "free" the punt bumped against the rotting timber of the wharf with the neat simultaneousness that was Rose's pride.

"It's the most romantic place," said Mullinger, holding the boat steady for the others to disembark. "I always think of 'Magic casements opening on the foam' when I see the lights in Drelincourt's windows. But tonight, it's all dark and deserted."

And on the word came a voice from the darkness quite near the boat. "Hullo," it said—"Hullo, you strayed revellers!"

And Anthony came forward into the circle of the lantern's light.

"Hullo, Drelincourt, that you?" Mullinger asked.

"Your acute surmise is correct. I say, Rose, I've got a fire. And something to tell you. Come along up to my place all of you, if Rose doesn't mind my collaring her party."

They went up, praised the fire, and clamoured for the news.

"In a minute," said Anthony. "You'll be surprised, I warn you."

Rose wondered what he was going to say. It couldn't be—? But of course not. She wondered how she should feel if he were to say, "I can't keep it to myself any longer. Rose and I are going to be married. At once." And then explain to her afterwards that he could not—absolutely could not—live without her any longer.

"Ladies and gentlemen," he said, "I propose that you should drink my health in champagne, which I went all the way to the Three Nuns to get. Today is, so to speak, the birthday of my life."

Again, Rose wondered.

"There is a corkscrew with a spike," he went on, "somewhere about. Bats will know where. And the doctor has in his knife one of those useful things for taking stones out of horses' feet with. And here's the champagne," he said, suddenly producing a large brown paper parcel.

"I thought the birthday of your life was the day you came into your money," said the doctor through the rustling of brown paper and straw. "I know it would have been mine."

"Not at all," Anthony assured him; and then a cork popped, and there were no glasses ready, and the wine foamed over and fell on the floor, and Bats wiped it up.

"That's unlucky, isn't it?" Mullinger asked—

If you spill your pot of beer,
Then your luck will disappear.

"On the contrary," said Anthony, "it's the luckiest thing in the world. (And besides this isn't beer, is it?) It's a libation to the gods of the laboratory. Most appropriate. Take beakers, if there aren't enough glasses. In fact, we'll all have beakers. That's appropriate too."

He spoke with a sort of quick joy that was not gaiety. His eyes were very bright, and his face very pale.

"Now," he went on, "I want you all to drink my health 'blind,' so to speak. I mean without knowing why it's the birthday of my life, and all that."

"Right O!" said Bats, standing up with the beaker in his hand. "Let us drink to the health of the mysterious but amiable Anthony Drelincourt—long life and happiness!"

"May fortune always smile on him," said Linda.

"May he live long and die happy," said the doctor.

"Success in life and love," Mullinger said—

May all the gifts the gods can send,
Ever upon his path attend.

"May he always have exactly what he wants," said Esther.

"May he always have exactly what he deserves," said Bats.

("Not that," said Anthony quickly.)

"May all his experiments succeed," said Rose, and, rounding off the chorus, "Long life and happiness!"

"Then they drank, and immediately began to shout "Speech! Speech!""

Anthony, holding his untasted bumper, raised it and stood up, facing the half circle of his friends, who still held their empty glasses.

"Ladies and gentlemen," he began, "the subject on which I have been asked to address you this evening is one which—oh, hang it all! It's only that—this time it's come off!"

"What?" said everyone but Rose and Bats. Rose said nothing, and Bats said, "The experiment?"

"Yes, the experiment. I've found out what I wanted to know. The thing's there. Done. Complete. Irrefutable. The time I went away—yes, it's all right."

They were crowding round him, proffering handshakes.

"Yes; when I had to go away, I thought everything would go to pot. Instead, it just quietly went on—and came out right. I was too impatient. I should never have done it if I hadn't been forced to leave it alone and give it a chance. And now it's done. It's the real right thing. And I'm the greatest man since Harvey—I'm not sure that Harvey's in the same field with me, if you come to that."

There was a murmur, inarticulate, congratulatory.

"Say you're pleased," Anthony urged. "Say it right out."

More murmurs—louder.

"Of course, we are," said Bats; "but you must allow for our struck-all-of-a-heapness. Look here, we really *are* all of a heap. Mayn't we fill up, and drink, all of us—you too—to your great discovery?"

"To the great discovery!" shouted everyone.

"To the great discovery!" cried Anthony. "I really have done it this time."

"The great discovery!" shouted the six again, raising their beakers.

"And I wonder," five out of the six told themselves as they drank, "whether this time he really has—this time, really, at last, discovered anything?"

The sixth was Rose. As her lips touched the thin glass, she said to her heart: "Yes. It's true. This time he really *has* done it. And he won't want me anymore."

Aloud she said, setting down the beaker: "Aren't we to hear what it is?"

"Oh, it's nothing," said the hero of the hour, setting down his glass with his left hand; "it's nothing much," he repeated lamely.

"Only it's everything," said Rose below her breath, standing by him.

"Yes. But really, it's only— No, I really can't. You wouldn't be interested. It would take too long to explain."

"Isn't it unlucky," Linda asked tactfully, breaking a silence near its beginning, "to drink from your left hand?"

"You were all shaking the other," said the discoverer; "and, besides, I can afford a little ill-luck tonight."

"That's the one thing that the richest man can't afford," said Esther Raven.

"Don't croak," said Drelincourt; "let's get your guitar, Rose, and you can all sing about love and roses and wine."

"If you've discovered anything new about *them*," said Bats, "you are indeed the greatest birth of time. What price Anacreon?"

"Bother Anacreon," said Drelincourt contentedly. "I'll get the guitar."

CHAPTER 10

The Missing Window

In the moment when Anthony Drelincourt knew that the secret was his—the secret for which he had striven so long, so strongly with such a delicate fervour, such an ardour of patience—he ceased to desire more. All the uses to which he had intended to put his discovery seemed now unimportant, puerile. He had attained! That was the one thing that mattered. As one in a dream, he locked the door of that underground room where the knowledge of his triumph had come to him, staggered up the damp, stone steps, and threw himself in the easy-chair in his laboratory. There, for a while, he lay, every muscle relaxed, every nerve quiescent, as a man might lie who has long struggled in deep wild waters, and has been suddenly thrown up by a wave, greater than he had believed any wave to be, on to a shore more tranquil than any shore of which he had ever dreamed.

He had attained to a knowledge that had been hidden since the beginning of time, except for glimpses vague or brief caught by people who had been called mad, and imprisoned—or called wizards, and burned at the stake. He had wedded the "philosophy of the ancients" to modern science. It was as though he had been labouring to bring together the mystic soul of the one and the splendid body of the other. And now here, suddenly, when he had been distracted by weaker and baser adventures, he returned disheartened to his workshop to find that the forces he had set in motion had, in his absence, done that which in his presence they had never done.

The result was achieved; the two were at last made one. The horizon of thought receded. Yet there was no longer room in his world for thought. The glory of his triumph overpowered all else and wrapped him in a warm glow, mellow as midsummer, radiant as sunlight. And the glory slowly ceased, or rather merged in that other, closer, more intimate enfolding of content, which held him as in a predestined nest, soft, warm, and grey as the down of the eider.

And from this he was roused by the voices on the river singing of romance and true love. "Of course, I must tell Rose at once."

He thought of himself sitting there, folding the content and the glory round him, with never a thought of Rose or for her. He clenched his fist, and hit his open left hand with it. He stumbled down his stairs and out across the wharf. The boat was receding.

"You fool," he said, "can't you at least try to behave like other men? How would Mullinger act if he'd found out anything? Well—no—not that exactly, but—Well, anyhow, he'd stand champagne."

He started off across the waste, and came back with the brown paper parcel, took it to the laboratory, lighted fire, and drew curtains. Then he went down to the wharf again. The boat was coming back now. Anthony struck the key to which he felt a successful discoverer and lover should, if he were like other men, seek to attune himself, when he cried aloud—

"Hullo, you strayed revellers!" and hugged himself on his close resemblance to the normal.

★★★★★★

It is not necessary to explain definitely the nature of Anthony's discovery; at this point of the tale it would not even be interesting. He was to use it later. But the need for its use is not yet. For the present, you see him contentedly returning to Drelincourt to prepare the way for his house-party.

Lady Blair met him at the station, wonderfully upright in a very high dog-cart. As he smiled into her old eyes, and pressed her little thick-gloved hand, and thanked her for coming, and climbed up beside her, and watched the groom tuck the driving rug round their knees, he felt that old thrill of pride at the successful way in which he was acting his charade.

"Really, any one would think it was real, almost," he told himself; "it is so very like real life as one has read about it. And yet one knows it's all illusion. No, thank you," he added aloud, to Lady Blair, who, wonderfully girlish in a large hat and white veil, was offering the reins. "I like to see you do it. You do it so beautifully."

"Drive, do you mean?" she asked, flicking a chestnut ear with a very smart whip.

"No, everything," said Anthony, almost expecting the applause of a large audience.

"But you *do* drive, don't you?" she asked.

And he answered soberly—

"No. I have never had the opportunity of acquiring the accomplishment."

"You will enjoy it," she said, smiling and gazing in his eyes at the dangerous crisis of cross roads, a motor, a wood-cart, and a tramp wheeling an old perambulator; "riding too; I am sure you will find that it is what you have longed for always—unconsciously, I mean."

"If these things were heritable, I ought to be an accomplished horseman," he said.

"Of course. And no doubt you will find that it comes naturally to you. Your father—"

"I was thinking of my grandfather," he said, suddenly coming out of the charade. "He broke his neck in the hunting field, you know. Worse luck for me!"

If Lady Blair did not say, "Tut, tut; why drag in your maternal grandfather?" Anthony heard it in her silence.

"You see," he went on suavely, "I owe it to my maternal grandfather that I was not brought up in the workhouse school. My father's people seem to have had no anxieties in that regard."

"My dear Anthony," she said, urging the horse to increased speed by what to Drelincourt seemed occult powers, "if an old woman might venture to advise—

"But of course," he said, "if there were one," and felt himself in the charade once more.

"Let the dead past bury its dead.

"Let dead dogs lie," he emended between his teeth.

"No, let bygones be bygones. When you are married, when you have sons, you will understand better the feelings of a father whose son—of course I know that your dear mother must have been the sweetest thing, the best of women; and your grandfather was prejudiced, no doubt. But it's all over now. Why rake up old grievances? You have Drelincourt, and I know you will be worthy of the Drelincourt tradition. It was your paternal grandfather's misfortune that he could not know this."

"Humph!" said Anthony. And he said it as it is spelt, which is unusual and startling.

"What did you say?" Lady Blair inquired.

"I said, 'Humph!' " Anthony replied. "And I meant Humph! Let me illustrate—Once, when I was travelling abroad, I engaged a sleeping-car. It was very extravagant, but I was mad with overwork."

She frowned ever so slightly, and he laughed with ever so slight a bitterness.

"I apologise for the sordid detail, so unfamiliar to you. But it belongs to the story. I undressed and went to sleep. At Lyons the train stopped—stopped going for good, I mean. It was 'All change.' A very wet night. I got into my clothes as well as I could. But before I was dressed, the officials turned the lights out, and dragged me and my odds and ends on to a swimming black platform. Then the train went away. And I found I had lost my watch and my purse. I carry a purse. I learned from Mr. St. Maur that gentlemen carry their money loose."

"How can you be so silly?" she said; "go on with the story."

"Infuriated by my personal discomfort and pecuniary losses," Anthony went on, warming to his narrative, "I called for those highest in office at the station of Lyons, and I reproached them calmly but firmly. 'I was told,' I said, 'that this train went to Marseilles. I was told three times by three officials of different ranks,' I said, 'that this train went to Marseilles, and, confident of the honour and probity of these officials, I went to bed. Now I find that the train doesn't go to Marseilles. I am turned out on your—I leave the adjective to you—platform. I have lost my watch and my purse, and I feel that I have caught the cold of my life.' They told me that I was mistaken, that no French railway official could have been so lost to all sense of personal honour as to deceive a traveller, especially a *Monsieur* so incontrovertibly *comme il faut* as this one. I replied, 'I have a cold in my head, and your statements are false. Who is the head man, the very top of you all? I will complain to him.' And then they said the thing that makes this tale à *propos* in this moment's crisis. They said—

" 'Oh, *Monsieur*, reflect. Do not complain to the Bureau. Rather

214

put yourself in the place of those unfortunates, those poor deceived officials, who, themselves *trompés*, informed you that your train did not stop till it arrived at Marseilles. Think, *Monsieur*,' they said, with what practically amounted to tears of emotion, 'think what must now be the feelings of those officials of varyingly important position—think of them, *Monsieur*, imagine their chagrin, their dolour, their despair, when they discover that they had deceived themselves in *renseinger-*ing a *Monsieur* so amiable, so distinguished, so entirely as it must!' Well! that's just it. What I felt then was just what I feel now when I hear you pitying my father's father for having been a mean fool."

The cart swung in at the lodge gates, and a woman, two boy children, and a girl child bobbed curtseys and touched forelocks.

"Don't vituperate!" Lady Blair said, managing reins and whip incredibly with one hand while she laid the other on his arm. "Of course, I understand. But one doesn't say those things, you know. All the same, you're wonderful. I didn't at all realise you till now. You have been so mousy, so polite. Do you know, I have always had a haunting feeling that you might perhaps, somehow, at some time, just by accident, as it were, be *too* polite. You don't mind my saying that, do you?"

"I adore your saying that." Anthony was already almost again in the charade.

"I knew you would," she said. "Well, you see, up to now I haven't seen the real *you* at all. You've been more like a character in a book, you know. Not at all like a real person. Or perhaps more like someone who was a real person, trying to pretend that he was a real person of quite a different quality. And now—"

"And now?" Anthony repeated, watching his park unfolding itself like a beautiful and extraordinarily realistic map; "and now—"

"Well-now. I'm sure (which I shouldn't have been yesterday), I'm sure that you'll understand me when I say—there is an infectious quality about your candour, my dear Anthony—when I say that you have originality, strength, personality. You'll do, my dear child, you'll do."

"Shall I?" he threw back. "Shall I? Thank you so much! I did, you know, so dreadfully desire to 'do.'"

"Don't play the Henry James trump," she said surprisingly; "the trick's yours without that."

"Then don't you play the Queen of Snubs. Let my mother's father alone," he said.

"I didn't," Lady Blair answered. "Oh, Anthony, I do wish——"

"What?" he asked. "If it's in my power to grant, it's yours, even to the half of my kingdom."

"What I wish," she told him, "is more than the whole of your kingdom. It's in another dimension."

"Tell me what you wish," he commanded, his eyes on the budding beauty of his new kingdom.

"Shall I?" she asked, and again the bright bay, responding to a signal quite imperceptible to Anthony, bounded forward. "Well, I will. I'm more than seventy. I whisper it because of Oddling sitting there all ears in his top-boots behind us. Because what I'm now going to say is rather in the nature of a love declaration. I wish that I were twenty so that I might marry you."

The charade feeling was overpowering as Anthony answered—

"I wish you were."

"But that's past praying for," said Lady Blair; "however, there are gleanings left. We might try friendship. Halves, and no secrets. I should like to be friends with you. Will you?"

"You're very nice to me today," Anthony said, and the chimneys of Drelincourt shot up through the trees; "let us be friends—to the death."

"Halves, and no secrets," repeated Lady Blair brightly.

"Halves, and no secrets?" he answered. "Right O! Then you'll tell me what the room was that was bricked up. What that boarded-up window belonged to."

The house's face was now plain to see in the gay spring sunshine. And he heard the horse's hoofs plash, plash on the damp gravel, in the little silence that hardly had time to settle before it took flight at her answer.

"Of course, I'll tell you anything. Only in return you must tell me things. About your fair lady, and your dreams and ambitions, and what you feel and what you think you ought to feel."

Anthony suddenly experienced the sensation that a man may know who walks on to a green lawn that looks firm and finds it a quaking morass. He caught at the staff of the Lie Absolute—the staff which looks so firm and which, in the moment of stress, so suddenly desperately betrays.

"I will tell you everything," he said, "everything. You shall be my sole confidant."

"Since that is all I can be to you," the wonderful old lady replied, "that is what I want to be. Perhaps it will save trouble if I explain at once that I have fallen in love with you—deep!"

"I, too," he said, once more lost in the charade, "over heads and ears. I will tell you all the secrets of my soul. And you," he added quite firmly, "you will tell me where that missing room is, and why it was boarded up."

"Of course, I will tell you anything. But as for windows. If there was one it must have been when there was the window-tax. All old houses shut some of their eyes in those days."

"Not with boards," he said; "the taxed windows were bricked up, not boarded."

They drew up in front of the beautiful grey face of Drelincourt. And a pause came like a full stop in their talk.

"Oh, well! Of course, you know best," she said, and the groom took the reins.

"After dinner," he said, in the instant before he alighted, "you will tell me the truth then."

"There isn't anything really," Lady Blair said; "but if we are to be friends, we are."

"And after all, it is my own house," he said, and wondered if he were being ungentlemanly.

"It's our own house," she said, and smiled at him like sweet-and-twenty. "I am a Drelincourt, too, you know."

★★★★★★

Sebastien greeted his master with something approaching enthusiasm, instantly and fervently demanding news of *Mademoiselle*, which they tell me a perfectly trained and newly engaged valet would not have done, nor a master accustomed to valets have tolerated. But Anthony was pleased. He went down to dinner full of interest in Lady Blair and in what she was to tell him. And a very silent-footed man came to him across soft carpets, and told him in a low voice that her ladyship had a slight headache, and begged Sir Anthony to: excuse her. So, he dined alone—and wondered.

And then he sat down in the library and reflected that Lady Blair was probably making up her mind what to tell him, and that the chance of her telling him what he wanted to know was remote. He had a feeling that she would try not to tell him anything that he could use. That she did not want him to know what he wanted to know— ought to know, since it was, after all, his house.

It was now perfectly plain to him that there was a space not accounted for between the library where he sat and the outer wall where the boarded-up window lay, blind under the ivy. Also, it was perfectly plain to him that that window had been boarded up for a reason, and that Lady Blair knew that reason and did not want to tell it.

"But she shall," he told himself.

The room was very quiet. No sound from the rest of the house could pass those panelled oak doors and the stiff curtains of gilded Spanish leather that hung in front of them. Only through the open window came the late talk of birds making their arrangements for the night, and the soft rustling of young leaves as the breeze ruffled the trees.

Anthony liked this room better than any room at Drelincourt. Not merely its noble proportions, the carved panelling of ceiling and chimney-piece, the subdued richness of its brown and crimson and gold, its chandeliers of antique brass and faintly purple copper, spoil of some old church rifled long ago. Not even the books themselves, shelf upon shelf of them, rising brown and ribbed with their gleams of gilding and warmth of red and green labels, nor the scent of the books, warm and mysterious and like no other scent in the world. Not the comfort of the chairs, nor the splendid daring incongruity of the vast Buhl writing-table. All these possessed charm, but they were not the charm of charms.

That was perhaps, in part, the charm of all libraries—the sense of the minds behind those ordered rows of brown leather backs ; of all the men who had done and thought and suffered, and then written their books, made their little scratch upon the sand of Time which the sea of Time not yet had obliterated. And further, in this room alone, of all the rooms in this house of his fathers, Anthony felt near to his work. Here alone he could feel that he, Anthony Drelincourt, was the same man as the Anthony Drelincourt who had studied in the white-faced house whose portal the pale wisteria overhung, who had worked in the schools and in the laboratory, toiled and agonised and failed—failed many times, and at last succeeded. In this room alone he seemed to be one person, not one of three or four.

There is a doubt, which I suppose we all know, a suspicion which comes now and then to the simplest of us, that perhaps we are not really quite so simple as we thought ourselves. We seem to see, now and then, that the man of Tuesday is not the man of last Friday week. But our various personalities seem to overlap, to blend, to qualify or obscure each other, so that we feel ourselves to be many-sided, but not many. With Anthony the lines of division were sharpened. With him there was no overlapping, hardly any shading off. He was a particular kind of Anthony at a particular moment, and without vagueness of transition would suddenly become another kind of Anthony, so different that each transition had for him all the effect of an awakening from a vivid dream.

In this room the different dreams seemed to steady themselves, to become part of a whole—not harmonious indeed, but not madly discordant; and the Anthony of the moment, whatever his mood, did really seem one with the Anthony of yesterday and of last year.

The mood of the Anthony of the moment as he sat here in the stillness of the May evening, was, at first, the calm satisfaction of the well and fully fed. He had ventured for the first time to order Wilkes to put down the coffee and leave it.

"All of it," he said, "just as it is. And you need not come back for it. I am going to work. I shall want to go on drinking coffee."

Wilkes retired.

"I'm not saying anything against Sir Anthony," he said later to the housekeeper; "for my part, I don't dislike the young man. But he can't be of an observing turn, or he'd know it's not my business how many cups of coffee he drinks. There wasn't any call for so much apologies."

"An affable gentleman, that's all," said the housekeeper. "To my mind, he's most handsome. And such a look of melancholy. He wants some good woman to take care of him. That's what he wants."

Anthony, at his third cup of coffee, felt his mood change to a childish but fierce curiosity about the room behind that boarded window. After all, it was his own house. He could break the panelling all to pieces if he liked. He lighted one of the wax candles in the silver candlesticks.

"I will investigate every inch of the place," he said, and carried the candle across to the wall of books that stood guarding the missing space. "If there's a secret room, it's my secret room, and I'm going to find it."

CHAPTER 11
The Secret Room

The mind once given to it, the puzzle was a very easy one, like a child's double-lidded pencil-box, or the cheap writing-desk whose secret drawer screams to you, "Here I am; please find me!"

At one end of the library, a door led to a small room, panelled in pleasant brown oak, and the window of this room looked out of that ivy-screened wall which Anthony had climbed to retrieve Rose's letter. At the other end of the library another door led to another and much larger room, whose windows, three in number, also looked out of that ivied wall; and from this room two other little rooms opened. The fire-places of all these rooms ranged round a common centre, and we all know that old chimneys take up a great deal of space. But still, the biggest chimney would hardly account for the difference between the length of the library and the combined lengths of the adjoining rooms. Anthony paced out the distances. Yes, there must be twenty feet or more missing. The chimneys could not account for all that. And besides, there was the window; that undoubted oblong of wood under the matted ivy.

Anthony looked closely at panelling and chimneypieces.

"There ought to be a piece of carving," he told himself; "the badge of your house, a lion's head or what not, that moves in your hand, and then the secret is revealed." And he went about, touching this and that carved leaf or scroll, and the warm wax ran over his fingers from the tall candle he carried.

In this way he examined the rooms beyond the library. The largest of them was luxuriously furnished with the pretty meretriciousness, the gilded graceful folly of the Second Empire. Glittering girandoles, consoles of ormulu and marble, chairs of carved and gilded wood upholstered in faded pink brocade, *escritoires* of smooth shiny marquetry, chairs and tables of *papier-maché* painted with flowers and gilt scroll-work, with rainbow insets of mother-of-pearl, an Aubusson carpet, a painted ceiling where cherubs sprawled, entangled in garlands of roses and loops of blue ribbon. Evidently the *boudoir* of some modish beauty of the eighteen-fifties. The panelling here had been painted white and its carved garlands gilded. New, it might have looked much too new, the gilding too gilt, the brocade too rose-coloured; inharmonious, probably, the tints of ceiling, carpet, and hangings.

But time had laid over all a unifying greyness, the discords had slowly faded to a very delicate and graceful harmony. There was that scent of old potpourri and mouldering wood which hangs about rooms unused. And yet there was no dust, the room was evidently "done" as other rooms were "done," daily. It was, somehow, like a room in a picture. No one could believe that any one lived in it, ever had lived in it. There was nothing worn about it—at least, if anything were worn, it was by time and not by service. Anthony had found this room in his first eager search for the inside of the boarded window, but he had not, till now, become aware of the room's personal character—its expression, as it were, the meaning of it.

Now, more quiet than the other rooms, it still seemed to be saying—

Yes, you are right; I have a secret and I mean to keep it.

Anthony heard it quite distinctly. He went back along the great library to where the tray was, and drank more coffee. And then he went back into that room that said it had a secret. As he went, he noticed, what he had not noticed before, that its door was part of the panelling of the library. But for its handle and finger-plates, it might have passed unnoticed. And at once he felt that he knew. He went through the little suite of rooms, and stopped in front of the panelled wall that enclosed the space where the boarded window was.

It was the same sort of panelling as that of the library. Holding the candle very close, he began to examine the lines of the moulding. And between two of the lines there was, without doubt, a narrow line of darkness, a crack. But nowhere could he find hint or hope of the secret spring which, to complete the adventure, must be there.

I do not know how to hope that you will forgive the Vandalism of his next act. The silence, the concealment, Lady Blair's silly reticence—the whole thing suddenly came upon him like a wave. And, after all, it was his own house. He set the candle on a table, put his shoulder to the panel and pushed. Something gave a little. And at that his heart began to beat like a schoolgirl's at a prize-giving. He turned round and kicked out, like an angry stallion, once, twice; and with a noise of cracking and wrenching and splintering, the panel yielded. He caught up the light and turned to see the dark oblong of a door. He had been right. He bent his head, for the door was low, and went in.

Nothing, just a little room like the others, only not furnished, and quite empty except for the dust of many years which lay on the floor thick and soft as any velvet carpet. There was the boarded window and the panelled walls—nothing else.

"How singularly rum," he said; "why should there be any secret about a little room? Why should its window be boarded up? Why should Lady Blair have lied to me about it? Ah!"

A little sound behind him made him turn sharply. And if that which laid a sudden hand on his heart were not fear, it was very like it. Through the dim *vista* of the Empire-furnished rooms a pale figure was coming slowly towards him; it made a soft rustling sound as it came.

A curious shiver disconcerted him. He felt suddenly cold. Then, as suddenly, the blood rushed hotly to his face, and he went to meet the thing, whatever it was, holding the candle high so as to throw before him as large a circle of light as might be. As the thing came nearer, he could see that it was a slender woman in pale trailing garments, with head down drooped and long loose plaits of hair. It came a little nearer yet and said—

"Oh, Anthony!"

"Why, it's *you!*" he said, with quite extraordinary relief; "do you know I quite thought you were a ghost!"

He took the little hand, and led its owner back to the lamp-lit library, where the ghost could be seen to be Lady Blair in a marvellous tea-gown of shell-pink soft silk, old lace, and black velvet ribbons. It was not till he had placed her gently in a chair close to the lamp that he could be quite sure that the long plaits she wore were part of an almost perfect wig.

She was panting, almost sobbing.

"Don't," he said. "What's the matter? Did the noise startle you? I'm sorry I made such a row, but I hate mysteries, unless I know I'm going to find them out. And I suddenly lost patience."

"Did you—" she asked. "You didn't see anything?"

"Only dust," he said; "what should I see? tell me."

"Yes," she said; "it's no use not telling you now. Only I very much didn't want you to go into that room. And really, there's nothing to tell. I wish you'd go and shut all those doors."

"You won't vanish, if I do? I believe you *are* a ghost, really."

"No—now you've done it, I must tell you, or you'll think it's worse than it is."

"A family monster, usually introduced to the heir at his coming of age, like the Glamis thing?" he asked.

And she said "No, no," but would he shut all the doors, *please*. So, he did.

As he came back, he wondered at her. In that dress, in that light, with that hair, she looked a girl. A wonderful illusion. It was only when one came quite close. . . .

"Yes, I really will tell you," she said. "It was foolish of me not to tell you before. But, you know, quite seriously, whenever that room is opened something terrible happens."

"But why?" he asked.

"Well, Drelincourt was an abbey once, and when it was taken away from the monks there was a curse. And that room—promise me you won't go in again tonight."

"Of course not, if you don't want me to."

"Well, that room is the only bit of the old abbey that's left stand-ing-that and the part below it. It was the little porter's room where the abbot stood to meet Henry's men, and he spoke the curse there. I believe it was a terrible curse. No; I don't know what it was."

"But what *happened?*" Anthony asked. "Something must happen. How does anyone know there was a curse unless something happens?"

"Well, I daresay it's all coincidence, but—"

"Yes?"

"Well, the eldest son of the Tobie Drelincourt who had the place first died suddenly 'By the act and visitation of God,' it says on his tomb in Latin, and his brother succeeded him. His eldest son, that was Howard Drelincourt, got his head cut off for treason. It turned out to be a mistake when too late, and I believe Queen Elizabeth was very sorry afterwards for the accident. Quite a boy he was, and his brother got the place. That was Anthony Drelincourt. He was the one who was Francis Bacon's friend. He was the first baronet."

"What happened to him?"

"The usual thing. He died without a son, and his brother inherited. He was accused of black magic, and burned."

Anthony thought of the book that Rose had given him, and a curious sensation like an inward flame, that warmed without burning, possessed him.

"Go on."

"Well, that's all," she said; "only by some curious accident Drelin-court has never been inherited by the eldest son."

"When was the room shut up?"

"It used to be shut up when I was a little girl. And when Sir Anthony—he was the eldest son and my cousin—came of age, he persuaded his father to open up the old place, and he used the place below—had it fitted up—"

"What for?"

"For a laboratory. And then——"

"And then?"

"Well, the eldest son had never inherited, it's true, but for several generations they'd died quietly, of ordinary things, like people there wasn't a curse on. And Anthony was engaged to be married. And a few days before the wedding was to have been, the girl disappeared, and he was found dead at the top of the steps in that little room you opened tonight. You are exactly like him. I wish you hadn't gone in there. It was horrible to me to see you there. You are so frightfully like him."

She put up both hands to her eyes, and he laid a hand on her elbow.

"Yes," she said, under her breath. "That's just it."

"Had the girl run away with someone else, or what?"

"Nobody knows. Nobody ever will know. Nor yet what killed *him*. The doctors just said heart failure. It's fifty years ago," she said, dropping her hands. "I didn't think I could be so silly. She—"

"What was she like?" Anthony asked gently; "pretty—nice?"

"Everyone adored her," said Lady Blair vindictively; "she wouldn't have given anyone a moment's peace if they hadn't. She was pretty, I will say that for her, and very attractive—and—well, you know, like a kitten that insists on being noticed. Sang to the guitar, and used to put gold-dust on her hair. Vain—heartless—and in the end he knew it."

"You think—"

"I think at the end he felt he couldn't live without her, and he wasn't going to try. He thought she was the only girl in the world."

"And she wasn't?" Anthony said stupidly. But Lady Blair caught his hand and said, "How you understand!"

And then, of course, he did, completely.

"How frightful for you," he said.

"Yes, because before she came—It's a dreadful thing, Anthony, to be an old woman, and have nothing beautiful to look back on—nothing real, I mean—only just to think how different everything might have been if only everything had been different. Well, that's all the story. And tomorrow you'll have the room locked up again, won't you?"

He reflected. "I simply can't," he said then, "and if it's been a laboratory, I'll use it as mine. And I promise you not to be found dead on the stairs. And aren't you hungry? I am. And it's frightfully late. And I had hardly any dinner—because you weren't there, I expect; and I'm sure you didn't have much, because you were feeling how cruelly you'd disappointed me. Couldn't we—? Only I don't know the way. And besides, I suppose in really aristocratic circles no one ever forages in larders?"

"I haven't for ages," Lady Blair cried. "Oh, come along! I know the way. You bring a candle, and I'll take one. We'll go like a procession of youths and maidens."

"Let's light the drawing-room fire, and have a picnic on the hearth-rug," said Anthony.

"Let's," said she, "and we'll forget all those sad old stories, and only remember that we're hungry and that there's something to eat in the house."

"If we can find it. It's like hunting for treasure."

"Just!" she said; "let me go first, and don't tread on my tail."

She led the way lightly, gracefully.

"You are about eighteen," he said, "and very charming."

"We are both eighteen," she said, "and both hungry. What more can we want?"

It was after the picnic on the hearthrug, among the cold chicken and champagne and gooseberry-pie and cream, that Anthony laid before Lady Blair his scheme for a house-party.

"I shall love it," she said, "and I am so glad that your Rose is tall and clever and handsome. I hate your little helpless, appealing women. Yes, Eugenia was little, and helpless and appealing. Yes, her name was Eugenia. Let's talk about what rooms they're to have, and what we shall do to amuse them."

So, they talked, till the birds were noisy outside and the blue-grey of summer dawn reached thin fingers through the chinks of the shutters.

"Why, it's morning," said Lady Blair, sitting on the hearthrug with her pink draperies round her like rose petals; "what a night of dissipation!" She sprang up, and held out both hands to him. "Goodnight," she said. "You've made me feel young again for an hour."

"And you," he said, "have made me feel old for ever! I shall never be as young as you, if I live to be a thousand."

"I wouldn't do that," she said—"not live to be a thousand, I mean. It's bad enough to live to be seventy-two."

"But supposing—" he said.

"Supposing one could go on living without getting old—the Faust idea?" she answered quickly; "that would be more horrible than anything. You would outlive everything—everything that makes life worthwhile. Did you ever hear of the Elixir of Life?"

He laughed. "Do you know, I think I must have."

"It's all nonsense, of course; but Anthony—my Anthony—was always dreaming about it. It's all nonsense, and if it were true, it would be intolerable. I'm glad *you* don't believe in those sort of silly things. You don't, do you?"

"Now should I?" he asked, and began to pick up the plates.

"Oh, don't trouble," she said.

"But won't the servants think we must be mad? Having supper on the mat, like cats?"

She opened her eyes very wide.

"My dear child," she said, "life wouldn't be worth living if one troubled about what they think. Whatever does it matter what *they* think? We're not villa-dwellers."

★★★★★★

When she had gone, he opened the long shutters and threw up the window and looked out on the grey and rose of dawn, above the trees of the park that stood up like fat rocks in a sea of pale mist. Anthony stood there looking out on all this tranquil beauty that was his own, and would be Rose's. And suddenly he thought of Malacca Wharf and the dreadful waste land where rubbish was shot, and the mean streets beyond, where Rose's biscuit boys lived in filth and poverty. And he felt what even the meanest worm of a rich man must surely feel at least once in a life, when he looks on his own life-lot and then on the life-lot of the poor. At such moments, one says, not with smug satisfaction, but with bitter shame—

Not more than others I deserve,
But Thou hast given me more.

"I must do something for those boys someday," he said, salving his conscience with charitable designs. But his conscience would not be put off. He turned from the window and looked at the comfortable grandeur of the room, and he thought of those other rooms.

"Oh, very well then," he said, as though in answer to the words of Another, "I'll send Rose a cheque today for her boys."

But the Other, once roused, was not easy to silence. He remained thoughtful, and presently he shrugged his shoulders impatiently.

"All right, I tell you," he told the Other, "all right; I'll go into the whole question. I'll talk it over with Rose. All right, I won't forget."

The sun had risen now, and the tops of the trees were golden, though still the park lay in misty shadow. keeper and two dogs passed across a *vista* of foreign conifers, and vanished.

He went back to the library and wrote his invitations, fixing times and trains, and put them in the box in the hall.

And now the sun was bright and the whole beautiful world awake.

"The servants will be up presently, I suppose," he said; "it seems silly to go to bed. Yes, of course. What else?"

He went back through the library to the *boudoir*, opening shutters as he went, and windows, to let in the air and light of a new day. In the soft radiance of early morning the Second Empire furniture looked, he thought, more ghostly than ever. The door of the little room had swung open again, and into its darkness from door and clouded sky-light came faint revealing light that still, however, left the darkness much to conceal. He went back for candles—tall new candles. Because, of course, what he wanted to see now was the place underneath that had been used as a laboratory.

And when he had the candles, and knew what he was looking for, which last night he had not known, he found easily enough the panelled door, that was only bolted, and that opened with a crack like a pistol-shot as paint parted from paint that had lain close to it for fifty years. The door moved slowly and complainingly on hinges long unoiled, and disclosed stairs that led down.

Remembering stories of vaults long closed, whose air was death to breathe, he thrust the candle before him into the darkness. Its flame swirled with his movement, but it burnt brightly, and he went forward. The stairs were of stone and soft with dust. They curved round as the stairs of turrets do. His hand on the wall felt dry stone, and the air, as he descended, was, though chill, not damp.

At the foot of the stairs was a door, shaped to the arch it filled—a door of heavy oak carved in a sort of rough linen pattern, and grey with age. It stood ajar. He pushed it open, and went through into a strange place.

A large octagonal room; high up, the walls were pierced by narrow lancets that let in air and no light. Pillars were ranged round it, which had evidently at some time supported a groined roof, but the groining ceased abruptly a yard above the spring of the arches, and the roof was not of stone but of wood, flat square boards, incongruous and unsightly. The walls, too, were match-boarded, covering the pillars, to a height of seven feet or so. Wood was fitted between the pillars at the top of the match-boarding, forming shelves, and there were other shelves below, and on them many bottles. Benches below bore the chemical apparatus that was "up to date" in the middle of last century.

There was a balance in its glass-house on a table, a baize cloth over it. A book lay open, with a pen on it, and an inkstand near. It looked as though someone had been writing in that book but a moment before, and had thrown down the pen, interrupted in his work by Anthony's approach. But that ink had been dry years and years before Anthony was born, and the hand that had written in that book had most likely never written anything more after that was written. Anthony blew the fine dust from the page, and read or tried to read.

But what was written there was written in a shorthand unknown to him; the chemical formulae, plainly distinguishable as such by their grouping, were written in some cypher, only at the end of all were words in ordinary writing, and not such words as one expects to find in the notebook of a scientist—three words written very hurriedly: '*Not death. She*— Then the pen had rolled across the page, leaving its dark trail. The writer must have felt Death coming to him, and have fled from Death to meet Him at the top of those winding steps.

Anthony felt very sorry for that man. Perhaps the news of her flight had come to him suddenly. He had not known at first that her going meant the end of life. He had tried to believe that he could bear it, and had gone back to his work. And then, even as he wrote the cypher-tale of his experiments, the truth came home to him. A man in a laboratory like this had no need to leave it to look for Death elsewhere. Only at the last, perhaps, he felt he did not want to die alone; perhaps he remembered the other girl, who was old Lady Blair now, but who then was young and loved him. Perhaps he had tried to go to her, and met only Death.

"Poor chap!" he said; "I wonder whether I should kill myself if Rose went off with someone?"—and instantly was ashamed of the question because the answer was so quick and so definite.

He looked round the room again. There were shelves of books, a mercury barometer in a long mahogany case hung on the wooden wall. There was a carved oak chest, grey like the door, and on tables and benches all a medley of dulled, glass-clouded bottles, papers disordered, retort-stands disconsolate.

Lamps with reflectors were fixed to the walls, the old Colza lamps that used to have to be wound up like clocks, responding to the winding by gulps and gurglings and tricklings of hidden oil.

A gaunt structure of chains, wheels, cranks, and pulleys against the wall at one side set Anthony wondering and examining. There was a wheel. He turned it, and with a rattling sound the slack chains stiffened to heavy resistance. There was a creaking sound, a cracking sound, from overhead, and then a sudden shower of dust like rain fell on his face and on the candles. Both candles went out. Anthony, in the dark, calling himself a fool, held on to the wheel and waited. Everything was quiet as death. If he let go the handle the machinery, whatever it was, might run down suddenly, with any sort of result unforeseen and undesired. If, on the other hand, he went on turning—A moment's reflection convinced him that no one would have set up machinery whose sole end should be to destroy the man who worked it. And curiosity backed reason. He must go on turning the wheel. But he would strike a match first and see what had sent the dust down on him.

The strong resistance which the wheel still offered warned him not to let it go. So fumblingly, leaning against the handle and still holding it with one hand, he tried with the other to get out a match and strike it. It is not easy to find your match-box, open it, get a match out and strike ,it, with one hand; but if you are careful you can do it. Anthony did it, and held up the little wax taper. By its light he could see fairly well the roof from which the dust had fallen, but he could not see what had caused the fall. He made a little torch of wax matches and dropped them carefully to the floor, where they burnt merrily—wax matches have this property. Then, slowly and deliberately, he turned the wheel a little, backwards and forwards. A fresh shower of dust fell, which put out his torch and made his eyes smart, but not before he had seen the effect of his efforts. The roof had moved.

Pleasantly surprised, he continued his investigations with scientific deliberation. Having let the wheel run very slowly back, until all was as before, he let go the handle, walked over and lighted the candles, made little dust shelters for them with two glass plates and some bottles, took off his coat, and then went back to his winding. And now all was clear. As he laboriously turned the handle, the roof slowly, very slowly, tilted up on one edge, like the lid of a box.

"This will be a long job," thought Anthony.

At the end of five minutes' hard labour the roof stood up vertically against the wall of the room above, and through the partially-obscured skylight of the roof he could see the vague blue and white of the morning sky. The little door which led to the stairs now opened on a space seven feet above his head.

Anthony, mopping his brow and thrilled with the enthusiasm of the discoverer, now first began to consider the meaning of it all. He examined the wheels and chains.

"The main part of the mechanism is quite simple, and merely consists of levers and chain-geared wheels enough to give sufficient mechanical advantage to enable a man's strength to move the roof. That means a pretty big advantage; hence the operation is of necessity slow."

And, "It must be jolly dry here, for all the steel-work to be in such good condition. The chains run quite sweetly."

And again, "Why did the other Anthony rig up all this business? He'd want the light, and the extra space would be handy for keeping the air clear of fumes, and the floor lying against the door up there as it does now would ensure privacy all right. He might have had the floor taken out, but I daresay he wanted the place to look unchanged from above. At any rate, it's all very neat." And his admiration for the machinery, which certainly was well-planned and carried out, caused him to murmur, "Very neat!" aloud, once or twice.

A quarter of an hour later his admiration was renewed when he discovered the function of a mass of steel-work high up on the machinery, which had, at first, seemed superfluous. The discovery was a relief, for the subconscious Anthony had for some time been wondering how the material Anthony was going to persuade the roof to return to its original position so that he might get out. He took up the old manuscript book and drew a rough sketch of the machinery with a little programme pencil that lurked in his pocket. With the help of his sketch, it was quite easy to find what should be the release, but, he thought, "I'll have to hang on to the handle pretty tight, or the thing will run down with noise enough to wake the dead."

Hanging on with the meditated tightness, he cautiously moved with his left hand the releasing lever, and, after a few futile attempts, found the right way to adjust it. But surprisingly, after one jerk the roof began to descend very slowly, and the handle, instead of pulling impatiently on his ready strength, merely turned slowly with well-regulated solemnity. After the first half-minute he let go altogether, and watched the roof slowly settle down with a subdued clanking and grinding.

"By Jove!" he said; "that affair up there must be a brake, and a very nicely regulated one too, judging by the uniformity of the working. Just push the lever over, and look on in lordly indolence. And when the things cleaned and oiled, it won't be very hard work to wind it up.' In his delight at finding it all so straightforward, he seized the handle and wound the roof up again, after which he lowered it once more with calm satisfaction.

Then he looked again, more closely, at the furniture of the room, if benches and apparatus can be called furniture; blew the dust from odd bottles and examined the labels, still clear under their protecting wax ; opened drawers full of wire, corks, odd lengths of glass tubing, empty bottles, clamps, and all the odd trifles that are found in all laboratories. Most of the bottles were the ordinary reagents of the organic and physiological chemist; but a few of them bore mere letters and numbers, E 11, and such like. The balance, its glass case clean and bright under the dusty protecting leather, looked a little antiquated, but it was a beautiful instrument; two microscope cases of bright mahogany gave, by their polished opulence, promise of fine workmanship within, but they were locked.

"I expect the lenses are not up to much compared to our modern stuff," he murmured; and, condensing his observations; "but things on the whole don't seem to have altered much in the last fifty years as far as ordinary apparatus is concerned. I shan't want much to make this place into a very efficient laboratory for the second Anthony."

He went back to the book.

"I must put Bats on to this," he said, turning page after page of unenlightening symbols, till, as he came once more to the three living words, "Not death—She"—the last convulsions of his second candle threw yellow waves over the old writing. "I'd better get out of this before the light goes," said he, and went up the stairs. "What an adventure! It's almost worthwhile being a Drelincourt and having an Ancestral Hall. Hope I don't meet Wilkes."

CHAPTER 12

Ancient History

And in the hall, he gave "Good morning!" to a startled Wilkes, who had hardly time before meeting his master's eye to adjust the butlerial mask over the face of a much intrigued and interested man. For Wilkes also, the morning had not been dull. When Sebastien discovered that Sir Anthony's bed had not been slept in; when others remarked that there were, on the drawing-room hearthrug, the remains of an informal banquet for two; that someone had opened the shutters, and that Sir Anthony himself was missing, the most delicious anxieties and suspenses agitated the servants' hall.

The letters in the box were sent off as usual by the morning postman, and it was Wilkes, always a bit of a Sherlock Holmes, who remarked that they had been written that morning. He made the remark in the pleasant housekeeper's room, where the morning sun was gay on plush and photographs and red geraniums.

"But how *can* you tell, Mr. Wilkes?" the housekeeper asked in almost awestruck admiration that yet had no incredulity in it.

"By the ink, Mrs. Simpkins," said the butler gravely. "By the ink; the blue-black writing fluid with which I fill the library inkstands with is not blue-black to commence with. It is blue first, and black after some space of time has elapsed—five or six hours, as a point of fact. Now the ink on those envelopes is still blue. You take my meaning? I shouldn't be surprised if something had happened."

"Don't say that, Mr. Wilkes," Mrs. Simpkins pleaded; "of course I know that in the midst of life—but perhaps he's only gone for a walk."

"In his evening clothes? Ho, no! Mrs. Simpkins." The butler was positive, with his thumbs in the armholes of his waistcoat.

Cook sent an emissary to inquire whether it was any good cooking breakfast, and Wilkes returned the majestic answer that, of course, breakfast would be served as usual.

"Shut the door—do," said the housekeeper, as the emissary went. "Now, Mr. Wilkes, just between me and you and the door shut—*did* you ever hear anything to make you say what you did about suppose something was to happen? Because her ladyship's maid—you see her ladyship's getting on, of course, really, and now and then she's let things drop. You're so clever, Mr. Wilkes, you ought to write a history of the County Families, telling the parts that the books leave out. You wouldn't put the real names, of course; just Lord H. and the Honourable Miss P. and a certain well-known Cavalry Major's lady."

Wilkes owned that he had thought of the idea himself sometimes. "But my duties," he pointed out, "do not leave me much leisure. But about the Family. Well, you and me *are* the Family, in a manner of speaking, if you take my meaning; and I am sure it won't go further."

"Not a word shall pass my lips," Mrs. Simpkins assured him, and thought how surprised her elder sister would be when she told her— "do go on."

"I have sent Charles and James out to search the park, also Oddling; and Mr. Mackenzie will send some men round by the home farm. So that all that is humanly active has been done, and I don't feel that I'm wasting time talking to you," he admitted handsomely.

"Thank you," said the housekeeper with gratitude, "and do sit down, Mr. Wilkes. Take the saddle-back chair; it's the easiest."

"At the same time, I will be brief, because Sir Anthony may turn up in time for breakfast, because, Mrs. Simpkins, the gist of the matter is this; this sort of disappearing and turning up again is hereditary in the family. My uncle fulfilled the office of butler at Drelincourt before my time, and he told me the facts. It appears there's a little room that's been bricked up since, owing to something of a fatalistic nature happening whenever the room was opened to inspection. And my uncle told me when I took the place that room wasn't to be so much as named. Well, the late Sir Anthony, the last baronet's elder brother, he had this room opened it seems, and messed about in it with liquors in bottles and chemical scents to a degree that my uncle said was poisonous. He and Miss Cecily—her that's Lady Blair now, having married Sir Wilson Blair later by her father's express wish, and not a say of her own about it—him and Miss Cecily were as good as engaged; very thick they were, my uncle says, very thick indeed. Miss Cecily's father's place being close by—Battle's End they had, that the Goldschmids have now—the young couple were thrown much together, and there is no doubt an attachment sprung up between the two."

"You *ought* to write for the papers," said Mrs. Simpkins, "really you ought."

"Not at all," said Mr. Wilkes, bowing as he sat, and now enjoying himself very much. "The young lady and gentleman appeared, my uncle says, to be all in all to each other; rides and drives and staying at each other's houses—she here more than him there, because of his chemical smells which she couldn't wean him from for more than a day or two at a time. And all went merry as a marriage bell till the foreign young lady came to light."

"How was it found out? "said Mrs. Simpkins eagerly, at once thinking the worst.

"Oh! I don't mean what you mean," Mr. Wilkes assured her; "it was all *ong ragle* and no scandal, seeing the youthful cousins hadn't been announced engaged. Miss Delmar was a distant connection of the family on one side, and she came on a visit to Miss Cecily, and later on here. Instantly she appeared on the scene, poor Miss Cecily's goose was cooked. I mean her chances of happiness were at an end."

"You mean he jilted her?"

"I don't think any of the family would go so low as jilting a lady, Mrs. Simpkins," Mr. Wilkes reproved; "but the understanding was entirely at an end. My uncle says he remembers Miss Eugenia, that was Miss Delmar, having a way with: her that nobody could resist—even him, a married man, and not of course quite equal in station. He says he would have got her down the moon out of the sky—that was his word—if she'd fancied it, and if he could have. So that shows. She turned everybody's head that came near her, even females. And Sir Anthony, from the instant he beheld her in cherry-coloured tarlatan at the Hunt Ball, it was all up. *Their* engagement was announced sharp enough, and poor Miss Cecily to be bridesmaid. It was the talk of the county. The wedding was to be here—all Miss Delmar's people being foreign on the mother's side, and her father dead, and Sir Anthony was

233

stopping at the Dower House and coming here every day."

"Didn't she interfere with his Chemistery?" Mrs. Simpkins asked.

"Not she. She was deep in it with him. First thing she does is to ask him to teach her how. So, they spent days together alone in the labatry he'd fitted up in the little room that had used to be bricked up. My uncle says she was like a rose just cut early in the morning.

"Sir Anthony fairly worshipped the ground she walked on, as the saying is. And anyone would have thought she did the same. They were a beautiful couple, my uncle says, and the admired of all. He furnished that room off the library purposely for her tarlatan the latest up-to-date furniture it was then, I believe—though it's all gone out now. You know, Mrs. Simpkins, the *boudoir* that's never used. Well, I must cut it short; it's close on eight, and if Sir Anthony doesn't turn up, I'm not sure but I ought to let the police know. Where was I?"

"The wedding."

"Yes, of course. Well, there wasn't any wedding. The day before it was to have been, everyone was very busy getting the place decorated, and arches in the park and so forth and so on; and him and her alone together, as usual, among the bottles and the liquors. His mother didn't approve because they wouldn't have a chaperone with them; but he said science couldn't be chaperoned, and it seems a young lady and gentleman may be alone as long as they like so long as there's enough bottles and jars and dull books with them. And no one suspected anything. And then he was missing at dinnertime—just like our Sir Anthony's missing now. And they went to call him, and there he was lying stone dead at the top of the laboratory stairs."

"I'm glad it's bricked up." Mrs. Simpkins shuddered. "Or else I should be afraid to go and see what might have happened."

"It was a dreadful blow, I understand," Mr. Wilkes said.

"Poor young thing," said Mrs. Simpkins, her heart with the bride of fifty years ago; "how did she bear it?"

"She didn't know it," said Mr. Wilkes; "she wasn't there. She'd disappeared. At first they thought she'd gone crazy, and run out when he fell dead, and began to scout for her accordingly. But it wasn't so. Because the doctor said he'd only been dead an hour; and her ladyship, his mother, had been sitting in the library since half-an-hour after luncheon. She used to sit there most of the time when they were down among the bottles; my uncle said it was as near chaperoning as they'd let her get. No, Miss Delmar must have eloped early in the afternoon before her ladyship went to the library. She must have told him all was over, or left a letter or something. And he couldn't bear it, so he killed himself, though they did bring it in heart."

"It *was* heart," said Mrs. Simpkins sentimentally, "and then?"

"Why, then all was horror and despair. Orders to stop building the arches, mounted man for the doctor; and Miss Cecily, who'd come at tea-time to be ready for next day, with an aching heart, no doubt, under her bridesmaid's exterior, she went nearly mad, they say, put her arms round the body, and they had to tear her away by force. She was very ill after that. A dreadful business it must have been."

"I don't wonder she was upset," said Mrs. Simpkins, "and that was her ladyship when she was young! To think of that! You'd never think it to look at her now, would you? And what became of the bride, after all? Where had she gone to? Who had she gone to?"

"Nobody ever knew. My uncle says she vanished as implicitly as though the ground had opened and swallowed her up. Nobody ever heard any more of her. Most likely she fled back to her foreign parentage. But it was well managed. Someone must have been waiting with a carriage and driven by the back lanes, and so got away unseen. You wouldn't have thought she could have been so heartless as it turned out. My uncle said no one would have believed it of her. She was always so kind to everyone. But love, Mrs. Simpkins, love laughs at—at all sorts of things, you know; and there's no doubt there was Another lurking in the background all the time."

"Poor young thing," said Mrs. Simpkins, "I wonder if she's alive yet, and if she was happy?"

"You may well wonder," said Wilkes. "Now if you were me, would you send for the police?"

"I'd have one more look first," Mrs. Simpkins advised.

"There are no young ladies in the case this time," said Wilkes hopefully.

"Oh! but didn't I tell you?" Mrs. Simpkins asked. "No, of course I didn't. Everything happening like it did put everything out of my head. Lady Blair told Miss Connolly this morning that Sir Anthony's engaged, and the lady and quite a house-party he's invited down. And she won't bring her maid. And none of the house-party's bringing their servants. I wonder what sort of people they are?"

"Now, mind you," said Mr. Wilkes, "I like Sir Anthony. Speaking as one man about another man, I like him. But you can always tell. He's been living in London, among a low lot, I shouldn't wonder. Artists and chemists and people like that. We mustn't expect too much from his friends, Mrs. Simpkins. He'll soon drop his low acquaintances as he gets used to the title and the property; and if his young lady is presentable tarlatan we shall do, we shall do."

"According to Sebastien," said Mrs. Simpkins, unmoved, "his young lady is something quite out of the common. I understood him to say she was a queen. Of course, she can't be that, but I expect it's his foreign way of saying that she is a princess."

"Titles like that," said Mr. Wilkes, "are as cheap abroad, I believe, as knighted the year he was mayor is with us."

"Sebastien told me," the housekeeper pursued, "that she was beautiful, like the beautiful day, and good as Madonna herself."

"Ah!" Mr. Wilkes explained, "he meant the Virgin Mary, these Catholics think such a lot of. Well, you take the upstairs and I'll take the down. We'll have one more look round, and if we don't find him I'll take it on me to send George for the police. If anything *had* happened to Sir Anthony, such as waylaying by a gang, it would look bad if the police hadn't been sent for."

Then Mr. Wilkes went out and met Anthony coming through the hall after his night of adventure, dusty from head to foot, with cobwebs instead of vine-leaves in his hair.

★★★★★★

The delicate rose-rouge stood up in strong relief on a very white face when Lady Blair heard how Anthony had ended the night. He did not tell her all. The secret of the machinery that the other Anthony had devised, that was the other Anthony's secret, and the new Anthony would keep it. And the note-book he had brought away with him and laid under lock and key in his room. And he did not tell of that. But he told of the laboratory and its fifty years' dust, and how he had broken in on its fifty years' solitude, and he invited her to come and see everything, before he perceived how pale she was.

"I wish you hadn't," she said; "I wish you wouldn't. No, nothing would induce me to go near the place. My uncle had the place fastened up again at once after *that* happened. Everything must be just as *he* left it. I know nothing good will come of opening it. I wish I could persuade you to have it all locked up again."

"I couldn't," he said honestly; "but I won't bother you to come down if you don't want to. I wrote this morning asking Rose and the others to come on Monday. I hope you'll like them."

"I always like young people," said Lady Blair, and her skin grew less like old powder-covered wax. "We must do something to amuse them. Would they like a dinner-party; just a few friends; because, of course, we're still in mourning for your uncle, poor dear. But we could ask a few nice people. Crowds of people have called, besides the ones you've seen. What do you say?"

"I'm a little out of my depth," he said. "But you swim beautifully," said she.

"I'm afraid I flounder a good deal. I think I would like to get used to the element before I ask my friends to plunge into it with me. I thought we might ask St. Maur, and that nice chap who collects beetles. I never heard his name. I never do hear people's names."

"Lord Alfriston; yes."

"I didn't know," said Anthony, a little dashed; "he seemed all right."

"That would make ten," Lady Blair said, "and only four girls. Wouldn't you like me to ask a girl or two and one or two more men?"

"You see," Anthony said comfortably; "it's like this. We're all brought up to think that a man's a man for all that, and that the rank is but the guinea stamp; and I hope I'm as democratic as the next man, and we're all equal before the law, and in the sight of, and all that. And, of course, you can read *The Manners and Customs of Good Society* by the butler of a duke, but it only tells you not to put your knife in your mouth, which you know before. And there's no getting over it; the worlds *are* different."

"You are Sir Anthony Drelincourt," she said.

"I believe you are right. But I wasn't always, and this world of yours isn't my world, and the atmosphere's different, the standard's different, the *sous entendu*s, the taken-for-granteds are different, the basis is different. Your lot have always had plenty of money."

"If you only knew," she sighed. "I could tell you stories—"

"About the distressing poverty of the aristocracy, and how hard it is to make both ends meet on three thousand a year. But the stories I could tell you are about people who have to decide whether they'll have a book or a breakfast, and whether, if you walk from Chelsea, you wear out more shoe leather than the two pence a 'bus would cost would pay for. We're all 'Ladies and Gentlemen,' of course; perish the doubt! but the point of view's different, so different that when I'm talking to your callers I feel as though I were a South Sea Islander just introduced to the oldest civilization in the world. Or else——"

"Yes—you must go into Parliament later on. Yes; or else——"

"Or else," he ended grimly, "as though I were a civilized man visiting savage tribes, making notes in my superior high-minded way of their curious superstitions, their reverence for their totems, which to me seem such silly odd little things. I find myself scientifically interested in their sacred books; the red-backed ones, you know, where the tribal history's written with that lofty calm the Initiate uses in writing of sacred things. I study the rites and ceremonies, what the temple slaves do, what the priests do, the high priest bearing coffee on a silver tray, the array of sacred vessels, each with its appointed use; the ceremonial robes of the priestesses, the—"

"Oh! don't rag us like that, Anthony," she interrupted; "it's all nonsense. We're all exactly the same, really."

"I daresay you are right," he said; "and that it's all nonsense. At any rate, it hasn't the seriousness of the other life where the 'bus fare and the boots loom so large. And if you go among savages, or if you're a savage and go among the civilized—if you go out of your natural environment, I mean—you've no choice but to accept the other people's convention, or try to make them accept yours. And I'm not at present prepared to do either."

"I think you make mountains out of—"

"The usual material? I think not. The people who go out of my element into yours can only keep afloat by colossal pretences. And those who come from you to us have a brief dip and go back saying how odd the Bohemian life is."

"But you and I get on so well," she urged plaintively.

"But then you and I are *us*," he said; "I'll say *we*, if you like, but us is what I mean. If the others were like you! Anyhow, don't let's have any strange girls. Only my friends and St. Maur and the beetle man."

Lady Blair was very charming to the three girls. Her tact fought with her natural disinclination to be out of doors without a veil, and tact won. She received them on the terrace, dainty in black muslin over white silk, with a very shady hat of white and black and red carnations at her slender waist. Rose, the most self-possessed of the three, appeared at first the most nervous, for Esther was concealing shyness under a mask of confidence, and was wearing her eye-glasses, which ordinarily she only used for writing, to look superior through. Whatever happened, she was not going to be patronised. Linda was frightened, which gave her an air of frigid disapproval.

Lady Blair asked kind questions about the journey. Tea was imminent, and a table gleamed white and silver at the terrace end.

Esther and Linda both wished they hadn't come, but Rose looked at Anthony, and thought that someday she would paint his portrait with that background of grey stone and ivy with the shoulder of distant Downs curving across the corner of the picture, and a bit of the park showing between the stone urns that brimmed over with trailing blossoms at each side of the gaps that the wide steps made in the line of the balustrade. And she looked out over the quiet beauty of the garden and park, and was glad that it was his. Also, she saw herself a ministering angel stooping from this heaven with gracious gifts of coals and blankets and soup to the deserving poor. Then she caught herself at it, and smiled. "We'll do better than that," she told herself. But she did not tell herself that this was too big and beautiful a home for one man and one woman in a world where other men and women lived in the mean streets beyond the waste that lies against Malacca Wharf.

The smile was still on her lips when she turned to answer Lady Blair's question.

"Yes, indeed, I like it," she said; "it's the most beautiful place I've ever seen. The terraces and the poplars and the fountains and the statues. It's like the background of a Watteau."

"Do you know," said Lady Blair, "someone said exactly that to me once before, just here, one day like this? Fifty years ago."

"Then I wasn't plagiarising, only quoting a classic," Rose said, and smiled again.

"It was a girl, too."

"I suppose girls' minds run on Watteau because of fans," Rose suggested.

None of the girls could have explained why they were nervous; in theory, of course, an educated woman is the equal of duchesses, but in practice the change from Soho to Ancestral Halls is disconcerting. Perhaps it is the sense of difference between the lives of those who earn their livings and those who not only don't earn them, but have never even thought of earning them. Perhaps it was a question of clothes, because William Bats and the doctor seemed quite at ease. As for Mullinger, his money, though made in Insect Powder, had taken him to many such houses as this.

Tea was not a merry meal, but it was not a social disaster. And after tea, Lady Blair said something about the lake, and they found themselves going down the terrace steps.

"I'll just slip away," Lady Blair told Anthony; "you'll have so many things to talk about. Don't be afraid, the old woman won't be a skeleton at the feast, except at such times as the feast materialises in mutton or teacakes. You and your friends are free of me till dinner."

"Don't be absurd," said Anthony; "though you're right this time, I shan't let you do it again. You've been a dear to them. By this time tomorrow they'll all love you almost as much as I do." He kissed her hand in the shelter of a great white rose bush, and she went back to the house.

He was a true prophet. When Lady Blair chose to be irresistible, no one could resist her. By the next tea-time she was calling the girls by their Christian names. And by the tea-time after that they had christened her their Fairy Godmother. The intense vitality that had kept her young so long delighted in their vigorous youth. The young men all professed themselves in love with her. She arranged all sorts of pleasures for them—boating, picnics, drives, and there was tennis and croquet, and going on, under and behind everything, the beautiful house and the beautiful weather, for the sun shone every day, and at night the moon was big and silvery over poplar and weeping willow, and lake and little temple, and all the sentimental detailed work of a long-dead landscape gardener.

Rose loved it all, the house, its pictures and rich restful elegance, the garden, the hills, the luxurious comfort of a perfectly-working household. And yet she was miserable. For here, among these surroundings, Anthony seemed less hers than ever. He was more uniformly affectionate, it is true, but uniform affection is tasteless food to a young woman in love. Rose felt that she would have been contented to be ignored by him for five days of the week, and beaten on the sixth, if, on the seventh, he would have held her in his arms and made her believe that love, resisted for six days, had, on the seventh, proved irresistible.

When they two were alone together, which was not conspicuously seldom, he would hold her hand and kiss her lips with a certain air of premeditation infinitely exasperating. His love-making was more than it had been, but less convincing. "*Un peu voulu*," a critic might have said. His lips found love-names for her readily enough now, but none of them had even the force of the earlier declaration that had discontented her. And never once did she see in his eyes the look they had worn when he gazed on her from the crystal.

"You are the luckiest of dogs, confound you," William Bats told his friend. "But I'd give all the rest of your great possessions for your library, and you don't ever use it."

"I often sit there," Drelincourt protested.

"Sit there!" said Bats in deep disgust.

Anthony showed his house to the Septet with the thoroughness of

240

a child exhibiting a new toy, reserving to the last, of course, the faded *boudoir* and the little room whose skylight had been cleaned, and the octagonal laboratory, now once again neatly ordered. But the working of the machinery he did not show, nor the book, nor did he tell them of the roof that moved. One must have some secrets even from one's best friend and the girl of one's choice; and this secret seemed at least as innocent as the secrets of most young men.

"And you give us leave to explore?" Bats asked. "That chest looks to me very much like the mistletoe bough."

"We'll find a key to it, never fear," said Anthony.

Wilfred Wilton found his chief interest in the herb garden, a curious winter garden of tropical and subtropical plants, mostly medicinal, which had "always been there," the gardener told him.

Nothing happened that was not good to live, and is not dull to chronicle, till the night when St. Maur and Lord Alfriston came to dine, and Lady Blair had the inspiration to make it a costume dinner. She turned out old chests and old wardrobes till heaps of old and beautiful clothes lay piled on the floors of the great bedchambers, beautiful clothes of the bygone days when not only women dressed beautifully.

"We'll all dress up," said Lady Blair gaily. "I shall be a *marquise*, and I hope somebody will be black Monsieur de Voltaire for a contrast."

It was at the end of that evening—an evening of joyous and successful folly—that William Bats, white in his Charles the First suit, came to Anthony, took his arm and led him to a window, and without word of warning said—

"Look here, I want you to know that I know."

"That you know what, you old duffer?" Anthony asked.

"About that body," said Bats, without further phrase.

Anthony said, "What body?" and laughed.

And Bats replied, not laughing, "The dead body. I've stood your guinea-pigs and monkeys, but when it comes to human beings—"

"We're going to do a minuet," Lady Blair interrupted, coming into the embrasure of the window where they stood. "Come!"

"In a moment," Anthony said. "Half a moment—may I?" And she left them again.

"Are you mad, or am I?" Anthony asked.

"I propose to find out later," said Bats quietly; "in the meantime you had better join the dance."

"On with the dance! Let joy be unrefined!" said Anthony. "Silly trick, you almost frightened me! Though I've no idea what you meant. Only *body* sounded bad."

He laughed and joined the dance, and Bats, left alone in the window, rubbed his chin doubtfully and fingered a little key.

The Discovery

"Goodnight, everybody. Now be good boys, and don't stay up till the grey dawn, smoking and talking." Lady Blair turned at the bend of the staircase to throw the last word over her graceful shoulder at the group of men who stood at the stair foot looking up at the bright flock she shepherded.

The evening had "gone like the change of a five pound note," as the doctor put it. Mullinger had found that Linda Smith could look pretty in the dress of a Dresden shepherdess, and he wondered whether she were not perhaps pretty even in her ordinary clothes, if one were to notice. Such discoveries, such speculations add new feathers to the wings of time. Lord Alfriston was astonished to find these girls, from a Bohemia unknown to him, quite as amusing as the dwellers in the Bohemia he knew, and much more intelligent.

Lady Blair had a genius for the lighting of interiors. No cruel revealing glare was ever suffered to spoil a scene for her. And the soft shading silks, of pink and pale apricot, made the fair women look like roses, gave to the dark ones the bloom and colour of nectarines. Each woman had been conscious that she looked her best, and every man had seemed to think so too. What more can one need to make an evening a success?

And now it was over, and the bright dresses and laughing faces showed for a moment against the dark panelling of the staircase, a massed bouquet of pink and blue and white, eyes that sparkled, and red lips that smiled, made vivid by the little blue and yellow flames of the candles, and the gleam of reflected light on the silver candlesticks.

"A charming picture," said Lord Alfriston, as soon as the picture had ceased to be.

"I hear you have discovered your uncle's secret laboratory," he went on, as they turned back into the library; "most thrilling! I've heard my father speak of that laboratory as being something very curious, but he never would tell me any more than that. I suppose he was bound to secrecy. They were great friends, you know. Thank you—a very little, and plenty of soda. I should very much like to see the secret room,

Drelincourt."

"I'll show it you now," said Anthony, picking up a candlestick. "Come on!"

"I wouldn't tonight," said Bats suddenly.

"But night is the time for these explorations, surely," Lord Alfriston urged, and Anthony said, "Why ever not?" and moved towards the door.

"Well," said Bats, with a sort of laugh, "I see I shall have to own up. I hid there when we were playing hide-and-seek, and it didn't strike me as very safe. I thought there might be some accident with those stairs, and I locked the room up. It was a confounded liberty, I know, Tony, and now I'm sorry to say I can't produce the key. Heaven knows where it has got to! I'm frightfully sorry."

There was a shade of annoyance in Anthony's eyes as they met those of Bats, but he said—

"All right, Bill. Don't worry about it. It doesn't matter. It will turn up all right."

Lord Alfriston also said it did not matter, and Mullinger said it was extraordinary how keys did get lost; and the doctor told a story of a boy who swallowed a key, and had worn it in his inside for twenty years, when a surgeon, operating for something quite different, had the unexpected pleasure of finding the lost object. And they all got sleepy, and said goodnight, and went their ways with their bedroom candles.

Anthony, alone in his great room with the funereal four-poster and the large inter-mahogany spaces, felt for the first time a thrill of complete satisfaction with destiny. What luck he had had! Some men went to their graves without ever having had a gleam of such luck as had shone on him. Everything had happened just as one would have chosen it to happen. He had known poverty, and so he could enjoy his inheritance as no man born to the expectation of it could ever have enjoyed. As to his family, he had known nothing and feared much. Well, that was all right. And the Idea, that had been with him, sleeping and waking, in his work and in his play, as a background to everything he did and thought and was, that had come near to him, suffered him to clasp and hold it. He was young, and he had done work that would make the greybeards of life and history seem mere children playing at science.

The work was done. He would do more, but this at least was done, and soon he would give his discovery to the world, his wonderful discovery, the greatest birth of time. In the meantime, how jolly everything was. Just a little while he would enjoy it, not looking before or after. Presently, when he had revealed his great secret—he would tell Bats first—when he had become famous, a life like this would be impossible to him. How pleasant the evening had been. They had danced and sung and acted charades, and played games, blind-man's buff, and hide-and-seek! What a house for hide-and-seek ! How jolly everything was. How jolly it was to be able to give his old friends a good time like this. And he would give good times to other people. His discovery would make him rich beyond any man's need of riches. He would be a millionaire, as they called it, and such a millionaire as the world had never seen. He walked up and down the room thinking. "What luck!" he said, "what luck! It's almost unbelievable."

Then there was Rose. He must marry Rose, and soon. She was a part of the simple and splendid life, the life which he meant to enjoy now, the life which, when once he had announced his secret, could never, in full completeness, be his again. And Rose was a dear, and really very beautiful. How the powdered hair and diamonds had become her. Yes, they would be married quite soon.

"Life's a glorious thing," he told himself; "but what a lot of rot they talk about love! One would think, from the way poets write about it, that it was something quite different from what it really is. All those hearts and darts and stars and roses; poetic license; but it's carried too far. I'll tell Bats the secret tomorrow. He deserves to know it first. If it hadn't been for him—"

He got his coat off and his waistcoat and his tie, and was fumbling with his collar stud when a little discreet soft tap sounded at his door. The door opened, and William Bats came in.

"Hullo!" said Anthony, dropping the collar stud; "never mind the stud, what's Sebastien for, anyhow!"

"Where is Sebastien?"

"In bed, I trust. I told him hours ago that I shouldn't want him."

"Then I can talk to you without being interrupted," said Bats deliberately.

"What's up?" Drelincourt asked, for Bats had shut the door in a stealthy but purposeful way.

"You know what's up. I told you. I must have it out with you, Tony. I can't sleep till I have. I don't like it. And I suppose we're friends enough still for me to tell you so?"

"*I* don't like it," said Anthony, "if you come to that. 'Still friends enough' sounds a little bit rum between us two, Bats, doesn't it? What have I done? Out with it."

"You know," said Bats deliberately. "I told you I knew. Of course, I always knew about the dogs and monkeys and things. But I didn't think you'd experiment on human bodies. At any rate I didn't think you'd do it *here*. Why, Good God, man, it was the merest luck that *I* found it. Suppose it had been anyone else? Suppose it had been one of the girls? Suppose it had been Rose?"

"Suppose *what* had been Rose? Found *what*? I haven't been experimenting on human bodies, here or anywhere else. At least not lately. You aren't drunk, I suppose. You never are. So, I suppose you're either kidding or else mad. And if you're kidding it's too late for larks, and I don't see any fun in it anyhow. And if you're mad, you'd better go to bed and see the doctor in the morning."

"Look here," said Bats, "you know I'm not mad, and I'm not a jackape to play the ass at two in the morning for nothing. You say you haven't been experimenting here. Well, then, someone else has played the fool."

"You're convinced, are you," said Anthony smoothly, "that I've not been leaving corpses about the place by accident? Now then," he turned angrily and suddenly on the other, "out with it. What the devil is all this rot about?"

"When we were playing hide-and-seek," said Bats very quietly, "I thought I would hide in your secret room. And I did. And then I remembered that Lady Blair had limited the hiding to the stairs and the hall and the sitting-rooms. So, I came out from under the end of the bench, and as I got up my shoulder caught in the barometer and it swung up on its nail, and something clicked. And when I stood up, I saw a crack in the wall and it was a door. The barometer is fastened to the wall and works a spring. I went in. I daresay I oughtn't to have, but I did. There's a little room, and inside that room, whoever put it there, there's a dead body. So now you know."

Anthony sat down on the sofa at the foot of the bed and looked at Bats.

"But there can't be," he said. "A body? Nonsense. There can't be," he repeated.

"I tell you I saw it."

"Some curious effect of light, I expect. I suppose you didn't go in?"

"Oh yes, I went in right enough. And I took a candle with me."

"Perhaps it was a statue or something," said Anthony vaguely, "because it couldn't have been what you say it was. It's impossible. These things don't happen."

"It isn't a statue," said Bats. "I touched it."

"You were upset by finding it. Marble does feel very like . . ."

"I wasn't upset, if you mean frightened. I was only furious with you for having such things in a house where there are women."

"But I tell you—"

"I know. I know. Well, what are you going to do?"

Anthony was putting on his coat.

"I'm going down," he said deliberately, "to find out what the devil's given you the impression of a perfectly impossible thing's having happened. There must be *something*. And it can't be what you say it is."

"All right," said Bats, "come on."

"You needn't come if you feel at all—what was it you said?—furious. I'm not afraid to go alone."

"Don't be a silly ass," said Bats. "I made a mistake. I thought what you'd have thought if you'd found what I found in any other physiologist's cupboard. Don't let's row. We shall have enough to do without that. I tell you the thing's there. And it's not been put there for any kind and wise purpose either. Someone's played this on you, and not to do you good. Come down and look. And then we'll see what's to be done. Or would you rather leave it till the morning? We can't do anything about it tonight, and now that I know that you-—"

"Thanks," said Anthony grimly, "when I do go to bed I want to sleep and not to lie awake wondering what the deuce has sent my best friend off his head . . ."

"I say," said Bats abruptly, standing with his hand on the door, "when I said I didn't mind when I found it, I was—well, it wasn't true exactly. I felt sick. I thought I'd gone off my head; and if I hadn't made sure, I shouldn't ever have been able to look myself in the face again."

Anthony pulled down his coat by the lapels.

"I know perfectly well," he said, "that I am not drunk. I have been drunk, I say it without shame, as one who has inadvertently ventured beyond his depth, and I know what it feels like. And yet all this is not sane common life. It's like a drunkard's dream of what he doesn't want to have happen."

"Old chap," said Bats, "it's quite simple. Somebody's played you a trick. Someone who doesn't like physiologists. What we've got to do is to find out who's done it, and why. Come on. Let's get it over."

They went on. Along the dim gallery, down the stairs which creaked a little and protested that this was no hour for any feet, even those of the master of the house, to be treading their shining surface; along the corridor to the door of the library, vast and quiet with its tiers of brown books and its heavy scent of leather and days long dead. Their candles showed in its spacious gloom like glow-worms in a forest.

They went, Anthony ahead, towards the Empire-furnished *boudoir*, that led to the staircase and the laboratory.

The predominant sentiment in Drelincourt's mind was annoyance. If Bats was playing a trick on him—well, that was annoying. If really the inconceivable had happened, and someone else in sheer spitefulness had played him a solid and definite trick—anti-vivisectionists and Brown Dog people were capable of it—that too was annoying. Especially now and here and thus.

Besides, it was late and he was tired, and the kingdoms and the glories and the powers were calling to him to lie down and rest on a bed of roses and laurels. The world was waiting for him. He had only to unfold his secret, and all the world must hail him victor, discoverer, master. And then some duffing outsider had suddenly tumbled a silly corpse into the middle of everything. Or perhaps hadn't. But in that case Bats, one's oldest friend, was as mad as a March hare, and that fact in itself was disconcerting and difficult to deal with. Yet Anthony found himself unable to take the position seriously.

"Oh, come on!" said Anthony, with the candlestick; "either you're mad or I am, and I should like to know which."

So, they went.

Bats fumbled a little with the key of the room.

"How finely you lied about it," said Anthony, "to Lord Alfriston, I mean."

"Oh, well," Bats answered, "if a thing's worth doing at all, it's worth doing well. I don't know what to think or what to do or what to say."

"Exactly," said Anthony, and then the door opened and they went in and down the stairs to the laboratory.

Bats twisted the barometer and the door opened. There was nothing to be seen.

Anthony told himself that he had felt certain there wouldn't be. Things like that didn't happen. He could not bring himself to expect anything but nothing. And nothing was here, sure enough, answering to his expectations. A black oblong, nothing more.

"Don't let it unnerve you," said Bats surprisingly. "No doubt there's a perfectly natural explanation. But in the meantime, here the thing is, and we've got to go through with it. Something must be done, and when you've seen it and made up your mind that I'm not playing an elaborate and silly joke on you, we can decide what to do. Look here," he said, leaning on the bench and holding up the candle so that he could see the other's face. "I am not playing the fool. So, hold tight to your nerves, if you've got any. Come on."

With that he stooped his head, for the doorway was low, and went into the inner room.

"You see," he said, holding the candle high.

It could plainly be seen that the room was another vaulted chamber, like the first but lower. In the middle of it, no couch or bed between it and the ground, lay a shape, to which a sheet or pale wrap of some kind moulded itself.

"Yes," said Bats, "that's it. Like to see the face?"

"Not by candle light," said Anthony. "If someone's trying to frighten us, a lay figure or a wax model could do the trick by candle light. I'll light the lamp."

A powerful sixty-two candle-power lamp stood on the bench. He lighted it with careful, steady fingers, and his friend stood in the doorway watching him.

"Now then," he said, "bring in that stool to stand it on."

Bats brought in the stool. Anthony set the lamp on the stool and looked around.

The room was vaulted like the laboratory, but it seemed to Bats that it must have been used as a chapel, for an altar of white marble, encircled with a metal chain, stood at one end. Carved on it, and gilded, was a sign that Bats did not recognise. It was a curious figure; two triangles, it looked like, with something else interlaced, and there were characters traced round it something like Hebrew, yet they were not all Hebrew. There were four long concave mirrors fitted into the old arches. There were tripods and copper dishes, a whole litter of strange objects. Bats had noticed these before, and Anthony did not seem to notice them now. The lamplight flooded the room and in the middle lay the still shape.

"Uncover it," said Anthony; "no, I will." But already Bats' hand was on the covering.

"It feels like powder," he said in a whisper, though he meant to speak aloud. "I expect we shook some dust down when we opened the door," said his friend; "gently there!"

And very gently Bats turned back the covering. A faint cloud of dust arose that made the candles look like stars in a fog, and the lamp showed like a moon in a night of mist. Slowly he folded the covering back till it lay across the knees of the figure. A sort of carpet of lambskin spread round it. Anthony fell on his knees on the soft skin and bent over the body.

"Bring the lamp here," he said. Bats brought it, set it on the ground by the head of what lay there, and stood looking down at that on which the yellow light glowed.

A woman! A young woman. Very pale, with closed eyes, dark fringed; arched, dark brows and a cloud of dark unbound hair that spread over the rug of white lambskin on which she lay. Her hands were folded lightly across her breast, as dead hands are folded. Her lips, pale and beautifully cut, were closed. She was not wrapped in grave clothes. Her dress was of pale red, with a V-shaped opening. Round her neck was a black velvet ribbon, and, attached to it, a gold pendant lay on the breast where no life stirred. The dress was unusual and complicated. She might have been one of the fancy-dress party that now already in this new happening seemed very long ago. Bats decided that the poor girl must have been rather good-looking when she was alive.

Anthony bent over her, laid his hand to the left side of her pale red bodice.

"It doesn't beat," said Bats; "I tried that."

Anthony laid his hand on the marble-white forehead where the black hair divided.

"She isn't dead!" he said. "She can't be dead! My God, how wonderful she is!"

"Wonderful?"

"Beautiful," said Anthony; "isn't she beautiful?"

"Yes—no—I don't know," said Bats testily. "Well, come along. Now you've seen it, you know I'm not humbugging you. Come back to your room and let's decide what we'd better do."

"We can't leave her here, you know," said Anthony; "she might wake and be frightened."

"*She* won't wake," said Bats a little sadly and very impatiently. "I wish she would. I don't think you quite realise what an infernal hole this puts us in, with inquests and all sorts of questions, and your experiments coming out, and all the old Brown Dog nonsense brought up. This dead girl—"

"I don't think she *is* dead," Anthony interrupted, sitting back on his heels. "Look here. Go and wake the doctor. I'll stay with her till you come back."

"Really? You want me to?" Bats spoke incredulously.

"Of course! Don't be idiotic. And, I say, you'd better lock the door of the room above and take the key with you. We don't want any of the servants or Lady Blair wandering down here. Fetch Wilton. See? Tell him there's something up and get him here quietly."

"You don't mind being left?"

"Good Lord, no, man! Why should I? He bent forward once more, and Bats very unwillingly took up his candle and went. He was not a nervous man, but he did not enjoy the traversing of the dark, high-ceilinged library, the sombre silent galleries, the stairs that creaked a very little and were full of shadows that danced to the movement of the candle he carried.

It is not an easy thing to wake a man from his first sleep and to explain briefly and convincingly that his presence is needed because a dead woman has been unexpectedly discovered in a secret room. But Bats did it, and he and the doctor went down through the still house, through the door that Bats had locked, and so, when he had locked it again, to the laboratory and that inner room where the marble altar was and the strange mirrors and the pale girl on the pale fur.

They found Anthony still leaning over her, only now his hands were laid on the dead hands.

"Get up, Drelincourt," the doctor said, with brisk matter-of-factness. "I can't make a proper examination with you there. Out of the way, man."

And he, in his turn, bent over the body. He touched her hands, her brow, her lips, her breast. Then he stood up. "No good," he said, "the poor girl's dead. How did she get here?"

"She's not dead," said Anthony quietly, "or if she is—I say! how long do you think she's been dead?"

"Less than half-an-hour I should say."

"But I saw her dead three hours ago," said Bats.

"That's impossible," said the doctor strongly. "Come on, you fellows, you can't do any good here. Drelincourt, come and see if you can find a tot of whisky. I feel to need it. And so, do you," he added to himself.

"You're certain she's dead?" Anthony asked, turning on the doctor a face as white as his own.

"Certain. Come along, do. It's all as rum as rum. Let's get out of this."

"Look here," said Anthony, almost stammering in a curious inexplicable eager anxiety; "I can't believe she's dead. I—you know I've studied physiology a bit. I should like to try—"

"You'll try nothing but a stiff glass of whisky," said the doctor, taking him by the arm.

"Let me cover her face," he said. "Go on, you chaps; I'll be up in a minute. I tell you to go. Am I the master of this house or you?"

"Oh, come on," said Bats; and as they went up the stairs the doctor said: "If he's not up in two minutes I go back. There's something here that I don't understand, and I tell you straight, Billy, I don't like it."

"You don't think—" said Bats, "because I'm positive he didn't know. He wouldn't believe she was there when I told him. *He* doesn't know anything about how she got there."

"He *thinks* he doesn't," said the doctor. "I agree there. But then he's off his chump, or near it. Did you see his eyes? Look here, I'm going back."

He turned, but Anthony was already at the stair head behind them.

"Give me the key," he said to Bats; "oh, it's in the door. Right. Go through. I'll lock it." He did, and the three went back to his great bedchamber.

On the way they found and brought up the tray with whisky and siphons. The doctor mixed for all three, but only two drank.

"Now don't worry," he said soothingly; "you go to bed and try to sleep, Drelincourt, and I'll sit beside you in case you wake up and want anything."

Anthony stared at him; then he laughed. "You old ass," he said, "I believe you think I've committed a murder and forgotten the details. Look here, this is something different, something wonderful, something you'll find it very hard to believe. I wish I'd told you all about it before. You'd have found it easier."

"I wish you had," said the doctor.

"Now look here," said Drelincourt; "I'm not mad. Feel my pulse, look at my tongue. Apply any of your absurd tests. I'm as sane as you are. And you never knew me lie. I don't know how that girl got there."

"Do you mean to say you don't know who she is?"

"I have no idea who she is."

"You mean to tell us you've never seen her before?"

"I—I—" he hesitated, confused a little it seemed; "it sounds silly, but I may have seen her before. But if I have it must have been—I mean I don't know where. But all that's beside the point."

"Good God!" said the doctor, "you'll find out whether it's beside the point at the coroner's inquest. Old chap," he went on more gently, "try to tell us all about it, and we'll try to pull you through. I believe in you, old man. I'm certain it wasn't your fault."

"You always were a good old duffer," Drelincourt told him. "Look here. Sit down, both of you, and try to understand. That girl *isn't* dead; or if she is, I can bring her to life."

"They'll never hold you responsible," said the doctor soothingly.

"Look here," said Anthony again, "if I don't go mad it won't be your fault. I don't know how the girl got there. I don't know who she is. But I know that I can bring her to life. It's the worst possible moment to tell you. But that's my infernal luck. I meant to tell Billy tomorrow. He'd have understood and believed all right then. You see, this is really my secret. This is my discovery. This is the thing I've been working at ever since I was a boy of sixteen. I've done it with rabbits; I've done it with a monkey; I've done it with a dead child I got from the hospital. He's alive and well at a cottage in Esher at this moment. And I'll do it for this girl. So long as she's not been dead twenty-four hours, and you say she hasn't. The thing's safe, safe, safe. Try to take it in. I can bring dead people to life. I can bring dead people to life! That's what I've discovered. And now you know."

"But look here," said Bats, humouring him, "if she died, she died from some cause, and that cause will be there and kill her again as soon as you've brought her to life."

"Do you think I don't know my business?" Anthony asked. "Do you think I've worked and sweated all these years only to be pantaloon to your harlequin? I know what I'm talking about. It's no use explaining to you anymore. You wouldn't understand. It isn't all physiology. And I'll tell you something else. The person who put her there knew she wasn't dead. Or at any rate he knew more than you do. Look here. Think of *fakirs*, who seem dead and have their noses and mouths stopped with clay and are buried and dug up again after months and come to life again. Try to realise that you don't know everything. And now get out. I want to go to sleep."

The other two looked at each other, and their looks said, "Ought we to leave him?"

He answered the look.

"Oh, very well," he said, "then Bats shall sleep on the sofa there. Will that satisfy you? Now look here. I'll tell you another thing. When you left me alone with her, I injected something into her arm. I shan't tell you what it was. But if I'm right and you're wrong—and I'm almost certain you are—then tomorrow, even a doctor, even you, Wilton, will be able to see that she's not dead. If she is—well, you can do what you like."

And on that the doctor went. Bats closed the door and came back to Anthony.

"Now," he said, "you'll sleep, won't you?"

"I wish," said Drelincourt, "that I hadn't injected that stuff. Because now Wilton will just think he was mistaken. I ought to have let a dozen doctors see her and declare that she was dead. Then I should have proved my discovery. Only I was afraid to risk the waiting—for her. Though really, I know it would have been safe enough. Only for her, everything ought to be safer than safe. Goodnight. I shall sleep like a tired dog."

He did. Bats lay awake. He was not so sure as the doctor was that the sudden finding of the dead girl had turned Drelincourt's brain. He was not so sure as the doctor was, for he had read more, thought more, seen more, heard more, and imagined far far more. He was not so sure as the doctor about anything. At the same time, it seemed to him good that Anthony should sleep and that he should watch. So, he watched. And his thoughts, even so, were not all of Anthony, nor of Anthony's discovery, nor even of the pale quiet form that lay on the yellow-white lambskin in that strange tawdry chapel-chamber.

CHAPTER 14

Moving the Chest

Anthony sat up in bed with the feeling that he was late for something. And when he sat up, Bats, on the sofa at the foot of the bed, sat up too and said, "Hullo!—sleep well?" Then Anthony remembered, and he lay back on his pillow and said: "We shall want a good deal of skilled diplomacy today, William. I wish the house wasn't full of all these people."

"If you take my advice," said Bats; "I've been thinking it over pretty thoroughly—if you take my advice you'll ring for Sebastien to bring your writing things and just sit up in bed and write a little note to the Inspector of Police, and send a man on a horse to Lewes with it before breakfast."

"What good will that do?"

"Why, don't you see? That body's been put there to get you into trouble."

"There's no one who would do it," said Anthony; "I don't believe I have an enemy in the world. Nobody's enemy but his own, you know."

"To get you into trouble," pursued Bats, unmoved. "If *you* don't let the police know, you bet the man who put the thing there *will*. That's what he put it there for, the brute. Send off the man on the horse and spike the enemy's guns."

"Your advice is admirable," said Anthony, "and I shan't take it."

"But why?" said Bats, rearing himself up on the blue sofa so that he could rest his elbows on the foot of the bed and contemplate the recumbent Anthony, who answered—

"Too much fuss."

"There'll be fuss anyhow," said Bats; "better be the author of the fuss than its subject. Good Lord, Tony, you must see that the thing's serious. And you say you think you've seen that poor girl before."

"I didn't say that," Anthony reminded him, "and I do see that the thing's serious. But in quite a different way from what you mean. You are an observant person in your own line, Billy. Did you notice the dust last night, when you lifted that veil thing?"

"Yes, why?"

"Look here, I am not going to tell you any more now; but I know more about this than you think. To begin with—I did tell you that though——I don't believe she's dead. What I'm thinking about now is that if she's to come to life, this isn't the best place for her to come to life in."

"It wasn't your selection," said Bats brutally.

"I think—I'm not sure, but I think I had better get her to Malacca Wharf."

"That strikes you as a suitable place for resurrections?"

"I've effected some there, however," said Anthony. "Suppose we get the others to go for a picnic, say we'll join them later ; then we get the carpenter to knock up a packing case, put her in it, the doctor and I take her to Malacca Wharf, and you join the picnic party and say I've had a telegram."

"There's only one objection to that. Whoever put the thing there will be on the watch, see you go off with a narrow six-foot box, the police will meet you at the station. *Avez vous rien a déclarer?* Won't that be nice?"

"You don't seem to see," Anthony lay placid among his pillows, "that whoever put her there would have to account for her. Supposing

254

that the person who put her there is alive. Yes. I know what I'm talking about. If I'm right, there's no chance of the police butting in. If you're right, the person who put her there will get the shock of his life when he accompanies your police to the fatal spot."

"But why?"

"Because she's not dead," said Anthony. "Now clear out, do you mind, before Sebastien turns up. We don't want unnecessary chatter."

There was a good deal of chatter at breakfast; the kind of chatter that sounds amusing when one is amused. The day was fine, the company pleased with itself. Lord Alfriston and Rose had been first to appear. Rose had said how jolly it would be to have breakfast on the terrace.

Lord Alfriston had said why not? and turning to the man busy among the silver paraphernalia of the sideboard, he asked whether breakfast was ever served on the terrace.

"Not in my time, my lord," the man answered. "I could ask Mr. Wilkes."

Mr. Wilkes, having an eye to the side on which the bread of the future should be buttered, had appeared in a stately morning dress to superintend the swift changes that ended in a white and silver table glittering in soft sunshine. Lord Alfriston had thrown gravel at Anthony's window, and, addressing himself to the resultant apparition, inquired, "What about breakfast out of doors?" Anthony had answered that breakfast out of doors was the dream of his youth and the fallacious aspiration of his riper years, and now here they all were, still vibrating to the last night's pleasant innocent intimacies and full of schemes for the completest enjoyment of the new and pretty day.

Miss Raven seemed to be unfolding like a marigold that, closed in the shade, opens frankly to the sunshine. Linda Smith had managed still to be in white and pink. If the dress was Rose's and had taken two ante-breakfast hours to alter and adjust, she and Rose alone knew it. Lord Alfriston and Mr. St. Maur were pleased explorers in a new social world; Mullinger, always happy with the Septet, was here radiant. Anthony and Bats were brilliant beyond their wont. Only the doctor seemed a little silent, a little abstracted. But in the froth of gaiety, real or simulated, a little silence and abstraction were easily hidden. It was a pretty sparkling picture, such as might have been painted by a Conder of clean instincts and a high spirit. Lady Blair had not broken through her rule.

"You know the adage," she had said the night before; "*Appear before breakfast, perish before tea.* Rose will preside." And Rose presided.

"It's all so much too near being perfect," Esther suddenly spoke to Anthony in a key lower than that of the conversation, which was in C Major. "Of course, I know this luxury's very wrong, and you're a wicked aristocrat, living on other people's toil, but it's the most perfect thing I've ever seen. And everyone's so nice. Are all the noblemen of England jolly? Or are we extra lucky? Do all people with titles live in this do-as-you-like way? Is it your atmosphere or the atmosphere of the upper classes?"

"I'm inclined to think it's yours," he said, "and Rose's, and Linda's and Bats and the rest of you. You must have brought it with you."

"Don't you feel," she went on, "rather like a *marquis* just before the French Revolution? If I were you, I should feel that something were going to happen, that it couldn't last. Suppose We heard a faint, far-away shouting, and it was the Great Voice of the People with pikes and guns clamouring for your blood at one of your picturesque lodge-gates?"

"They won't clamour," said Anthony almost sadly; "they haven't sense enough. They wouldn't touch a gun; they touch a cap. Pull a trigger? Not they! They only know how to pull a forelock."

"Then you're not afraid."

"No," said Anthony. "I don't think I am."

"Is there no dark passage in your past," Esther went on, in a hollow voice, "that calls you to beware?"

"I haven't heard it," said Anthony, laughing.

"Then you feel no thrill of apprehension when you perceive the uniform of the local constable appearing and disappearing among the trees of your park?"

"Constable?" said the doctor sharply; "where?"

Esther pointed. "But *you've* nothing to be afraid of," she told the doctor. "It's the wicked baronet whose accomplices have betrayed him; the head of the secret coining gang."

"There *is* a policeman, though," said the doctor earnestly; "what can he want?"

"To make an appointment for Sunday with one of the under house-maids," said Lord Alfriston, "under cover of a report about poachers."

The policeman was now seen to be approaching across the smooth path, the sunlight glinting on his buttons. A pang of sickening doubt shot through Anthony. Suppose Bats were right, and someone—it was inconceivable, but then any explanation was inconceivable—suppose the whole thing was a plot to get him into trouble—suppose this man had come to arrest him-him, Anthony, how would it be with *her?* He believed that she lived. But, after that injection, she would not live another day unless he was at hand to continue the treatment, the same treatment that had succeeded with the bird, the monkey, and the little boy now so happily alive at Esher. He sprang up.

"Come on, Billy," he said, "let's go and hear about the poachers."

Bats followed him.

"If you're right," said Anthony, quick and low, "if that man has come to arrest me, say you're me, will you? It will just give me time to get to her and make the next injection. She'll have to come to life here, of course; infernal nuisance. But if she's left for another twenty-four hours, she *will* be dead. Keep him as long as you can. I can barricade myself into that lab. for long enough to make everything safe for *her.*"

The policeman was out of sight when they got to the end of the terrace. They ran down the steps and saw him making for the side door.

"Don't let him get at the house," said Anthony.

"All right! All right!" said Bats impatiently. "Hi! Hullo!" he shouted.

The constable turned his head, then himself, and walked heavily towards them.

"What do you want?" said Bats, when they met.

The man saluted and fumbled in his pocket.

"He's got a warrant, or whatever it is," Anthony told himself; "and yet it *can't* be."

"I wished to ask Sir Anthony Drelincourt," said the policeman, still fumbling.

"Yes?" said Bats.

"If you would be so kind, Sir, to support the police *fête* on the seventeenth of next month in aid of the widows and orphans of members of the force?"

"Oh, rather," said Anthony, and laughed aloud. "I thought you'd come about poachers or something like that," he added, to explain that inappropriate laugh; "glad it's only a *fête*. Here, let's have the tickets."

A glad-hearted policeman went down the drive chinking gold in his pocket.

"Something like a gentleman," he told himself.

"Look here," said Anthony, "I shall give myself away if I don't look out. It's your doing, Billy. You and Wilton between you. You must run that picnic, as I said, and let me get clean away. And I'll think of some excuse for our not going with them to the picnic."

"Let me send for the police, like a sensible chap," said Bats.

"It's impossible," said Anthony earnestly; "I can't go into it all now. There's a lot more to it, Billy. But even if you're right and I'm a silly lunatic, there are three of us to swear to finding her. None of us can get into any row over it. There are no risks. If there were I should do so just the same. It's much the most important chance I've ever had. I tell you there are things—Talk about something else, will you? We mustn't arrive in silence."

When they got back to the terrace, the whole party was engaged in gathering roses with which to pelt Lady Blair, who, in the wonderful chestnut pig-tailed wig and a blue *kimono*, was leaning out of her window. She looked about twenty-five, and the powder did not show at all at that distance. She kissed a little pale hand to the two as they came within her range of vision.

"The top of the morning to you," she called; "and what's the programme for today?"

"Isn't there a ruined abbey, or a castle or something?" Drelincourt called back; "today was made for a picnic."

"Of course, there is. Both!" she said. "I'm coming down to organise the picnic. It's absolutely *the* thing. Is it a popular idea? or a little unsupported project of your own?"

"It's *the* thing," said everyone. And Lord Alfriston said: "I could find it in my heart to be the person named Whitehead."

"Who was he?" asked Esther, who didn't know. Lord Alfriston recited the immortal words—

> There was a young person named Whitehead,
> Who never knew when he was slighted;
> When he went to a party
> He'd eat just as hearty
> As if he'd been really invited.

"Thank you," said Anthony. "I think that is the most touching compliment I ever received. Of course, I hoped you could stay and would."

"Concealment is at an end," said Lord Alfriston; "I have been hoping ever since I came yesterday that you wouldn't be able to part with me this morning."

Lady Blair had disappeared.

"I'm so glad to see you still at large," said Esther, who seemed somehow like somebody else; "the coining industry is not yet ruined."

"I am spared," said Drelincourt, "for the moment. He had a writ or a warrant or whatever it is in his pocket, but my face and manner disarmed him, and he pretended that it was a subscription to a skittle alley for the use of disabled policemen that he was after."

There was a chorus of laughter.

"Wouldn't it be pretty and romantic of us to go and feed the swans," suggested Bats, collecting bread from the table. And the chorus broke up into duets.

"Look here, Rose," said Anthony, the moment he and she were alone together in the swan-ward procession. "Something rather unusual has happened, and the doctor and I have got to go to London. I want you to keep things going. You and Billy can do it. I don't want explications, or to have to lie in detail to the whole lot of them. And there isn't time to lie artistically; and there isn't time to tell the truth to them. There isn't time to tell the truth to you."

"It's nothing horrid, is it?" she asked. "You might tell me, Tony. Just in three words."

"Three thousand wouldn't do justice to it. No, it's very exciting; it's to do with my work. It's really the chance of a lifetime. I *can't* tell you anymore. There isn't time. But I'm going to say we'll join you at the abbey, or whatever it is. And then I shan't. Bats will turn up alone, and say I've been telegraphed for to go to London on urgent business. I'll try to get back tonight. I shan't be able to really; but he'd better say that. I don't want to break up the party; they seem so happy!"

"Yes," said Rose; "but I wish I knew."

"You *can't* know now. It would take ages. We're just upon the others. Back me up, there's a dear, and play up for all you know to keep things jolly. And don't say a word to anyone. You shall know all about it in time. I couldn't make you understand without a lot of explanation."

"All right," said Rose cheerfully; "if it's about your work I know I should want to be a good deal explained to."

"I wish we'd been the first lovers," he said, with unusual tenderness; "you'd never have got turned out of Paradise for silly curiosity."

"How well you know me," she laughed, but she thrilled to the tone, and stroked his sleeve furtively with two fingers. Also, she flushed a little, remembering shamefully how she had pried into his laboratory against his wishes—and found Mr. Abrahamson.

"I wish you weren't going," she said. "Do you know, I sometimes wish you hadn't any work. I should like just to live here and spend your money. What a time we'd give my biscuit boys! That's the best of having been poor. One knows how to spend money. These rich people don't. And I do like swans," she ended, as they joined the group by the lake. "They are the only people who can be greedy gracefully."

Anthony got away from his guests and waited in the hall till Lady Blair came down the stairs, charming in grey muslin and pink roses. Her face, fresh from the clever hands of her maid, was a masterpiece veiled by chiffon.

"You look like Aurora," he said, taking her hand at the foot of the stairs. "Just come into the library a moment, will you? I want to conspire with you."

"There's nothing I love better than a conspiracy," she said, making soft eyes at him, quite prettily too, for all her years; "unless it's a conspirator."

They were alone in the library.

"This picnic," he said, "you'll make it 'go,' won't you? I have some important letters to write. So has Bats. And the doctor has to do his column of medical answers to correspondents for *Lily of the Valley*. It's the way the poor live, you know. So, you must start without us. We will take the little car and join you at the ruin, or whatever it is. Only I shall get an important telegram and have to go to London, and the doctor will go with me. Bats will come and tell you, and you will be much surprised and disappointed."

"I'm both already," she said.

"I hope to get back tonight," Anthony went on, "but, as a matter of fact, I know I shan't be able to. I'll do the rest with telegrams. It's a question of some of my experiments, and I don't know how long it'll take."

"Must you go?"

"Absolutely. But I don't want to break up the party. Everyone seems to be having a good time. And I want you to keep it going till I get back, and to expect me every day for certain. Will you?"

"How delightfully mysterious. Of course, I will. But I want to know a little more. Is it really experiments? Or is it something you've suddenly got to adjust; some old entanglement, perhaps? I'm secret as the grave? And if I could help in any way?"

"If you could, I'd ask you like a shot," he answered, and added with intentional disingenuousness, "I don't know how you guessed. But it *is* an old affair. You won't talk about it to anyone, will you? especially not to Rose."

"My dear boy," said Lady Blair, "anyone would think you were talking to a girl. If I haven't learnt to hold my tongue by now, I'm afraid I never shall learn it."

"So *that's* settled," said Anthony. "I never can make up my mind whether you're most like the fairy godmother or the fairy princess. But anyhow . . ." he carried her hand to his lips. . . . "Get them off as soon as you can, won't you?" he said.

"You're very handsome this morning," said Lady Blair, "and very— what shall we say?—*interested.*"

"I'm intolerably interested," said Anthony quite truthfully. "I want to get the matter settled."

"Don't be too interested," said Lady Blair; "these old entanglements—I could tell you a story—the man had to marry the young woman, and he was engaged to a Really Nice Girl. These last meetings, you know—so dangerous."

"Exactly. I'm taking Wilton with me," said Anthony. "I cannot excuse him."

"That's very wise," Lady Blair said; "it's the despairing parting *tête-à-tête* that ruins a young man's life. Now don't worry. Trust me entirely. And get back as soon as you can to your fairy princess and your fairy godmother. Where is the fairy princess, by the way? Your beautiful Rose."

"Feeding the swans, of course. That one. Where should a fairy princess be? Unless she's talking to the poor entangled prince. I suppose I am a prince, if you're a princess."

"I'll tell you what you are," said Lady Blair; "you're different. And if I were Rose, I should get the wedding day fixed."

Anthony felt suddenly ashamed of himself.

"Will you drive?" he said. "What carriages shall I order? I'll go round to the stables myself. Oh! but I'd like to."

And, on that, got away. Lady Blair would have made an excellent commanding officer. Within an hour of Anthony's appeal, she had her flock arranged, her hampers ready, her carriages at the door. In a flutter of smiles and ribbons and gay last words, they drove off.

"Thank God!" said Anthony, on the terrace as the last carriage vanished among the trees. "Now, Wilton, come on into the library. I suppose Bats told you what I mean to do?"

"It's an insane thing," said Wilton slowly. "The police—"

"You can give me up to the police if you like," said Anthony; "but, unless you do, I'm going through with it. Come on."

The Empire room within the library was a safe place to talk in.

"I've looked out a train," said Wilton; "there's one at 1.7. And that idea of carpenters and packing cases is rotten. You don't want any more people in it. There's an inlaid chest in the hall. It's only got tennis rackets in it. Couldn't you be taking that up to your rooms in London with apparatus in it—if you like."

"Can you and I move it?"

"I should think so," said Wilton; "but why make a secret of *that*? You rather want to make a show of it. Ring for your footman. Tell them what you're going to do. Tell them to have a cart or something ready to take it to the station."

"Has it got a lock?"

"Yes, a modern one. The key of my bureau fits it. I've been attending to that. And I thought I'd meet the telegraph boy, and bring you a telegram while they're bringing the box in. I've got an old red envelope."

"Good!" said Anthony. "You are some good after all, Wilton."

"Then when they've brought the thing in here, we can carry the body up and put it in and lock it up. I'm a fool to help you, I know, but I—"

"Don't try to excuse yourself for one of the very few sensible things you've ever done," said Anthony. "Ring the bell, then, and let's get it over." He gave his orders to the servant whom the bell summoned, and the chest was brought in.

"Will you want any straw or packing of any sort, sir?" the man asked. "Or could I pack for you ?"

"No, thank you. I'd rather see to it myself," Anthony told him. "And I'm not to be disturbed. I have letters to write."

The man went out, and Anthony, having waited till he had passed across the library and closed its door behind him, locked the door of the little *boudoir*, set the lid of the chest wide, and led the way to the staircase.

In the laboratory he paused and stood a moment with his hand on the barometer.

"If I'm right, Wilton," he said, "you must prepare for a shock. It's rather decent of you to help me, backing my hand blind like this, and I'll tell you what. If you still think it's a case for the police when you've seen her again, I'll—well, I'll promise to think it over." He could not bring himself to say more than that. And now he turned the barometer round and the spring clicked.

"Best light the lamp before we go in," he said. And the lamp was lighted.

Wilton himself could not have told you what he expected. If he had been asked, he would have answered that he expected to find everything as they had left it last night, but this could not have been the fact, because, when he looked round the vaulted room and perceived no change, he experienced a faint sensation of disappointment. He did not know that it was disappointment, but it was.

Anthony closed the door. "Now," he said, "I want you to examine her heart and lungs. Satisfy yourself again that she *is* dead. We were all a little startled last night. I want your cool, measured, morning opinion. Go ahead, man."

The doctor obeyed. The examination was more searching and more prolonged than the last. But the verdict was the same. Only it was given in a different tone, and in different words.

"I find no sign of life," said the doctor. "I fear she is dead." And he said nothing more about the police.

"Well then," said Anthony, "I'll carry her up."

"I'll take the feet," said the doctor.

But Anthony had already stooped and gathered up the body as one gathers up a sick child.

"Bring the lambskin," he said, standing up and shifting his burden so that most of the weight was on his left shoulder. "So: go first and show me the light."

The doctor obeyed. And when Anthony had mounted the stairs, staggering a little, and came out into the Empire room, the doctor set down the lamp on a console table where it burned palely in the sunshine.

"That's right, put the fur in the box," he said. "Put those sofa cushions in first. That's it. Now keep the lid steady. Right!"

He stooped and laid the body in the woolly nest, smoothed the dark hair, and arranged the hands across the quiet breast.

"The lungs are not acting? You're sure of that?"

"Quite."

"Then more sofa pillows. There must be no chance of bruising her against the chest."

"But if she's alive?" said the doctor. It was his first concession.

"But you say she isn't. And anyhow it's all right for a few hours. We must travel in the guard's van with her. Fetch up some odds and ends from the lab., will you? To look as though we'd been packing apparatus. Strew some straw about. There's a case of glass under the bench downstairs."

"Yes," said Wilton. "I say! The way the arms fell over your shoulder——"

"Yes, I know," Anthony interrupted; "you'll have to come round to my view. Hurry up with that straw."

Anthony spread the veil over the face in the chest, and gently laid the sofa cushions on it, and folded the ends of the lambskin up over all. Then he shut the lid.

"Now," he said, when Wilton came back with the straw, "just lock it, will you? while I go down and collect one or two things I need."

He went down and began to put together certain objects from the inner room.

The doctor, left alone, lifted the pillow and the veil for one more look. Hearing Anthony returning, he hastily lowered the lid and turned the key. But it would not turn; something obstructed it. He tried again; something resisted, yielded, the lock turned, and he took the key out. Then he saw that what had withstood him was a fold of filmy red stuff which, overflowing from the chest, had caught in the lock. It showed more fully at the side of the lock. He did not want to unlock the box again, so he tore at the stuff and a piece came away in his hand. He drove in the broken edges under the lid with his penknife.

"Locked? Right!" said Anthony. He had a bundle of knobbly things in a cloth.

"I'll cut up and pack these things in a bag," he said. "You ring and tell them to bring the cart round, and we'll see the chest taken down ourselves."

They did. And they reached the station in time to oversee the lifting of the chest from the cart. It was an easy matter for Sir Anthony Drelincourt to arrange to travel up in the guard's van beside the chest that "contained valuable apparatus." Wilton kept him company. The journey was tedious. Both men were tired, and responded with effort to the guard's subservient commonplaces.

The glory of the day faded as they neared London, and it was under grey skies that Wilton sought out a greengrocer near London Bridge, who—one of the porters assured them—"kept a van." Anthony remained at the station guarding the chest, and was an object of deep interest to a girls' school on its way to the Crystal Palace. After a very long time Wilton came back with the van and two beery satellites. The traffic was heavy and the eastward journey slow. Anthony, with the calmness of a man the natural impatience of whose temperament had been schooled to quietness by his stronger will, sat by the driver looking straight out over the horse's ears. It was Wilton who criticised the driver's choice of route, and besought him, more than once, to "hurry up."

"The 'orse is doing of 'er best," the driver always answered; "it's a bit thick today, you see. We're a-gettin' on now."

And so, at long last, skirting the mean streets and the waste ground, the van stopped at the big gates of Malacca Wharf; the gates were jerked back on their rusty hinges, and the carved chest was carried across moss-grown stones, up the stairway, and into the laboratory, already dusty with solitude.

"Thankee, guvner," said the major satellite, wiping his forehead with the back of his hand; "I don't mind if I do. It's bin as 'eavy a job as ever I done. Full of gold and silver, I s'pose." He laughed and spat on the half-crown that had been Anthony's largesse. "I'd as lief carry a corfin," he said. "Thankee, sir!"

CHAPTER 15
Three Telegrams

The filling of a chest with any object which you may wish to remove, the superintending of its removal from your Ancestral Halls in Sussex to your laboratory in London, may present difficulties; but the task is simplicity itself compared with playing a conspirator's part at a picnic when your fellow conspirators are far away and you, besides being afraid of committing yourself, are racked with a thousand curiosities and anxieties in regard to the conspiracy, its cause, its progress, and what the deuce is going to be the end of it all.

William Bats carried out Drelincourt's programme, and Lady Blair played up beautifully: was surprised and desolated to hear that Anthony had been called away to London, and assuaged and comforted to hear that he would return that night if possible. The other guests behaved quite naturally: except Rose. Rose said nothing whatever at first. And then she said too much, regretting Anthony's absence with transparent falseness, and saying how much too bad it was of him, till Bats longed to shake her. He did mutter, as he offered her salad, "Don't overdo it;" but she did not seem to hear. Fortunately, the picnic party was enjoying itself, and Bats perceived that only he and Lady Blair were observant of Rose.

One picnic is very like another. This one was at Bodiam, and the cloth was spread in the courtyard of the old castle. After luncheon everyone wandered except Lady Blair, who said she would like to sit quietly for a little while and think of the past.

"Ruined castles always make me think of the past," she said. "The ravages of time, you know. And the past *is* the past, whether it's fifty years ago or five hundred."

So, they left her. And she went to sleep at once. The ravages of time are wonderfully resisted by sleep. And Lady Blair had this much in common with Napoleon and the Iron Duke, that she could take sleep as she found it, by the minute or by the hour.

The rest of the picnic party divided itself into couples, as all well-regulated picnic parties should do, and began to explore. Lord Alfriston and Miss Raven found the old punt, and went round and round the broad moat that is half choked with water-lilies under the shadow of the tall towers. Mullinger and Linda Smith found the scaling of the crumbling walls worthwhile. Miss Royal and Mr. Bats stood and looked at each other.

"Well!" said she.

He replied like an echo. "Well?"

"Let's climb a tower," she said; "or no, let's climb on to that bit of broken wall by where they say the refectory used to be. Then I can smoke, and if any tourists come, I can see them in time and hide the cigarette. In towers people come upon you unawares. I must smoke."

"You're feeling like that, are you?" said he, for it was a recognised convention that Rose only smoked when she was worried. ("One must smoke or drink," she was used to say, "and drinking would be disgusting, whereas smoking is merely repulsive")

"Yes; exactly like that," she said, setting hand and foot to the climbing of the mound. "There, now you get up on the other side. That's it. Now then, what's the matter with Tony?"

"Tony?" he echoed blankly.

"Yes, Tony! Not you or me or Mullinger, but Tony. What is it?"

"What's what?"

"Of course, if you won't tell me, you won't," said Rose; "but it's no use repeating what I say like a parrot. Something has happened to Tony. Something important. And I want to know what it is."

"How should I know?" he said. "How should I know that anything has happened?"

"Do you know why he's gone to London?"

"No," lied Bats loyally. It was the first lie he had ever told Rose, and he did not enjoy it.

"Now look here, Billy," Rose was saying; "don't be crusty and tiresome. Anthony was different this morning. Didn't you notice it? I can't make you understand if you didn't notice it. But he was different. And I wonder whether it had anything to do with his going to London. Has it?"

"I don't know what you mean, and I don't know where he's gone. And I don't pry into his business."

"You mean I do? Of course, I do. I ought to. You pretend to be fond of him."

"I don't."

"And yet you can't see that he's no more fit to take care of himself than a baby."

"I wonder how you'd like it if anyone said that of you?"

"They *couldn't* say it of me. Why didn't you go with him?"

"*My* name isn't Whitehead," said Bats.

"Well, mine is," said Rose, her head turned away from him. She was picking bits of moss from between the stones and pulling them to pieces: the cigarette had gone out. "If I'd called myself his friend, I'd have gone with him. Billy, do be nice. I'm awfully worried about him. I want you to tell me something."

"Well?"

"Has he ever been in love with anyone else?"

"You really think I should tell you if he had?"

"No, of course not, but you might tell me if he hasn't."

"I should tell you that if he had."

"Oh, don't be clever! Tell me, has he?"

"On the distinct understanding that I should say the same whether he had or had not, I don't mind telling you that to the best of my knowledge and belief he's never been in love with anyone."

"Not even with me?"

"You know I didn't mean that," he answered, knowing that he *had* meant it, though he had not meant to say it.

"If you hadn't—I mean if I hadn't-I mean if I didn't feel sure that he hadn't cared for anyone else I should feel as though he *had* cared for someone, and that this going to London is something to do with *her*."

"I may set your mind at rest then," said Bats, "because really I don't believe he ever has."

There was a silence. Then Rose said: "I'll tell you one reason why

267

I'm worried. Old Abrahamson told my fortune for me once. He looked in the crystal. And I looked—

"And saw—your fate? Anthony?"

"I saw Anthony, yes. But Abrahamson saw something else. It was that day I brought the coffee, and we sat on the stairs. Do you remember?"

Bats remembered.

"Well, I went into the laboratory after you'd gone, I don't care," she said, answering some voice that was not hers or Bats. "I don't care. I shall tell if I like. I got Ben Levi to send a telegram to Linda and she sent me one. And I told you it was from the *Glorious Weekly*, and you went out with the illustrations. Then I got my key and went into the laboratory."

"When you knew he didn't wish it?"

"Yes. I wanted to find out *why* he didn't wish it."

"How extraordinarily dishonourable," said Bats deliberately.

"Yes, it was. I'm glad you know it, though. I wanted to tell Anthony, but I was afraid if I did, I should let out what Mr. Abrahamson said."

"What did he say?"

"He came almost as soon as you'd gone. He seemed much less English than usual—very mysterious; and he looked in the crystal and he told me the man I cared about would ask me to marry him that day. And Anthony *did*, that very evening. So *that* came true. Then he said that the man I cared about would be very rich, and *that* came true too. So, it looks as though there were something in it, doesn't it? And it's that that torments me. Because if two things have come true, the others may."

"What were the others?"

"He said something about a strange sorrow. And he said if wealth came to my—to him, I mean——I ought to make him refuse it. And I didn't, of course, when the time came. And he said it was a matter of life and death. And then he pretended not to believe it and went away."

"What did he see in the crystal? Didn't he tell you?"

"He said he saw something he didn't understand. He said he saw a beautiful woman—dead."

"*What?*" said Bats, almost falling off the mound.

"It wasn't *me*," she went on ingenuously. "Some other woman. And it was after he'd seen that, that he pretended not to believe in it. So, I know the strange sorrow had something to do with *her*."

"I see," Bats forced himself to say.

"So, I wondered whether Tony's going today had anything to do with anyone else he'd cared for. I thought she might be dying and have sent for him. He might have told me. I shouldn't have been jealous or horrid about it."

"Not if she was really dying, you wouldn't. No!" said Bats.

"Billy. You are fond of me, aren't you?" said Rose quickly. "Because if you are, don't say unkind things. I feel so helpless. As if I were alone at sea in a boat without oars. You know I've always felt so strong. As if I could always trust myself to keep going and to have a dozen people hanging on to me and keep them going too."

"I know," he said, "and so you have."

"Yes, but," she went on, "it's not like that now. I feel like a person that's lost its way. I've always felt as if—well, don't you know, sort of George Eliot-y about Fate—as if one made one's own fate, and that people who were unfortunate were really only silly. I always felt I could do anything I wanted, and that other people ought to be able to too. If I wanted any one to like me, they always did."

"I know," said Bats again.

"Until," she was going on, but Bats' voice seemed to awaken her. She stopped short. "I'm talking an awful lot of nonsense," she said; "the cigarette must have got into my head. Oh! it's gone out and I've broken it at the waist. Give me another. What I was trying to say was that I'm anxious about Anthony. And I know it's silly. But I wish you were with him."

"He's got Wilton."

"Wilton's no good. *He'll* look after Wilton. But you'd look after *him*. It was Wilton going too that made me wonder whether he'd gone to see someone who's ill."

"You're worrying yourself about nothing," said Bats. "I believe Anthony's gone up on some business connected with his great discovery. And he'll tell you all about it if you ask him, I've no doubt."

"I never like to ask him about his work," said Rose. "I simply can't understand it, and when he takes a bit of paper and a pencil and says he'll make it as simple as ABC, my brain spins round like a—what are those tops that go crooked?—yes, a gyroscope."

"Cheer up," said Bats. "I suppose the wives of geniuses always have a poor time. And I suppose that there's something that compensates. He probably thinks it's a noble reticence that makes you not ask questions about his work. When really it's your gyroscopic mind."

"Yes," said she, "and it's hateful, isn't it, when people think you much nicer than you are?"

"I don't know," said Bats; "do you? It works both ways, doesn't it?"

"I suppose that's clever," said Rose. "Look, the Fairy Godmother is signalling. It *can't* be tea-time already. Yes, I can get down all right."

It seemed to Bats that he had had enough for one day. But Destiny thought otherwise. It elected that he should occupy the second seat in the little motor. The other seat was Lady Blair's, and no sooner were they alone in the little motor's whirring luxury than she opened on him with—

"What's the matter with Anthony?"

Mr. Bats wanted to be quiet, wanted to think, but he roused himself to defend the position with—

"What do you mean?"

"He seemed different this morning," said the terribly observant old lady. "More vivid, more alert. As though something wonderful had happened to him. I've seen the look before," she sighed.

"Then you ought to know what it means better than I, who can't even recognise it from your description."

"But that's just it," said she. "When I've observed that look before, it's been because the young man who wore the look had just fallen in love."

"It's not that, at any rate."

"I understand from Anthony," said Lady Blair, "that you and I are at present his sole confidants in the matter of his engagement to our magnificent Rose. What a girl, what strength, what force of character, what integrity, what noble beauty!"

Bats felt half-inclined to say "Thank you!" and more than half-inclined to say "Don't be impertinent, woman!"

He said neither.

"So of course, it can't be falling in love that's given him that queer look. It's not the look of an engaged man, you know—I know that look well enough, a sort of exalted sheepishness. No, the look I mean is when a man has just that minute discovered that there's only one woman in the world; a sort of beautiful madness. But of course, that's all over in this case. I do wonder what the transfiguring influence could have been."

"Science, Madam," said Bats severely. "Science is a mistress whose least smile transfigures the world to her devotee. I have seen our friend lost to the world before now by some sudden luminous *aperçu* in the matter of bacteria or crystals or a dog's inside."

"Yes, I know," Lady Blair interrupted. "But you waste your eloquence. You can't throw dust in my eyes, or crystals either. Have you ever heard of the resurrection of love?

Love we deemed dead rises again,
Greets us re-risen,

". . . .or whatever it is."

She looked at him keenly. "In my opinion a young man would look just as our Anthony looked if someone he had loved and parted from 'for ever,' as they say, had suddenly let him know that it wasn't for ever. But in that case, what a pity about our Rose!"

"You may dismiss that idea from your mind," said Bats very decidedly; "there's never been anyone else."

"Then, from an old woman's sentimental point of view," said Lady Blair, "there's never been anyone."

"I don't know what you mean," said Bats, hoping he spoke the truth.

"Well, my dear Mr. Bats, you are a man of the world, and it is ridiculous to pretend that Anthony is really in love with that dear girl. He doesn't understand, as far as she is concerned at any rate, the ABC of love. How do I know?" for Bats had made an interrogative movement. "How do *you* know? Why, my good young man, we've both of us been in love some time or another, I suppose? We know what the real thing is like, don't we? Come, say what you think, you can trust my discretion."

"I should like to say, if I might, with every circumstance of respectful humility, that I can't believe Anthony's sentiments to be any of my business."

"Quite the right attitude," said Lady Blair, unmoved; "but you know, seriously, Mr. Bats, you can't help taking an interest in young lovers; and the only thing that upsets you is talking about them. Of course if you tell me you've never thought Anthony's sentiments—what shall we say?—inadequate, I shall believe you But you won't tell me that."

"I shall, though," said Bats roundly. "I never have speculated on his feelings. And that's my last word, ma'am, please."

"Bravo!" said Lady Blair. "I didn't think you'd got it in you. Well, of course all this is in confidence. And no doubt you're right and I'm wrong, as you usually are."

This familiar and agreeable tag, so unexpected on the lips of Lady Blair, ended the second martyrdom of the sorely tried Bats.

"I don't think I gave anything away," he told himself, as he dressed for dinner that night; "but what a woman! And what a situation! Well, no more *têtes-à-tête* for me, thank you."

And even as he said it, a tap at his door opened a third *tête-à-tête*, this time with the nervous apologetic Sebastien. Sir Antonio had taken no clothes, no robe of the night. Did *Monsieur* think that he, Sebastien, ought to take or send what was needed? Yes, a telegram had arrived. Sir Antonio was detained in London. Would *Monsieur* have the goodness to advise? *Monsieur* briefly advised inaction. Sir Antonio had gone to his rooms in London. He would have everything there which was needed. Sebastien might rest tranquil. Sebastien withdrew, thanking *Monsieur* infinitely.

★★★★★★

"Now," said Anthony at Malacca Wharf—he spoke to Wilton, his hand on the closed lid of the chest—"I'll explain as well as I can. But first pull the dark blinds down and help me to bring my mattress in here, and we'll get her out. There's no hurry, really. But we may as well get everything in order at once."

They brought the mattress from the bed in the little room and laid it on the floor. Then the chest was opened, the pillows removed, and the two men, taking the corners of the sheepskin and lifting it, lifted the body as in a hammock.

"Now," said Anthony, "there's another injection due. Just let me." He stood at the bench a moment, then bent to the body and did something to its arm, his hands moving quickly and certainly under the veil.

"Now," he said again, "it's like this. I'll give you the technical details later if you like, but just now what I want you to understand is this. This lady is not dead now. But you and Bats are right so far that she *has* been dead. If you look at me like that, Wilton, I shan't be able to stand it. Just take what I say, will you, for the moment. I'll give you proofs and details later. For the moment make up your mind that what I say is so."

"I'll try," said Wilton, sitting down on the *prie-Dieu*. "Well then, I'll just say this. The person who put her there knew as much as I do, and probably more. Why he put her *there*, I don't know, nor yet when. But her condition corresponds with a condition which is reached at a certain stage of my process, and I know what is the next stage, and I know how to induce it. But there are a few things I don't know. One is how long she has been like this."

"That's important, I suppose?"

"It's most important. Because the longer she has been in this state—I can best express it as a trance-state, just on this side of death—the longer it will take to restore her. And the interval between the injections should be determined by the knowledge which we don't possess, of the length of time she has been in this condition. I can only go cautiously. Now, if anything goes wrong, if I make any mistake, make my injections too soon or too late, we shan't save her. And then there may be trouble; and I don't want you to be mixed up with it. So, I'm going to thank you for the way you've helped me, and ask you to clear out and get back to Drelincourt as sharp as you can."

"Likely," said Wilton.

"But I'd honestly rather you did," said Anthony. And the other said—

"No doubt. But if you think I'm going to have you spend the night watching a dead woman, with your brain and nerves in the state they are in, you must think me a rum sort of doctor."

"All the same," said Anthony uneasily, "I'd rather you went. She isn't dead, you know. And if she were, I'm not a child or a fool."

"If she weren't dead," said Wilton slowly; "if she came to life, I mean, don't you think she'd rather come to life with a medical man at hand than alone in a strange place with just you?"

"I didn't think of that," Anthony owned; "but the fact is— Well, Wilton, you think I'm mad now. And you'll think I'm madder before I've done. But the fact is, it's not all chemistry and physiology. It's—well, I don't know what you'd call it—psychic influence, magic, willpower, life-force—they're all nice words. There are things I must do if I'm to save her. And to you they'd look like the most childish hanky-panky. Another thing. I'm not sure how it would be to have anyone here who wasn't in accord. Will you, like a good chap, go?"

"No further than your bedroom," said Wilton. "I don't mind waiting there if you want to be alone. I was a fool to help you in this, but I mean to go through with it. When will you begin?"

"Not before tonight. I must choose the time when the vital forces are weakest and easiest to control. Nothing can happen now, for hours. Let's go up to the Three Nuns and get something to eat. No, don't uncover the face. You wouldn't see any change. It will be hours before anything happens. Come, let's lock up and go. We must pass the time somehow. An early dinner and some music, if there's any to be got at the Queen's Hall. I want not to think for a bit. And then if you still insist on seeing the whole thing through, well——"

When they got back to Malacca Wharf at half-past eleven, they found Sebastien sitting on the doorstep with a suitcase by his side and a kit-bag at his feet.

"I thought you would want your night-robe, Sare," he said; "so I bring it."

"Good Lord!" said Anthony under his breath, "this is the last straw!"

"Thank you, Sebastien," he said aloud; "it was very thoughtful of you. But for the future please remember that I wish you to stay at Drelincourt unless you have orders to the contrary. I have no bed here for you."

"I can sleep anywhere," said Sebastien eagerly; "on the floor, outside *Monsieur's* room. I need no covertures, Sare!"

"You will sleep," said Anthony deliberately, "at the Bridge House Hotel, London Bridge, and you will stay there till you hear from me. Goodnight! No, I will carry the things up myself, thank you. Good-night, Sebastien."

★★★★★★

Wilfred Wilton can never be induced to talk much of that night. He retreated, as he had undertaken to do, to the little bedroom, and lying on the naked spring mattress with a rug over him, he listened to the hollow sound of Anthony's footsteps on the echoing wood of stairs and floor. The stairs spoke loudest and longest. For Anthony went up and down them more than once, and as he came up there was something in his step that told of weight carried with caution. Then there were movements in the laboratory, and the light that showed under the door increased. Then Anthony came into the bedroom and took off his boots and got into slippers, talked a little about ordinary things, and ended with the suggestion of a drink.

"No, you'd better not come out," he said; "I'll bring it in." Then through the half-open door there was the splash of spirit and the spurt of soda, and Anthony came back, glass in hand. Wilton, for reasons of his own, did not drink that whisky. When Drelincourt was gone, he emptied the glass outside the window-sill, and it trickled silently down the house wall. Then he lay down again with eyes closed and breathing regular.

Presently Anthony came in again softly, seemed to hold his breath and listen to Wilton's breathing. Then he went out and closed the

274

door. And for a very long time, as it seemed to Wilton, there was silence. And then a low voice spoke, Anthony's voice, disguised in the cadence of a language Wilton did not know. Faint scented vapours invaded the room, sweet, pungent, unrecognizable. And the light that shone through the ground glass above the door varied in colour and in intensity. Wilton listened, and looked, consciously hostile. He hated the whole business. This is all that Wilton will tell you. But I believe he knows more. He says he did not sleep.

And when it was daylight and he got up and dressed and went out, the body lay on the floor, very still; and Anthony, asleep in the armchair, started up at his entrance, and came towards him, looking like a ghost.

"No change," he said; "did you sleep well?"

"I haven't slept at all," he said. Anthony, looking closely at him, saw that he spoke the truth.

"So that was it," he said slowly. "I must try again tonight. Wilton, don't! You don't know how everything hangs on a thread. If you won't go away and won't go to sleep. What did you do with the whisky?"

"So that was it," said Wilton, in his turn.

"It wouldn't have hurt you," said Anthony. "If you won't go away and won't go to sleep, at least don't oppose me. Wish me well. Wish I may succeed."

"I can't," said Wilton. "It's all rubbish. I ought never to have allowed myself to be drawn into this. I shall wire to Bats and see if you can't be got to hear reason. Even now it's not too late to tell the police. I'll explain the delay by saying you've got sunstroke or something. Drelincourt, don't be an idiot."

"All right, I won't," said Anthony; "let's go and get some breakfast."

As they breakfasted, Drelincourt wrote a few words on an envelope. "Have that telegram sent, will you?" he said to the waiter.

They spent the morning in the laboratory. Anthony was at his bench. Wilton went out, for a breath of fresh air, he said, but he was back in half-an-hour trying to read. And between them lay the quiet prone figure, its outline further shrouded by a white sheet laid over all. It might have been a mere heap of loose linen that lay there.

At noon a little quiet tap took Anthony to the door.

"It's Sebastien," he said over his shoulder, and spoke to the man quickly and softly in French. Wilton could not hear or could not understand what was said; only he thinks he heard Sebastien say something about being at the orders of *Monsieur*, and then Anthony said,

"Come out a minute, Wilton," and Wilton went out, and there was Sebastien at the top of the stairs. And he and Anthony suddenly came towards Wilton together. Sebastien had a coil of rope over his arm; he came straight on, never looking to right or left. Wilton stared at him, and the next moment Anthony had caught his hands, and Sebastien was binding his wrists together with that cord.

"I'm most frightfully sorry," Anthony was saying; "but you leave me no alternative. I can't and won't submit to have my whole life's work ruined because you think you know everything."

They tied his arms and ankles with close knots.

"Now, Wilton," said Anthony, "I don't want to gag you, because I believe gagging hurts; but by God I will if you don't give me your word not to call out."

"I suppose you know," Wilton, pale with rage, addressed himself to Sebastien, "that this is an assault. You can be sent to prison for it. And you shall be."

"Yes, Sare," said Sebastien respectfully.

"I am awfully sorry," said Anthony again.

"You'll be more sorry still before you've done," Wilton told him.

"Go downstairs a minute, Sebastien," Anthony said. Then to Wilton: "I trusted you and then you impede everything, actually stop it, and threaten me with the police. I can't act otherwise. Will you promise to hold your tongue? Don't refuse out of pride or temper. I *must* gag you if you don't. And I hate to do that."

The interested doctor in Wilton struggled with the angry and outraged man in him. He looked at Anthony.

"All right! I promise," he said, with an effort. "But for how long?"

"I don't know. Thank God, you're seeing reason. Wilton, there's not one man in a thousand would have had the pluck to promise that, for fear I should think he was a coward. I'll never forget that. Now, Old chap, you see what it means to me. I'll stick at nothing. Let me untie the cords. Just promise you'll go away for the afternoon. Let's call it a joke. I'll tell Sebastien it is."

"No," said Wilton. "Oh, this is absurd, Drelincourt. Don't behave like a penny dreadful. Untie my hands."

"I wish Bats was here," said Anthony.

"So, do I," said Wilton. And, as if he had come from the depths of Sussex suddenly by the magic of the speaking of his name, Bats appeared at the foot of the stairs in the noisy act of overwhelming the opposition of Sebastien.

"What's all this tosh?" he said, throwing from him the faithful but ineffectual Helvetian, and coming up. "Guarded stairs and, Good God, Tony! it's about time I did come. What's it all about?"

"Drelincourt insists on my leaving him, and I contend that he's not fit to be left. That's why I wired to you," said Wilton. "Untie this rope, Bats. I'll leave him all right now you're here."

But Anthony had caught Bats by the arm.

"Look here," he said, "you can understand. Wilton—I know he's acting for the best, and all that rot. Take him away, take him for a walk. Let me have the place to myself. Good God in Heaven! it is my place, after all, isn't it? Take Sebastien away."

Sebastien had discreetly remained below.

"Very well," said Bats; "but we shall come back. Or look here, I have the key of Rose's house to see after her letters. We'll wait here. Telephone if you want us."

"Right!" said Anthony. "Now go, like good chaps. I'll apologise later, Wilton."

He went into the laboratory and shut the door. They heard the key turn.

"He's quite mad," said Wilton, as Bats took his knife and cut the cords, and he rubbed his wrists fretfully.

"If he is," said Bats, "I'm for humouring him. He'll certainly go off his head if we don't."

"It's not fair to the girl," said Wilton.

"What girl?" said Bats.

"The dead girl," said the doctor. "I don't bear any malice about the rope. If he's mad, he can't help it, poor chap. But the dead girl."

"But if she's dead—"

"But suppose she isn't dead?"

"Oh!" said Bats, "his madness is infectious, is it? You believe the girl isn't dead now, do you?"

"Of course, she's dead," said Wilton; "but—oh, well, come along."

They went to Rose's house, a dusty little house it was, and lacking her presence, a dreary little house. They sent Sebastien out to buy food, and when he timidly explained that he could "make the kitchen," they let him cook it for them. They smoked and they read. Wilton fidgeted and moved about restlessly, and more than once he said—

"We ought to go back to him, we ought to go back."

And always Bats said: "No. I've seen him like this before. It always ends all right. Wait till he rings us up."

And the day wore on. And still their ears waited in vain for the tingle of the telephone bell. It was evening when the two men, reading in the parlour, and Sebastien patiently doing nothing in the tiny kitchen, heard a step on the flagstones outside, and a key rattling in the lock of the front door. They were all in the little passage when the door opened. Rose stood on the doorstep—Rose, pale and dominant.

The three men retreated a step or two. She came in.

"What is it?" she said. "What's the matter?"

"I thought you wouldn't mind," said Bats. "You know you gave me the key when I was staying at Tony's, and you said then I might use the house to cook in when you were out. And we had to wait somewhere."

"But you said you had to go and see your aunt who is ill," said Rose.

"One must say something," Bats urged. "In point of fact Wilton wired for me, but I didn't want to go into explications with Lady Blair."

"But why?" Rose asked. "Why, why, why? Why is Sebastien here?"

"Sir Antonio telegraphed to me at the hotel," said Sebastien.

"But why have you come up?" Bats asked.

"Oh!" said Rose, "Sebastien telegraphed for me!"

CHAPTER 16

Achievement

No later cross-questioning of Sebastien ever elicited any explanation of his action, first in following Anthony with undesired suitcases, and, secondly, in sending to Rose a telegram which took the curious form:

"Sir Antonio is at Malacca very strange Sebastien."

But questioning Sebastien was, in the first awkwardness of the meeting of those four in the narrow passage, the last thing to interest Wilton and Bats, just as the arrival of Rose had been the last thing they could have anticipated. Neither of them could find any words that seemed likely to help the situation. Rose took hold of it.

"Come in," she said. "Sebastien, wait in the kitchen. Now," she said, shutting the door and standing with her hand on its handle, "what is it? What's the matter? Where's Anthony?"

"Anthony's in his laboratory, conducting an experiment," said Bats patiently.

"But why are you here? Why did Wilfred come to London with Tony? Why did he wire for you? Why all this silly mystery?"

"Why did *you* come up?"

"Don't I tell you?" said Rose. "Sebastien wired. I thought Anthony was ill. Poisoned or blown up or something. Is he all right?"

"Perfectly," said Bats. And Wilton carefully said nothing. He would have gone out and left Bats to invent explanations, but Rose's hand was on the door.

"Don't behave like babies," said Rose. "Wilfred must have had *some* reason for wiring to you."

"It's Anthony's experiment," said Wilton feebly.

"Very well," said Rose; "it seems I can't get any sense out of either of you. I shall go to Anthony for an explanation." She was turning the handle when Bats' hand closed over hers.

"No," said Bats; "that's impossible. Look here, Rose. If Anthony's interrupted now it will be very bad for him, wreck everything. He's got an idea. I don't think it's a correct one, but if he's not allowed to prove that it's incorrect, he'll always think that it was right and that we made him muff it. And all his life he'd go on hating anyone who interfered at this moment. Don't you see?"

"A wrong idea? He told you what it was then?" she said, like lightning, and shook her hand from his.

"No, I happened to find out."

"And Wilfred, too; did he find out?"

"Don't," said Bats evenly. "Let Wilton tell Sebastien to get you some tea or something."

She looked blankly at him. Then—

"Yes," she said, "please. Would you mind?"

She took her hand from the door and stepped back. Wilton, without a glance at either of them, went out.

"Rose," said Bats, the moment they were alone, "*don't!* How can you expect to make Anthony happy, if you're going to spy and bother every time he has an idea? You know he always rushes off after a new idea. Life with him will be impossible if you're going to behave like a baby and whimper and go on saying: 'You might let me look! Oh, do let me look!' No man could work with a woman like that hanging on to him."

"You're trying to brace me up, as they call it, by being rude. What are you doing it for? What is it I've got to bear or got to hear? What has happened to him?"

"Nothing whatever," said Bats, and once more hoping he spoke the truth. "But I'm very fond of him and I'm very fond of you, and I don't want you to make a mess of everything." He led from any suit; the game seemed lost in any event. Afterwards he asked himself why it should have seemed to him that winning the game meant deceiving Rose; keeping her in ignorance about the dead girl. If the dead girl had been a living rival, he could not have felt more tensely the need to keep Rose from any knowledge of the dead girl's existence.

Rose had pulled off her hat and thrown it on the table: quite automatically she ran her fingers through her hair, to make it take on those loose waves that suited her face so well. She always did that when she took off her hat, and she did it now. Suddenly her hands dropped.

"Billy," she said, and it seemed to Bats that she almost fawned upon him, "I know I'm behaving like an hysterical schoolgirl. But it's that crystal. There was something strange and terrible to happen after he'd got his money. And when I got that telegram from Sebastien—oh! why did he send it if there was nothing wrong?—when I got it, I felt the thing had come now. And I wanted to help Anthony."

"When a man wants a woman's help, he asks for it," said Bats, blessing Wilton for Wilton's absence.

"Does he? Always? I feel that if I went to him now, I could save him."

"*Dangerous guides, the feelings*," quoted Bats. "Rose, don't be womanly. Not now. You're right so far: this is a crisis in Anthony's work. You can make him muff the whole thing. Be reasonable. Have some tea and laugh at the whole thing with Anthony tomorrow. You can't believe in that crystal nonsense. Not *you*, Rose, you can't!"

"I know I can't," she said, "only I do. All sorts of horrid things happen, explosions and blood poisonings and—

She looked at him a moment, frowned, bit her lips and covered her face with her hands.

"Thank God!" said Mr. Bats silently; "you can always manage a woman if only she'll begin to cry."

Rose went blindly towards the table and sank into a chair beside it, her elbows on the table and her head in her hands. He came and stood beside her.

"Don't," he said; "don't, dear!" and touched her hand. She caught his and laid her forehead on it, and he felt her tears warm upon his palm. "Now I wonder," he said to himself, "what particular sin I'm paying for now? Whatever it is, the price seems excessive." And Wilton might come in at any moment.

"You're overwrought," he said; "you've been worrying and fancying. Everything's all right."

She clung to his hand convulsively.

"Oh! how I wish you'd say something I could believe," she sobbed.

Bats racked his soul to grant her wish. In vain. So, he stood there in an awkward silence, and felt that Wilton's tact in keeping away was becoming almost tactless. Then he found himself saying: "Give Anthony a chance. If he doesn't tell you tomorrow, I will. I promise you that. Only he wanted to tell you himself. He's going to ring us up the moment he knows whether it's all right. I always thought you were so brave. And here you are making yourself ill about an old fortune-teller's foolishness. Cheer up! Everything's all right, believe me."

Through his last words something else spoke.

"Oh!" she cried, and jumped up, almost throwing his hand from her, "there's the telephone!"

It was, in fact, the telephone which had spoken. And before Bats could think of anything sensible to say or do, the receiver was at Rose's ear and she was saying, "Yes?" hoarsely.

"It's Drelincourt," said her lover's voice; "is that Wilton? Come over at once, there's a good chap. It's all, right. She's moved. She's breathing. She's alive!"

So much she heard before Bats, by sudden force, tore the receiver from her and held her away from the machine while he put the receiver to his own ear.

"What's that?" he said, and heard in a tone of inexpressible joy and triumph—

"She's alive. She's breathing. That you, Bill? Send Wilton. I was right. I must go back to her. Make Wilton come. He'll forgive all that silliness. Send him now."

Bats hung up the receiver, still holding Rose from it with his other arm.

"Be quiet," he said to her, in a voice she had never heard, and shouted, "Wilton! he says it's all right."

Wilton put his head in at the door.

"All right, I tell you," said Bats, answering the other's look and tightening his grasp of Rose, "go over at once. It's life."

Wilton went.

"Now," said Bats. He loosed Rose, but he stood between her and the telephone. "I hope you're satisfied."

"She?" said Rose gasping. "She? I knew it. I knew it."

"I suppose I must tell you now that you've eavesdropped into the middle of the whole story," said Bats, at his wits' end. "It's a poor woman they thought was dead, and Anthony's succeeded in reviving her by some new process. Now are you satisfied?"

"But—why wasn't I to be told?"

"I thought you didn't like dissecting-room stories," said Bats brutally.

And Sebastien came in with the tea.

"I'm sorry," said Rose flatly, when he had gone out; "but I suppose you can't understand. If you were as fond of anyone as I am of Anthony, you'd understand then."

"If being fond of people makes one want to interfere at every crisis of their work, I hope to Heaven no one will ever be fond of me," said Bats tartly.

Then Rose deliberately blew her nose, wiped her eyes, put her handkerchief in her pocket and smiled at him. The smile was beautiful. She was not one of those women who are disfigured almost unrecognisably by tears.

"Pax!" she said. "Let me give you some tea. I'm sorry I made a fuss. I'm going to be a perfect Griselda for ever and ever. And," she added, smiling still more brilliantly, "you won't tell Tony what a fool I've been, will you?"

"That's a false move, Rose," he said. "You should never ask people not to tell. It puts the idea into their heads."

"But you won't," she persisted, and her eyes, he saw, were still full of tears.

"No," he said, "this once I won't. *I* don't want to worry the man's life out by letting him know what he's got to look forward to."

She laughed, not quite steadily, but still she laughed. "I *said* Pax," she said.

★★★★★★

When the door had closed and latch and lock clicked home; when the departing feet of his two friends and his servant had, echoing, died away on stairway and flagstone, Anthony Drelincourt stood a moment, breathing hard. The enthusiasm of the experimenter, thwarted by the conscientious tiresomeness of the doctor, the half admitted hopes, the half-resisted fears, anxiety, curiosity, and a thousand little undefined impulses, attractions and repulsions, all these swimming in an overwhelming ocean of something new, something unknown, something which he strove in vain to understand and to reckon with, all these had driven him to a condition nearer frenzy than it pleased him to remember. He stood there disconcerted, ashamed, and bitterly conscious that he was now in no condition to attempt the control of the forces which he believed to exist, and believed himself to be, at his best, able to master.

There were certain things that could be done now, even by one whose self-control had been shaken and whose hand, though trembling, could be schooled to steadiness; another injection, the ignition of certain resinous gums and spices, the lighting of certain tapers. These things he did without removing the sheet from the face of the body.

Then he retreated to the far end of the room and sank into his chair, every muscle relaxed, and stayed there seeking to relax his mind also, to wash from it all traces of the agitation and anger that had distorted and enfeebled it in his encounter with Wilton. It was a long time before he succeeded, but at last he rose, made certain preparations, drew back the veil from the dead girl's face, and, without ever touching her, began the "treatment" which, succeeding the hypodermic injections, the strokings of the forehead, the application to nostrils and ears and lips of strange, strong, sweet-scented liquids, must, if his faith were to be justified, restore to life this pallid, death-still body.

The extremest mental tension was of the essence of the treatment, a tension so great as to obliterate all bodily consciousness. Yet that kind of mental tension is physical also, and, as he stood gazing at the dead face, the sweat poured off his forehead, and every now and then he brushed it from his eyes with the back of his hand. But presently this ceased, the mind took full possession of the field, and his body ceased to protest its weakness. The consciousness of power awakened in him, doubt and fear shrivelled and vanished like dead flowers in a glowing furnace, confidence of triumph possessed him, growing, growing, till it seemed to fill his being. If ever a man felt like a god, it was Anthony Drelincourt in that hour. And he might have been a god, a god carved in some transfigured splendour of marble, as he stood at last, all the prescribed gestures and passes made, motionless with hands outstretched over the body of the girl.

When the moment had come, he spoke, strange words, slow and intense. His voice shaped itself to something like a low toneless chant, words indeed, but words of no language that is taught in the schools. Words that have been handed down from Mage to Initiate through generation after generation, since days before great Babylon was a little village, before Nineveh reared her towers to the stars, before the

Hittites set the first stone of the first city of their mysterious civilization, the civilization which time has wiped away as a child wipes from a slate a little sum done wrong.

The chant, in an invocation that was almost a cry, ceased. Silence filled the room.

Now—now—now! Here was the moment. If not now, all was in vain; the faith of the man's life a worthless trifle trampled in the dust. Now—now—now!

His eyes fixed on the dead face, wavered for the first time. Something fiery yet enervating, like chloroform and sunshine mingled, flushed through his veins. "No more," he told himself; "I can do no more."

And as he told it, a sound broke the throbbing silence, a little light sigh. And he had not sighed.

"Now," he said again, concentrating all his soul and spirit in the command. "Now!"

And the dead woman's eyelids fluttered, opened an instant and closed again.

The thing needed was at hand. He had seen to all that. A phial and a glass. He filled the glass, raised her head and held the glass to her lips. Her lips accepted the brim of the beaker. She drank. Her eyes closed again.

Rigid with an inconceivable joy and triumph, he turned away, left her there lying still, living, with eyes closed and quiet hands. There were certain ceremonial washings of his hands and face. Anthony performed them duly and came back to where she lay. Kneeling by her he set cold fingers on her brow and spoke, this time in no strange tongue.

"Awake," he said, "it is time."

And the body that had been dead, moved; the hands fluttered, the eyes opened, gazed a moment wildly, unseeing. Then she raised herself on her elbow and her eyes met his.

"Is it all over?" she asked, and her voice seemed to him to be like no voice his ears had ever heard, and yet to be a voice whose echoes had been always in his heart.

"Yes, it is all over," he said.

She put one little hand on the floor and raised herself by it till she was sitting on the floor, her face looking up to his as he knelt beside her.

"I *do* feel different," she said. "I feel more alive, a thousand times.

I did not think it would be so. But you knew—you. And it is truly a fact accomplished?"

"Yes," he said, trembling now in every nerve, but resolute to show nothing but strength, calmness, trustworthiness.

"And now," she said, "I live for ever?"

"Yes," he said soothingly, "yes."

Then the unexpected, the not by any chance to have been fore-seen, happened. She smiled full into his dazzled eyes—oh! she was a thousand times more beautiful than he had thought her, a thousand times more beautiful than he had thought any one could be—laughed a low laugh of perfect contentment and happiness, flung her soft arms round his neck, and, laying her soft cheek to his, breathed softly—

"Oh, my love!"

His heart checked and stumbled, but his arms went round her. What else could they do when hers round his neck seemed to know themselves in their natural home? He held her a moment thus, and the world seemed to spin among a sea of stars and roses. Quite as mixed as that were Anthony's thoughts. Or had he any thoughts at all? Perhaps not. He knelt there, holding her to his heart that beat as it had never beaten in all his life. Her face lay against his; her shape, slender and delicately warm, nestled in the curve of his arm. She tightened the clasp of her arm round his neck, moved her face a little, and smooth warm soft lips sought his and found them. Stars and flowers and all the world whirling to a wild wonderful music unimaginably beautiful, just not heard, but imminent.

"Oh, my love!" she said again; "oh, my love!" She caught her breath, and he felt her tears hot on his cheek.

As one picks up with tongs a red-hot cinder that has fallen on the hearth, Anthony's brain caught hold of Anthony's heart, lifted it, sought to set it back where it should be. Not with Rose. He never thought of Rose, did not so much as remember that a human being named Rose existed in this same wonderful world with him. What his brain told him was that She—there was only one—must rest, must not agitate herself with emotion, must be calm. Yet how answer these words of hers with words of less worth? That was impossible, and he did not even try. Yet what he felt was surprise when he found himself saying—

"My love, you mustn't. Be good. Be quiet. You're not out of dan-ger yet." And then he said, just as Bats was, even then, saying to Rose, "Don't! please don't!" and "You mustn't cry. It's bad for you."

"It's only joy," she said, and clung to him.

A sudden wild fear assailed him. What if, after all, having brought her back from the dead, he should be powerless to keep her? What if, weeping and clinging to him, the new life he had given her should wane, sink, fade out? Up to this point he had known what to do. Now he did not know any longer. Wilton; why had he driven Wilton away? Of course; Wilton was at the other end of the telephone. He came back to the old life, the old self, with a sickening, bewildering half-turn. Yes; he had done it: he had raised the dead. Her breast pressed to his, softly palpitating with life, witnessed to his triumph. He had brought her back. She had been dead. He knew it. He had known it from the beginning, though he had told these fellows that she was not dead, because it was the simplest way of getting them to understand what he wanted to get understood. She had been dead. And he had gone down into unknown deeps for her, like a second Orpheus, and brought back an Eurydice, not his. But she thought herself his. He trembled and clasped her closer.

"Don't cry," he said; "ah, don't!"

In the bringing of her back he must somehow have impressed his personality, himself, on her mind, so that when she clasped life again, she, with life, clasped him. He had done what he knew how to do. He had brought her back. But now? He was adrift on a sea of wild possibilities, impossibilities; and her arms were round his neck. He put his hands up and loosed those clinging hands.

"Listen!" he said, in a new voice of authority; "listen. You must listen. And you must do what I say."

"Have I not, always?" she asked. And her pale face met him appealing over their clasped hands as he knelt and looked at her.

"Collect yourself and listen," he said; "it—it has taken longer than was expected. Things have changed."

He saw by her eyes that she hardly heard his words. But hers showed that she had heard his tone.

"What is it?" she said. "Are you angry? What have I done? Did I not submit? Did I not do all that you say, though you know how I was afraid."

"No, no; don't, dear," he said. The tender word could not help getting itself spoken; it was the only answer to her appealing eyes. "Of course, I am not angry. How could I be? How could I be anything but—? Ah! you know," he said. But he was awakening to the world as he had known it, the old dull world that had not in it this wonder with the eyes that seemed to live in his, the arms that went round his neck as though that were their right.

"Listen," he said again; "it has taken longer than was expected. Things have changed."

"How long?" she asked, and not waiting for the answer, hurried in the vital question, "not you—you have not changed? You love me like before?"

What could he say? The new life that he had not created, of course, but recreated, seemed to hang on his words.

"You know," he found himself saying, "you know," and his hands clasped hers closely. But he himself did not know.

"Do not be afraid," he went on. "I only ask this. Will you trust me?"

"I always trusted you," she said.

"Trust me entirely. Do exactly what I tell you. It is not yet safe. There are things to be done for you, to make your new life safe. There have been changes——"

He hesitated. In face of her obvious delusion that he was her lover, that he was the man who had induced in her the death sleep from which he, Anthony, had roused her, he could not tell her the truth. Yet something he must tell her.

"Don't try to understand now. I'll explain later. What I want you to understand is that things have happened, things are changed. Your life isn't secure, no, not even now, unless you see a doctor who knows what to do for you. And the only doctor I can get is one who doesn't know everything about us; doesn't know that I—that you—that we—"

"That we are lovers," she said simply; "but I will tell him."

"That is just what you must not do," he said. "I can't explain why you mustn't. You must pretend that you don't know me, that I am a stranger who has happened to be able to revive you from a trance."

"You—a stranger; but—" she breathed, clasping his hands more earnestly.

"It is as I say," he said. "Trust me. Can you trust me?"

Her eyes answered him.

"It's impossible to explain now," he said; "there isn't time." And then, for the first time as he remembered how he had used those very words to Rose, he remembered too for the first time what he was to Rose and what Rose ought to be to him. He stumbled on blindly: "The only thing now is to see a doctor. I'm going to call him. If you let him know that you—that I—"

"I know," she said; "but the doctor knows. Everyone knows."

287

"This is another doctor," he said. "Trust me, believe me when I say that everything depends on his not knowing, on *everybody's* not knowing that"—he hesitated and the end of his sentence came like the caught breath of a spent runner—"that we love each other."

"Truly?" she said.

And he answered: "Truly. Things are different. See, you are in a strange place. All is changed."

"Except our love," she said.

"Except our love," he repeated.

"I see," she said, looking round; "it is a strange place. But it is a laboratory. And the candles are there and the altar. In the heart of it it's the same. You told me——"

She faltered and swayed a little as she sat.

"You understand," he said; "no one must know. It is our secret. If anyone knows yet that we are lovers, we shall be parted for ever."

He saw himself humouring the wild illusions of this girl whom he had raised from the dead even while her touch on his hands set every nerve in his body vibrating to the tune of heaven and hell.

"I do not understand," she said, and her voice was faint and grew fainter as she spoke. "I do not understand, but I obey. No one shall know from me, my lover, my Master."

She shivered and swayed towards him. He caught and laid her again on the couch of lambskin. He hesitated a moment, then bent over her, still hesitating.

"It is the last time," he told himself. "Wilton will restore her memory, her senses. Then she will know that it is not I whom she loves."

And, with a pang of such agony as he had never dreamed possible, his lips sought hers.

"Oh, my love," she murmured, withdrawing her lips, "I think I am dying. I can't leave you. I can't—not after everything—not——"

Her face had grown once more death-white, her voice trailed away into silence, and Anthony, springing up, rushed to the telephone.

"Wilton will know what to do," he said, as he held the receiver to his ear.

★★★★★★

Wilton did know what to do. And under his ministrations the colour came back to pale cheeks and lips. She opened tired eyes on the two men, only to close them again in sleep.

"I never would have believed it," said Wilton, "never!"

The two men were talking in whispers at the far end of the laboratory.

"Well, you were right," said Wilton generously.

"And, I say," said Anthony, "you won't go talking about it, will you? You see it's my secret. It's my lifework. It's my great discovery."

"I won't," said Wilton grimly. "One thing, no one would believe me if I did."

"I'll make it all public in time," said Anthony feverishly; "but I do want to choose my own time."

"Of course," said Wilton. "Have you found out who she is, or how she got there, or anything?"

"I thought it best to send for you at once," said Anthony. "You see I didn't know how to deal with the case at all after a certain point. So, I just called for you. And I can't thank you enough for not bearing malice about my imbecility this morning."

"Oh, that's all right," said Wilton.

"Well, I won't keep you any longer. Thanks awfully. Goodnight, old man," said Drelincourt. But Wilton hesitated.

"I say," he began awkwardly, "she'll wake up presently, you know. I expect she'll be quite conscious; not wandering, you know, as you said she was at first. I know the scientific mind doesn't bother about Mrs. Grundy; but *she* will, when she wakes, you know."

"I don't quite understand," said Anthony. He was aching in every limb, worn out in every fibre of soul and spirit. Sleep seemed to be now the only good thing in the world. "Do speak plain English. I'm tired out."

"Well, then," said Wilton roundly, "when she wakes up and finds herself alone with a man in his laboratory in the middle of the night, she won't like it, if she's the girl I take her for. There ought to be another woman here."

"But how can I get another woman at this hour of night?"

"*I* can get you one," said Wilton, with a pleasant sensation of hidden archness. "You leave it to me. And when she comes, you'd better clear out. You might go over to Rose's house. Bats is there. And leave the patient and the woman I'll send you to spend the night here. And in the morning our patient will be able to tell us a good many things, I shouldn't wonder."

"Are you sure your woman is trustworthy?" asked Drelincourt, glancing at the sleeping girl in the lambskin. I couldn't do with a fool, you know, in an affair like this."

"Oh, she's no fool," said Wilton, hugging himself in his tact and sagacity. "She'll be a pleasant surprise for you. Goodnight, old chap. No, not another word about this morning. I quite understand."

Was it all innocent archness on Wilton's part? Or was there, deep down in the subconsciousness, a desire to be even with Anthony for that morning's outrage? Did Wilton *feel* anything?—he could have known nothing. Was it ingenuous friendship—or what was it? Those are questions which the doctor himself could not have answered, problems to which Anthony later tried in vain to find a solution.

Anyhow, what happened was this. Wilton walked quietly across the deserted yard of Malacca Wharf, and broke in on the talk of Bats and Rose with—

"The experiment has been successful. And Anthony wants you to go over for a moment. No, not you, Bats; it's Rose he wants."

"It's me he wants?" said Rose; ". . . oh!"

"I didn't think Rose cared so much," Wilton commented, when Bats, having escorted her across the yard, came back silent and cross.

"I didn't suppose you did," Bats snapped, filling his pipe.

"I like giving people these little surprises," said Wilton.

"Surprises?" Bats paused, pipe in hand, to ask.

"Of course, I didn't tell him it was Rose I was sending," said Wilton, laughing triumphantly. "I said I'd send a woman."

"God help all fools," said Bats. "He didn't know she was coming? You've tumbled Rose right into the middle of *that?*"

"I love doing little good turns to lovers," said the doctor; "anyone could see how the land lay between them. We won't go to bed till he comes, will we? He's coming across as soon as he's seen the 'woman' I promised to send, and arranged for her to look after the revived person for the night. Won't he be surprised? What's up?"

For Bats had risen and made quietly for the door. But at the question he came slowly back.

"It's too late now," he said, "I can't do anything," and he felt for his matches.

"What do you want to do, you silly old interloper?" said Wilton jovially; "it's the crowning moment of Anthony's life. Didn't you know that he and Rose were keen on each other? I've seen it for ages. They'll come to an understanding now, you'll see. What a scene! The great experiment successful. The girl of his heart to tell all about it to. And the witching hour. It's beautiful! It's perfect! What luck that she happened to be here! It's God's own chance!" "And you," said Bats in silence, "are God's own ass! And I've got to sit here and look

290

at you. And she's there. And Anthony will introduce her to the new-comer with, 'Here's a dead body come to life.' And I can't do anything. Oh, it's a beautiful world, full of beautiful people. Damn!" he added thoughtfully and aloud.

"Burnt yourself?" asked Wilton sympathetically.

CHAPTER 17
Lies

Rose, all aglow with joy that, in his triumph, it was to her he turned, that in the crowning moment of his life it was she whom he needed, ran lightly up the long stairs and tapped at the laboratory door.

"It's me," she called; "it's Rose. May I come in?"

To the last he was grateful to her for having called out. It gave him a moment's grace, the moment which it takes to cross a room and open a door. Had she merely knocked, and had he, expecting a charwoman or district nurse, opened the door to find himself face to face with his betrothed, the situation might have slipped beyond his control. As it was, he was able, the door safely closed between him and the girl who called him her love and clung to him as by right, to meet with some semblance of natural surprise and pleasure, the only woman who had a right to cling to him.

"My dearest Rose," he said, quite as convincingly as he ever said it, "how splendid and how amazing," and he held out his hands to her and kissed her. Never had the charade feeling been so strong.

"What's happened to you?" he went on; "why aren't you at Drelin-court? Is anything the matter? Did you want me?"

"Wake up," she said, and pinched his ear. Yes, she had every right to pinch his ear, he reminded himself. "You're in one of your dreams, dear. But even you can hardly have forgotten that you told Wilton to send me over, because—oh, Tony, I am so glad the experiment is a success. Let me come in, and tell me all about it."

"Wilton seems to have told you," he said, and wondered if Rose could help noticing the toneless quality his voice had suddenly taken on.

"Jealous?" she said. "Did he want to be the one to tell his own secrets?"

The agitation of the long journey, the reaction from anxiety to joy had shaken Rose into an intimate playfulness that Anthony had never seen in her before. He wondered why he had ever thought her strong

291

and sensible. And she felt the impulse of repulsion in the weakening clasp of his hands.

"I'm wandering," she said quickly; "of course Wilton didn't tell me anything. He left it for you. He just told me you wanted me; that you'd succeeded. And I was very proud that you wanted me, at a time like this," she ended, once more the Rose that he had always known, alert, competent, dignified.

"My dear girl," he said, "I do want you. I always want you. And Wilton must have guessed that I did. And I suppose he knew you'd come up. Of course. They were waiting at your house. But in point of fact I thought you were at Drelincourt. Why aren't you?"

"Oh, I had to come up," she answered impatiently; "don't bother about trifles, Tony. Tell me what it is you've discovered, or succeeded in, or whatever it is. And do let's go inside."

"Not yet," he said. "I want to tell you first. Wilton offered to send me a woman to help me in a little difficulty. I— But I'm keeping you standing, dear. You must be tired, the journey and all. Let's sit down on the stairs."

They sat down.

"I'm very glad it's you he sent," Anthony made himself say; "because of course I want above all things to tell you everything." And as he spoke, he cursed Wilton's officious folly, and his own lying lips; and wondered desperately how little it would be safe to tell this girl who nestled confidently against him as they sat. "I trust you so completely," he said, taking a perverse pleasure in elaborating the lie.

"Oh, don't! wait a minute," Rose said, and moved a little from him. The memory had come sharply to her of that time when she had sat on those stairs with William Bats, and how she had schemed to get Bats away so that she might spy and pry into Anthony's laboratory, and surprise, if she could, and if there were any, his secrets.

"You oughtn't to trust me," she said; and told, in detail, why. To him the confession lacked interest, but his imagination helped him to forgive her gracefully. "And now," he said, "I want to tell you. My great discovery is this—at least this is part of it (his sudden snatch at truthfulness surprised and interested him)—I have found out how to bring to life people whom other people believe to be dead."

"How splendid!"

"You know for thousands of years people have tried after this. You've heard of the Elixir of Life and things like that. Well, I've been trying it on for years, and I've succeeded. I succeeded with guinea-pigs and birds and a monkey."

"Were they *really* dead?"

"Yes. I know it's hard to believe, but it's true. And then a child that they thought was dead at the hospital. He's alive and jolly now in the country. And then, it was yesterday, I got a telegram."

"Who from?"

"One of the doctors at Guy's," lied Anthony readily, "a chap who's followed my experiments with the greatest interest. And they wanted me to try another subject. It's a woman who was given over for dead. And she's here. And I've revived her. Wilton helped. She's all right, but very exhausted and feeble. And then of course I wanted a woman to look after her. And Wilton said he'd send me one. I thought it would be a district nurse or something. And instead—it's you! Wilton must have guessed—dear!" he said, and wondered at himself.

"But I can do anything a district nurse can do," said Rose, her confidence in her own competence asserting itself. "And I'd love to help you. Let's go to her, poor thing. Who is she? A poor woman, I suppose, as it's a hospital case?"

"She's a lady," said Anthony, "and I think it's rather a peculiar case. I have an idea who she may be; and if so, it's a most extraordinary coincidence. She's asleep now. But you see—of course, when she wakes, she'll feel a bit awkward in a strange place with no other woman. I ought to have thought of that and had someone here in readiness."

"Your Guy's doctor ought to have thought of that," said Rose indignantly, "but it doesn't matter. I'll stay with her. Oh, Anthony! I can hardly believe it. They really thought she was dead. And you restored her. How splendid you are."

She put her arm around his neck and kissed him in tender congratulation.

"It is rather jolly," he said, and laughed. But he had to stop that at once.

"She'll want clothes," he said, "a nightgown and so on, and tomorrow some clothes must be bought for her. She's in a sort of fancy dress. It was a sudden seizure, and that's how— Oh, Rose!" he broke off suddenly, "I'm dog tired. Go over and get a nightdress for her and whatever you want yourself for the night. And don't question her. She's very feeble still, and it's all rather mysterious. I am so tired."

He leaned his head on Rose's shoulder, as a tired child leans against its mother. "I can't talk anymore," he said. "If I may sleep at your house—may I?"

She put her arm round his shoulders with a gentle protective gesture. "You poor boy; yes, of course. I'll go at once, dear. No, don't come with me. Go back to *her*. She might wake and be frightened at finding herself alone, poor old thing."

"You think of everything," he said, standing up with his hand on the door; "but she isn't old. At least I don't think so," he added, and wondered why he could not have let well alone, when Rose said—

"What it is to be a scientist! I wonder you ever realised that *I* wasn't ninety."

"I know I'm unobservant," he said; "but she *is* young. I'm almost sure of it. You'll bring hairpins and brushes and soap and sponges, and all the things women want for dressing, won't you?"

"Don't fuss," she said, and went.

She would have liked her house to be spotlessly clean and ruthlessly tidy since Anthony was to have the run of it. And she knew too well that in every room but the parlour there would be sheaves of everything that ought to be neatly arranged, lying loose round. And there was no time to make her house neat for her lover's eyes. Nevertheless, as she made the choice of things needed for her own toilet and that of the stranger and threw them into a bag, she hastily collected by the armful the odds and ends of clothing, drawings, and mixed litter that encumbered her rooms, threw them on to the bed, and when chests, tables, bureaux were all clear, knotted the quilt round the miscellaneous clearings, and dragged the bundle into a cupboard which she locked. She put fresh sheets on the bed and a clean quilt, hastily dusting the tops of things with her handkerchief.

"Ten minutes can't matter," she said. Then she called out to Bats, and he came up for the bag.

"Anthony must sleep here," she said; "see that he does, will you? He's tired out. You and Wilfred must manage somehow. Isn't Tony wonderful! He can do things like that, Miracles really, and yet not notice if the person he's doing it to is old or young. Oh! and I say, you'd better tell Wilfred about Tony and me. He must have guessed it, or he wouldn't have sent me there as a surprise-party. And he may as well be told. I don't mind everyone's knowing now. It was only at first when I thought we might change our minds. But now I know we neither of us shall, I don't care who knows about it."

Bats lifted the bag.

"That all?" he said.

Drelincourt had lighted all the gas jets, and the laboratory windows shone, yellow oblongs in the night.

"Sure you don't mind looking after her?" Bats asked, as they reached the warehouse door; "not afraid or anything?"

"Of course not. Why on earth should I?"

"Telephone if you want anything," he said.

"Of course," she said again, and wondered why people were so silly. To her the adventure was thrilling in itself, and charming because she was now in the position which she always desired. To her responsibility, the exercise of her powers, the looking of others to her for help, was the breath of life, or at any rate its fullest joy. And that she should be doing things for Anthony; that he should be leaning on her; he who had always so wilfully and strongly stood alone! This was life as she saw it. And the woman in her was glad, furtively, that she and the man she loved were, for this night, exchanging homes.

Anthony met them at the door, brisk and businesslike.

"Got everything you want?" he asked. "Right! Now, Bill, you take the feet and I'll take the head; get hold of the mattress—that's right. We'll lift her on to the bed."

They lifted her and carried her into the little room that had been a counting-house when Malacca Wharf was alive.

"Now," said Anthony, coming back and going to the bench, "come here, Rose. This glass, with the card on it labelled 1, you give her if she wakes. And if she wakes, ask her if she'd like to be undressed and go to bed. If she says no, let her be. If she says yes, help her to undress. No talking, mind. She may want to talk. She's got all sorts of delusions. But quiet's the thing. I think she'll sleep all right. When she wakes in the morning, give her what's in this other glass labelled 2. And ring us up. We'll bring breakfast over. Keep her head low. Only one pillow. I think that's all."

"Yes," said Rose.

"Sure you don't mind. It's awfully good of you," he added, as an afterthought.

"I love to do anything to help you, you know that," she answered, low, because of Bats standing patiently by the door.

"Telephone if she seems ill or anything. But she won't. Goodnight."

"Goodnight," said Rose. "Goodnight, Billy."

Bats went out. Anthony following, turned at the door and came back. He felt that he owed Rose something for this unquestioning service so willingly rendered.

"Goodnight," he said again, almost as lovers say goodnight.

Rose, left alone, locked the door and went about in a business-like way, lowering most of the lights. Then she let down the gold and black table, set the bag on it, and unpacked carefully and methodically, setting everything ready on convenient chairs. Her best nightdress, the one with the most and the prettiest lace, she laid on the work-table.

"I suppose one ought to air things," she said; "but this glorious weather—they can't be damp."

She rather prided herself on being in no hurry to go into that other room. But at last she stepped to its open door and looked in. The little room had its gas alight.

"So, this is where he sleeps," she told herself, and then went forward to look at the form that lay on his bed.

"How *could* he not have known she was young?" she asked herself, as for the first time she saw the delicate dark beauty of that quiet face. She sat down on a chair at the foot of the bed and looked. Rose was "no good" as an artist; Esther Raven had been right; but she was artist enough to know beauty when she saw it.

"I *am* glad she's saved," she said; "how dreadful if she had died—all that beauty wasted and thrown away."

And she sat quite still, looking, looking.

If you look at a sleeping person long enough and earnestly enough, that person wakes. Suddenly large dark luminous eyes returned Rose's scrutiny. Neither spoke. For a long minute they looked at each other.

It was not till the girl on the bed moved her hand to her head that Rose spoke.

"You are to have some medicine now," she said, and fetched it.

The other girl raised herself on her elbow and drank.

"Thank you," she said, as Rose took the empty glass from her; "I am sorry to give you so much trouble."

"I am very pleased to do anything for you," said Rose, and both voices were ice-cold.

"Is *he* there?" the girl in the bed asked, her eyes questioning the open door.

"No, he's gone to bed; he is very tired," Rose answered. "It has taken hours to revive you."

"Yes, of course," the other said, and was silent.

"Don't you think," said Rose, "that you'd be more comfortable in bed?"

"Yes, but—oh, I see—this is a bed, is it not? Yes. Thank you."

"I will help you to undress, if you like," said Rose, hating herself for the sudden and intense repulsion which this beautiful vision inspired.

"Thank you," said the vision again.

"I'll get the things," said Rose, and went into the room, calling upon herself to be reasonable. She was clear-sighted enough to realize exactly what that pang meant which she had felt when those eyes opened, when that voice—a very beautiful voice she hated to have to admit—asked for *him*. And she was level-headed enough to tell herself that jealousy—yes, it was that; she was certain of it—was nothing short of insane. He had never seen this woman before; he had not even known whether she was young or old.

"For shame!—he might be any ordinary young man," she told herself, and added, veiling the egoism in a wordless vagueness of thought; "you might be any ordinary young woman instead of the strong, sensible, competent, compelling person that you are!"

She gathered together the needed objects from chair and table.

"And besides," she said, with no vagueness now; "poor thing, how confusing and terrible for her. A strange place. Strange people. I must get her to like me and confide in me. She will need a friend."

So Rose, stifling the first instinctive repulsions of her whole healthy nature, went back to the woman who had been dead and was alive.

"You'd like me to bathe your hands and face," she said gently, kindly, dropping scented drops into the wash-hand basin; "and I'll brush your pretty hair, and plait it. You mustn't trouble to do anything. Let's play that I'm your maid, shall we?"

The other smiled. "How kind you are," she said. "I am foolish. Just now when I woke, I was afraid of you."

"You weren't really awake, not quite, were you?" Rose was laying the soft sweet sponge on the other's forehead and hoping for enlightenment. She had promised not to question her charge. But her charge might speak, unquestioned, and throw some light on her personality, her identity, and the circumstances that had brought her here. She did.

"You are more gentle than my maid," she said. *That* was enlightening. The stranger was, at any rate, of the class that has maids.

"What is your name?" she asked, as Rose brought soft towels.

"Rose."

"It is very beautiful, like you," said the other; "my name is Eugenia."

Rose could not remember where she had heard that name before.

"You must not talk so much," she said, feeling how good it was of her to say it. And Eugenia answered—

"I know: he said so. But we must know each other's names, my kind beautiful nurse. My dress—oh yes—it's the red one. It hooks at the back."

It did. But as Rose unhooked it the stuff tore, gave way rather like tinder, and as she withdrew the skirt, fragments of frayed red fell all about her.

If this had been a fancy dress it was a very flimsy one. But also, very thorough. For under the dress the clothes were as strange to Rose as the dress itself. The white clothes were of linen, heavier than anything Rose herself wore, and trimmed much less elaborately. And the stays-Rose fumbled in vain for the fastenings. Her fingers met a broad hard surface two inches wide at least—wood, it felt like—where the fastenings should have been. A little patience revealed the fact that the things fastened at the back, and had to be unlaced from end to end. The stockings were of white cotton, rather coarse, with open-work at the feet and a pink edging at the top.

Rose noticed all this with a growing sense of confusion.

"What a beautiful nightgown," the stranger said, lying back on the pillow and looking at the lace ruffles on the sleeves. "How kind of you to lend me such a beautiful thing. It was laid by in the drawer for your wedding, is it not?"

"*No*," said Rose hotly.

"Ah! I am sorry. You have no doubt more beautiful ones in your trousseau. I have in mine much fine work, my own sewing. All girls prepare for their wedding long before, is it not?"

"You mustn't talk, you know," said Rose; "let me put my arm round you. Now stand up and I'll pull the sheepskin away and then you can get into bed."

The girl stood up, and Rose, with one arm round her slender shape, dragged away the sheepskin. Something hard fell and rolled away under the chest of drawers.

"All right, get into bed. I'll pick it up afterwards."

Rose took away the lambskin, folded the girl's garments, set them in a neat pile and laid the torn red dress over all.

"Now go to sleep," she said. "Call me if you want anything. I shall be in the next room. Goodnight!"

"Good night," said the girl in the bed, a little forlornly; "won't you kiss me? I feel so lonely and lost. It's all so different."

She stopped—Rose kissed her and felt arms round her neck.

"There, there, it's all right," she said; "I'll take care of you."

She turned out the gas and went back into the laboratory where now the gas jets strove with the grey of dawn, wrapped herself in a shawl since the dawn was chill, and sat down in Anthony's armchair to watch out what was left of the night. She was very tired, and she roused herself suddenly from a pleasant languor that was creeping towards sleep to wonder what it was that had rolled away on the floor; a brooch or a button, most likely. Anyhow she would go and see. It would stop her from going to sleep. She went, fumbling under the furniture among the grey shadows, and came out into the laboratory with something in her hand. A ring. She took it to one of the gas jets, turned the light full on, and looked at her find. It was her ring, the ring that Anthony had given her.

The ring with the beryl and the chrysoprases.

"How clumsy of me," she thought; "what a good thing I heard it fall. I shouldn't like to lose you," she said, and kissed it. "Silly!" she said, and put it on.

As it slipped with less ease than usual on her finger, she heard herself called.

"Rose, Rose!" and hastened back to the bedside. The stranger caught at her hand.

"My ring," she said; "I want my ring. Did you see it when I undressed? He laid it on my heart when—I forgot—I mean it was on my heart. I heard something fall—was that it?"

"It was my ring that fell; this one," said Rose.

The small hands fingered it in its place, then pushed Rose's hand to where a shaft of gaslight struck through the door and made a yellow bar on the bed. "But this *is* my ring" she said. "He gave it to me. You mistake, dear Rose, is it not?"

The quick "No!" was stopped on Rose's lips by the agonized anxiety of the other's voice. "Humour her in everything. She has delusions," Anthony had said. So, Rose just said, "I suppose I was mistaken," took the ring off and put it on the finger which Eugenia held out.

"It's so large for me," said she, sighing contentedly; "he's going to have it altered. Only we always forget." Then she kissed the ring, as Rose had kissed it three minutes before. "It's very silly, I know," she said, sighing contentedly, and smiling up at Rose, "but *you* understand."

"Oh!" said Rose suddenly.

"What is it?"

"Nothing," Rose answered. "I've just remembered something. She walked to the wash-hand-stand. Her rings were there, as she had laid them when she poured out the water and scented it for Eugenia's washing. And there was her engagement ring. She turned, with it in her hand, to see its counterpart on the other woman's.

She went back into the laboratory, trembling and faint, glad to sink into the chair, with her hands pressed against her heart that fluttered.

Another ring, exactly like hers. And "he" had given it to this woman? Who was "he"? The woman had said, "Where is he?" and Rose had thought she meant Anthony. Had she? Had Anthony given her the ring? If not, how came there to be two rings so alike as to deceive even her, who had worn one of them for more than three months? How had this woman come here? Could Anthony have told her anything but the truth? Impossible—and yet——

One sees well enough the endless ebb and flow of questions, doubts, surmises that broke across Rose's heart in those hours of growing dawn. When it was, beyond all doubt, daylight with sunshine, and a sky of deepening blue, Rose made a careful toilet, bathed her eyes so that no one could have guessed that she had not only watched but wept, made her hair and dress neat, and resolutely sat down to read. She found *The Eyes of Light*, and did her best to lose herself in that gay and alluring work. But all the time she was saying to herself: "I will trust him. I will. I will. I will. I won't ask a single question. Not even hint one. He couldn't have lied to me. He couldn't!"

And when he came at eight o'clock with coffee for her, she was brave enough to meet him with a smile. And his first words were, "Rose, I told you a lot of lies last night."

CHAPTER 18
The Truth

"Hush!" said Rose, proud to be able to speak quite calmly; "she's asleep."

"Shut the room door, then," said Anthony; "I must speak to you." Then when Rose had softly closed it, he said—

"Look here, I don't know why I did it. I've been trying to find out most of the night. And I think it was mainly because I thought if I told you the truth last night it might frighten you. I was a bit unnerved myself. But if you'd like me to tell you the truth I will."

"I think I should like the truth," said Rose evenly.

In quite a few words he told it, from Bats' discovery of the body to his triumphant resuscitation of it. And then he stopped.

"Is that all?" she asked.

"That's all the facts," he said, "but there are conjectures. It's—there's something about it I don't understand. But I'll tell you the rest, Rose. Only don't misunderstand."

"I won't misunderstand," she said quietly.

"But your coffee's getting cold," he said. "You had no supper last night. You've had no breakfast. I'm a brute."

She poured out a cup of coldish coffee and drank it.

"Now," she said. And still he hesitated. The recital, with Rose's eyes upon him, seemed almost impossible.

"You understand," he said at last; "she was very weak. She couldn't have stood any shock. When she came to, she thought I was her lover. And I let her think so."

"Did she kiss you?" Rose asked, in a low voice.

"Yes," said Anthony.

"Did you kiss her?"

"Yes," he repeated miserably. "It wasn't possible to do anything else."

He spoke like a man on the rack. Rose gave the instrument another firm turn.

"Was it just when she revived, when she was confused? Or had she time to—to see your face and hear your voice?"

"Yes, plenty of time."

"I see."

"Rose, dear," he said; "do have your breakfast. I made the toast for you myself."

She laughed. "How funny life is," she said.

"But, Rose; you aren't angry. It's a delusion. And the moment she's well enough I must explain it to her. But I daren't till then."

"And that's why you're telling me the truth now. You want me to stand by and see that girl treating you as if—and you behaving as if you loved her. What do you think I'm made of, Tony?"

"I thought you'd help me," he said simply. "It's not my fault that this has happened." And to himself he said, "Well, whatever happens now, at least it's not *all* choked up with lies."

"What I don't understand," said Rose deliberately, "is how she ever got into that secret room. Someone must have brought her there. You are sure you know nothing of it? It wasn't you brought her here?"

"I suppose I deserve that you should doubt me," he said bitterly; "but I've told you the truth. I've never seen her before. But I've seen a portrait that is very like her. Oh, Rose, don't look at me like that. My dear, splendid Rose, don't! I've never seen you cry before."

"You thought I couldn't, I suppose," she sobbed; "and you haven't told me all the truth now. *What about the ring?*"

"What ring?"

"The ring she's got. Exactly like mine. She said '*he*' gave it to her. And she talked about weddings. Tony, for God's sake tell me the truth. I believe I shall go mad if I can't feel that you're speaking the truth."

"Before God," he said gravely, "I am speaking nothing but the truth. I know nothing of any ring. But if there is another ring like that it only confirms what I am beginning to believe." He stood a moment looking gloomily at her. Then, in a sudden revulsion of pitying tenderness, he went to her and put his arm round her, and drew her head to his shoulder. "There, there, dear," he said, "I want to tell you everything, but how can I if—? Don't make everything so awful for me just now, just now when I want your help so much; when I can't do without you."

It was the strongest appeal he could have made. And Rose answered to it.

"I—I'm rather tired," she said, taking the comfort of his arm about her, and his shoulder against her face; "I'm sorry. I won't be silly." And for the second time in twelve hours she dried her eyes, put away her handkerchief very definitely, and smiled.

"Now," she said, "I'm going to have my breakfast, and you must tell me everything that you haven't told me. And don't think I'm being horrid if I ask questions. You want me to know everything that *you* know, don't you? Cold? Well, it is rather. Is that the saucepan? I'll warm the coffee, and you must have some too."

Thus, determinedly did Rose drag into the scene those domestic details which so often qualify drama and blunt the edge of tragedy. She smiled again. And Anthony, in a spasm of gratitude, tried to return her smile.

"Now," she said, when two cups of coffee steamed on the table between them; "I suppose you've got used to the idea. But I haven't. I can't believe somehow that she got into that cupboard, or whatever it was. I know you say so. And Billy and Wilton saw her there too. But it seems to me as if you must have been deceived. Isn't there something they call collective hallucination? When a lot of people think they see a ghost or something, or when Indians throw a rope up into the air and it seems to stick fast and they climb up it and vanish and pull the rope up after them and they vanish too?"

Anthony shook his head. Rose munched flabby toast to show that she was now prepared to consider the subject from a common-sense standpoint.

"No," he said. "I think it's something much more interesting and unusual than that. To begin at the wrong end, because I feel you're still worried about that though you're pretending not to mind. Her taking me for her lover. I think her lover was with her when she died. And you know to restore her to life wasn't just drugs. It was lots more—an enormous spiritual and mental effort—to recall her soul. Or however you like to put it: to make her live again. It took all there was in me, of mind and spirit, every ounce.

"When I revived that boy, I told you of, he seemed extraordinarily attached to me. I didn't think of that before. It makes things clearer, talking them over with you. He did seem very fond of me—is still. That confirms my theory. It seems to me the only explanation is that in that intense application of all one's spiritual and mental force one somehow impresses oneself on the patient, who of course is quite helpless, with all the will-power in abeyance. It took a much greater effort to bring her back than it did for that boy. And I think that effort impressed my personality upon her so that when she became con-scious, she believed that I was her lover. It's a lame theory, but it's the only one I can formulate at present."

To Rose the theory was infinitely comforting.

"But will it last?" she said. "You must tell her some time, you know; when she's stronger, I mean," she hastened to add, lest he should think her unreasonable.

"Of course, the moment she is strong enough. But my theory is that this impressing of my personality on her would have been impos-sible but for her weakness, and that as she gains strength this delusion will fade, especially if she does not see me again."

Rose's heart leapt up. "And what I want you to do is to keep her with you till she is quite strong, and then if the delusion's gone, well and good. If not, I'll dispel it by telling her the truth."

"You're very much in love with the truth this morning," she said, but not bitterly. "Of course, I'll keep her, if she'll stay. Well?"

"Now to go back to the beginning. How did she get there? Well, I gather from the condition of the secret room and the things I found there that the person who put her there, whoever it was, knew as much as I do about what I've called my great discovery. In fact, it's plain that someone else discovered the secret of life before I did. I'm not sure that there haven't been two. And I'll tell you why in a minute. But first, I think my great-uncle Anthony had discovered it, because that lab. at Drelincourt was his, and this room opening out of it had things that belong to this secret, heavy things like mirrors and so on, that couldn't possibly have been brought in secretly since his time. He must have put them there, and he must have known what he was doing when he put them there.: They were all arranged for the working of the—the treatment, the first stages of it, that is. The body of that woman was brought in somehow, by someone who knew of that room, and knew that it was fitted for the early stages of a certain treatment. Who that person was I don't yet know, but we shall know, because he was the lover of that girl."

"You said you didn't know if she was young or old," Rose interrupted.

"Only last night, when I was lying to you."

"Sorry," she said, and put her hand on his.

"Either she'll recover her senses and tell us who she was, or he will come to look after her—unless-unless anything's happened to him. If he's alive he'll come."

"Well?"

"How he found out about the place; how he got he: in, I can't begin to make out. But he got her there and he began the treatment. Then he must have left her, intending to return, and not been able to return. Something must have happened. Perhaps a change of servants, one of them may have been abetting him. Perhaps my going to Drelincourt—but no, that wasn't it."

"Then if you—I mean if Bill hadn't found her, she'd have been dead—I mean really hopelessly dead, like the dead people they bury, in a few days." Her voice thrilled to the horror of it.

"No," he said slowly. "You see, it's like this. I'll try to make it plain. My secret isn't just bringing people to life. It's much bigger than that. I'm almost afraid, now it's come to the point, to tell even you. My secret's the thing the old philosophers were after. It's the Elixir of Life. Don't begin to think I'm mad, because really, I'm not. Did you give her the second medicine this morning?" he broke off to ask.

"Yes, at half-past seven, when she woke. She went to sleep again at once. Go on."

"You can't set a limit to the possibilities of science, mental or physical," he went on. "You can't estimate the strength or the nature of the forces that are all about us. There's a hard core of scientific scepticism, and round it—wonders, and the belief in wonders. How do you know what strange actions and interactions follow, when once, ever so little, you pierce the thin veil that divides the material from the spiritual world? Of course, I know it's unusual in a Christian country and an enlightened age to believe in a spiritual world beyond the material one. Yet many have believed in it. Or rather in the not-to-be-separated two-in-one of the material and the spiritual. Rose, you believe in miracles. Well, miracles have been done, and are being done, by the people who see that there isn't a hard and fast line between the body and the soul, the material and the spiritual; any more than there is between mineral and vegetable, vegetable and animal. There have been men in all ages who have claimed to be able to raise the dead."

"Yes," said Rose patiently, "go on."

"Let me think a moment. It's so difficult," he said, with a sublime candour that kept her silent, "to remember that you don't know anything about anything." It was difficult. It is difficult to realise that to others an idea, a thought is new, inconceivable even, when that idea has lived for long years in one's heart and mind. All through Anthony's school days, his days at college, in work and in play, always at the back of his mind had been this one thought: the Elixir of Life. To find that, to succeed in that search wherein so many had failed, to equal Paracelsus and Pythagoras and to excel them, to bring science to the aid of psychology, and to transmute science into what the ignorant call magic.

"To use "magic" (he never found a better word for the thing he used), to use magic and science side by side, above and below, acting and interacting, and so to achieve. There had been in him from the first that certainty of ultimate achievement without which no great scientific or psychic discoveries are made. No man who does not believe in himself and his work ever discovers anything worth the discovering. The explorer who faces all dangers to get beyond the mountain range that till now has been the limit of the known world, knows that he will succeed, or die. And if he die, in the effort, who shall say that he has failed, since Death does not end all? Anthony Drelincourt sat a moment in silence. Then he said—

"It's like this. You can't put eternal life into a body that's subject to disease and to the wasting of the tissues and the other things that mean old age. Of course, eternal life means eternal youth, or eternal prime, let us say."

"Yes." Rose felt as though she were in a very difficult dream.

305

"So," he went on slowly, "before you can give the life, you have to destroy the tendencies, the liabilities to disease. You have to render the patient immune from all diseases. And you have to—how shall I put it—take from and add to the bodily tissues till they become something different and yet the same. It's simpler perhaps to say, till they become immune from decay. Now these processes are difficult for this reason, that they cannot be performed on a living body. You follow?"

"I'm trying to understand," said Rose humbly; "go on."

"The life in the body, for some reason that I can't quite make out, resists to a degree that makes quite half the process impossible. So that life has to be destroyed, and immediately on death the processes of purification begin; the processes which, in their result, defeat old age, disease, and death. I believe old Anthony knew all that I know, and the Anthony of the sixteenth century knew more of it. It was in that book you gave me, almost all that I had found out. It was a little different in some of the details, but practically the same. It was in cypher, you know. Bats worked it out. He got the clue from one of those Bacon cyphers he's always at."

"Yes, I know," said Rose, impatient of Bats and his cyphers.

"And there was a little bit more in my uncle's writing. That was a cypher too, and Bats got at it. And it was *that* that put me on the right track. I owe that to you, Rose," he said, and stopped.

"Do you see," he went on in a moment, "you can only—how can I put it—build life on the foundation of death. You can't build a new life on the old life. Now the person who put that girl in the secret room, put her there because that room was a place he knew somehow of, ready and prepared for what he had to do. He took her there, and when she was dead—"

"Do you mean that he killed her?" said Rose, in a voice of horror.

"If you put it that way. The life went out. Then instantly he began the work, arrested the body's decay, destroyed the potentialities of disease, treated the tissues so as to render their deterioration impossible. And then, something happened. I don't know what. He could not get back to her, and she has been lying there, awaiting the last ministrations that should restore conscious life."

"It sounds most awful," said Rose; "suppose you hadn't come."

"That wouldn't have mattered, so long as someone had come someday. Her body was not dead when we found it, in the ordinary sense of 'dead.' It was simply prepared for the new life, decay arrested, and the other ministrations completed. She could have stayed there for years. And," he hesitated, "you know," he said quickly, "I think she had been there for some time."

"How long?"

"I don't know. It might be a long time. Rose, the veil that covered her was thick with dust."

"Her dress," said Rose, in a very low voice, "fell to pieces when I took it off, Tony. I can't help it; I don't like it. It's horrible."

"The idea will be beautiful to you when you get accustomed to it," he said; "it's new to you now. Think of the wonder of it, the—"

"Don't!" she interrupted. "Have you told me everything *now*?"

"Not quite," he said. "You know that my uncle was engaged to be married, and the girl disappeared?"

"Tony," she almost screamed, if one can scream in a whisper, "you don't mean she's been dead all these years; that she's that girl that disappeared. I can't bear it; I can't!"

"No, no," he said soothingly; "of course not. She ran away from my uncle. I expect she was afraid of these things, as you are. Would you run away from me, Rose, because I've made the most wonderful discovery a man has ever made?"

He laid his hand on hers.

"What I think is this: that girl ran away. She married someone else, and this is her daughter. There's a portrait of the girl who ran away. This girl is like it. The girl who ran away was working with him in his laboratory. She knew his secrets. She must have told her daughter, that girl we have here. And the girl must have told her lover. He must have known a good deal himself, by the way, or he couldn't have used what she told him. He and she decided to take the chance of life without possibility of disease or death. They got in somehow, and then he went away and couldn't get back. That's what I think."

"And the ring?" asked Rose.

"The beryl and the chrysoprase are part of the treatment," he said. "You lay them on the patient's heart at the very beginning."

"She said he had put it on her heart," said Rose, "but it's exactly like mine."

"You see," said Drelincourt, "your ring most likely belonged to my Uncle Anthony; it has his initials on it. The girl who ran away from him may have had its mate, and it would descend to her daughter. It seems to me it all fits on."

He looked at his watch. "Good heavens! why did you let me go on talking like this? She ought to have had food an hour ago. I'll go and get something—beaten-up eggs, I should think; and you take it in to her, and we'll clear out and you can take her over to your house. And, Rose, she'll want clothes." He was fumbling with his pocket-book.

"I can't!" said Rose.

"But of course," said Anthony obtusely, and he dragged out some banknotes, "I can't let you pay for her. Here—if you want any more—"

"I mean I can't do it," said Rose. "I daresay it all seems beautiful and natural to you, but to me—oh, thank God you didn't tell me last night. I couldn't have stayed with her. Tony, I'd die for you, gladly. But I can't do this. I can say I will, but I know I couldn't stand to it if I did. I can't have a dead woman to live with me, not even for you. She put her arms round my neck last night."

She spoke in extreme agitation.

"But, Rose," he said, "you're too sensible."

"I'm not sensible; I'm not, I'm not," she said, a little wildly. "You must get someone else—the dust of years—and that horrible red dress. What was the name of the girl who ran away?"

"Eugenia," he said.

"That's her name too! A horrible name. It's like death, somehow."

"You're talking nonsense," he said sharply. "Come, 'Rose, this isn't like you. My Rose that's so brave and clever and good."

"Don't!" she said; "that sort of thing's no use. Have you told Bats all this?"

"I've told no one but you," he said reproachfully; "and you're going to fail me."

"Tony, Tony," she said in an agony, "I don't want to fail you. I'd do it if I could. But I can't. It's stronger than I am. I daren't!"

"At least," he said coldly, "you'll carry the girl's breakfast into her. She's alive enough to need that."

Rose hung balanced between terror and returning self-control.

"Yes," she said, "I'll go and get it. No, you shan't go. I won't stay here alone."

He shrugged his shoulders and she went.

But in the yard, in the sunshine, she turned on herself and hated herself for a shifty fool.

"He has trusted you completely," she said. "You wanted him to lean on you; he is leaning on you. And you give way."

Bats, anxious-eyed and elaborately cheerful, met her at the door.

"Anthony's told me everything," she said; "more than he's told you, much more," and could have laughed as she said it at the pitiful jealous pride that spoke in her words, "and I've come for her breakfast. Beaten-up eggs, he said."

"Wilton said they'd be needed," said Bats. "I've got them. And milk."

Beating up eggs was somehow incredibly soothing; the presence of Bats was soothing; his talk too. Wilton, when he appeared, calm and friendly, was soothing also. Rose began to feel as one supposes a horse may when, having shied at some unspeakable horror, he is led close to it and perceives the unspeakable to be, in the concrete, at wheelbarrow or a post painted white. "I have been a fool," she said, watching Bats complete the egg-beating. And when he said, "Half of this is for you," she took it meekly.

Bats carried the tray across the yard.

"I wish," she said, "you'd come in. Tony's told me how you found her, and all that. And it's upset me a little. I suppose it's silly. He wants me to keep her at the little house for a bit till she gets better. And somehow, oh, Billy, it's awful to be a fool—I told him I simply couldn't."

"I should think not indeed," said Bats.

"I feel hateful," said Rose; "but I can't explain it. Only I know if I kept her, I couldn't go on with it. There would come a time, tonight most likely, when I should rush out and leave her. Oh, say what you think. You can't despise me more than I despise myself."

Bats did not say what he thought. Instead he said—

"Of course, I'll come up. Anthony's always in the clouds. We must think out some practical scheme. Of course, she must go back to her friends."

The idea that the stranger *had* friends was in itself vaguely comforting to Rose.

"And Wilton must see her presently," said Bats; "see if she's fit to be moved, and all that. Now look here, Rose, don't you worry. Because Wilton and I are here, and," he added with a not too obvious afterthought, "and Anthony. You've not got it all on your shoulders, you know."

"I know I always think I'm so necessary and important," said Rose humbly, "but Anthony does seem to want me."

Again, Bats did not say what he thought. They went up the stairs together. Rose entered the little bedroom with much the feelings one might have who explored a mausoleum alone at midnight. Yet, when her eyes fell on the quiet face of the stranger, she experienced again and more strongly the feelings of the horse who has unreasonably shied.

She laid her hand on the shoulder of the sleeper, warm and slenderly rounded under the thin nightdress, and said, smiling with a conscious effort into the awakening eyes, "I've brought your breakfast. Do you feel better?"

"I feel quite well, quite," Eugenia said; "how kind you are."

She sat up and threw back her hair which had loosened itself from the plait Rose had woven last night. She took the proffered glass and drained it. Then, "Where is *he?*" she asked.

"He is not far off," was all Rose found to say.

"I must see him, you know," she said, "as soon as I am dressed. I have important business to talk with him."

The poor little pretence was transparent to Rose, who knew her strange delusion.

"I will tell him," she said. "But your dress is torn. I must get you one of mine."

"Your dress will not fit me," said Eugenia, smiling. "You are great like a queen. I am small like—

"Like a fairy," said Rose kindly, and again smile answered smile. Poor little thing! How could she have been so heartless, so imbecile? Rose asked herself. This girl before her was no deathly terror to run from, shrieking, but a living, breathing, friendly fellow-creature to be helped and—yes, she was stroking the little hand now—to be petted.

"I have a loose gown," she said; "we can draw it up at the neck. It will trail a little, but that's graceful. I'll go and fetch it."

"You won't be long?" Eugenia asked. "Oh, I am so glad to have a friend like you."

Rose passed softly through the laboratory, only answering Anthony's inquiring look with a whispered, "I'm going to get her a dress. She's asking for you. You'll have to see her." She felt very brave and very trusting as she said it. Somehow, she must pay for this morning's folly and cowardice. Anthony should see that she trusted him.

The dark blue dress, embroidered in pale cornflowers and their grey-green leaves, became Eugenia's dark beauty as a frame becomes a picture. When she was dressed, the dark hair banded neatly, Rose left her a moment and came into the laboratory. Bats was looking out of the far window.

"You must see her now," she said to Anthony; "I'll bring her in."

"Rose," Anthony caught her hand. "I see I was asking too much. It's all right, dear. I'll wire to Lady Blair. She'll be able to see to things.

She's the only woman friend I have, except you."

If anything had been wanting, this was it.

"Nonsense!" Rose said briskly. "Of course, I'll do everything. I was out of my mind just now, I think. I was tired and—"

"You're an angel," he said. And she crossed to Bats.

"Wait for me outside," she said. "She wants to talk to Anthony. She thinks she has 'business' to transact with him. It's a delusion, of course, but it's got to be humoured."

Bats went, Rose hesitated a moment. She longed to tell her lover she "trusted him entirely," but she refrained. She would not detract from the price she was paying for her suspicions and cowardice.

"I'll bring her in," she told him, instead.

And Anthony Drelincourt had the experience, not easily forgotten, of seeing those two women come through the door and towards him, with their arms round each other.

"There," said Rose, placing Eugenia in a chair. "All right? Good. Sit down, Anthony. Telephone if you want anything, won't you?"

With that she left them. It was perhaps the proudest moment of her life. As soon as the sound of Rose's feet had died away on the stair, Eugenia rose. Anthony, whose emotions defy analysis, sat still in his chair. She moved towards him, a little feebly, a little uncertainly, and still he sat like a statue. With a little rush her transit ended. She was on her knees by him, her arms round his neck. And again, the world was stars and roses, meteors and thorns. It was not pleasure that thrilled him, rather the faintness of a mortal agony. But his arms enfolded her.

★★★★★★

"It was silly of me to be frightened," said Rose to Bats, "but I can do it all right. I don't know what made me so silly. She's a dear, isn't she?" said Rose, feeling herself a heroine.

"If you have her at your house, I shall be at the laboratory all day and all night," said Bats. "I can get across in half a minute, or less."

There was something to lean on here. Rose felt it. And Bats had meant her to feel it. She made little plans for taking care of Eugenia, keeping her happy and amused till her friends could be found, laughing, talking, almost reassured.

But there had been, it seemed later, no need for reassurance.

"My idea was right," Anthony told Rose later; "she *is* the daughter of the Eugenia who ran away. No, she can't remember any details about how she got there. She thinks she'll remember if she goes to Drelincourt. I'm going on at once to prepare Lady Blair. I *can't* tell *her* the truth, Rose. I hate lying, but it's impossible. If I told her the truth, she'd never believe it. I shall say we found Eugenia in a hospital, and I'm bringing her home because she's a relation."

"Whatever you like," said Rose, hating the familiar "Eugenia," of which he seemed unconscious.

"Will you and Bats bring her on by the five o'clock train?" Anthony went on. "And here's that money. Buy her clothes. And boxes, you know, to put them in."

"You can't buy clothes like that, to fit," said Rose. "Don't you remember what you told me about men's clothes?"

"Oh! Lady Blair's maid can make them smaller," said Anthony, with the memory of a slender shape in his arms; "do the best you can, Rose. I'll never forget what you've been to me in all this—never."

"I am not likely to forget either," said Rose to herself. To him she said: "The seven o'clock train. The five's impossible. And even so, I shall have to leave her alone nearly all day."

"Wilton will be here and Bats and your char. And she'll sleep most of the time," said Anthony. "Get everything she's likely to want. Everything. Is that enough?"

She counted the notes he had given her.

"I should think so," she said drily. He had given her notes for three hundred pounds.

"I shouldn't have thought it safe to carry so much money about," she said.

"I never feel it's safe to have less," he answered; "you never know what may happen."

"No," said Rose, "you never do, do you?"

CHAPTER 19

Eugenia

There is a pleasure in spending money, even if you are spending it on someone else's trousseau. Rose enjoyed herself, entered thoroughly into the work in which she had engaged, and looked back with scorn at the hysterical girl who had met her lover's claim on her help with, "I can't do it!" Careful measurements enabled her to buy clothes that would, more or less accurately, fit the other girl. Even hats—the head once measured and the face kept well in mind—were not impossible. For shoes, she took with her one of those Eugenia had worn, a slender satin thing with a sandal of perished elastic cord. She bought everything that a girl could need, from silk stockings to silver-backed brushes, and back again from tortoise-shell combs to scarlet slippers. It was a beautiful trousseau.

Rose had a taxi-cab and kept it waiting and collected things in it. At the last shop she deposited the collection, whirled away and bought the trunks and bags, at the same shop where Anthony's had been bought, whirled back with them to the last shop where everything was waiting, had everything packed, save the walking dress, hat, gloves, shoes, that Eugenia was to wear, and then gave the word that should cause her to be whirled to Malacca Wharf. As the taxi slid down St. Martin's Lane, a sudden impulse made her stop it at the shop of Mr. Abrahamson. He had written to her, only two days before, that he had more books with the same bookplate. She might buy them for Anthony; with his own money. He wouldn't mind. He ought to be pleased.

The old man came from the remote recesses of piled books as she darkened the door.

"You come to see the books," he said; "yes?"

"Yes; thank you for writing."

He laid the books on the counter, a half-dozen or so of dusty volumes in worn brown calf.

"See," he said, fluttering the leaves of the topmost one, "the bookplate and the name in all."

"Where did you get them?" Rose asked.

"From a person of no account. Where *he* obtained them, I shall know later."

"And how much?" said Rose.

"They are not for sale," Mr. Abrahamson told her, and quickly, to meet her fallen face; "if Miss Royal will accept them, it is old Abrahamson's marriage gift to Miss Royal."

"Oh! but I can't," she said; "I mean it's too kind of you; but—"

"You will not deny an old man who has now left so few pleasures; ah! so few, so few!" He spread a sheet of brown paper and began to arrange the books on it. "The enchanted chariot waits again," he said. "You will take them?"

"I don't feel it's fair."

"Not fair to grant me this little pleasure! Your betrothed, he paid me that hundred pounds, you know."

"Did he?" said Rose, relieved by the news from a sense of obligation which she did not like.

"Of course, I told him when I promised about the book. If it should bring him money; but I didn't know—"

"He told me it had enabled him to make a priceless discovery. Priceless," he repeated meditatively.

"Yes," she said, "oh yes. And I don't know how to thank you."

"And you are happy?" the old bookseller asked, looking at her across the little heap of volumes. "And he is happy? His discovery has brought him joy; not?"

"I—yes—I think so."

"And all is well—none of the nonsense I saw in the crystal?"

Rose remembered what he had seen—a dead woman.

"Part of it has come true," she said slowly, and shivered. "But what *I* saw, hasn't."

"You are sure? Yes? Ah! it will come." There must be in life what you saw in the crystal. It was I who saw amiss. Things that could not be, that should not be."

"I wish," said Rose abruptly, "you'd just tell me one thing. Did what you saw in the crystal end happily? Did everything come right?"

"I saw all wrong," he said, tying the string of the parcel. "I saw the impossible, the not to be believed. I saw death cheated by the wit of man. And no man's wit can juggle with death and life, Miss Royal. Think of it no more. You love and you are beloved, and this is your marriage gift from the old man who knew that love was on the way to you. No, no; I myself will place the so worthless offering in the enchanted chariot of the princess."

He carried the parcel out, and Rose, at the door of the taxi as he turned from placing the books within, gave him her hand, and on a quick impulse, both hands. A lingering errand boy with a basket was much intrigued by the little group, the dusty old man in his worn black, the brilliant young lady in the blue muslin and the hat of flowers.

"The God of my fathers protect you," he said. She gave him that smile of hers; it was all she could give him, and at that moment it cost her much.

"Poor child," he said to himself, as he turned back to his wilderness of books; "poor child, poor child! Yet the end is peace."

Rose, whirling once more in the enchanted chariot, was the battlefield of what used to be called "a thousand conflicting emotions." Strongest, perhaps, was the sense that she had not, after all, been weak. She had been able to respond to her lover's claims on her. She was doing what he wished her to do. And so, the taxi whirled on to Malacca Wharf.

Eugenia, still in the blue gown, was seated in Anthony's chair, holding, it seemed, a little court. Bats and Wilton were on each side. Rose was aware of a new quality in the picture before it broke up at her entrance. The two men came forward to take the parcels she carried.

"Take them all into the next room," she said briskly. "Come, Eugenia, you must change your dress at once. The taxi's waiting outside. There's none too much time." And Eugenia came obediently.

It was rather annoying, after all the trouble Rose had taken, that Eugenia did not like her dress, and found the shoes clumsy. But the silk stockings she liked, and the white cloth coat and the mushroom hat and the scarf of dark blue chiffon.

Rose caught Eugenia's eyes in the glass; they met her own with a troubled wistful expression.

"What is it?" she asked a little impatiently; "aren't the gloves the right size? What is it?"

"You are sure," Eugenia said, "that it is so that ladies dress? You would not buy me clothes except such as ladies wear?"

"Of course not," said Rose. "I've bought you absolutely the best things money can buy."

"Whose money?"

"His money." Rose wished she could have given any other answer. "I've bought you two trunks full of the nicest things I could find."

"Ah, that is so kind," said the other, "but you know I have a beautiful trousseau of my own. It needed not to buy so many."

"But if you do not know where your trousseau is?" Rose could not help saying.

A troubled look clouded the dark eyes. "But I do know," she began. "No, I mean you know best. Thank you, dear Rose, for all the trouble you take, for all your kindness. I am ready now. We go?"

Anthony met them at the journey's end. Wilton and Bats were on each side of Eugenia, and he got a word with Rose.

"Lady Blair was awfully upset," he told her. "She's gone to bed. Esther and Linda, I had to tell all of them then, of course, they're frightfully interested. Best get Eugenia to bed as quickly as you can. I hope to God bringing her to Drelincourt's the right thing. It seemed so this morning. But now I don't know."

"He looked harassed and old.

"I've got some books for you," Rose said, rather than say nothing; "old books that belonged to your uncle. Mr. Abrahamson got them for me for a wedding present. Wasn't it sweet of him?"

"Do you know," said Anthony, who had only heard her first words, "I sometimes wish I had never seen a book, never learned to read. Yes, I brought the big motor. Keep her warm; these evenings are chilly."

"I got the clothes for her," said Rose.

"Oh!" he said; "were they what she wanted?"

That was Rose's reward for the long, well-organised, well-executed shopping.

"She's not seen them all yet," she answered, and with that they reached the motor.

"Another little train," said Eugenia.

Sounds of laughter and talk came from the open window of the billiard-room and struck on Rose's ears with a curiously desolating sensation. She had been through these pains and terrors, and these, her friends, had been merry and jolly all the time. She did not know what sort of welcome she had expected at Drelincourt, but not this. She felt as children feel who are sent to bed in disgrace and hear "the others" laughing and talking just as though nothing had happened.

They went up the steps, and Wilkes met them at the door.

"You'll come straight to bed," said Rose, taking the hand of the little white-coated figure, and drawing it through her arm; "this way."

She led Eugenia to the stairs, too full of the desire to play perfectly the part of Anthony's guardian angel to pause even to put the commonplace question, "Which room?" If she thought about it at all, she supposed that she would. find a maid waiting on the soft-carpeted corridor. But no maid was there. Rose turned to the right, intending to go to her own room and ring. Her door was the fifth in the corridor. But Eugenia stopped suddenly at the third door and turned the handle. It was locked.

"Not there," said Rose; come to my room. Then we'll ring and find out where your room is."

"This is my room," said Eugenia, resisting the gentle pressure of Rose's arm.

"No, no," said Rose. "Come, it isn't far." And Eugenia's resistance yielded.

The maid who ought to have been waiting came in answer to Rose's ringing. The room prepared for Eugenia was next to Rose's; a wardrobe had been moved, and a door was revealed connecting the two rooms, and beyond Rose's room was a sitting-room in which a table was whitely spread. Supper appeared here, appeared before Eugenia had even removed her hat and coat. The two girls ate together at the table by the window.

Rose watched Eugenia eat chicken and sip champagne, and wondered how she could have been silly enough to shrink from this gentle charming little person, who ate and drank heartily as a child and daintily as a bird.

Supper over, she leaned across the corner of the table and took Rose's hand caressingly.

"I feel I shall love you very much," she said; "you are so brave and strong and beautiful. And so kind, so very kind. But I feel that you cannot love me because I am forbidden to speak. He has told me that I must say nothing that is real. And I do not know how to speak; I am stifled with all this mystery."

"You have been ill," said Rose, pressing her hand; "everything will seem quite different when you are well again."

"That is what they say when people are—what is it? insane, is it not?" Eugenia spoke with a sudden terror in her eyes. "You don't mean I'm *that?*"

"No, no," Rose reassured; "only you are fired with your illness, and of course everything seems different."

"Yes," said Eugenia, looking around her, "everything is different. This room is different."

"The doctor said you were not to talk too much."

"Ah, that you all say," said Eugenia, with a movement half-petulant, half-despairing. "Well, I talk no more. I go to my bed, sweet Rose. And tomorrow I must talk with Mr. Drelincourt, and tell him that I am not ill, and that I cannot live in silence. I choke in it. I stifle. I want to tell you everything, dear Rose. May I not tell you?"

Rose had many weaknesses, but in this moment, she yielded to none of them.

"No," she said very decidedly. "Of course, I'd love to hear anything you'd care to tell me, but not if it's bad for you. The doctor said, don't talk. And you mustn't talk. Come, I'll help you to bed."

Rose joined the party below. They were full of polite questions for a few moments; but soon it was plain to Rose that their interest in her journey, and in the newly discovered relative, was only a matter of politeness, mingled with curiosity. When they found that she had nothing to add to the story Anthony had already told them, their interest flagged. Lord Alfriston was still of the house-party. Could it be only the day before yesterday that he had covered his request that he might be asked to stay by a quotation about a Mr. Whitehead? It seemed impossible that one could have lived in so little time, so much. He and Esther and Linda and Mullinger seemed in this little time to have, on their part, also lived much. They seemed to have cemented themselves into a quartet which Rose could only contemplate from the outside.

Mr. St. Maur had gone; Lady Blair was invisible; Anthony was deep in talk with Bats and Wilton. The three had given her but the briefest greeting when she entered the drawing-room. And now the quartet, having done its duty by her, fell back on allusions to little things that had happened after her going away. She was "out of it." So quickly, so completely, one dropped out. She left the group of four and went to the window and looked forth. The moonlight was casting black shadows of the vases on the terrace. Beyond it, poplars stood tall and sentimental. Somewhere to the right a late nightingale sang fitfully. The voices behind her sounded detached, far away, like the voices you hear in the garden of an hotel where you know nobody.

"No one really wants me," she told herself; "not even Anthony." And as she said it a voice behind her said—

"You're very tired. Why don't you go to bed?"

It was Bats, of course. Anthony and the doctor were still in earnest talk at the window farthest from that where Rose stood.

"I'm choking; I'm stifling," said Rose suddenly. "I wish nothing ever happened. Oh, how different everything was before Anthony got his money. What's all this mystery? What's—No, I don't mean to worry. Only everything is detestable. What's going to become of her?" she said. But at the back of her mind the question was, "What is going to become of *me?*"

"She stretched out her arms towards the night and breathed deeply, as though indeed she felt stifled.

"I hate all mysteries," she said; "and I hate you, Billy, for catching me with my guard off! You're always doing it. Go away. Send Anthony to me. It's a dignified position, isn't it?" she said, laughing drearily, "to have to *send* for him? Oh, go away! You make me say things I hate myself for saying."

She turned her face from him and looked steadily out into the moonlight. When next she turned her face, it was to look into Anthony's.

"I couldn't come before," he said; "I was trying to make the doctor understand."

"She says," Rose told him, disdaining to accept or reply to his excuse, "that she must see you. That she wants me to love her and that

I cannot while she is forbidden to talk freely to me. Don't you think it's rather silly to limit her in this way? Why not let everything go on naturally? I should have thought talk would be a relief."

"One doesn't know what to do or think," said Anthony wearily; "but I thought I'd better not talk to her again, by ourselves, I mean. I thought you wouldn't like it. And I did think it best for her not to talk. Good Heavens, Rose!" he said, with sudden heat, "don't you see that she'll go and tell everyone that I'm engaged to her? And it doesn't seem fair to her to go warning everybody that they mustn't believe a word she says."

"The mistake was bringing her here," said Rose. "If I'd only not been a coward! It's simply insane to pitchfork that poor girl and her delusions into the middle of a lot of strangers. I ought to have kept her at Malacca."

"It's no use crying over spilt milk," he said; "she's here. And we must make the best of it. By the way, did anything happen—before I came, I mean? Because when I arrived Lady Blair had gone to bed with a headache. She got up on purpose to see me."

"*I* don't know what happened," said Rose. "I wasn't here, you know. I was with her—and you," she added more graciously.

"Of course, you were. I must ask the others."

"Then goodnight," said she; "the others are just a little bit too much for me tonight. I'm tired, Tony."

She gave the words a note of appeal.

"Of course, you are, my brave, clever, sensible Rose," he said remorsefully. "It's my fault. But if you knew—"

"Oh, I know," she said, made herself smile at him, and went. He crossed to Esther and put his question about Lady Blair. "I don't know," she said; "she seemed depressed all day. And the evening before, too. I think she was annoyed about the straw."

"The straw?"

"Where you'd been packing, you know. And it hadn't been cleared up. She let one of the footmen have it about leaving the room in such a state. I suppose things like that do upset you when you're old and when you've always had footmen to do every little thing. But, Anthony, do tell me about this new relation you've discovered."

He told his careful, guarded little lies.

"What a rum world it is, though," was her comment. "Fancy going to see an interesting case and then it turns out to be your own flesh and blood! I hope she's all right again now?"

"It was a curious sort of seizure," said Anthony; "she has not quite recovered her memory. Treat her like a child who's forbidden to tell a secret, will you? I'm afraid if she taxes her brain by trying to recall things——"

Rose, deep in one of those dreams wherein Anthony looked as he had looked in the crystal, and spoke as he had never in this world spoken, and kissed her as one kisses the goddess who benignly stoops with unhopedfor respondings, woke to feel lips still on hers, a butterfly touch, instantly withdrawn; Eugenia's touch.

"I couldn't help it," she said, "you looked so pretty asleep."

Rose rubbed her eyes. "And you," she said, "how pretty you are. What a pretty dress. Where did you get it?"

"It was in the room beside mine," she said. "It is a little dressy for morning, but it is mine and it fits me. I could not find any of the others."

It was a blue silk dress, very full in the skirt, very pointed as to the bodice, with trimmings of black and white, and a collar of white lace. It fitted Eugenia as though it had been made for her.

"It is a French chest of drawers," she explained. "The lowest drawer is not with a lock. It appears part of the case. The other drawers are locked. The dress is new; still in its silver paper. I have never worn it. But it was not well packed."

She smoothed its creases carefully.

"It was in your room?"

"Yes. Next to where I slept. The door was bolted, and they had set a wardrobe over it. But the maid who called me moved it. And I helped. You see now how I am strong."

Rose dressed with the miserable certainty that Eugenia's brain had been touched by the strange happenings that had befallen her. She must tell Anthony. It was not safe. The girl ought to be in an asylum. Her heart welcomed the thought while repelling it.

She was late for breakfast. Only Esther was there. The others were out on the terrace. As Esther poured the tea Rose slid to the window and looked out. She could see a glint of blue, surrounded. A glint of pink, solitary. Linda in the pink and white gown—how fresh she had kept it—was leaning on the balustrade alone. All the men were surrounding the blue silk with the black and white trimmings.

"Your new friend has a way with her," said Esther, handing tea.

"Yes," said Rose at the sideboard, hesitating in a choice of foods for which she had no desire; "isn't she beautiful?"

"They all seem to think so," said Miss Raven. "And so, do I," she added hastily. "But she's very helpless. She couldn't do anything for herself at brekker. Her bread had to be buttered for her, and her marmalade I put on her plate, and her peach peeled. She makes me think of the ladies who were toasts, don't you know—

"That regal indolent air she had,
So confident of her charm.'"

"Does Lord Alfriston admire her too?" Rose asked, coming back with something she could not have named on a plate.

"It looks like it," said Esther. "But it looks like it with all of them; even with Saint Anthony, which is absurd. Q.E.D."

Rose wondered why she had only just begun to notice that Esther was a little vulgar. Esther thought it strange that she had never before perceived Rose to be malicious.

There was a silence. Then—

"She treats the place as if it belonged to her," Esther said, "and the people too," she added.

"She's an invalid, you know," Rose made herself say, and tried to feel loyal; "they're always privileged."

Esther had put her elbows on the table and her chin in her hands.

"Things never stay as you want them," she said. "It was all so jolly, and a new person does change things so, don't you think? If I had my way, I'd never make another new acquaintance. They upset things so."

"I didn't find Lord Alfriston upsetting; did you?" Rose asked.

"No; but then he's just as if he'd always been one of the Septet, much more than Tony ever was," said Esther.

And this time it was she who thought Rose vulgar, and Rose who thought her malicious. And another silence fell.

Rose was surprised to find Esther's hand in hers; Esther's face averted.

"Rose," she said, "do help me. Do keep her away if you can. I've never been so happy in my life as I've been here. You're all right. Everything's printed and bound and indexed for you. But my life's in manuscript, and she'll go through it with a red pencil. Yes, I know it's not like me, Rose. But I'm afraid of her. I wish she hadn't come."

"She's had," said Rose, consciously tactful, "a long illness. I expect she's frightfully glad to get out and talk to anyone. You know, the bird-out-of-a-cage feeling."

"And why does she wear fancy dress in the morning?" Esther asked. "It isn't fair. Besides being silly. And look at Linda, completely

321

out of it. And only yesterday she was—"

"Don't be a goose," said Rose, and went out to join the others.

Eugenia in the blue silk looked as out of place in the group of men as a tropical bird in a pigeon-loft. She smiled to greet Rose, but Rose saw behind the smile a tired anxiety.

"Ah!" she said, catching at Rose's hand. "Now my old friend you are here, I must leave my new friends. We have so much to say, so much to arrange, is it not?"

And she led Rose towards the house. The moment they were out of earshot of the group she turned feverishly to Rose. "You come to deliver me from a dream. I understand nothing. I cannot bear it. You must find him. Tell him I must speak with him. I cannot live so—in a dream that I do not understand. Come, this way," she said, dragging Rose towards the library. "In the little room here, we can talk with no interruptions." She went quickly to the Empire room.

"You explored this morning then?" Rose said for something to say while she was thinking what to do.

But Eugenia took no notice. She loosed Rose's hand when the room was reached, and said—

"Go now. Tell him to come now. I cannot understand, and I cannot bear it. Yesterday should have been my wedding day. This I tell you, because I would not have you think me unreasonable. I wait for him here."

"And you must go," Rose told Tony two minutes later, when she had overtaken him with Bats walking silently in the rose-garden; "it's no use. She says you told her not to talk. And that she doesn't understand anything and she can't bear it."

"You know what I told you," said Anthony, as Bats fell behind to smell the roses; "she thinks——"

"I know," said Rose; "you'll have to tell her."

"You send me? You tell me to go to her? Rose, it would be better if I went away."

"Nonsense!" said Rose briskly; "don't be a coward. It's got to be faced."

Anthony could find no words to explain to Rose what he knew and she did not know—what it was that had to be faced.

"All right," he said lamely, "I suppose I'd better get it over."

"Much better," said Rose encouragingly, and went to join Mr. Bats among the roses.

CHAPTER 20
Fifty Years Ago

The sun shone full on the window where Eugenia stood waiting. The blue silk spread round her like a full blue rose. She made no move to meet Anthony, only her eyes were on him as he closed the door and came across the room to her. When he reached her she smiled and said, "At last."

"You wanted to see me," he said stupidly.

"And you; did not you wish to see me?" she asked, as with perfect knowledge of the answer.

"Of course, I did," he said.

"Only that?" she said. "Only so?" and challenged him with her pretty eyes.

He could find no weapons save words to meet her challenge. So, he said very awkwardly: "I mustn't. It wouldn't be fair. There are things I must tell you."

"I forgive them all," she said. "You need not tell me. I know you could do nothing I should not forgive."

"I wanted to wait till you were quite strong," he said, "but——"

"I *am* strong. It is as you told me. A little weakness after the sleep, such as the butterfly has when first it is born, then the lightness and the confidence of a perfect creature for ever."

"I did not tell you that," he said.

"You have lost your memory while I slept," she said, "but I will bring it back. It will come back after—Anthony, can't you send all those people away, so that I may do for you what you did for me?"

"I have done nothing for you," he said, "except to awaken you. And you can do nothing for me."

She trembled and turned pale.

"What is it?" she whispered. "Anthony, I am afraid. You are changed. You do not love me now? Has the great change made me so that you do not love me? No, no, no. It is not possible. Say that you love me, dear. I am afraid. Say it. You do love me still?"

"I mustn't say so," was as near as he could go to the plump negative to whose utterance, he tried to nerve himself. "I don't know how to tell you—don't—oh, my God—I can't tell you!"

She had come to him, put arms about his neck, laid her cheek to his. "Dearest," she said, "it doesn't matter. Nothing matters except our love. Have you lost all your money? Is it that? Do you think I care?

Don't be afraid to tell your Eugenia who loves you."

"You don't love *me*," he said. And it sounded almost like the jesting lie of a lover. "Listen," he went on, "sit down here on the window seat and let me hold your hands. So. Now tell me, how long is it since you were put to sleep?"

"Two days, no, three," she answered. "I thought that. But you say it was longer."

"Much longer. And I am not the man who put you to sleep."

"But Anthony—"

"Listen," he said, and expounded as calmly as he could that theory of his about his personality being impressed on her mind in the moment of her awakening.

"But that's nonsense, dear," she said gently; "you are you and I am I, as we always were. I do not understand what it is that you want me to believe. Or why. We both know the truth. Why try to make me believe lies?"

Her soft eyes caressed him; her hands fluttered in his hands like doves. It was harder than he had thought it would be. Yet he had known it would be hard. He looked at her, and her eyes filled with tears as they met the passionate sad tenderness of his.

"What is it?" she breathed; "my love, my love! What is it?"

He was no nearer making her understand that he was not her love. "See," he said, with a sudden inspiration; "let us suppose that I have forgotten everything—that I do not remember you—only since you awakened. Will you tell me, as if I did not know, who you are, and who I am? And about the sleep?"

"But yes," she said; "I see now. You said there were risks, but I did not understand it was for you or I would never—My poor Anthony. You have forgotten all? Everything?"

"Yes," he said. "Who am I? Who are you?"

"You are Anthony Drelincourt," she said patiently, as one humouring a child, "and I am your sweetheart Eugenia Delmar. You found out the secret of the lasting life, and we shut ourselves up in the little vault."

"When?" he asked eagerly.

"The day before our wedding. You remember. We wished to make sure that we should never part. You arranged the altar and the lambskin and gave me the drug and you kissed me and I surrendered my will to yours. Oh, Anthony! You told me it would not hurt. It hurt like death. But you were there, holding my hand, and I did not call out, did

324

I? I was brave, yes? And then you kissed me through the beginnings of a dream, and then I slept till you woke me in a strange place and told me that I had been asleep longer than the three hours that were to have seen the new life made. How long had I been asleep?"

"I don't know," he said. "I mean what day was it?"

"The twenty-first of June, of course," she said wonderingly.

"And the year?"

"Why, this year, of course."

"What year is this?"

"You forget even that? My poor boy! But I will take care of you. It is the year eighteen hundred and sixty-six," she explained gently.

"In the year eighteen hundred and sixty-six you were put to sleep?"

"Yes, dear, yes. Don't agitate yourself."

"You have slept a long time," he said difficultly. "I am afraid to tell you how long."

"Days?"

"More than days. More than weeks."

"But it is summer still," she said, touching the rose at her breast.

"More than months. Eugenia, it's possible, but I can't believe it. Tell me more. Who was in the house when you were put to sleep?"

"Your brother Bartholomew and your mother. She was sitting in the library. And Cecily Drelincourt, your cousin, you know, that was to have been our bridesmaid."

"All that," he said, "I knew. I might have transferred my thought to you. Tell me more."

"I knew your secret; how the floor was raised to barricade the door. And I know all the ways of the house and the garden. Blindfold me and I will show you that I know. Or send for your brother or Cecily. They will persuade you. It is terrible to-have forgotten, but I will remind you of everything, and presently you will remember."

He found himself kneeling before her, holding her hands, gazing into her eyes.

"Oh, my God," he said, "if it were only as you think. Be brave and listen. I *must* tell you. I wish to God I could take you away somewhere where you need never know. Even now, perhaps—" His hand tightened on hers. What was Rose? What was a promise of marriage? What was anything, weighed in the balance against this love that life suddenly offered? He could take her away. What was money for but to buy happiness? Take her away to some distant place, some island in the far seas, and she need never know.

"Tell me what?" she said, stroking his hair with hands that thrilled.

"I will tell you nothing but that I love you," he said. "Whatever's true, or isn't true, I love you. I know what love is now. I didn't before. Kiss me, my love, and tell me that nothing shall ever come between us, nothing, nothing."

She told him what he asked, crushed in his arms, her heart against his.

"You'll marry me tomorrow?" he said at last, releasing her and drawing back to let his eyes drink in the beauty and the love of her face.

"But yes," she said, "and then you will remember. And I will do for you what must be done so that we live for ever, together."

Both had risen and were standing face to face, his hands on her shoulders and hers on his breast.

"I've been a fool," he said, "forgive me. But I'm sane now. There's nothing in the world but you."

She laughed softly, gladly, and raised her innocent lips to his. And the door opened suddenly. And Lady Blair came in, saw them, and the light word of apology on her lips froze there. She looked again, closed the door and came towards them.

"So, this is the new relative?" she said contemptuously. "You lose no time, Miss Delmar."

"Who is this person?" Eugenia asked coldly.

"Present your new friend by all means," said Lady Blair.

"This is Miss Delmar, my promised wife," Anthony said. "Eugenia, this is Lady Blair."

He was trying to catch Lady Blair's eyes, but she had no eyes for any but Eugenia. And Eugenia was saying in tones of ice, "To what are we indebted for the pleasure of Lady Blair's company?"

"You are very like your mother," said Lady Blair. "I congratulate you on carrying on the family tradition. Your mother also came to this house. She also broke another girl's heart, as you are doing. Does Rose know of her good fortune yet?" she asked Anthony, and stood there, her poor old face white under the rouge, and the roses in her muslin hat nodding to her trembling.

"You don't understand," he said, "dear Lady Blair, leave us. I'll explain later."

"No explanation is needed," she said; "the situation explains itself. Yes, I will leave you. I will leave your house and take your poor broken-hearted Rose with me."

"Who?" said Eugenia to Anthony, "is Rose?"

"You know Rose."

"But why should she—? Is that what you have to tell me? Tell me then later when this lady shall have left us."

"I will tell you," said Lady Blair. "Forty-six years ago, your mother came to this house. Anthony Drelincourt had loved, or almost loved another girl who would have died for him. As soon as he saw your mother . . . faith, honesty, honour . . . he forgot them all. He threw everything away, for your mother. And she—she amused herself by breaking my heart, and his. And then she left him on the eve of their wedding, and he died of it. That's your mother's record. And she is like her, Anthony," she went on; "so like her that I can see the old Eugenia in her as if she were a looking-glass. Even the dress—how did you get that dress?" she asked.

"It is my own dress," said Eugenia composedly, kindly even, and in a low voice she said: "Anthony, I am sorry. Why did you not tell me she was deranged? My mother died in the Madeiras. She was never in England."

"That was your grandmother," the old lady said; "your mother— Anthony, I will tell you, so that you may know what it is that you are sacrificing Rose for. The night before this girl's mother ran away, I went to her room. I humbled myself. I told her how I had always loved Anthony, and how he would have been happy with me, and I begged her—oh, it's too long ago for me to have any shame about it—I implored her to go, to leave him, to give him up to me. She never loved him as I did. And she listened, smiling to herself, the Jezebel, and making a hairpin red-hot in the candle-flame and making little holes in the wax with it; and when I could say no more, she laughed and said she was sorry for me. And then she said: 'Give him up! I would throw you and all the rest of the world into hell and cross over your burning bodies to get to him. That's what love means. Take your milk and water to another market.'"

"Cecily told you that," Eugenia said, looking down; "I have been very sorry for that."

"Told me?" Lady Blair echoed, and drowned Eugenia's later words. "I was that Cecily Drelincourt. I have carried the mark of those words for fifty years or near it. And your mother told you, I suppose? And now you come here to break another girl's heart as your mother broke mine. Now you know what's in her blood, Anthony; and I've warned you."

"You told me all this before," said he. "Dear Lady Blair, please, please be calm. You don't understand."

"And I," said Eugenia, "do not understand either. Is this Cecily's grandmother?"

"I tell you I *am* Cecily," said Lady Blair, and stamped her foot.

A faint shadow of some horror not yet apprehended crossed Eugenia's face. She moved her lips, but her opening "But" was lost in Lady Blair's next words.

"The mother took my love, and the daughter takes you. Oh, Anthony! all the nonsense I've talked! *You* understood, didn't you, that to me you're the son I've never had, the son I should have had if that woman had not come between my lover and me?"

"I understood," said Anthony, and Eugenia said a little faintly—

"Stop; don't say any more. I'm sorry you're unhappy. But I don't understand. You don't mean to say that you were Cecily Drelincourt, the same Cecily that was to have been my bridesmaid, that asked—I didn't hear you right, did I?"

"Give him up," said Lady Blair, clasping her hands on which the veins stood out blue; "forgive anything I've said and give him up. Don't take him away from me. She began to cry the tremulous quick tears of age.

"Don't," said Eugenia with deathly quiet. "What was it you said, Anthony? About my having been asleep for more than weeks? Was it years? Not years, Anthony; not years!" She clung to him with the terror of a child lost in the dark. "It's not true. It can't be. But when she said, 'Don't take him away,' her voice was like . . . Anthony, I can't bear it; I can't! Tell me was it years? What year is this?"

"It was Lady Blair who answered: "Nineteen hundred and eleven." Her mouth hung slackly, the tears had dabbled the rouge, and her figure seemed to have shrunk, fallen in upon itself.

"Is it true?" Eugenia asked, in a whisper.

"Yes," he answered.

"I've been asleep for fifty years, and Cecily, *that's* Cecily. Am *I* like that?" she ran to a mirror, "but of course I saw this morning. I am myself. But everyone else has gone. Oh, horrible, horrible! Why did you wake me?"

She was coming back to him, hands outstretched, but she stopped short.

"You're not old. Did you sleep too?"

He shook his head.

"Then you—then you—who are you?"

"Your lover, dear," he said, and moved towards her. But she drew back.

"No, no," she cried; "you are someone else. You didn't know me. You don't know me. Don't come near me. I'm a ghost. I'm not real. I've been dead for fifty years. Cecily, if you are Cecily, you know me. You're real. Oh, help me, help me!"

Lady Blair only stared and shook her head and wept. Anthony, at his wits' end, stood between them.

"It is true," he said to Lady Blair; "she is the Eugenia who wronged you. She has been in a trance for a long time. She never ran away." He told her very plainly and quietly, with a purposeful choice of commonplace words, all that had happened. He could not be sure that she understood. But when he ended, she said—

"If you and she are not mad, and this is true, she should have a scar on her hand, and she can tell me how she came by it."

"You picked up a stiletto from my dressing-table," Eugenia said slowly, "and tried to stab me with it. It went into my hand and you were sorry." She held out her hand, palm uppermost. There was on it a little scar, not quite healed.

"You see," she said, "it's fifty years ago to you. To me it's three days ago. Oh, you loved me when I first came, before Anthony did; help me now. I've nobody but you."

Lady Blair seemed to awaken the tottering, shrunken old woman seemed to expand, to straighten to something that was, quite recognisably, Lady Blair.

"I found a bit of her dress," she said, "among the straw. I wondered. But I never thought. Fifty years. Your Anthony's dead."

"No!" the girl almost shrieked.

"Yes, *that* is his nephew. You belong to my time, not his."

"No, no, no!" a wail of anguish ran through the house.

"I am not dead," he said. "Whatever else has changed, I have not changed. I am Anthony who loves you. I have always loved you. I always shall."

She looked at him and spoke softly.

"It *is* you," she said; "you may have died as she says, but you have come into the world again to wake me. Don't I know you? It is you—but—it's all in vain. I know it."

She shrank from him. Lady Blair came forward with outstretched hands.

"Oh, my poor dear," she said, and enfolded Eugenia with a tragic tenderness. "I can forgive you anything now I know you didn't desert my Anthony."

Eugenia clung to her. Anthony left them together.

★★★★★★

He went out into the garden and, shaken out of all self-control, told his story to the first person he met. It was the doctor. Anthony fought the other's unbelief, beat down his rational distrusts, till he felt that he had overpowered him, convinced him.

"And I love her," Anthony ended. "I didn't know what love was like before. What am I to do? I must tell Rose."

"You never loved Rose," said the doctor slowly.

"No. I know that now. But I thought I did. And to have to hurt her like this—oh, my God!—but I can't do anything else."

"I have the honour to wish you good morning," said the doctor.

"You mean, Anthony looked at him in wonder; "you mean that you don't believe *yet?*"

"I mean that I believe that at last you have fallen in love, and that you've arranged all this elaborate melodrama to cover your breaking with Rose. But you might have spared yourself the trouble. She won't believe your twaddling fairy stories about Sleeping Beauties. And I think Rose is jolly well rid of you, at any price. If you want to know what I believe, it's that. So now you know."

He turned away and left Anthony standing there.

To him presently came Bats. And to him Anthony told, in far fewer words, what he had told the doctor. Bats listened, nodded now and then. "And Rose," Anthony ended; "my poor Rose. I do love Rose too, Billy. I thought I loved her as men do love. I didn't know."

"It may help you a little," Bats said slowly, "if I tell you that I'm certain Rose never loved you either-not as you and I mean when we say 'love.' You piqued her; you were indifferent. The rest of us were at her feet. Oh yes, I'm there with the rest, if you care to know. That sort of pique has passed for love with many a woman before Rose. And as for the other; Drelincourt, I've told you many a time that it was dangerous. I tell it you again now. You've done what you set out to do, and you've found—her. But there are some things that are . . . not allowed. I don't know how the judgment will come on you. But it will come. You've got beyond the line that we're not allowed to go beyond. These things can't be."

"I mean to marry Eugenia," he said. "I've won, all along the line.

330

If I've not got to hurt Rose, there's nothing in the world but splendid happiness."

But Bats shook his head.

"We're not at the end yet," he said.

Chapter 21
The Old Love

Anthony went slowly back to the Empire room. It was empty. He sat down on the window seat where so little a while ago he had held his world in his arms. His world. Deliberately he repeated the words. For they were true. Science, psychology, the great mysteries, honour, fame, friendship, nothing mattered but this.

"I must have loved her in some other life," he said, as so many have said before him, so many suddenly realizing the strength of the unknown god, blindingly made manifest. "There must have been another life, when she and I were together. She could not otherwise, in the very first moment of my seeing her, have become the heart of my heart."

For he perceived now what before he had not realised, that at the very first sight of her pale face lying so still in that still and hidden chamber, he had, as it were, become alive. Lines he had never understood sang themselves just past his hearing. How did the thing go?

Hair in heaps lay heavily
Over a pale brow spirit pure.
      ******

And lo, a blade for a knight's emprise
Filled the empty sheath of a man.
      ******

He looked at her as a lover can,
She looked at him as one who awakes,
The past was asleep, and their life began. "

Yes, that was it, or near it; "*a blade for a knight's emprise.*" How foolish to think that work and fame were worth nothing. They were worth everything, since he could give them to her.

"She belongs to my time, not yours," Lady Blair had said. A saying meaningless. She belonged to *him*, and what had time to do with love? "Love's not Time's fool," he said, and realised with almost a smile that for him, as for the other lovers at whom he had mocked, the only language was the language of lovers and poets.

"And all the time I was mocking at Love, here it was in me, my very self, waiting to come to life, just dormant like some live thing that waits for the spring sunshine to awaken it; like *her*, who waited to be awakened." Again, he almost smiled as he saw to what a bathos of egoism his metaphor was leading him. His fancy busied itself with his future—their future—drinking in the dream of a long life spent together, of youth's rose-crowned banquet, of a prime, vigorous and splendid, and of the gentle tender peace of an old age side by side.

Then the thought struck him with a sudden buffet. She would not grow old. She had been down into the valley of the shadow of death and had come back having conquered death and broken the arrows of old age. She would be always young. And he—he would grow old and grey; and all this life that he looked to to draw them closer through a growing twilight till death's kind darkness enfolded them—all this life in the dream of which he had gloried, this life would be like a wedge mercilessly struck home by the years, driving him and her further and further apart. In this new enlightenment, Death, whom he had sought to conquer, appeared to him as a friend outraged and for ever estranged. He did not want to live for ever on this earth. He wanted to live the allotted time, as other lovers lived it, to see her children grow up, and know the tenderness that grows with the waning of youth and beauty. He had been wrong. His discovery was a useless one: who wanted to live for ever? Yet had he not made it, he had never found her, who alone made life worth the living.

The voices of Esther and Linda and the others came to him through the open window like the voices of actors in a play in which he, far off in the gallery, had ceased to be interested. He sat there a long time, thinking, dreaming, musing. And in and through the web of musings, dreams and thoughts, ran the golden thread of this new magic of love, now at last discovered. What were any of his discoveries compared with that? So, he thought, sitting there very still.

To him there came Lady Blair, a strange Lady Blair, aged and no longer gay.

He roused himself from his triumphant musings to go to her.

"My poor boy," she said gently.

"Why poor?" he asked, a sudden terror catching at his heart. That was how people spoke when—, but that fear at least was groundless. Death could not touch his love. And now the thought that he had hated came to him as a friend. "Why poor?" he repeated.

"Because you've got yourself on to a plane where the impossible looks as though it could happen. But it can't, my dear, it can't."

"You've been talking to Bats," he said, and she told him, "Yes, and he sees it as I do."

"But it's no good," said Anthony, "seeing things as each other does, and all that. She's here; I'm here. I shall marry her tomorrow."

"She won't," said Lady Blair; "she—"

"You've been advising her," he put in hotly.

"Yes, advising her to accept the thing quietly, get used to this new world you've brought her into, marry you and be happy. She won't. And she wants to leave Drelincourt."

"Then she must marry me. You don't suppose I can let her out of my sight?"

"I will go with her," said Lady Blair. "I am on your side, Anthony. I want you to be happy. Only I know in my soul you never will be."

"Ah! don't croak," he said almost gaily. "Do you think it's possible for anyone to come through what she has come through and then— nothing?"

"I don't think you realise," said she, sitting down very wearily beside him. "You've been telling people. That doctor will talk. He doesn't believe you. But he'll talk. And other people; if they don't believe, they'll think the worst, as he does. And if they do believe— It seems so odd to be sitting here in the sunshine and talking of things that can't be true, and yet they are. If people do believe that she's a woman who died fifty years ago. . . . Tony, you know how people feel about the dead—the horror, the mystery, the wild unreasonable terror!"

"We shan't want—anyone else," he began, but checked at the third word. "But *you* don't feel any horror?" he said.

"I'm an old woman," said Lady Blair, "and I am too near Death to be afraid of it. And I knew her when she was alive before, Tony. No one else is alive who knew her then. She feels that too. She feels that in time even you will shrink from her. God knows what the rights of it are. She says she's been dead all those years. You say so. I know it can't be true, and yet I see it is. My old brain's muddled." She put her hand to her head. "She asked me to tell you all this. To tell you that she knows the best thing she can do is to go away. She wants to go away with me. She wants me," said the old woman, and her voice shook and her hands. It was as though old age, so strongly resisted, had in an hour done the work of half a lifetime.

"And," she added, "I want her. She knows all the people I knew when I was young. There is no one else left but her and me. Let us go away together. Don't hurry everything. Let her have time to find herself, to see if she can live in this new world you've dragged her back into."

"She's got to live," he said roughly, "whether she likes it or not. Of course what I found out was too fine a thing not to have some damned counterbalancing terror. Just as the rest of us must die, whether we like it or not, she must live, whether she likes it or not."

"I hear what you say," said she, "but it doesn't seem to mean anything. My head's going round."

"My poor dear," said Anthony, and came to her and kissed her withered cheek. There was no paint on it now. "Don't let's talk about it anymore now. Go back to her. Stay quietly with her. I cannot let her go away. I will wait as long as you like. I will not ask to see her till she wants me. But she must stay here. I must get rid of all these people. And I must tell Rose."

But Bats had told Rose.

She was waiting on the terrace when Anthony came out, and she came to him quickly.

"Don't," she said; "I know. Don't tell me anything. You've quite enough to bear without telling me things that'll break your heart to talk about. I know just how you feel. You're bracing yourself up to get it over. Billy has told me. He said it was the only thing he could do for either of us."

"How splendid you are," he said; "you don't reproach me? don't hate me?"

"Reproach you?" said she; "oh, my poor boy, it's bad enough without my reproaches. Even now I can't believe it's true. And yet I knew in my heart the moment I saw her that it *was* true. And nothing's any use, and everything's all over, and I shall never be happy again, and you've never been happy at all."

The remembrance came to him of an hour at Malacca Wharf when he had held, for the first time, his world in his arms.

"I not happy?" he breathed; "oh, but I have been happy"

They stood facing each other with nothing left to say. Rose could not leave him in that empty silence.

"There's one little thing I'd like to tell you," she began quickly, "before I go. Oh yes, of course I'm going. Do you think I want to stay? I had a letter from Abrahamson this morning." Tony drew a deep breath, as one who begins to recover from a swoon. To talk of Abrahamson and letters was the first step back into the world of everyday, the world where he meant to live. The world in which he had passed the morning was the world he meant to leave, meant Eugenia to leave. He welcomed the commonplace daylight warm world of everyday things. "Yes?" he said.

"He has found out where those books came from. And, he thinks, the ring. Oh, these Jews have ways of finding out things. I don't know how he knows, but he does. It was a man who was in your uncle's service at the time of his death. He must have stolen the books when your uncle died. And the ring. And sold them. He told his landlord once that he had expected the books to be gold and silver to him, and then found they were in some language he couldn't read. Russian he thought." So, she spoke, almost placidly.

"The cypher," said he. "Rose, I think I see. This chap must have taken those books; and my uncle, perhaps he could not remember the formulae, couldn't revive her, perhaps he only missed them when he had gone too far in the treatment to stop. Perhaps the shock of finding them gone killed him. He had written three words in the laboratory book, 'Not death—She—'

"Yes," said Rose, "yes." Then lamely, "I thought I'd tell you. I mayn't perhaps see you again, you know."

"Oh, don't say that," he said mechanically. He wanted to stay a little on the low-level ground where one felt nothing, to breathe a little and rest. "Where are the others?" he said; "did you all have luncheon?"

"Yes, Lady Blair sent word not to wait; that Eugenia was ill. The others are all gone. Billy got them off. Lord Alfriston took them to London in his motor. There's no one here but Billy and me."

Anthony gazed at this girl whom, a week ago, he had supposed himself to be about to marry. And he knew, whatever Bats might say, that she had loved him.

"Oh, Rose," he said, and "Oh, Rose, Rose!"

"The house feels as if there'd been a funeral," she said, and shivered.

"You are wonderful," he said; "some women would have made me suffer to the utmost they could inflict. You are an angel."

She did not speak for a moment. Then she said: "Tony, perhaps you'll think some day and be sorry for what you've done. About me, I mean. Think you ought to have gone on with it, you know, and things about your honour and all that. I want you always to remember what I'm going to tell you. I didn't know it then, but I know now that it was all over for me from the moment you told me of your discovery. I could never have married you after that. I should have been afraid of you."

It was bravely said. And he believed her. Perhaps she believed herself. Perhaps, on the other hand, what she said was true, only she did
not know it for the truth.

"Thank you for telling me that," he said. "And I do love you, Rose.
It's only that I didn't know that there's only one sort of love worth
offering to a woman."

"The stars and roses you used to make fun of?"

"Yes," he said, "the stars and roses."

★★★★★★

Drelincourt was emptied of its guests. All had gone, even Rose
who wanted to stay and Bats who had decided that she should not.
He took her back to Malacca Wharf, got Esther Raven to stay with
her and came to see her every day.

"No, her heart isn't broken," said Esther to him one day when
Rose was busy with the biscuit boys, "but it's badly bruised. Poor dear
brave splendid Rose. That he should have preferred that little dowdy
insignificant relation—I would never have believed it, never."

The doctor had told Esther the story that he did not believe and
she had not believed it either. Bats had told no one anything. Rose
had told no one anything.

"She bears up wonderfully," said Esther; "just goes on with her
work and the boys and her Mothers' Meetings and things. I don't suppose she'll ever marry. She'll never get over it. And yet she keeps such
a brave front. I love courage."

"So, do I," said Bats, "the more by token that it's my only virtue.
No, I have one other. I can keep a secret. Can you?"

"Yes," Esther answered alertly.

"Then I'll give you one to keep. I mean to marry Rose."

"If she'll have you," said Esther incredulously.

"One has instincts," said Bats. "When I put the revolver to her
head Rose will give in."

"The revolver—?"

"It's just a way of speaking. When I tell her that I mean her to
marry me, Rose will marry me. It's the only way to manage these
strong self-reliant people."

"She'll simply laugh at you," said Esther. "I don't see anyone bully-
ing Rose into marrying a man she doesn't love."

"Nor do I. Perhaps I forgot to mention that I also intend that Rose
shall love me."

"She never will," said Esther with conviction.

"I don't know. I sometimes think . . . Love soaks in, like water into rock, you know. If you go on loving people long enough before they find it out, when they do find it out it's soaked into their very souls."

"Do you mean?"

"Always. From the first moment I saw her. But you won't tell her that. I shall tell her, when the time comes. And then you'll see."

"I never shall," said Miss Raven. But Miss Raven was wrong.

"I tell you all this," said Bats, "because I want an ally. Abuse me or praise me, I don't care which you do. Only I want you to know what you're doing. And in return I'll ask you to tea when Lord Alfriston comes. He is coming, by the way, next Wednesday. And Linda and Mullinger. I am becoming a matchmaker."

"You are brutal," said Miss Raven, flushing, "and I shall not go to your hateful party."

But Miss Raven went.

★★★★★★

A hushed stillness, like the stillness of death, had settled over Drelincourt. Lady Blair and Eugenia kept to Lady Blair's rooms, and for three days Anthony wandered like a ghost about that quiet house of his and the glorious gardens, thinking, thinking, thinking.

On the fourth day Lady Blair came to him.

"Eugenia is happier now," she said. "She does not cry so much now. And she says she will see you soon. She asks a great many questions about some little boy. She says he was given up for dead and you revived him. She wants you to have the child here. She says that she and the child would understand each other. She is very insistent about it. Where is he?"

"With a clergyman and his wife at Esher. Sebastien shall go for him," Anthony told her. "But is she more reasonable?" he asked quickly. "Does she see yet that she and I . . . If she and I keep apart, the whole thing's been for nothing. Won't she see me? I have been patient," he said impatiently. "Yes, I think I have been very patient. Won't she see me now?"

"She will see you when she has seen the boy," said Lady Blair. "You will send for him today, won't you? I think what she feels most is the horrible loneliness. I am the only one. This child—she feels she has some kinship of common suffering with him. It seems that dying, before it is your time to die, hurts horribly."

"I did not know," said Anthony. "I thought it was rest."

"I hope you never will know," said she. "I must go back to her. She likes the roses you send up. Yes. I've implored her to see you, but she says she must get used to her own soul first. I don't know what she means."

Anthony sent for the child, and Sebastien brought him, a little boy of six or seven. Anthony would have liked to see the meeting of these two beings who, alone, had tasted of the first-fruits of his discovery. But Lady Blair had given orders that the boy was to be brought straight to her rooms. And Anthony, still alone, saw and heard nothing of the meeting. Though alone, he was not lonely. The reaction from the intense emotion left him at peace. Eugenia lived, he lived, and he wandered without restlessness about the gardens whose paths had known her feet.

Lady Blair came to him sometimes, and from her he heard of Eugenia and of the child, and of the love the two had for each other. And once from his window, he saw her and the boy in the Dutch garden. They looked like mother and child, he thought, with a sudden pang. In this separation of her choosing, he was almost contented. The string of emotion, stretched almost to breaking point, was now all relaxed. That she should be in the same house with him was enough. It would have been almost enough, he felt, that she should be in the same world. He felt like a man who, in a shipwreck, has saved his dearest treasure and himself, and is content to know her safe, and to await quietly and with a solemn gratitude the time when she, rested and restored from that wild fight with death, shall come quietly to his arms.

And at last she came. He had been cutting roses—he sent roses to her rooms every day—and his hands were full of them as she came towards him through the flowering bushes. And when they met, he let the roses fall and took her hands across a heap of red and pink and white. There was a wooden seat round the trunk of a weeping ash on the turf at the end of the rose garden, and thither he led her, keeping her hand in his hand. The weeping ash made a green and gold bower for them, and the world was well shut out. There she crept into his arms and they clung together, even as those shipwrecked ones might have done.

"You have kept me waiting a very long time," he said.

And she answered, "A very long time," and clung to him yet more closely. "Anthony, I have thought and thought, and prayed and prayed. And I have come to see that what I feared from the first is true. It is not possible."

"What is not possible?" he asked, sick with a sudden fear.

338

"That we should be together. That we should be married. It is not possible. We are not mates. I have been on the other side."

"And I? Have I not been on the other side? How else am I here, the man you loved, when the man you loved died years ago?"

"It is not the same," she said. "You came and went by the gates of birth and death. But I am not of your kind. I feel as though I were a ghost who loved a mortal. I am afraid."

He tried with fond words and the eyes of love to move her from this fear. In vain.

"I did not know how deep the gulf was, how very deep and wide, until the child came. Then I knew. He and I are of one blood. I am not strange to him as the rest of the world is strange. He is not strange to me. He and I are happy together. You and I would never be happy."

Anthony spoke.

"No," she answered. "I know you love me, and I thank God for it. But you would not love me long. You would be afraid. You would say to yourself someday, 'This is a dead woman I hold in my arms,' and I should feel you shiver and shrink . . ."

Again, he spoke.

"And this too," she said; "have you thought of this? You will grow old, and I shall be always as I am now. Horrible, horrible! I look forward. I see our children . . . do you think I have not thought of that? Your baby to lie at my breast," she caught her breath; and once more Anthony spoke, a very few words.

"Yes," she said, "I know. And when our child grew older; I should be still the same; and when our child was a man, and looked to find a mother faded with a life of love and care for him, like the good mothers of other men, he would find only me with my intolerable fixed unnatural youth!"

She listened patiently to his passionate pleading.

"Do you think I don't say all that to myself?" she asked. "Over and over and over. And always the answer is the same. We are of different worlds. We must part."

"Beloved," he said. "There is an antidote. It is in that book."

She shone and sparkled like a stream that the sun strikes from the edge of a cloud.

"To make me a real woman again? Oh, Anthony!"

"It is not a true antidote," he said. "At least not as I have used it. I tried it—on the bird and on other things —and the answer always was . . . death."

"It might not be so with a human soul," she said; and he said—

"Do you think I am going to risk it?"

"*I* would," said she, "to be a real living woman; for your love . . . oh, I would risk far more than death."

Then he talked to her, quietly, reasonably, commonsensibly about the wonders of science and the power of man's will.

"You take this too much as a miracle," he said. "By and by it will seem nothing to you or to the world. Electricity seemed a miracle once, and we send sixpenny telegrams. One comes to take the most wonderful magic as a matter of course. Look at the X-rays, and wireless telegraphy and . . ."

"No steps come back," she said. "I have crossed the threshold of death, and this which has come back belongs to the other side."

"Your feet only touched the threshold," he said.

"They crossed it," she said, "and the child, he too has been where I have been. He sleeps in my arms. When he is there I do not dream. I am afraid of my dreams. They are all of you."

"And you and he are of one blood, you say?" Anthony asked, suddenly seeing light in the great darkness.

"Yes, he and I, but not I and you; oh, my dear love, not I and you!" She wept on his shoulder.

"Then the way is plain," said he, holding her softly. "I shall go where you have been. I shall—Eugenia—you were to have worked the charm for your lover when he had worked it for you. You knew it all— if you have forgotten, I will teach it you again. Will you do this? Then at least you can never say that there is any gulf between us."

"It is a terrible sacrifice that you ask me to let you make," she said.

"Yes," he said simply, "but I want you more than anything that can be sacrificed."

"And everything that I care for in myself says No. It is not—oh, Anthony, don't you understand?"

"It may be wrong," he said doggedly. "I don't know. Yes—I do know. God would not put any secret in our way, and then forbid us to find it out."

"But to use it?"

"Well, if it is," he said, "am I nothing to you? I would go through hell for you. Will you do nothing for me? I tell you you shall do it. You are mine and you shall do it."

"I must do what you command," she said, and trembled.

"What? Then I command you to marry me tomorrow," he said,

and a sudden flush of triumph dashed his pale face.

"I must do it if you say so. I love you," she said. "But I could not live afterwards. The first moment you left me alone, I should find a way out."

"There is no way out," he said. "You are safe from disease and old age. Let me take you as you are."

"I must do as you say," she told him again.

"Then I say do this. Make me your peer, your equal. And whatever terrors the future may have we shall share them together."

She wrung her hands in an agony. "No, no, no," she cried, "don't make me do it! Let me take the antidote rather. It would not kill me."

"If I did," he said slowly, "and it did *not* kill you, you would be old, old, old, like Lady Blair."

"Then at least I could die," she said, like one who perceives a loop-hole not undesired.

"You are going to live," he said strongly; "you are going to live for me. And I am going to live for you."

But she trembled and shivered.

"That room," she said. "That horrible vault. I could not face it. The floor was up and we were cut off from everyone. The machinery needed a strong man. Were you suddenly faint, overcome? Did you try to get help and were met by that barricade, and died before you could get help? Was that it, Tony?"

He covered her wide eyes with his hand.

"Hush!" he said. "We are just a man and woman who love each other. All the rest that has happened is less than nothing. Only you think that there is a gulf between us. I know of none. But if there is one, I am going to leap it. And you are going to help me. And it shall not be in that room. It shall be out here, in the moonlight. The full moon helps, you know. It must have been a full moon when you were put to sleep. At the full moon. You promise?"

"I must promise if you command," she said again. And even then, he was not warned.

He clasped her in his arms, and once more the world spun in a wild splendour of stars and flowers.

CHAPTER 22
The End

William Bats, leaping from a whirring taxi-cab at London Bridge Station, almost knocked down a hurrying stranger who, turning, showed the face of a friend and became Mr. Abrahamson.

"Sorry!" said Bats. "Oh, it's you, Mr. Abrahamson; I'm in a frightful hurry to catch the 8.50. There's something wrong at Drelincourt. Excuse me."

Mr. Abrahamson walked beside him into the station. "I will escort you if I do not intrude," he said, and followed Bats to the booking-office, and when Bats had taken a ticket, Mr. Abrahamson took one also.

"You find first your train," said he. "Then I have a little talk with you."

Bats found an empty carriage. Abrahamson spoke to an official. Next moment the carriage door was locked on the two men.

"You are going my way?" Bats asked, surprised.

"I go your way," said Abrahamson. "You go to Drelincourt and you say there is something wrong. May I ask in sympathy if our fortunate physiologist is ill?"

"I don't know," said Bats shortly. He was in no mood for talk.

"You go down then," said Abrahamson, with a sudden kindly interest, "for the only real reason, the unreasoning impulse. I also. It is the only guide. Not the reasonable impulse which you by analysis can explain and justify, but the one which you can neither justify nor explain. The impulse that permits not itself to be analysed and explained, only recognised—and, if you are wise, followed."

The train started.

"I'm afraid I don't have those impulses," said Bats, interested in his turn. "I am going because I have had a telegram. It arrived last night and I did not find it."

"It is from him?" Abrahamson asked.

"There is no reason why I should not tell you," Bats began, but the other interrupted.

"Yet you say to yourself it is no business of mine, and that I ask too many questions. My young friend, Nathan Abrahamson does not ask idle questions. I know many things. I have foreseen much. You and I are perhaps on our guard because we do not know what the other knows. Yet I know you know much, for Miss Royal told me that it is you who transcribe the cypher. And I have attained my knowledge by another path. And I am now in this train to go to the young Anthony to warn him, if there should still be time."

"Of what?"

"The unreasoning impulse I call him," Abrahamson went on. "Perhaps it is another name for what my fathers were used to say, 'Warned of God in a dream.' The impulse came yesterday at noon. It came last night, very strong and clear, but I would not listen. And this morning, for the third time. And now I go, and I fear I have been false to the light."

"I don't understand," said Bats.

"Once before in this matter I was warned. That time I obeyed. I went to Miss Royal. I made her gaze in the crystal. I warned her. But I did not tell her all. I had pity. If I had told her. . . . But I was false to the light."

"Miss Royal's engagement is broken off," said Bats, without feeling irrelevant, "and I will show you the telegram. It is from Lady Blair who keeps Drelincourt's house."

The Jew took the bit of pink paper and read:

To William Bats, Esq.,
Falstafe Chambers,
Dean Street, London, W.
Please come at once you must come there is something different you must come tonight motor if there is no train do not fail most urgent come I am afraid.

Cecily Blair.

"And you received it?" he said.

"Half an hour ago."

"There was no further telegram this morning. No?"

"There wasn't time. I left at a quarter-past eight."

"We will talk no more," said the Jew. "Meditation is best, to clear and calm the mind, to cleanse the courage and make endurance strong. Mr. Bats, I fear that this train is carrying you into the land of sorrow. Let us meditate in silence."

He closed his eyes and spoke no more.

Meditation was, in that hour, the last thing Bats wanted. He resolutely opened the book he carried and tried to think that he understood what he was reading, and whether he understood or no, the book served its purpose. It was an anodyne that he wanted, and to the Western mind meditation is no anodyne.

There was no carriage to be had at the station. The two men walked over the fields and through the park, Mr. Abrahamson still in meditation and Bats intolerably anxious not to meditate.

They were met on the terrace by Wilkes, and as soon as they saw his face they knew.

"Yes, sir, the worst as could be, sir. Poor Sir Anthony and the young lady and the child. All three of them dead, sir. They seem to have been at some play acting or another, and accidents happen so quick. But Lady Blair, she requested me not to enlarge, sir, but just to show you up as soon as you arrived and she will tell you herself. You was expected last night; I wish to God you had, if I may say so, sir. This gentleman to wait in the library? Quite so."

Wilkes led the way to Lady Blair's sitting-room, and Bats went into a darkened chamber where a little heap of dark clothes cowered in the corner of a sofa. The maid who sat in a chair nearby got up and went as Bats came in.

"Will you ring, sir, please, if anything's wanted," she said, lowering her respectful voice to the key of the darkened room.

Lady Blair's voice sounded changed, harsh and low, such strange breaks and hesitancies.

"I want to tell you how it happened and I am very weak. Don't interrupt with questions. I woke in the night; the child was calling 'Eugenia' again and again. I got up to go to him. My door was locked on the outside. I called out to the child but he did not hear me, or else he would not answer. And I heard him go down and I heard the French window open. And I looked out and called to him. But he would not listen. He was going straight to *them*."

"But where were they?"

"Down by the lake I saw them. It was a still night, very moonlight. . . . I read my first love-letter by moonlight," she said, and stopped.

"Don't give way," he urged her. "Tell me. Go on. You saw the child—"

"They were down by the lake. I could not see who it was, but it was they. I know now. There was a white patch on the ground, and candles all round it, and someone in white moving about. And the child went through the shrubbery in his nightgown."

Again, she paused.

"I don't understand being able to tell you all this," she said wonderingly.

"And then?"

"The child got quite close to them. He was running, and I suppose one of the candles caught his nightdress, because there was a flare, and then it went out suddenly, and there was a sound of water, and everything was quite quiet, just the white thing lying there and the candles, nothing else. And I could do nothing, nothing. From the first moment

I knew what they were doing. They were trying to make *him* like *her*. You've seen all the things, the things that were found when you found her. They tell me there was a lambskin and an altar. And she was trying to change him into what she was. But she couldn't. Oh, thank God, she couldn't!"

"But why didn't you ring?" asked Bats, "rouse the house—do something?"

"I thought you knew," she said simply. "When I first got to the window and saw the white things by the lake there was a sort of numb blankness, and then I watched and felt I couldn't move from watching; and when I felt I *must* move, I couldn't. I shall never move again."

The shawl fell back from her face, and his eyes, now grown used to the dim light, saw that it was all twisted and crooked.

"The gardeners found them, and they sent up to me, and my maid sent for the doctor. And he came and told me Anthony was dead. Me? Oh, the doctor says it's paralysis, and I shan't live long. Thank God for that," she said, "and they found Anthony dead and the girl and the child were in the lake. The swans were scolding and flapping and they went to see what it was. I told them to leave everything for you to see. I am alive still, in my brain. I wish I'd been able to go altogether and to go before he did. You were his friend, you will see to everything. Oh, one thing more. He told me sometime he had made a will, leaving you something. I wanted to say . . . don't refuse it . . . because of any silly scruples. I want everything to be as he wanted it to be. Goodbye! I'm glad somebody's going to be happy. You'll be good to that Rose girl. I shan't see you again. Ring for my maid, do you mind? Goodbye!"

Bats went out into the sunlight and down to the lake. There everything was green and sparkling and the blue water laughed to the blue sky.

On the grassy promontory that jutted into the lake lay quiet things covered with white cloths. There was just enough breeze to lift the corners a little and lay them softly down again. There were the lightless candles, there was the altar; there on the grass in bands of white cloth fastened by long nails to the grass was the sign that had been traced on the floor of that dark room where he had found the lady of Anthony's life, in the death-sleep. All was, here in the sun and the glowing summer life, even as it had been in that dark and secret chamber.

Someone lifted a corner of a sheet and he saw the face of his friend. He was glad afterwards that he had seen it with that look upon it. They replaced the sheet, and Abrahamson and another man came to him out of a group that had in it the gardeners, Wilkes and the same local constable who had come up that day to sell tickets for the *fête*.

"This gentleman is the doctor," said Mr. Abrahamson; "he will tell you what he thinks."

And the doctor told, with many dull words, how the unfortunate baronet had been rehearsing for a play, something Greek, most likely, the doctor thought, probably a pastoral drama to which he would have invited the villagers, and the child's clothes had caught fire and the lady had plunged with him into the lake. "They were extricated from the fatal stream near the bridge," he said. "Poor Sir Anthony! He was probably playing the part of a dead Greek lying in state, and some sudden shock—perhaps the child screamed—caused a cessation of the heart's action. I shall be, of course, happy to give the necessary certificate. Very sad, yes—very. In the midst of life, we are in death. Yes, yes. I will call on my way home and see the undertaker," he said, "unless you would like to call in a firm from town."

"I will see to all that, thank you," said Bats. "You are sure he is dead? There must be no funeral till there is no least possible doubt that he is really dead. It might be a trance, mightn't it?" Bats put it to the doctor and hung on the answer. To have his friend back, safe as of old, and all this like a dream when one wakes; the thought had but time to brush his heart before he remembered what life would mean to Anthony, after that dream.

"Dead?" The man would have laughed but for the professional sadness demanded by the occasion. As it was, he choked the laugh into a cough. "I am afraid there is no doubt about that," he said. "Unfortunately, or fortunately, I know my business. I have heard of trances, my dear sir, but they are things doctors do not come across."

"Have no fear," said Abrahamson softly, "your friend is dead."

The old Jew, of his larger and deeper knowledge, pieced the thing together for Bats when the lake-side had been cleared of the strange pitiful show and they paced there together in the sunshine.

"As I see it," he said, "the child missed his friend in the night and followed her out. Perhaps he came at the moment when life in your friend was extinguished, before the woman began the incantations and the needle-prickings of the destroyers of death and disease. And the appeal of the child and the flames caught her from even her lover and she and the child perished together."

"Then," said Bats, "if the child had not run out . . . if she had not left Anthony to go to the child . . . he would have been alive now. She would have succeeded."

"No," said the other, weighing the word, "and no, and no. She could not. Waste no regrets, my Bats. The child came with an angel to bring him to them. But for the coming of the child, she would have lived to know that she had killed her lover, and lacked the power to bring him to life. She had surrendered all her will to him before she passed into her own death-sleep. How then could she control the powers of death and hell as he had done for her? They died in ignorance; that was the best that life could have given them."

"But," said Bats wretchedly, "if you had come in time—if I had had the telegram last night."

"It all makes nothing," he said. "I saw not that before. But now I see. She could not have lived; the child could not have lived. Death let them go as a cat lets go a mouse, to snatch at them again. Man is such a little thing and he plays so foolishly among the giant greatnesses. Disease he can conquer, yes, and old age, but Death has many arrows in his quiver. She died because her allotted time was come, as you and I will die. Disease and old age? Yes, these he reckoned with, conquered them with infinite labour and the arrogant theft of forbidden things. God is not mocked. The child and the maiden were safe from sickness and from age, but who could secure her from the elemental forces, the lightning and the deep waters? It could not have been otherwise. Thus, it must be with those who are bold to lift the curtain and adventure among forbidden things."

"It seems such waste, such stupid senseless waste," said Bats. "His great thoughts, his fine body that loved life, all the friendship, the aspiration, the love . . . all thrown away, gone, wasted for ever."

"Who says that it is wasted?" said the Jew. "It is his body that has served its turn and is cast away. The great thoughts, the friendship, the aspiration, the love; can we say that these die? Nay, rather, these shall not die. These shall live in the Courts of the Lord, for ever.

LEONAUR

ALSO FROM LEONAUR
AVAILABLE IN SOFTCOVER OR HARDCOVER WITH DUST JACKET

MR MUKERJI'S GHOSTS *by S. Mukerji*—Supernatural tales from the British Raj period by India's Ghost story collector.

KIPLINGS GHOSTS *by Rudyard Kipling*—Twelve stories of Ghosts, Hauntings, Curses, Werewolves & Magic.

THE COLLECTED SUPERNATURAL AND WEIRD FICTION OF WASHINGTON IRVING: VOLUME 1 *by Washington Irving*—Including one novel 'A History of New York', and nine short stories of the Strange and Unusual.

THE COLLECTED SUPERNATURAL AND WEIRD FICTION OF WASHINGTON IRVING: VOLUME 2 *by Washington Irving*—Including three novelettes 'The Legend of the Sleepy Hollow', 'Dolph Heyliger', 'The Adventure of the Black Fisherman' and thirty-two short stories of the Strange and Unusual.

THE COLLECTED SUPERNATURAL AND WEIRD FICTION OF JOHN KENDRICK BANGS: VOLUME 1 *by John Kendrick Bangs*—Including one novel 'Toppleton's Client or A Spirit in Exile', and ten short stories of the Strange and Unusual.

THE COLLECTED SUPERNATURAL AND WEIRD FICTION OF JOHN KENDRICK BANGS: VOLUME 2 *by John Kendrick Bangs*—Including four novellas 'A House-Boat on the Styx', 'The Pursuit of the House-Boat', 'The Enchanted Typewriter' and 'Mr. Munchausen' of the Strange and Unusual.

THE COLLECTED SUPERNATURAL AND WEIRD FICTION OF JOHN KENDRICK BANGS: VOLUME 3 *by John Kendrick Bangs*—Including twor novellas 'Olympian Nights', 'Roger Camerden: A Strange Story', and ten short stories of the Strange and Unusual.

THE COLLECTED SUPERNATURAL AND WEIRD FICTION OF MARY SHELLEY: VOLUME 1 *by Mary Shelley*—Including one novel 'Frankenstein or the Modern Prometheus', and fourteen short stories of the Strange and Unusual.

THE COLLECTED SUPERNATURAL AND WEIRD FICTION OF MARY SHELLEY: VOLUME 2 *by Mary Shelley*—Including one novel 'The Last Man', and three short stories of the Strange and Unusual.

THE COLLECTED SUPERNATURAL AND WEIRD FICTION OF AMELIA B. EDWARDS *by Amelia B. Edwards*—Contains two novelettes 'Monsieur Maurice', and 'The Discovery of the Treasure Isles', one ballad 'A Legend of Boisguilbert'and seventeen short stories to cill the blood.

LEONAUR

ALSO FROM LEONAUR

AVAILABLE IN SOFTCOVER OR HARDCOVER WITH DUST JACKET

THE COLLECTED SCIENCE FICTION AND FANTASY OF STANLEY G. WEINBAUM 1—INTERPLANETARY ODYSSEYS by Stanley G. Weinbaum—Classic Tales of Interplanetary Adventure Including: A Martian Odyssey, its Sequel Valley of Dreams, the Complete 'Ham' Hammond Stories and Others.

THE COLLECTED SCIENCE FICTION AND FANTASY OF STANLEY G. WEINBAUM 2—OTHER EARTHS by Stanley G. Weinbaum—Classic Futuristic Tales Including: *Dawn of Flame* & its Sequel The Black Flame, plus The Revolution of 1960 & Others.

THE COLLECTED SCIENCE FICTION AND FANTASY OF STANLEY G. WEINBAUM 3—STRANGE GENIUS by Stanley G. Weinbaum—Classic Tales of the Human Mind at Work Including the Complete Novel The New Adam, the 'van Manderpootz' Stories and Others.

THE COLLECTED SCIENCE FICTION AND FANTASY OF STANLEY G. WEINBAUM 4—THE BLACK HEART by Stanley G. Weinbaum—Classic Strange Tales Including: the Complete Novel The Dark Other, Plus Proteus Island and Others.

THE COLLECTED SCIENCE FICTION & FANTASY OF JACK LONDON 1—BEFORE ADAM & OTHER STORIES by Jack London—included in this Volume Before Adam The Scarlet Plague A Relic of the Pliocene When the World Was Young The Red One Planchette A Thousand Deaths Goliah A Curious Fragment The Rejuvenation of Major Rathbone.

THE COLLECTED SCIENCE FICTION & FANTASY OF JACK LONDON 2—THE IRON HEEL & OTHER STORIES by Jack London—included in this Volume The Iron Heel The Enemy of All the World The Shadow and the Flash The Strength of the Strong The Unparalleled Invasion The Dream of Debs.

THE COLLECTED SCIENCE FICTION & FANTASY OF JACK LONDON 3—THE STAR ROVER & OTHER STORIES by Jack London—included in this Volume The Star Rover The Minions of Midas The Eternity of Forms The Man With the Gash.